An Infidelitous Earth

Brandon Smalls

Published by
Melange Books, LLC
White Bear Lake, MN 55110
www.melange-books.com

An Infidelitous Earth ~ Copyright © 2017 by Brandon Smalls

ISBN: 978-1-68046-404-7

Cover Design by Lynsee Lauritsen

For my Mother, who gave me the passion to hunt,
My Father, who taught me the code,
And Jesse, who saw my strength before I did

The Hunter

A familiar feeling, flying through the wilds with the moon smiling overhead. Its teeth gleamed and pulsed with the shifting of the clouds as it drank in the hunt. Below, a man's frantic steps broke winter's silence. Behind him soared a grotesque predator. Its webbed wings beat with the same calm as its heartbeat until the creature began to close on the human form fixed in its great, grey eyes.

The wood thickened, the brush broadened, and the beast set down on all fours to continue the pursuit, churning up ice in white cascades. The man before it ran with pure determination in his breast. His heart quaked, injecting pure adrenaline into his limbs, quickening his pace and sending his eyes into quivering fits.

"I know you, Stoneslayer." With legs pounding into the snow the beast gained, growling. "I know what you have done."

The man did not turn. He did not talk. He did not tremble. His focus was set on his long and triumphant stride.

"Your hands are black with the blood of my brethren." It was close now—close enough to pounce. "You will suffer for them."

The Stoneslayer emerged into a clearing in the wood moments before his pursuer, finally slowing as he did so. The monster, too, came to a halt. Its jowls glowed, dripping with mercuric saliva that caught the moonlight and cast it back through the dark in silver streams. The beast split the sky with a snarl. The man edged away from it, removing his overcoat. As he did so, the moon revealed a row of knives concealed within the lining.

"Don't bother with those," the gargoyle remarked, rearing back on its legs. It towered at eight feet. Its horns curled upwards to nine feet. Its

1

wings arced upwards to ten. It was daunting, even in comparison to the admittedly large human that now looked up at it.

Without so much as touching a weapon, the man threw down his coat and stepped backwards past the center of the glade. The gargoyle matched his composure and followed him across the moonlit expanse.

"You are a strong man," it rattled, closing the gap, "but your strength and your cunning are uneven." It stopped short. "I am no fool." The gargoyle's tail lashed from behind, striking the earth between them and recoiling in a single motion. In an instant, a mechanism planted in the ground triggered and a counterweight fell outside the glade, pulling a roped bundle of sticks and leaves skyward, sans gargoyle.

His blood seethed. The last of his restraint waning, the man backed up against a tree at the edge of the clearing and slid a knife from his boot.

The gargoyle watched him as he moved away. "You cannot trap a true hunter," it mocked him. "We are—"

"Stop talking." He lifted his dagger and, for a moment, the wood reclaimed its silence.

"We are the eyes of the nigh—" The gargoyle darted to the side as the weapon came streaking past its face. It continued to fly an unprecedented distance before finally biting into a tree. The blade drove in all the way to its hilt.

Still eyeing the gargoyle, the man grunted and drew a knife from the opposite boot. "You know why it's so easy to kill gargoyles?" He turned to a second rope affixed outside the glade and began sawing away. "You're so cocky." He brought the knife clean through the cable, severing it completely, and stood back.

Within seconds, a wide cluster of netting sprang up from the ground and spread above the entire area. In its center, a large hole flew around the gargoyle before tightening high above and enclosing it in a cage of rope. The animal swiveled around, scanning the trap but finding no discernible gap large enough for it to crawl through, before snapping its eyes back to the man in black.

"Why are you smiling at me?"

"Someone done went and got himself trapped," the man laughed.

"You think this will hold me?" it roared. "A minute at most."

"That's the idea." The hunter discarded his weapon and pulled himself through the side of the cage; the holes were just large enough for him to fit. He stretched his neck and clenched his fists. This felt too familiar.

His prey faltered. "*You.* You think you can take on a gargoyle unarmed?"

"I got arms," he boasted, marching towards his victim.

"I will tear you apart." The beast spread its wings wide and let loose a shrill bay.

"Come with it, then."

The gargoyle's wings shot backwards, propelling the demon within inches of its foe. The hunter reacted inhumanly, ducking under its talons and taking firm hold of its tail. Before the gargoyle could react, it was on its back, breathless. A single, pain-laden gasp escaped its throat.

"How?" it heaved, struggling to stand.

The hunter lurched towards it, simpering. His chest swarmed and swelled. He came at the beast with a feint, forcing its retreat. His offhand flew twice as far, catching its stony jaw straight on. Its head flew to one side, then the other, then back again, beset by a battery of punches. One last straight sent it sprawling to the ground once more. Before the hunter could capitalize, it had flapped itself to its feet. Now it fought on all fours.

"You always try that," the man mused. "Never works."

It leapt like a lion in spite of his words, its teeth forward and its arms spread, anticipating a punch. The hunter dropped to one knee, vaulted the beast over himself, and turned to see its tail come flashing across his face. The impact sent him spinning once, twice, thrice through the air before hitting the ground.

He rolled onto his back as quickly as his body would allow, still seeing double but just in time to ward off the gargoyle's eager claws. Hand in talon they grappled, matching each other's strength as the creature whipped its argent tongue across its teeth and leaked toxic spatter into the hunter's eyes. He closed them in time to avoid the poison's effects, but that bought him little time. The gargoyle's weight and leverage began to prove overwhelming. Soon, his arms began to shake.

3

With few options, he brought his heel up into the beast's ribs four times before gaining enough ground to throw it to the side. Freed, he scrambled to his feet and scraped the saliva from his eyelids. He dared not open them until he was sure that he was free of the toxin. Even so, he could sense his prey's breaths filling the forest. He smelled its metallic stench drawing closer. He heard the all-too-familiar sound of unfolding wings and counted milliseconds in his head.

Entirely by instinct, he chose a direction to sidestep, turned his frame, and caught the gargoyle's arm and leg in a single movement. He poured out the rest of his strength to lift the demon, twirl it in the air, and drive his opponent's face down into the ground. He felt the quarter-ton beast go limp, and finally he released it.

Still gasping, he cleared the remaining fluid from his eyes and opened them. They widened as he watched the tail hurtling across the ground too fast for him to escape. It swept his legs out from under him, knocking him onto his back and forcing whatever air he had left from his lungs.

Exhausted, he turned on the ground to confront the beast, realizing that it was entirely unconscious—its tail was thrashing about on its own.

"Fantastic," he wheezed, sliding away. Melting down through the snow, he turned his gaze to the great, white observer above. "It's over," he said and spat blood to the side. "Why are you smiling at me?" He did not smile back. He lay for several minutes, watching his breath emerge and dissipate into the frigid air until his growling stomach interrupted his dream state.

The hunter stood. He bound his prey with enough rope to hold a dragon, cut down his trap, and took a moment to admire his handiwork. Of all the gargoyles he'd ever captured, this one would be the last.

Then he waited until his heart matched the calm of his lungs, and he began at length to drag the beast back through the wood towards London, the moon at his back and a bloodstained smile on his face. He smiled in spite of the fear that lingered when the adrenaline had gone all away. Unease waxed within him. It was the unmistakable sensation that the hunter himself was walking into a trap.

Part I
On Tracking

Chapter One
The Call to Arms

Mr. McCrary,

I hope that this letter finds you well. It was fairly difficult to locate you on such short notice, so I assume that your time off since New York has been restful. However, your services are now required in London.

I am Walter Brimford, the executor over Western Europe, and I need your help.

I understand that you are North America's foremost hunter, with a résumé that impresses even me. No doubt then your skills would prove invaluable should you choose to assist in the matter at hand.

That said, please understand this is a very sensitive issue. I am reluctant to disclose any specific details in such an insecure medium, and your discretion would be appreciated regardless of whether you decide to accept my invitation.

If I've piqued your interest, please make your way to London no later than the seventeenth of December. Enclosed are the following: two first class plane tickets on a flight leaving from Berlin on the thirteenth (I have heard that you worked with an accomplice whilst in New York), a cheque totaling four thousand dollars US (for any inconvenience and to thank you for your consideration), and a card with the address for our operation.

Rest assured, no expense will be spared in contending with our current threat. You will be rewarded considerably for your assistance.

Brandon Smalls

Once the threat has been dealt with, I can personally promise that you will never have to work again as long as you live.

Lastly, in order to demonstrate your renowned talent, I would ask that you procure a piece of architecture to bring with you to the briefing. I am a fan of gargoyles. They hold such secrets in their icy jaws.

Regards,
Walter N. Brimford
Executor Mythic, London

Chapter Two
The Executor

"Mr. McCrary?" the voice fluttered into his dreams. Its timbre suggested a woman who'd learned to use her voice as a weapon as well as a shield. It furthered her intents and masked her motives with all the effectiveness of the hunter's cloak and daggers. As he analyzed her words—searching them for every detectable piece of information from which he could derive meaning—it failed to occur to him that he was the one whom she was addressing.

"James, is it?" James. The personal touch of her dulcet accent sent his mind into memories—to thoughts of home. As the receptionist nudged him, the serenity of his escape fled, leaving only the discomfort of stinging eyes, bruised ribs, a likely concussion, an empty stomach, and the even more troubling realization that he'd fallen asleep in an unfamiliar setting.

His head tilted up and, eyes opening, he met her gaze and sighed. "Yes?"

The receptionist's physical decorum matched the mental picture he'd already drawn up. She stood with immaculate posture, looked to be in her late twenties, and dressed like a professional, no doubt the product of a strict upbringing and meticulous training. With short, tidied hair and a demeanor befitting a dominatrix, she seemed too confident for such a menial profession. Having never worked directly with an executor, James did not fully understand the structure of such an outfit. He merely understood his role in these sorts of operations and knew that anyone associated with an executor was more than they appeared to be.

"Mr. Brimford is ready for you."

"What are—"

"I'm a reader." She smiled.

"Oh." He hesitated. "I wasn't—"

"Guarding?" they both said simultaneously. "It's okay. I'm good at what I do."

"Hold up." James stood, slapped himself awake, and took stock of his surroundings. The ground floor was empty save for the two of them. He presumed that most of the garish building was strategically vacant. He closed his eyes, opened them again, and then looked back into hers. "Now go."

The receptionist-reader folded her arms and laughed. "Are you doing a number or a color?"

"You tell me."

"Four."

"Easy. Wh—"

"Some sort of green."

"Hold on," he closed his eyes again, refocusing. "Okay, n—"

"A red three hundred eighty-seven. And now the seven is blue." She raised an eyebrow. "Done?"

"I'm kind of worn out, you know," he pouted. "Long night."

"That's what you get when you play with gargoyles."

His jaw slackened. "Wow. Memories, too?"

"Well, I do work here. We hear about it when gargoyles are dragged through the lobby at four in the morning."

"See, that's cheating," he posited.

"Maybe," she conceded. "Although, I did see when he knocked you flat out with his tail…while he was unconscious."

"Jesus," James chuckled. "Glad you're on my side."

"You're on our side already?" She handed him a bag of luggage from the ground before returning to her desk.

"Thanks." He collected himself, slung the bag over his shoulder, and shuffled out of the lobby. As he neared the sizeable elevator at the north end of the hall, he turned. "Which—"

"Thirty!" she shouted back.

8

"Wasn't guarding!" he called out, ducking into the elevator.

Assessing the lift, he found that although from the outside it appeared to be a passenger elevator, it was more likely a freight elevator with a weight limit well over two thousand kilograms meant for conveying much more than human passengers. He examined the array of buttons on the control panel and was not surprised to find that a number of the floors required a key, including the two basement levels. Walter Brimford's courier had taken his gargoyle quarry down to one of those levels, he remembered, then left him alone in the lobby overnight to wonder. Anything else on those levels had to be just as dangerous.

Shaking the thought, he selected the thirtieth floor and leaned against the side of the elevator. It stirred to life with some effort, climbing the side of the building into the London sky. Around the tenth story he noticed a massive gash in the opposite wall of the elevator. By the twentieth he'd inspected it closely enough to know that it was not the claw mark of a gargoyle; it was far too deep. By twenty-six he'd ruled out harpies and lycanthropes, and by the time he reached the thirtieth floor he was certain that he knew what had caused the scar.

He turned to the elevator doors as they parted and questioned the handgun that greeted him. "Did you have a dragon in here?"

The man with the gun lowered his weapon and corrected him. "Rakshasa."

"Hmm." James strolled out of the elevator and into the corridor beyond, past his equally-composed would-be assailant.

"Come," the man managed in an indeterminable dialect, replacing the pistol and stepping past the guest.

"I've never seen a Rakshasa before," James said, following the stranger to a pair of regal doors at the end of the hall.

There came no reply. The man ran his hands along the doorframe as if searching for a hidden switch. The sound of static crackled through the air as an iron box above the entrance clicked and unlocked the door.

James took note of the event, overflowing with questions but striving to keep his excitement to a minimum.

"Walter," the atypically-tongued man said as he slid the doors apart. "The hunter."

Light bounded into the windowless hallway, blinding James as he crossed the threshold. As his eyes adjusted, he struggled to scour the room as he'd been trained. Even as the stranger introduced him he began to make out the finer details of the office.

The room was large, even for that of an executor. He counted off the dimensions in his head according to his own system: Three-second stride to either side of the room, four to the back. Quite maneuverable. The lofted ceiling granted him twelve or so feet of headspace but denied a flying creature any distinct advantage. The back wall was made up of a single sheet of glass, likely bulletproof but not unbreakable. Just in front of the large pane lay an umber desk, likely ancient, littered with maps and books too old to be referred to as anything other than tomes.

Shelves engorged with books stood on either side of the office interior. A ladder leaned against the east bookcase. Luxurious carpets that would yield or deny traction had been placed here and there. Slick wood paneling ran along the edges of the floor. The rest of the room was bare.

As Brimford's assistant broke off the last word of his introduction, James detected the executor himself rising from behind his desk.

"Welcome to London." The two met in the center of the room and exchanged handshakes.

The hunter winced at Walter Brimford's grip. The older man had matched this grip against every sentient and animal creature imaginable and had emerged victorious—or at the very least alive—in each encounter. In spite of his old age, he was an intimidating man. Even the shadow of death kept its distance from him. His forged birth certificate stated that he'd been born on the second day of March in 1940. According to the document, he had only made it halfway through his fifties, yet Walter Brimford was, in actuality, seventy-six years old.

His hair had finally begun to whiten in recent years, a shift that made him appear all the more menacing. He kept it trimmed and combed back in a style suggesting his antiquity. His lupine-green eyes, though tremulous, boasted a certain sharpness. Most characteristic, though, was the leery-eyed grin he held in place, interrupted only when he laughed. Men had come to fear that crooked smile.

James knew none of this except for what he felt in the oddly aggressive handshake.

The two broke contact, squaring off without words.

After a moment, Walter nodded to the briefcase in James' hand. "I trust you didn't encounter any issues getting your..." he paused and cocked his head to the side before continuing, "*arsenal* through customs?"

"No, sir." His response was crisp—militarily so.

"I respect a man who does things the old-fashioned way. Guns are messy, even for men like me."

"Executors, sir?"

"Executors, hunters, and what have you. Earthers are becoming more and more suspicious by the day." He made his way back to his desk chair. "We're entering a new era, James. A more modern era. Earth's twenty-first century. It's only a matter of time before we're discovered."

James shot the strange man standing next to the bookshelf a sidelong glance. "Is that why I'm here, sir? Are there people asking questions?"

Walter cleared some of the papers from his desk. "No, not quite yet."

He rummaged through the litter of documents until he was able to produce a compact disc. "Xiang?" The third man in the room retrieved the CD and went to play it.

"I need you more for your tracking skills than your killing skills. I've got Xiang here for that. Xiang?" The man had just finished entering the disc into a music player.

"Sir?" A symphony of classical music bombarded the room from a set of speakers overhead.

Walter winced. "Could you turn that down a touch?"

"Sir," Xiang complied.

"And did you introduce yourself to James?"

Xiang nodded to the hunter.

"Xiang is my courier."

"And a lightning elementalist?" James added.

"Oh, yes, yes," Walter perked up. "One of the best. He's never failed me. He used to hunt for Mythic in the '80s. Brilliant fighter."

"I'd love to see what he can do." Xiang studied James with a statue's posture. The hunter returned a glare just as stony.

11

"Well," Walter sighed, "he's forbidden to cast within my office. And I also ask that you refrain from throwing any knives. But," the old man leaned over his desk and clasped his hands together as he tittered, "I'd love to see the two of you spar."

James' overcoat came off before Walter had completed the proposition. It clanged powerfully against the floor with the weight of a miniature armory inside it. "I don't see why not," the hunter said.

Xiang's clay countenance melted as he stepped away from the bookshelf, unstrapped his gun holster, and removed the shades that concealed most of his face. His frame hung thin and lithe, wrapped in an oversized dress shirt and loose slacks. He stood several inches shorter than James. His hair was long and black, face haggard and scruffy, eyes dark and discerning. He wore a chain with a pale blue diamond around his neck.

"What is he, second generation?" James asked, stretching his legs.

"First," Walter contested. "He came to Earth as a child eighteen years ago."

"Huh," he mused, pausing. "Maybe this won't be as easy as I thought."

Walter let slip a laugh. "Oh, no." He'd been holding in his laughter for some time. "Not nearly."

At the sound of his boss's chuckle, an impish smile carved its way across the courier's face. The gem tied around his neck glowed a brilliant, cerulean hue.

"I thought you didn't let him cast in here." James turned to the executor as the diamond's light grew ever-brighter.

Walter struggled to contain himself. "Well, not directly," he said, doubling over. "He's a reflexist," he managed at length.

"Oh." James swiveled to see his opponent and flinched.

The courier-reflexist clapped his hands together, summoning a wave of electricity that shot up his arms and down his spine. His body reacted at first with shock then settled into a familiar tension. He experienced a brief convulsion before becoming still again. The light of the gem faded and the room sank back into the warmth of the sun.

"So how fast does that make you?" James assumed a combat stance, wary of the reflexist's abilities.

Xiang smiled and spoke at double his ordinary cadence. "Very fast."

He spun as if he were dancing, his feet finding the floor in an uneven yet sophisticated pattern. One, two, three, four, one, two, three, four, one, and he was already upon him, arms outstretched for the first strike.

James winced, lowering his body, but Xiang's attack was a feint. His legs whipped around his waist lightning-quick, catching his target in the shoulder and knocking him to one side. The hunter spun to face him and brought his fists up to defend against the ensuing onslaught. Xiang's jabs were rapid and smooth, finding an ounce of flesh with each hit even when James deflected them. He pressed James towards the back of the room, countering any attempt at retaliation with the decisive strikes of his palms.

At some point in the barrage, James landed his first blow, meeting the reflexist's gut and driving him a few feet backwards. So far, the score was twelve to one.

In the interlude, James inhaled a soothing breath and felt for his foe's next move. He'd been in it long enough now. His blood was flowing and that feeling was returning; that familiar feeling which turned Xiang's next lightning strike into a glacier. James took the punch to his chest purposely, absorbed the blow, and pulled Xiang into an arm hold.

The courier took a moment in the hold, allowing his straining captor a taste of victory before catapulting his weight backwards and forcing the two of them to the ground. He slipped free of the grip and leapt to his feet just in time to catch James' fist in his open palm. James launched the other hand out and met his opponent in a fierce grapple.

Xiang stood almost a half a meter under him, twenty kilograms the lesser man, but still held his own. Gradually, though, James began to press his advantage.

"You know who wins in a grapple, right?" he grunted through a smile.

The reflexist matched his grin. The gem around his neck started to glow. James seized, fell onto his back, and shuddered for a few seconds.

"The elementalist. Every time." Xiang returned to his normal level of metabolism and moved to the bookshelf while James regained control of his muscles. Meanwhile, Walter cackled at the display before him, his laughter juxtaposed against the soothing tones of Dvořák's *New World Symphony* that still boomed around them.

The executor-turned-hyena took one final look at the courier-turned-lion then cast his gaze back to the hunter-turned-gazelle before his laughter finally subsided.

"The knives make a b-big difference," James stuttered after one last residual shock.

"Of course," Walter said, collecting himself. "Thank you, Xiang. Check up on our guest in B2."

The courier nodded and took his leave.

Walter leaned over his desk to address the grounded combatant. "Please accept my apologies, James, insincere though they may be."

"It's fine." He made his way to his feet.

"I wanted to give you an idea of what you can expect." His voice turned. The somber words twisted his smirk away. "The beast we're hunting, I would not pit five Xiang's against."

"What is it?" the hunter asked, eager to learn of his prey.

Walter's attention wandered. "He was my last courier before Xiang." He fixed his eyes on one of the weathered tomes on his desk. "He's human, but a powerful fire elementalist." He looked back to James. "And an ancient."

The hunter felt fire surge over his scalp as he heard the word. The executor watched his eyes shiver and recoiled from the sight himself.

"Frightful, indeed," he comforted James who returned to stoicism by burying a thumb in his fist. "He's one of Adure's descendants. I don't know how many generations down."

James took one hand to his forehead, massaging away his apprehension. He could feel his heartbeat bursting through his temples. "When did Adure come to Earth?"

"Not Adure. His son left Mythopia a century ago."

His mind spun. The mention of their mutual homeworld, the ever-elusive world of Mythopia, led his consciousness into a trance. James had seen it in dreams, smelled the oceans in nightmares, walked the plains in mystic visions. It was connected to Earth through a number of rifts both transient and untraceable. At some point in history or prehistory the worlds had been much closer, allowing creatures to spill over onto either planet up until the portals had started to disappear. Now the two worlds were separate and had developed accordingly.

Earth existed in a state of oblivion, unaware of its sister sphere and the unwanted wonders it had left behind when the planets diverged. The advent of modernity had rendered thoughts of dragons and magic obsolete, even unthinkable. The separate subspecies of humans left behind eventually diluted into the mainstream population but took it upon themselves to protect the creatures of Mythopia from widespread scrutiny.

In time, all manner of beasts and humanoid creatures alike learned to live in the shadows of human society, remaining merely as apparitions, fairy tales, and myths in the eyes of those who walked in the light.

"He and I had been working together for some time. We were investigating the increasing number of portals across Earth."

"The two worlds are reconnecting," James offered, familiar with the phenomenon.

"It would appear so." Walter stood and made his way to the window as if he expected to find the defector on the London skyline. "I'm not sure what set him off, but I know that with the knowledge and power he has he is an incredible threat to our existence on Earth." He turned to face the hunter. "He took something from me. A weapon. A gemstone I fear could bring this entire city to the ground."

"I'll get it."

"What he has, no man was ever supposed to use. Whatever he's planning, we can't allow him the opportunity to go through with it."

"Tell me where to start."

Walter found his smile again. "Take this." He motioned towards one of the tomes. "I've compiled a set of documents, annotated and otherwise, that should help to explain what's going on. In the meantime, I need you on our first lead immediately."

James picked up the manuscript and rustled through the mangled pages. "Where?"

"A pub in Camberwell. An associate of ours—Robert Fletcher—will be there to meet you."

The hunter wasted no time. He gathered up his coat, placed the tome in his briefcase, and began to make his way out the door as soon as he understood his assignment.

"And James?" He turned to face Walter once more. "We spoke with the gargoyle you brought in this morning. Suffice it to say, we discovered when our opponent intends to act." Walter dismissed his smile. A moment of stillness filled with an array of string instruments in full accord prefaced the revelation: "We only have three days to find him."

James nodded and exited the room. He waited for the elevator to come up thirty-two floors, all the while enveloped by thoughts of the overwhelming task before him. A gargoyle was one thing. A skilled elementalist was another. An *ancient*, a being imbued with strengths and abilities so astounding that not even full-blooded Mythopians understood them—that was something else entirely.

Thirty floors down he emerged into the lobby, still wrapped in concerns. His focus did not break until he passed by the receptionist-reader. She sat at her desk with a stack of documents pushed aside for the sake of a large book.

"Hey," he said, effectively bringing her eyes up from her novel. "You know a good place for a steak?"

She laughed and shrugged. "Sorry. Vegetarian." He sneered and started for the exit. "See you around, James," he heard from behind him. "Good luck."

"Thanks, Michelle," he responded and marched on.

She returned to her reading, only then realizing—"I never told you my name."

His back already to her, the hunter lifted his free hand, tapping himself indicatively on the head before waving goodbye.

Chapter Three
The Promethean Pendant

James,

Long ago, there lived a horrid king who ruled his subjects with fear and cruelty. Renowned for his brutal tactics and fiery anger, King Salus controlled much of Mythopia, from the edge of the Greatwood to the deserts of Raforia and beyond. The people, terrified of his might, did nothing to stop his reign. Anyone who conspired against him was put to death without incident, incinerated in fires so great that the smoke could be seen across the entire kingdom.

Salus maintained his power by granting his soldiers great privilege and amnesty from the law. Together, they suppressed the common people for over thirty years.

The queen—the beautiful and chivalrous Timone—saw the evil in her husband's heart and lamented, for it was through their marriage that he had gained his power. She resolved to end his reign and employed numerous assassins to try and take his life. With each failed attempt, though, the king grew more and more paranoid. His demeanour grew colder, his acts more wicked, and his trust waned. Soon, even his most dependable men were subjected to the same atrocities as the commoners. Many more were burned alive.

Timone, at last realizing that her husband was too powerful to be silenced directly, sought the counsel of her brother, the shrewd Aegis. He told her of a charm with unusual properties he'd acquired. Whenever the wearer became too angry, the ruby pendant would erupt into flame.

"But beware," Aegis admonished her, "for the Promethean Pendant will consume all in its reach, regardless of its bearer."

Thanking her brother for his help, the queen departed at once and went to the side of her husband. She presented the pendant to him, declaring it a tribute to his glorious strength and legendary fury. Salus, though, sensed her deceit and thrice refused the gift. He saw the intention in her heart and after the third attempt commanded her to wear the ruby herself.

Her heart sank, but Timone knew that she must sacrifice herself in order to save her kingdom. She latched the pendant around her neck and at once unleashed all the rage she'd been hiding for years. She lashed out at the king severely, swearing to end his reign no matter the cost. As she shouted, the ruby began to glow crimson red and the air grew warm.

King Salus took the queen by her wrists and ordered her to cease her seething anger, only bringing himself closer to his own demise.

Without warning, the queen burst into brilliant red flame. The fire spread instantly to her malevolent husband, and the two were bathed in fire. Both perished within seconds.

Aegis, despondent for the loss of his dear sister, took up at once the mantle of king and swore to correct the damage his brother-in-law had done. He wore the Promethean Pendant over the course of his entire reign to ensure that he would rule not with anger and hate but justice and compassion.

This is one of the most popular fairy tales still told in Mythopia today. It is the first recorded use of elementality. What we once attributed to sorcery we now know to be the gem reacting to its corresponding emotional state, granting its wearer the power of pyrogenesis and pyrokinesis. Of course, it would be some time before Mythopians learned to control the elements in any capacity. Thus, many similar stories arose over time.

The man we're looking for has a gem a hundred times the size of the Promethean ruby, his fury dwarfs that of Salus, and he knows what he is doing. Be on your guard, James.

*   - W.B.*

Chapter Four
The Initiate

"Who are you?" The Scotsman seemed more discrediting than confused. He examined his new associate as he pulled a knife-laden briefcase out of the back of a taxi and grimaced at the weight.

"James." The hunter tightened his coat and shut the boot of the car. "You're Robert?"

He ignored the question, hefted the briefcase over to this 'James,' and tossed a few pounds to the cab driver. "No offense brother, but aren't we supposed to be incognito? I don't know if a..." He paused and looked James over, choosing his words carefully as the hunter's face soured. "I'm just not sure that a tall, black man with an American accent really qualifies..." The tall, black American stared him down. "...as subtle. I'm sure you qualify."

"Don't call me 'brother'."

"Oh, sorry," he laughed. "You know, it's a black thing in the states, but here it's reserved for friends." He managed a strained smile and extended a hand. "Friend?"

James waited for the cab to roll back into the sleeted streets before he grabbed Robert's hand and faked a smile. "Let's get to work."

"Right, then." The chatty barkeep shook off his earlier apprehensions and motioned to his pub behind them. "Shall we get warmed up? My treat."

"Got any steak?" the hunter muttered as he followed him inside. "I'd kill for a steak."

"I've got lager," Robert countered.

Inside, the tables were empty save for a handful of regular denizens. They kept to themselves, strange and silent one and all. As Robert ducked behind the bar, James couldn't help but murmur, "Who are these people?"

The barkeep came up with two glasses and filled them with lager simultaneously. "You don't know?"

With a shake of his head, James took a glass and took a few gulps.

"Oh," he went on, noticeably concerned. "We're initiates, brother." He downed his beer as James choked on his.

"We? We're?" He looked over the downtrodden assortment of souls populating the pub. At a second glance, they looked more destitute than ever. Sunken eyes and heavy beards. Crushed spirits crushing spirits.

"I thought Mr. Brimford told you. I'm not Mythopian." He filled his glass again. "Far from it. I've only known about you lot for a few months."

"They're not working with us, are they?" James tried to lower his voice.

"No, no." Robert paused and drank some more, starting his second glass. "This is a sort of haven for initiates. Like I told Mythic, I think that's why the courier's been coming here."

James' eyes narrowed. "Xiang?"

Robert grunted, losing confidence, and pulled a bottle of whisky from the shelf. "Casey's!"

Thankful he hadn't been in the middle of a swig, James took away his new friend's glass and demanded with subdued gravity, "Who the hell is Casey?"

"Obviously," Robert began, wide-eyed, "there has been some severe miscommunication here. Brimford sent you here to capture a courier, and you don't even know his master's name?"

"Capture…" he muttered, "a courier?" he snarled.

The lazy heads in the pub bobbed and swiveled, catching the tiff in dreary eyes before turning back to their drinks.

Taking a beat to recover, James grasped the severity of his situation. He reached into his briefcase for Walter's tome and leafed past the passage about the Promethean Pendant he'd read in the taxi.

On the very next page:

James,

Robert Fletcher is an initiate—an Earther introduced by some means to our secrets. While some are detained and adjusted in order to protect our interests, a minority is selected to further them. This process...

He rummaged through the details he already understood, finally coming across a crucial piece of information he should have been privy to some time ago:

Casey has employed a courier of his own. Though the courier's identity remains a secret, we do have reason to believe that a Mythopian visiting the Grey Gargoyle has been actively recruiting initiates for some cause. This could likely be the connection we need to determine both the nature of Casey's operation and its specific details, as well as the scope of the endeavour.

"Learn anything useful?" Robert leaned over him, his recovered drink in hand.

"We've been in here for two minutes. How many of those have you had?"

He eyed the amber glass for a few seconds, shrugged, and took another drink. "If I still have the count, then clearly not enough."

James thumbed through a few more pages, making sure he wasn't missing any other vital clues, then stowed the tome and turned his attention back to the initiate-alcoholic.

"When does he usually show up?" Both pairs of eyes shot to a clock on the far wall.

"About this time," Robert replied, squinting.

Half past one. Walter hadn't had enough time to debrief him in person, instead relying on James' particular set of skills to push him to victory. However, in this instance, he was operating out of the dark—a circumstance no hunter liked to be stuck in. He had no time to set any effective trap, no intelligence about his prey, and—he looked to Robert, the half-drunk Earther with his head tilted at the wall clock as he attempted to take another drink sideward and spilled it up his nose—no support.

"Robert," he said, somewhat discouraged, "can you at least tell me what this guy looks like?"

"You got it, brother," he said, choking. Then he slammed down his glass in a show of triumph, splashing it all over the bar. "Sorry." He grabbed a rag from behind the counter, explaining, "I'm a little nervous. I've never actually worked with a Mythopian before." James felt a pair of eyes bounce to him. They belonged to the man in the nearest corner of the pub, the one with a drink in hand. He made a mental note of it.

Robert held his hand at eye level. "Small guy. Carries an umbrella— big black number—even when it's sunny."

"Probably bulletproof," the hunter postulated, forming a more complete picture of his victim with each detail.

"Ya think?" Robert's mind raced. "Is that gonna be a problem?"

"No." The calm of his voice reassured the initiate, if only a little. "What else?"

"That's all I've got." He paused. "Sometimes he comes with cards he gives to the fellas he's been bletherin with."

James brought his speech down to a whisper. "Has he given anything to anyone who's here now?"

Robert's eyes shot downwards, his jaw going limp. "In the corner. With the red hair." The hunter knew better than to make eye contact with the man who'd been watching him this entire time. His best option was to allow the scout to think he had an accurate stock of the threat then deny the advantage later. The only thing worse than cornering one animal was cornering two.

"You think he'll warn the courier?" As he looked up, James could see the fear creeping into the Scotsman's bright, brown eyes. He then thought he might be confusing that anxiety with nausea.

"I need to have a look around. Stay here. Watch my shit. Act natural."

"Here. Shit. Natural. Got it."

James left the pub, drawing as little notice as possible. Robert ran his rag across the countertop, shaking, trying to behave as though everything was all right. Then he locked eyes with the red-haired initiate in the corner of the room.

The desperation in his eyes evaporated. He was no longer another faceless husk. This was a servant of the enemy, one of Casey's soldiers. As his gaze constricted the timid man, he rose and strode over to the bar.

"I need to use your phone," he murmured, looking down to keep Robert's eyes on his.

The other initiates watched, sensing the moment's gravity, weighing whether they should flee or remain still, invisible.

"Maybe I could make the call for you?" he attempted, swallowing his words. The fiery-haired initiate held his dead-eyed gaze. "No?" Robert broke off the stare. "Hell with it," he muttered, abandoning his protective stance over the telephone. He grabbed a tumbler, poured himself a glass of whisky, and acted natural.

Chapter Five
The Courier

James caught sight of the courier walking along the opposite side of the street as he cleared the pub. The man was the only person for a mile who was carrying an umbrella, either paranoid of snowfall or prepared for something else entirely. The hunter sized him up like he'd been taught, taking in the way he held the umbrella, which would suggest whether it was a weapon, a shield, or a combination of the two; his dress, which might betray his elemental preference; and the way he moved, which would reveal his fighting style.

The courier's steps were sluggish and sloppy, as if he weren't accustomed to walking. He held the umbrella like anyone else would have. He even managed to look cross about it, appearing to be just another Londoner let down by the local weather report. He dressed like a common businessman in an overcoat: suit jacket, vest, slacks, dress shoes, a shirt and tie. Here was a man who understood the power of anonymity, but he was not without tells.

His coat, like the hunter's, hung open in spite of the cold. Otherwise they wouldn't have quick access to their weapons. For James, his daggers. For the courier, likely a gun. A quick scan of the man's arm confirmed his suspicion. His right arm hovered too closely—too rigidly—to his body.

James bore similar indicators. He strode with all the confidence of a demigod, a man who'd seen and conquered everything. The tension in his hands betrayed him, as well. He looked to be someone who was used to clutching something—a gun, a knife, or even a sword. Even in the English winter his coat was too large and bulky to be comfortable. It unmistakably concealed his defenses. His boots, likewise, were alien— all-purpose treads designed to grant traction on even the slickest surface, a mainstay of the melee fighter. Had the courier been expecting an attack that day, he would have cross-analyzed his opponent and understood him completely. Fortunately, though, he was late for his engagement and hurried across the icy road into the Grey Gargoyle, not once stopping to check his surroundings.

After sighing relief and ducking behind a corner, James set about defining the rest of the battlefield. He didn't have much time before the courier either escaped or took Robert as a hostage. Discarding any façade of normalcy or civility, he bounded down the street, identifying buildings, gated alleys, walls, and dead ends. After a brief circuit, he wound up back at the pub, taking stock of its back exit. It led into an alley with only two viable escapes: the street-side opening—a red door topped with barbed wire—and a pipe that ran up the neighboring building. He didn't have time to test it but did not expect to use it, anyway. He tried the backdoor, which was of course locked, before rapping on it.

Sure enough, a few seconds later the door flew open, just missing his shoulder. Robert peeked out from behind it, more disheveled than ever. "God, it's good to see ya, lad." He stumbled backwards. "Might've had another drink."

"Just the one?" James caught him and propped him up.

"Might've been a double," he joked, working his way back to the front of the pub. "Treble. Trible?"

James stalked in behind him, dipping a hand into the lining of his coat, and began to focus. He tried to slow his heartbeat and conserve the adrenaline for when he needed it, but this fight might be over fast. *Very* fast.

"They know you're here," Robert hiccupped, grave. "This is it, brother. I couldn't stop him. He was on the phone saying you were here."

The hunter nodded, taking the lead as they emerged into the pub just as the door chimed, heralding the courier's exit. James could still see him through the glass windows, his umbrella over his shoulder. He took no time to react. He bolted straight for the door, sighting the fiery-haired man rushing from his table. James threw his arm forwards at less than half force, leveling the traitor-initiate. The man sprawled, unconscious, to the ground.

"Call Xiang to pick this guy up," James roared as he thrust open the door.

"Jimmy!" Robert shouted after him. "Watch yourself!"

No time to stop and listen. The hunter was determined to intercept his prey. If he could not take the role of the lion creeping in the grass, then he would adopt that of the cheetah and overtake the courier by force. Regardless, he would always strive to be the predator. It was his nature.

He saw at once the courier at full sprint down the sidewalk close to the pub's back alley. James matched his pace with speed left over, positive that he would reach him in only a few seconds. Then his prey did something unexpected.

The courier knew this area, without a doubt. Why he would allow himself to be cornered, the hunter could not ascertain. Nevertheless, he sped in blind pursuit when the courier turned into the back alley and shut the red door behind him, trapped like a swine.

James let his adrenaline take charge. The battle would be upon him in seconds. He reached the red door with his coat flapping behind him, glistening array of daggers in plain view. The bystanders, the innocent men and women who saw him racing after his prey, faded into the air, out of mind, irrelevant to the hunt. Any repercussions—any witnesses—meant nothing now.

He struck the door with considerable force, snapping the wood frame that held it into splinters, and emerged into the alley. His jaw was clenched, his eyes were wide, and he was ready for anything.

Except this. James stuttered to a stop, the adrenaline rush dropping as quickly as it had arisen. The alley was empty.

He cursed and charged on towards the pub's back door, his vigor deterred. Had they left it unlocked? A sudden pang of concern washed over him as he thought of Robert left to fend for himself in the front of the pub. He tugged at the door handle, expecting it to come free, but instead found it still secured. He turned, puzzled, and froze at the sight of the opening of the alley.

There, with the umbrella casting him in shadow, stood the courier.

He did not speak. He stayed still and silent only to gauge his opponent's response. Presumably unimpressed, he took a pistol from inside his coat and fired.

James dropped instinctively to a crouch, faster than any Earther could ever dream to react. He could sense the silenced round by sound and feel as it whirred over his head and into the door behind him. His hand already in the lining of his jacket, he had only to direct the projectile as he launched a throwing knife at the assailant.

The courier answered appropriately, ducking out of the alley doorway to avoid being impaled, and James took this one and only opportunity to escape. His adrenaline back at full tilt, he catapulted himself off a trash skip and jettisoned up the side of the next-door building, shuffling up the gutter pipe at an incredible speed. He felt the shots around him, one in the pipe, another in the wall, one through the tail of his overcoat.

With milliseconds to spare, he threw himself over the building's edge and onto the rooftop. He had no idea how the trap had been reversed or how much time he had to adapt to his new environment, but he knew that at the very least he had to determine what kind of elementalist the courier was.

He cycled through the five disciplines in his head: fire, water, earth, lightning, and wind. Which one the courier wielded he couldn't be sure. He went back through them one by one, resolving to find an answer.

If it were earth, he could have simply gone through the wall of the neighboring building and doubled back to the alley. This would mean that an engagement on solid ground would favor the courier the most.

Halfway through his appraisal of fire, James got his answer. He heard a gust howl up from below, the sound of a single flapping wing. He turned as the courier rose above the rooftop, umbrella in hand. His free hand was extended to command the wind, a glowing emerald ring on one finger.

James reached for his knives without delay, aiming a trio directly at the floating courier. He in turn waved his hand to the side, and the current beneath his umbrella left, diverting to protect his front. The knives parted as they neared him, trailing off to each side and into the distance.

The courier reached for his sidearm as he dipped then dropped to the roof. He landed with superb grace in spite of the height of his fall, the slope of the rooftop, and the icy terrain. In less than an instant he had his gun trained on the hunter's chest. James darted down the side of the roof, taking cover behind a chimney as the voiceless assassin fired a salvo of suppressed shots across the rooftop. James made a note of each shot fired and tried to determine the make of the gun, but he came up blank. Frustrated, he made another dash across the rooftop the moment he heard a lull in the firing.

He made his way behind another chimney, thankful that he was in London and not on the desolate roofs of his native New York. Another two shots. At this point, he had the option of continuing to flee until he had a terrain advantage, or he could make the bold assumption that his foe had emptied his magazine and would be vulnerable for a few seconds.

He wisely selected the first option, listening to another triplet of suppressed shots ring into the roof tiles as he bounded off the edge of the building. He'd measured the distance when he had surveyed the area. In retrospect, it wasn't nearly as short as he'd thought. Four meters across, he started to wonder if he'd survive if he fell.

His entire body took the impact as he struck the concrete and caught the edge of a window frame. He clambered onto the roof of the building with what wind he had left and hid behind an air conditioning unit before his opponent could bring his gun to bear again.

Tucking his umbrella under his arm, the courier sidled to the edge of the roof. James could hear him in the static void of winter, fumbling to reload his gun.

"92FS?" he queried, trying to confirm a suspicion. "You're a fuckin terrible shot," he taunted when no response came.

The courier chuckled. "You taking the piss? You having a laugh?" came his firm English accent. "Are you left-handed? Cause I'm not." The wind elementalist devoted his primary hand to his umbrella. His left—the same one adorned with his emerald—was what he fired with.

Weapon loaded, he chambered the first round with some difficulty. "You're quick for a big guy. Shame you don't have anything to fight back with." James stayed silent. "Nothing personal, mate. I've got to do this." His emerald lit up as he extended his umbrella and stepped off the rooftop. The wind picked him up like the outstretched hand of God and ferried him to the building above. "I promise I'll make it quick," he said over the tumultuous air before settling on the second rooftop, that of a flat with an assortment of A/C units in the center and a sheer drop off the opposite side into the parking lot.

With a burst of energy, the hunter sprang from cover, showering the courier in a rain of knives. The latter moved to protect himself, summoning a fierce tailwind and deflecting them all, but in the process, he'd lowered his weapon. He'd lowered his guard.

As he approached him, James crossed his arms and reached deep into his coat. He drew twin fighting knives from their holsters. The two blades, Yin and Yang, shrieked into the air and descended upon the courier. The man brought his pistol up to shoot and lodged the muzzle into the hunter's gut, pulling the trigger.

The weapon fired and the round raced forwards into the white sky above, striking nothing. James twisted, catching the courier's arm between his elbows and wrenching the gun from his grip. Yin and Yang met in his left hand, his right finding the pistol. He twirled it, one-handed, into position and aimed it straight at the courier's head.

The battlefield fell into a sudden hush. On one side, the hunter stood poised for victory, the product of a glorious chase, a brazen dash, and a fortuitous strike. On the other crouched the courier, his hands resting on his umbrella, ready to react at any instant…but at this range, what was the point?

James stood fast, knowing that he only needed to uphold this balance for a few moments before the man at the end of his iron sights buckled and submitted. Then it happened again.

His senses darted to the last time he'd fired a gun, the last time he'd tried to take a life with a half-hearted pull of the trigger. It hadn't been a target or a bounty. He recalled the smell of pine, the frozen silence of a snowcapped country, the sting of subzero air on bloodstained skin. He remembered the eyes of his victim—not afraid, not angry, just

29

disappointed. He could feel the ice rushing from the sky to numb him. He could taste the blood that channeled into his gaping mouth as he panted. And all around him he could sense the approving eyes of his allies, united in bloodlust, demanding that innocent blood be spilt against white hills on the basis of some half-truth he'd never been fully sure of.

He must have lingered in his mind for a moment too long, or else the courier had intercepted his thoughts more easily than he could anticipate. The defeated man's brow wrinkled. He tightened his grip on the umbrella, testing the hunter's resolve. His trigger finger did not move.

Without another thought, the courier slid a blade through the tip of his umbrella and sliced at his attacker, catching him off his guard. The blade grazed his right shoulder, making a shallow incision. The gun fell from his hand and clattered to the ground. James managed to kick it to the edge of the roof before stepping back to dodge a second swipe.

The courier stood tall, assuming a fencing stance while James redistributed his daggers and took a stance of his own. The fencer-courier lunged, forcing his opponent a great distance back. The hunter backpedaled right into an A/C unit, momentarily losing his balance and affording his foe a prime opportunity. His stabs were precise and measured; seldom did he wager a reckless attack. His range prohibited any attempt at a counterattack, and his speed took its toll on the hunter's stamina.

As James became more and more accustomed to his opponent's style, though, the opportunities made themselves manifest. He sidestepped one of the courier's thrusts, seeing it as the perfect chance to hurl Yang towards him. The courier was unsurprised, deflecting the blade with a flick of his wrist and a pocket of pressurized air. Yang spun through the air and landed a good distance away—too far away to retrieve. He saw the hunter's hand dive into the side of his coat to pull another dagger and lunged, disregarding his defense for the first time. James twirled to the side, catching the blade in his coat but sustaining no injury, and watched as the umbrella turned rapier tore a set of throwing knives from the lining. He fumbled to catch one of the weapons as they plummeted, but the courier's assault allowed no chance for their recovery.

30

Once he ran out of throwing knives, James' ability to fight would be severely hindered. It was only a matter of time before the aeromancer's impregnable defense and faultless form overwhelmed him.

James sidestepped a blow, wheeling the fight back to the A/C units, determined to reverse the advantage. He took Yin in his left hand and reached his right into his coat, just far enough to draw a lunge. The courier obliged, thrusting his blade right through the thin aluminum wall of an industrial air heater. The hunter took the extra half-second he'd just gained and tore the umbrella away from its wielder.

Stumbling backwards, the courier's calm evaporated as he glanced around for a weapon. His eyes caught the throwing knives discarded on the ground then the ones hurtling towards him. A wall of wind repelled them. An instant later he saw the hunter, surefooted and enraged, stampeding towards him, one fang primed and ready.

He widened his stance. The ring on his finger glowed verdant green, intensifying to a level unseen as of yet throughout the battle. The courier brought one arm forward, shot the other back, and ushered forth a column of air so powerful that it forced James onto his heels as he raised Yin to strike.

The courier launched his back arm forward to meet the other, calling a rapacious torrent of wind. The surge struck James head-on, driving him a few meters backwards.

It was all the hunter could do to point his body and drive through the wind tunnel. If he turned to escape it, he'd be blown over the side of the building. He trudged through the howling gale step by step, all the while enduring rush after rush of air.

The elementalist summoned every last bit of strength he could muster, pushing his art to heights he'd never before attempted. Each time he brought his back arm forward, another wave of intense pressure shot into the column, battering James in a deafening burst.

"Don't fight, bruv!" the courier strained to be heard over the clamoring wind. "Die! Die! Die!" he repeated with each wave.

James let his arms fall backwards, let his coat slip off into the vortex. It caught the current and blasted across the rooftop. His drag reduced, the hunter paced on, fighting the force with a tenacity that doubled that of his adversary.

He gained, closer and closer, three meters, two meters…

The courier's heartbeat quickened. His blood turned to acetone.

"You know who I am?" He put all of himself into the storm that raged on the rooftop. "I'm the man who brought down Archadus," he bellowed, referencing a dragon so great he had terrorized England from the shadows for decades. "I am Gerard Jones! I am a legend!"

James reached forwards, now within centimeters of his prey. Yin's cold steel was a hair's length from piercing Gerard's outstretched palm. The blade howled louder than the wind, hungering.

The courier faltered for a moment before shaking his head. *No*, the hurricane seemed to roar. He reared back, preparing himself for a final gambit.

The hunter's eyes widened.

Gerard Jones leapt into the air. His arms and legs extended, commanding a wind so great that not even James McCrary could stand against it. It hit him square in the chest and knocked him into the air.

He gave in to the current. He had to. He struck the ground with force, nearly dislocating his injured shoulder, and continued to move at an alarming speed. Yin had left his grip seconds ago. His hands darted over the cold, smooth concrete on the roof, fighting for a hold—anywhere—but finding none. He leveled out just as he smashed against the lip of the roof and toppled over the edge.

Gerard breathed for a moment, rediscovering his calm. He stood carefully and straightened his tie, fixed his jacket, smoothed his wind-scrambled hair. Then he went to retrieve his gun. Pausing as he lifted it from the ground, he looked across the rooftop and decided to take Yin and Yang as trophies. Satisfied, his new weapons tucked inside his jacket, he readied the pistol and went to the edge of the roof to finish whatever nature and gravity had left up to him.

He hopped onto the edge and peered down, finding nothing on the ground below. Instead, he felt a fearfully powerful grip around his ankle. All sense of balance left him as the hand tore him from the rooftop and swung him through a glass window on the side of the building.

James kicked out the glass that remained in the frame and followed his prey into the apartment below, happy that he got to be the lion after all. Shards of glass littered the body. Blood poured across the linoleum floor. The hunter nudged the courier with his boot to ensure that he was out, took the emerald from his finger, recovered his blades, and smeared them with his victim's blood before securing the apartment. He could hear two-tone police sirens wailing from the street towards the Grey Gargoyle and knew that he needed to hurry. Silenced shots were more than loud enough to draw attention. A windstorm on a rooftop maybe more so.

"You know who I am?" he called from the next room, mocking the accent. "I'm the man who brought down Gerard Jones." He reentered the room with a set of sheets and a garbage bag and then set about disguising his fallen opponent. "I'm a legend."

Chapter Six
The Fall of Vaos

The famed courier Illius' delivery of word of the victory at Ponsithia was the feat that effectively ended the War of the Falling Sun, the legendary struggle that ended the Elven Age, tearing Mythopia apart and dividing it for the rest of history. His penetration of the CotA lines was the only way to relay the message to the besieged capital of Raforia to lash out against the Cultist forces in concert with the elves en route from Ponsithia.

What follows was penned by the famed bard Ynir, who watched the hero run through enemy ranks from atop the mile-high wall of the city. Aside from Vaos and the ancients themselves, he is widely regarded to be one of the war's greatest legends.

- W.B.

Lo! and see the agony he wracked upon our foes
Hark! unto the gallantry with which he mended woes
The man who saved Raforia as he from westward rose
Illius of the elven with his emerald aglow

A score of mighty warlords stood by me on the walls
A sea of silver longswords below in scattered squalls
Illius of the elven, through the shifting, swirling sand
Tore swift across the hostile ground with emerald in hand

An Infidelitous Earth

The Cultists went to meet him, eighty thousand at the least,
Determined to defeat him, with their allies in the east
They galloped all around him, on horseback and afoot,
Took seconds to surround him in the sand and ash and soot

From high above the carnage we watched them as they raced,
Each man-at-arms oblivious of the ruby on his waist
We saw the glint from miles away and cheered his glorious name
The courier took a fighting stance and showered them with flame!

The horses reared into the air, their riders fell from grace,
And even from the wall we saw the smile on his face
Illius drove his fire like a dragon scorned and spurned,
And struck a path straight through the Cult with every louse he
burned

In concert with the ruby charm his emerald beamed bright
And shaded him from missile harm around its verdant light
The Cultists barked and fled away as fire pushed them back,
But through the boiling air we saw the eastern line attack

A waterfall of dragons came in answer to their cries,
Undaunted by the courier's flame with malice in their eyes
The drakes let loose a torrent of the elements they breathed
The fire, ice, and poison struck the earth which swelled and seethed

We bore a frightful witness as the greens' miasma rolled,
In terror, frightened witless as the blues unleashed their cold
And cringing with the sound of reds and blacks exhaling gas,
We saw the dozens drowned in heat and frost and poison blasts

But oh! the shout that came about, so thund'rous and resplendent
When we beheld Illius rising unscathed and ascendant
Aloft and o'er the perils of the battlefield below
Right to the wall of Rafor with his emerald aglow

Brandon Smalls

He neared the endless coil that we'd draped across the wall,
Began to climb the battlement in battle gear and all,
Assisted by the archers that our general assigned,
But in the heat of battle, Cultist arrows cut the line

He toppled to the surface, using wind to break his fall
And hurled a hundred curses as he turned to see them all
A sea of eighty thousand came to quell the courier's words
And we could not assist him with our bows or with our swords

The general insisted that we not release our ranks
And forced us to stand passive as the horde came at his flanks
The courier stood silent as he drew his shortblade out
His enemies grew violent as he opened up his mouth

Illius drew a mammoth breath, and much to their dismay
He let howl high a battle cry and charged into the fray!
With titan ire and dragonfire he set upon his foe
Illius of the elven with his emerald aglow

They stuck him with a spear and sword when four of theirs he'd
felled,
But he his present fear ignored and to the bulwark yelled
His missive, carried by the wind his emerald invoked,
Came crashing through the rigid air as he his message spoke:

"Vict'ry o'er the azure flame," his weary lips imparted
Just as the life left from his eyes, before his soul departed
And in the tepid stillness, through the ashes in the sky,
We saw a host of gryphons swarm towards us in reply

A thousand winged allies came stampeding from the west
And we unleashed our army at the general's behest
Then through the Ebon Gate the Knights of Rafor charged the Cult
And pinned them in the middle of the field as a result

And hearing that their god had seen the light at Adure's hand,
The Cult of the Apocalypse took wing and fled the land
Pursued by Rafor's valiant men and plagued by Zephyrus,
The Cultists met their fated end and fell to the abyss

And to this day Raforia pays homage to the elf
Who rescued all Mythopians by sacrificing self
His gemstone hangs atop the city, so that all may know
Of Illius of the elven with his emerald aglow

"I found it," Robert interrupted him, pulling a piece of tattered parchment from the red and white bundle of sheets. James shut the tome and tucked it under the seat of the initiate's car. "But he's lost a lot of blood, brother." The sobering Scotsman glanced to the shards that littered the backseat. "We've gotta get him to hospital."

"He's going to Mythic. They'll take care of him." James reached out for the message, the next lead in his hunt.

"I can't make heads or tails of it." Robert turned the paper sideward and tried to read it in the low light of the alley they were parked in. Shrugging, he handed it over to the hunter. "What do ya think?"

James stared at the writing on the parchment, eight words meant for the courier's allies and no one else. Eight words no more menacing than a verse in a poem. Eight symbolic words strung in syntax that sent an old god's azure flame down his spine.

"Vaos lives in the blue fire of London."

"What does it mean?" Robert leaned in close to find his friend's face weak with worry.

"Cultists," came James' voice, shaken. "The Cult of the Apocalypse."

Chapter Seven
The Torturer

The hunter's pace did nothing to mask his fear as he shoved aside the doors leading into Mythic. He moved like prey, feeling every eye that found him. Robert filed in after him with a body still tangled in red linens draped over his shoulder. He was nowhere near as cautious.

"Jimmy? Little help, brother?"

"Michelle," James murmured, ignoring him. Mindreader or otherwise, it was clear to the receptionist that he'd just discovered something significant. He motioned to the courier. "Get him into the basement. Get him some help."

Wordless, she kicked off her heels and hurried to assist the sobering initiate.

"Thanks, lass." Robert smiled. She sensed his foremost thoughts and shot him a severe look. "Something I said?" he asked innocently.

Ahead, James hailed the lift and waited for the other two to make their way across the lobby. They then set Gerard down inside the elevator.

"I appreciate the help," Robert panted. Michelle took a key from her blouse pocket and inserted it into the lift's control panel, unlocking one of the lower levels. "Would you believe he hasn't said a word in twenty minutes? All the way down here it was like talking to a bleeding stone. This is a fancy place, by the way. I'm Robert." He extended his hand to the reader, but she and the hunter were already exchanging words.

"We do have other offices in this building," she said. "You can't just bring in bodies at midday."

"Like my wife," Robert prattled on in spite of them, "not much of a talker, that one."

The hunter's eyes remained straight ahead. Neither his mouth nor his mind yielded a word. "What's going on?" Michelle asked, impatient.

"Cultists," James replied, stone-faced. Robert's comment had segued into a lengthy anecdote that neither of them noticed.

"I see." Michelle turned her attention forwards as her voice fell out from under her and the elevator chimed.

Robert gawked as the doors opened and a sharp screech rushed in between them. "What was that?" he asked, turning to James.

"Just a gargoyle," the hunter reassured him. The Scotsman's pupils dilated and the blood drained from his face. "It's fine. He's probably tied up." James hefted the roll of sheets and started down the long white hallway before them.

"Probably?" Robert stammered. "Probably is good enough for you when there's a gargoyle involved?" He retreated to the back of the elevator, his eyes still wide with animal panic.

"Come on," the hunter commanded, pivoting to face him.

"I—" he hesitated, eyeing the hunter carrying a dying man without an ounce of discomfort on his face. "Right, then." He shot Michelle a glance. "Ladies and hunters first," he joked, extending his arms to show the way. Her nose wrinkled as it picked up the strong scent of cheap whiskey. She wasted no time sidling past him.

As she did, James watched the initiate's eyes drift down her frame. "Focus, Robert," he grumbled.

Even without her eyes on him, the reader could feel the thoughts creeping up from Robert's blood. Four seconds into the corridor and her patience was already stretched tightly over the complacent smile she flashed at him as she turned.

"What'd I do?" His eyes stayed up while his thoughts stayed low and his stream of consciousness continued to radiate from his libido. Michelle wasn't responsible for all of his adrenaline, however. She recognized the telltale fear in his voice when the moans in the next room began to louden. So did James.

"Here," he said, offering Robert Gerard's body to distract him.

Somewhere in the tumult of his mental disarray, the initiate extended his arms to take the courier. At that exact moment, the gargoyle's roar flooded the passageway. He recoiled instantly with the wounded man loose in his grasp, and Gerard dropped to the concrete floor.

Robert's ambient thoughts came to a standstill. "God Almighty, I hate that sound." Michelle sighed, thankful for the relative silence, and moved to help him with the body. "Sorry," he whimpered, "I *am* just an Earther." In that instant, their eyes met. The reader expected a torrent of emotions, a few lewd thoughts, a crass remark, but sensed only: *What beautiful brown eyes.*

Caught off guard, she felt her breath fall into her gut as she pushed the courier into the Scotsman's arms and made for the door. Beyond it they could hear low, droning music that did nothing to cover the gargoyle's cries. Robert's mind and mouth stayed quiet while the noise in the next room rose around them, filling him with fear just as it pacified the two veterans.

James opened the door to reveal a circular chamber cast in scathing, artificial light. Rock and roll blasted from inside. The floor, walls, and ceiling were bare and white. The latter left barely enough room for a tall man to stand beneath. The creature in the center of the blank void had been forced onto stony knees. Its arms, legs, tail, and wings had been bound, its jaws bolted shut. Its viscous, grey ichor drenched the cement floor in a wide perimeter.

Above it stood the courier Xiang, painted in red and black. Covered in the beast's blood and his own, he looked to be a proud warrior poised over an assured kill. He looked over his shoulder to see the newcomers, greeting them with a scowl.

"We need the room," Michelle demanded of him over the clamor as she circled the gargoyle. Her tone indicated her disdain for the torturer and his craft.

James' eyes adjusted slowly to the light, but he could hear the gargoyle straining. Robert crept behind Michelle like a pup, too paralyzed to voice a single concern. Gradually, the light in the hunter's eyes faded so that he could see the reader and courier planted opposite each other, defiant in spite of their mutual allegiances. "This man needs help," he reminded them. "I don't know what this is, but we don't have time for it."

Xiang grunted, then snorted, and finally stepped over his captive, striking him in the neck with one heel to invoke a pathetic yap.

The grappling match between James' curiosity and his pity was enough to turn his stomach. He saw Xiang toss something down—what looked to be a handheld blowlamp—next to a stereo playing a cassette of '80s glam metal. On top of that he noticed two neat lines of white powder and a baggie to match.

"Well, that's something," said Robert, happy to have a milder vice. He looked up at the gargoyle to see the left side of its face watching him, the right side having been seared to a pulp. His stomach softened. He struggled to maintain his vision and his grip on Gerard as he hurried after Xiang and Michelle who were already at the door on the other side of the chamber. "James?" He watched the hunter approach the gargoyle, stand over it.

"Go on," the hunter told him. "I have to see Walter."

"Right. Come get me when you're done." The gargoyle stirred, leaning towards the hunter in challenge. Robert found himself moving to the exit before the choice could occur to him. "As soon as you're done."

James nodded to him as he left then turned to face his earlier prey. Broken and mutilated, it didn't strike the hunter as a trophy. This was a caged animal; the most unpredictable kind.

"Is this necessary?" he asked. He could hear Xiang returning from the next room.

"Is what necessary?" the torturer-courier sneered in his deliberate tempo.

James answered him with a scowl. "It's a little much."

"Since when does the Stoneslayer have love for gargoyles?" Xiang squatted down over his stereo and pulled a rail of the white powder through one nostril before standing and politely offering the other line.

"Thank you, no."

"Whatever it takes." He shrugged and turned back to admire his welding work. "I'm wrapping up. He's been in and out, but this has helped us."

"Sure," James said and started towards the lift before Xiang could offer him something more revolting or more tempting. "Let me know when your heart stops."

"I can restart my own heart," he said with a confidence that almost inspired inquiry.

The best hunters were masters of survival above all else.

Chapter Eight
The Gemologist

Left with his concerns, the hunter's mind flew back to the task at hand: catching the renegade ancient. Tracking a man was easy enough, though this was no ordinary man. Even an ex-courier the hunter could understand. A Cultist, however, was something else entirely.

The Cult of the Apocalypse was not a religious sect. It was a theocratic army. A conglomerate of heretics Earth-wide and Mythopia-wide led by a deceased god and a set of faceless prophets. It was effectively indestructible. How it maintained its ranks remained a mystery to even the highest Mythopian authorities. At any point in time, though, its agents were presumed to number into the tens—if not hundreds—of millions. It wasn't just its size, however, that made it frightening. Not since their defeats at Ponsithia and Raforia had the Cult emerged in any significant numbers. Its soldiers made it worrisome. Its ideologies made it dangerous. Over two hundred years of silence were enough to make any undying entity terrifying.

If this was the uprising, the return of the Cult, the rekindling of the fanatic fervor that had almost destroyed a world that was *prepared* for it, then Earth could not hope to endure it.

After thirty-one floors of desperate rumination, the lift opened into the plush hallway preceding Walter Brimford's office, a stark departure from the bleach-white torture chamber that was B1. Passing along the soft burgundy walls textured and trimmed with gold, most would've been soothed. James boiled.

With Xiang indisposed, he had no way of opening the executor's electric lock. When he reached the end of the antechamber, he rapped the door with a clenched fist. Moments later, the executor appeared with a pair of jeweler's glasses strapped to his head. "You've come back."

James rolled past him and paced next to the desk which had been cleared of all its reference material and refitted as a jeweler's station.

"Don't sound too surprised."

"Oh, I do apologize," he said with a laugh, taking the barb in jest. "Also sorry Xiang wasn't here to let you in. He's downstairs with our gargoyle guest. Say that five times fast." He repeated it thrice.

"I caught the courier," James interrupted, flustered.

"Of course you captured the courier," he simpered, weaving his way back to his chair. "No courier could compete with your incredible combat capabilities."

The hunter answered his playfulness with silence, distracted by the matter at hand and the array of gemstones on the executor's desk.

"Ah," Walter said, noting his curiosity, "I'm something of a gemologist. Dabble now and again. Sojourned in Mythopia for a time studying in an elven lapidary. Can I get you something? A nice sapphire or a diamond, perhaps?"

"I don't cast," James replied curtly, his face swelling with contempt.

"Really? I was under the impression that you did."

"Used to." Choosing not to linger on the subject, he went on: "How much money do you have, you can just buy up gems whenever you need them?" Though the cost of each element-controlling gem was not terribly restrictive, the sheer volume of demand among Mythopians often mushroomed the prices. A novice fire elementalist could burn through a thousand dollars' worth of rubies in less than a day of training.

Walter sat, his youthful smile now retracting into a static grin. "I've worked hard for my wealth, James—bled for it." He took a pinch of sequin-sized diamonds from a sieve and let them trickle between his fingers. "Now I use my money and influence to make this world a safer place."

"Yeah," the hunter scoffed, "training psychopaths like Casey to cast fire."

The warmth fled the room.

"There are always investments that go sour, Mr. McCrary. You of all people should know that."

James flinched. "The fuck you mean by that?"

"You and the financial straits you find yourself in." Walter watched James recoil from the assertion. "A prodigy of a hunter groomed by some of the greatest, yet not a red cent to show for it. There must be something that swallows up all your profits. Why else would you need a job that pays like this one?" The hunter settled into the accusation, still feeling its bite, but reined in his reaction. "What is it?" the executor plowed on relentlessly. "Drugs? Gambling? We all have our addictions. Casey's after the same thing. He's only—"

"You think he wants money?" James leaned across the desk, pulled the Cultist parchment from his coat, and threw it down. "He's a Cultist, Walter."

Walter's lips straightened. His eyes ran over the damning evidence lying before him once, twice, and again. "Oh, Casey. It's true, then," the old man muttered.

"You knew about this before you wrote me."

The executor sighed. "I couldn't be sure."

"If it was ever a question—"

"I could have killed him, yes," the executor's tongue lashed, "when I started to suspect. Or could've tried, at the least. It was weeks before he left. I didn't..." he paused, turning to the window before continuing, "I didn't have the presence of mind to stop him. Or the heart, I suppose. You have to understand, James, that there have been Cultist flare-ups in London for centuries. If we jumped at every shadow in the street, we'd exhaust our resources in a matter of years. This business is all triage."

"Does New York or Paris know?"

"God, no. I've cried Cult too many times to bring them in on something this close to home. If they actually smelled an uprising, New York, Cairo, Paris, Athens, Rome, Berlin...they'd all come down on this city with an iron fist."

James paused, considering the option. "Might be that's what needs to happen."

Walter turned with reddening eyes and a childish smirk. "Friend, you don't want another Chicago Fire or sack of Rome in this day and age. We've reached a troubling threshold. We can't deal with the Cult that way anymore."

"Throwing money at the problem won't make it go away."

"No," he said, laughing at James' naivety. "Not this time. I thought Casey was after Mythic, just another disenfranchised employee trying to escape to a nameless island for the rest of his life. I should've known he was more ambitious than that." He looked up from his desk and saw, for a moment, the judgment in James' eyes. "Don't think that I'm an idiot. Money works most of the time. I funded the expedition that hunted Archadus."

James nodded, unimpressed. "And now Gerard Jones is bleeding out in your basement." He took the emerald ring from his pocket and tossed it in with the rest of the collection.

"Christ, he was the courier?" Walter dropped his head to his fist. "This circle of trust just gets smaller around my neck."

"Good thing I'm handy with a knife." James was smirking as the executor looked up at him, seeing that his hand was outstretched. "Let's get this done."

"All right." Walter agreed with a handshake. Still, he hesitated to go on. At length, though, he conceded. "Let me tell you why you're here."

He pulled a sheet of paper from one of the desk drawers and laid it flat across the bare portion of his desk. It depicted a robust stone of a peculiar cut and color with notes and measurements drawn around its edges. According to the footnotes, the gem had to be at least the size of an apple and several times heavier.

The hunter's eyes iced over. He did not blink for some time. He studied the paper before asking, somewhat apprehensively, "What is that?"

The executor regarded the diagram with silent horror and sharp reverence; a twisted worship of the stone's likeness. As he explained, his eyes remained transfixed by it. "I took this from the Cult forty years ago when I was in the old world. It would seem that after all this time under Mythic's protection, the Cult found a way to retrieve it. This is the gem Casey stole. It's the largest of its kind, the single rarest gem on this Earth—the Eye of Vaos."

The ancient moniker again plagued the hunter's thoughts. "Vaos."

From the stories he'd heard of the Cult's draconic god, he knew that this translucent, black stone was too small to be one of his eyes. Nevertheless, the gem's image disturbed James. It was as if it watched him even without a pupil, studied him, relaying information back to a remote mind somewhere in the aether. "What kind of gem is that?"

"It does not respond to ordinary manipulation. As far as we can tell, it doesn't control any of the standard five. Popular speculation is that it governs a sixth."

A sixth element. James felt his knees weaken.

Having appeared behind him, Walter interrupted his thoughts with a hand on his shoulder. "Of course, the novelty of this information should impart all you need to know about its confidentiality. Mythic controls only a handful of these gems. As always, your discretion is appreciated." He backed off.

"Mythic doesn't know it's missing," James deduced.

With his back turned, Walter shook his head. "You, Casey, and I are the only ones who do, as far as I can tell. And it must remain so."

"Well, you bought my silence," the hunter vowed, "and I know a good way to keep Casey quiet."

"You'll get your chance," he promised, turning with a devil's smile. "In just a few days," he reminded him. "And then this—" he alluded to the courier's message still crumpled on his desk. "'Vaos lives in the blue fire of London.' Couldn't be less cryptic. It's obviously referring to the waterworks, but that doesn't get us much further."

James took on a vacant stare. "How you figure that?"

Shrugging off his disbelief, Walter elaborated: "Cultists are always harping on Vaos and his legendary blue fire. In every manifesto and codex I've come across, they've called it the water of the apocalypse. So, the message is that Casey is hiding underground. In the sewers."

His pride hurt from not having deciphered the code himself, James chalked it up to Walter's extensive knowledge of the Cult. "Then we look underground."

"Go ahead." After a moment's pause, the hunter turned to leave. "I'm kidding, James. We can't canvas the entire London sewer system in three days. It's tens of thousands of kilometers long."

"You'd be surprised how lucky I get," James responded with a sidelong glance.

"We have to dig up every piece of information we can while we've got the upper hand. Casey won't sit for long without word from Gerard."

In a moment of inspiration, a ripple of apprehension rolled across James' face. "I know someone who can help us." The executor stared expectantly at him. "Emily Galloway."

"The elf?" Walter smiled, surprised by the hunter's resourcefulness.

James widened into a triumphant stance. "We're old friends." The statement resonated with more emotion than he meant to let on. "If anything is going on with the waterworks, she'll know."

"Good," the executor breathed. "Good. I'll go to market and look for anyone who's been buying up earth and water gems in any capacity and, in the meantime, have Xiang sit on the courier."

"I'll see Emma tonight," James volunteered and moved to leave. "Emily," he corrected himself.

Walter chuckled, inviting a glare. "It was women, then," he teased.

Turning to look over his shoulder, the hunter asked, "What was it with you?"

The executor took in air then thought better of it. In spite of himself, though, he offered an answer. "Gems," he said. "The gems. The power. Always."

Satisfied, the hunter exited into the luxurious hallway with garish walls and gaudy moldings, now seeing a hall of champions instead of a nightmarish squandering of wealth. For reasons he did not understand, he felt the compulsion to run his fingers along the western wall, noting the texture, basking in the aurulent light cast from overhead and underfoot.

When the elevator doors opened, Michelle and Robert stood in its frame. They found the hunter held captive by the corridor's walls.

"Gerard?" he asked, seeing the reader's blood-soaked blouse.

"Stable," she reassured him. "He'll live as long as Xiang keeps him that way."

"That's a good start," James began, his head turning back to the walls. "Robert, do you know where Club Tranq is?"

"Tranquility?" Michelle asked, puzzled.

The Scotsman's head tilted. "You thinking of doing a little dancing, brother?"

The hunter joined them in the lift and pressed the button for the ground floor. "There's someone I need to see." He held his smile tight as they were brought down, even though his eyes echoed sorrow. All at once it dawned on him that the thought which had lifted his spirits even in the face of certain apocalypse was of Emily.

Chapter Nine
The King

In my youth, I corresponded for a time with a prominent Mythopian figure: the current king of Raforia, George MacArthur. His moniker may come as a shock. Suffice it to say, the people of Raforia have a certain predilection for Earth's culture. After an early and marginally successful military career, the king adopted the title "MacArthur," as the American general was one of the foremost military commanders at the time. The surname has belonged to the royal family ever since.

MacArthur was usually referred to as the king, but at other times "The General," and sometimes "The President." This infatuation with America has always entertained me, especially in recent years with the US's current enemies, as the Raforians are tied ethnically to the people indigenous to Saudi Arabia, Afghanistan, Iran, and the like. George's original name was Junaid. Junaid al-Aziz.

He invited me, in some capacity, to join him on a campaign (a desperate publicity stunt to garner public favor) to root out and exterminate the Cultists hidden in the nobility of the neighboring Kingdom of Salamance. I obliged him, as I had never visited Mythopia and was eager to study the native gems firsthand. It was 1968 when I disembarked through the Belizean-Raforian gate in what was then British Honduras. It wasn't until many years after my return that I received a missive bearing the king's seal. What follows is the letter George MacArthur sent to Earth just before the last documented portal collapsed. Before it arrived, we had no idea just how dire the situation across the stars had grown.

An Infidelitous Earth

Walter,

Do you remember when we stormed Son'Qila? It was a good day. The days now don't compare. No one knows about that like we do.

You were already in the city, ready beyond the walls, when they denied me entrance. Karim bellowed up to the gatekeeper shaking like a new recruit. He must have never seen a dwarf in full plate before. He was worse than you when you saw your first dwarf. "I thought they were small!" you said. "He's two meters even!" "Yes," I said, "he's on the short side, this one." Still, the gatekeeper would not let us pass. "Here I come," Karim said. "Ready or not."

Have you seen a city wall crumble before you? The sound delights me. Karim and the other earthshapers blasted the portcullis from the barbican. We charged. No matter what, we would not stop.

The bells rang for their morning prayer. Our shouts drowned them out. Their soldiers came down the rampart. We buried them. I blew my dragonshorn and Hellsmouth flew in from the sea. Their archers turned just in time to see fire rain from his jaws. We went on like that, fighting.

Talon and fist, we fought until we met you at the Golden Square. That you must remember. The fighting was thick by then. We didn't have the men to sustain it. The streets were narrowing—Hellsmouth's fire couldn't reach. We moved to the keep where the city would open up again, but we took more licks than we could give. It was a tough fight, even for the king.

Of course, the Archduke of Whatever the Fuck was there at the bridge with all his knights. He must have hoped for some brilliant dance of steel. A duel, I think he wanted. He asked if we meant to declare war. I answered him with the sound of my horn. Hellsmouth answered him with the sound of his fire. I left you with Karim to hold the bridge, and I went on into the golden keep. There was nothing to be afraid of.

Vaos, though, did not live in the gold walls of Son'Qila. I told you that we found the marquess and his family there, butchered. Most of that was the truth. The children were dead when we found them, but the marquess was nowhere to be found. I did not murder them. All we found alive were serpents.

Keep thinking the uprising is centuries away. Keep telling your children they're safe. That city reeked of the Cult. You're no safer than a king is.

It is coming.

Safe times are gone along with the good, but we still have something to fight for.

From the beginning, someone baited us into that trap. There was no Siren. There was no King of Serpents. Now the marquess leads every city east of the desert in open war against us. The nations that claimed to be our allies in the war against the Cult have abandoned us. The Elf Queen and her mages, the Lord of Legend, the Dragonlords—traitors every one of them. I have sacrificed my health and my kingdom's safety to protect this world, and we have nothing to show for it.

Everyone will see soon enough. You'll see on Earth as we see here that total war is inevitable. When it comes, the Cult will slip onto every battlefield. They'll infiltrate every city. They'll inhabit every court. The Knights of Raforia will be ready. Will the knights of Earth be ready when it comes too soon?

I lost contact with King MacArthur after the Belizean-Raforian gate collapsed. After that, portals became shockingly scarce. What correspondence we did receive revealed that the alliance between the nations had failed and that Raforia had become an isolationist state, extending aid only to nations that paid tribute to MacArthur. Furthermore, we learned that armies consisting of Salamancian soldiers led by the Marquess of Son'Qila had begun encroaching on Raforian and even Ponsithian territory. That was in 1986.

- W.B.

Chapter Ten
The Elf

They could hear the bass from blocks away. The deep, deep rumbling that thumped through the sidewalk and up into their chests only drew them closer. The streets were dark, lit by the occasional lamppost, the glistening snowflakes, and the slowly waxing moon above. Ahead, though, they could hear the music and the crowd, they could feel the beat, and they could see a spectrum of flashing lights from the next street lancing through the shadows.

The hunter and the initiate turned the corner and saw at once the nightclub rising out of the earth like a great pyre. Club Tranquility. The entrance roared whenever the doors opened. A few patrons filtered out every so often, but the queue of Londoner-moths being drawn in from outside was immense. The line stretched all the way down the block to the end of the street where the two onlookers paused, gaping at the spectacle.

"Christ Almighty," Robert cried, slack jawed, "it's more popular than I thought." He turned to his companion, adding, "It's half ten on a Monday!"

James peered over his companion's head to see a stampede of men and women sidling past them and into the line. "We're not waiting." He motioned for Robert to follow and stepped out into the street. They walked alongside the line for half a kilometer before they reached the front, a hundred scornful pairs of eyes fixed upon them. Robert forced a smile and waved to them, attempting to placate the crowd, but only invited insults.

The patrons jeered at the out-of-place visitors, targeting their obvious weak points. Robert wore dated and burly winter wear while James had his thick coat to counter the cold and conceal his weapons. Conversely, the people awaiting admittance were dressed in what they thought to be appropriate attire for the occasion. They wore tight-fitting jackets and coats over thin dress shirts and short skirts, shivering on the pavement.

Amidst a wave of slurs and derogations they made their way to the entrance where a cluster of bouncers stood and watched the street with wary eyes; sentries at the castle gate. The hunter stepped over the velvet rope on the edge of the walk. Robert ducked under behind him and came eye-to-forehead with the tallest guard who stuffed a hand into his chest and snapped, "Oi!" Having commanded the intruder's attention, he continued in an East London dialect, "Queue starts back there, mate." He pointed his thumb to the tail end of the line.

James ignored him, motioning for his accomplice to head on inside. "I'm a friend of Emily Galloway," he shouted over the restless mass waiting in line.

The bouncer, unmoved, laughed and replied, "I'm sure she'll be appy to see er old friend once e's wai'ed in line." He motioned again.

"I don't have time for this." The hunter stood his ground while Robert began to float back onto the street. "Just let me in."

The bouncer rolled his neck and shoulders in a show of intent and said with volume, "I'm not gonna tell you again." The two squared off, locked in a mental draw, while the people at the front of the line grew more and more impatient. In his peripheral, James could see the two guards at the doors approaching. The lead bouncer said once more through gnashing teeth, "Back. Of. The. Queue."

"Yeah, sod off," a short man with too much gel in his hair and too much goatee on his face called from the sideline. The hunter shot him a glance. The man-mouse flinched.

Another red-nosed patron, though, joined in on the abuse, her hands wrapped around a fur shawl. "We've been out here for hours, arsehole!"

Under his steady pretense of rage, the hunter calculated in an instant the parameters of his situation—distances, targets, terrain, and tactics. He determined that he had sufficient room for the maneuver he had in mind. He determined that he could cause an upstart without harming any of the women nearby, the ones who continued to test his patience with a chorus of shrill yowls. Finally, he determined that the bouncers were close enough for him to carry out his plan without any hitches. So he did.

The man with the sloppy scruff could not have possibly seen him coming. The hunter was upon him in a blink. It must have appeared to him that the six-foot god-knows-how-many-inches man had simply skated across the ground towards him. So he didn't react when the titan grabbed him by the collar and hoisted him into the air. He couldn't perceive it quickly enough. He couldn't react until he felt himself hurtling towards some unknown object in the distance. To him, in that moment, it looked like a bouncer.

A trio of enraged men bolted from the line, shrugging off the shock of the other bystanders while the bouncers came from behind. James let them all throw their first blows. He knew well enough that he'd dodge the bulk of them and that any punches that *did* make their way through couldn't compare to the dwarf that used to knock him flat with a slap to the temple, the gargoyle that had once broken his nose with a cement fist, or the drake he'd seen topple a car in one charge. It almost felt like cheating.

He felt a straight to his chest glance off as he twirled away from the center of the storm and shoved a bouncer into the group in one measured motion. Trapped in his course, the thick security guard that had first delayed him found himself moving headlong into a collision with the rest of the combatants. The six-man pileup, in turn, obscured the hunter's escape as the bouncers and patrons clawed over each other in the maddening cold.

James slipped back past the velvet rope and shot a glance at Robert, still standing dazed in the street. "What part of this," he repeated his gesture from earlier, "did you not get?"

The initiate jolted to attention. "I'm just the chauffeur," he defended himself before following James through the doors of Club Tranq and into the belly of the bass-laden beast.

Just inside the heavy metal doors stood two more security guards, oblivious to the bedlam outside. The new pair of visitors slid past them into the club's atrium and looked over their shoulders just in time to see them peeking out at the scene. Upon seeing the situation on the street, they ducked outside without exchanging words.

"Nice work there, brother." Robert winked and patted him on the back.

He couldn't help but indulge the amiable initiate. "Thanks, brother," he said, affecting his best Scottish accent.

"Is that what I sound like?" he asked as they pressed on to the entrance hall.

In the first chamber, they discovered a bar, lounge seating, bathrooms, and a large gate leading farther into the club. Through the portcullis, James could see the massive dance hall populated by no fewer than half a thousand people. The techno blaring from the chamber pulsed in tandem with an assortment of multicolored lights high above the atrium.

Besides that, only a few neon blue lights lining the ceiling illuminated the room. The soft tones soothed the hunter's animal tendencies. Artists had carved a series of elaborate moldings and installed beautiful murals on the walls, an intricate array of scenes from high medieval chivalric romance. In the fresco that caught his eye, the hunter could make out a battle between a proud, long-eared man and a vicious armored foe. The elf held a sword in one hand and an iconic emerald pendant in the other.

He smiled to himself. All around him he noticed familiar themes, locales, and persons and felt, for a strange moment, at home. The next moment, though, he remembered his purpose and made his way to the man taking drink orders across the room.

"I'm looking for Emily," he rasped over the pervasive music.

The bartender turned his attention from another customer at the mention of her name. He stood just an inch or two shorter than James, dressed in a long, classical azure robe and a number of ornate pieces of jewelry. A pair of shining sapphires swung from his ears, the sight of which took both James and Robert aback.

"You're an elf!" the initiate exclaimed, forgetting himself. He pointed to the slender, pointed ears protruding from the man's long, blonde hair before looking to James for confirmation.

The bartender glowered at him, taking the reaction in stride. "Yes," he managed at length. "That's the theme of the club." He indicated the mural of Illius on the opposite wall. "Elven culture." He made sure to gesture symbolically at the mention.

James and Robert exchanged puzzled looks and turned back to him. "But you're an actual elf," the latter contended.

"It's a costume," the barkeep replied, agitated. "They make us wear them. Did you say that you were looking for someone?"

"Aye," answered the initiate, "someone to tell me I haven't gone mental."

"I need to speak to Emily," James said, commandeering the conversation. "She owns the place?"

"Galloway?" The hunter watched unease swell behind the elf's expression as he looked to the entrance of the club where he saw no one standing guard.

"My name is James McCrary," he declared, attempting to calm the employee.

"*The* James McCrary?" came his astounded response. Even with the music in the foreground his voice sounded throughout the entire atrium.

"No, that's his cousin," Robert retorted. James punished him with a jab to the ribs.

"I'm Leon Sharpe," the elf said, eliciting a response. The hunter stood silent for a moment, unsure of where he'd heard the name before. "My sister is Sabine Sharpe," he went on, elated.

"From Berlin?" the hunter inquired with an inkling of a memory.

"Yes!" He struggled to contain his excitement. "You saved my sister's life."

The hunter shrugged, a small grin creeping across his face. "Just a little lindworm, man." He spent a moment trying to think of something to add in the case for his modesty, eventually shrugging again with a laugh.

"So humble," Leon chuckled. He turned to Robert, informing him, "This man is a legend in Berlin. He took on a dozen gargoyles at once with nothing but knives and a garnet."

"I didn't know you were a geomancer," Robert said, his interest piqued. "I've never seen you cast."

His smile subsided. "Yeah, I used to." Again, he searched for words to further his thoughts, finding none suitable amongst those bubbling up in his heart. His mind, though, lingered elsewhere. "So, is Emily here?"

"Miss Galloway's office is in the back," Leon told him, finally calming down. "I'll take you." He looked off into the distance and called a replacement over. "Can I get you anything?" Leon asked the two of them as he made his way around the bar. "Complimentary, of course."

Robert stifled a smile. "Whisky sour?" he petitioned him, holding up a finger. A look from James led him to reconsider. "Neat, then?" The hunter moved away as Leon started off to the club's main room. "I'll bet they have steak here!"

"Later," James said as they emerged into the fray.

The elf couldn't help but declare, "You know, James, my sister is quite fond of you."

He used the ensuing jump in ambient noise as an excuse not to respond. They came presently into the dance hall—the primary chamber of Club Tranquility, the epicenter of the entire establishment—and the beauty of it astounded James. In every direction, he saw elves talking and dancing along with their sister species.

Some of the patrons wore what were obviously fake elf-ears, rubber costume pieces that pointed straight up. With some, though, that particular piece of anatomy proved to be more convincing. A select few were unmistakably of Mythopian descent and couldn't be more at home in this indifferent environment. Here was the tolerance every Mythopian craved from the world with none of the adversity. It was as if they belonged.

"This is unbelievable," James thought aloud.

"Isn't it?" Leon concurred. "Miss Galloway is making London into the new Serendipity. A home for elves everywhere."

"How many here are elves?"

"At least thirty work in the club. Hundreds live in the city, maybe more. Miss Galloway plans to bring them from all over Earth." Leon turned to regard him as they sidled around the dance floor towards the back of the club. "We may be only a few months from revealing ourselves to the world."

The hunter's brow wrinkled. "Mythic won't let you."

Leon giggled out loud. "They can't stop us. Besides, they're more concerned with Earthers not finding out about dragons and gargoyles. They won't mind if word of just one race gets out. What's more, the humans accept us here. They'll accept us out there too, if we give them the chance."

James turned back to see the crowd of revelers twisting in euphoric trances, swaying and swerving and sliding. Outside of this club they were separate, man and elf, one living in daylight with freedom and abandon, the other in shadow, forced under hoods, hats, and long hair. Despite being one of the closest relatives to humans, a vast distance remained between them.

"What's to stop the other races from following your lead?" James asked.

"Nothing," Leon told him with an unflappable smile. "This world is big enough for all of us. It's time we learned that."

The hunter kept his doubts private. It seemed a lovely notion, however delusional. *But the world*, he thought, *does not welcome its guests or its immigrants. The world rejects.*

They soon came to a door guarded by a pair of elven sentries around the back of the nightclub, beyond the dance hall. Leon approached them first. "James McCrary to see Miss Galloway."

One of the sentries nodded. "She's been expecting you." Leon turned, surprised, and motioned for James to go inside. Robert followed, only stopping when one of the elves placed a hand on his shoulder. "Why don't you wait with us?" The initiate looked to his friend for instruction.

"I won't take long," James promised, turning through the back door and heading up the long flight of blue stairs towards Emily's office.

"So," Robert started once he'd left, "how's elf life?" All three ignored him. "About that whisky…" he mentioned to Leon.

One of the elven sentries pointed towards the entrance to the dance hall. "Where is Mendel?" His partner looked to him, equally confused.

Robert, too, looked towards the front of the club where he saw of a pair of elven bouncers hastening to the entrance. "Must be one hell of a fight," he said to them, shrugging.

Leon's ears stiffened. Off in the distance, he thought he heard something like a rushing flame.

Chapter Eleven
The Lover

James' heart was quivering, but not for the normal reasons. Ordinarily he could control it. He could manipulate the rate at which his blood pumped, could regulate the epinephrine in his bloodstream, could focus his eyes when they wanted to blur from excitement. Now, though, he could hear his heart beating above the muted music back downstairs, and he couldn't do a thing about it. It was an unfamiliar feeling.

As he reached for the door, he felt his heart tunneling down into his stomach, searching for something in the way of solid ground. Each time he inhaled he felt closer to suffocating. He pushed it inward anyway, breathless as the light came in from her office and bathed him in warmth.

Emma, he said in his mind, but could not for the life of him speak the name aloud. *Emma*, he tried again, fruitlessly.

"Jim," she said, smiling, as the door closed behind him.

He felt the joy pacing inside him. He felt his wild heart wriggling in his ribcage. "Emma," he cried at long last, and smiled.

She'd been sitting cross-legged in the center of her office, meditating. The moment she'd heard his footsteps her concentration had dissolved. Now she stood with one hip out, a few meters away, her teeth glowing as radiantly as ever. Her smile electrified him, sent a charge down the length of his spine, and evoked a physical response. He at once began to march towards her.

In his head, he kept saying her name like a mantra, over and over again. *Emma. Emma. Emma.* She did the same with his. *Jim. Jim. Jim.*

She bit her lip as he approached and closed her eyes tight as he took her up into his arms, pressing her into his neck with the strength of a great, black wolf.

James gripped her as tightly as his heart commanded, knowing that she was strong enough to take it, and he hesitated to let her down. When he did, though, after a long, blissful instant, he peered into viridian eyes, lingering in them while Emily watched his lips.

Then something else struck the hunter's spine all at once. He took a step back. "What happened to your ears?" He studied them for a moment. They weren't long and pointed as he remembered them but short and round and ordinary.

Emily looked up, surprised at first. "I got them cut." He stared back, stone-faced. "Plastic surgery. Just to make things easier."

"Oh. You…look good," he said, letting his feelings diffuse into the words.

"Thank you," she replied without confidence, still scrutinizing him.

His full senses restored, the hunter glanced around the room. Emily Galloway's office was exactly the sort of environment he would expect a water elementalist to inhabit. What light there was came from the lamp on her desk, the row of small windows at the top of the back wall, and the colossal water tanks on either side of the room.

They were mostly empty, save for a few exotic fish that floated about, relaying their calm to the room's inhabitants. Each tank stretched from the ground to just below the ceiling, effectively wallpapering each half of the room. She'd decorated the front and back walls with the same iconic murals that adorned the rest of Club Tranquility.

The floor was hardwood. Emily had been sitting on a small, square mat during her meditation—a common practice among hydromancers, as they depended on composure for their discipline.

"I came to talk to you about the waterworks," James said once he'd gotten the lay of the land.

"Oh," she said, almost giggling before his silence stole her smile away. "You came…to talk about the waterworks?"

He thought about confirming this then thought better of it. "I—"

"I haven't seen you in ages." Her tone warped.

"I'm working for Mythic. We're looking for someone. It's

important. I could really use your help right now."

"Would you like something to drink?"

"Water." Something in her voice had set his teeth on edge. He couldn't be sure if it was anger, but he knew he'd never heard it from her before.

She took a pair of drinking glasses from behind her desk and set them down. A sapphire ring on her left hand lit up quickly, and with a wave of her hand she began to condense the vapor in the air. Water began to appear in floating globules. These she commanded into the cups. The action soothed her, but even so her mood remained tenuous at best.

"I love your water," he reminded her. "So pure."

She feigned a smile back and handed him a glass before circling back to her desk. "And now you want to hear about the waterworks."

The hunter took a sip of his drink and nodded. "There's a pyro in London right now. I need to stop him right away."

"And you think he's hiding in the sewers?" She stared him down with a furrowed brow and an illegible attitude.

"Have you heard about anything in public works? Missing workers or engineers?"

"What are you now, a detective? One of Mythic's dogs?"

"I'm old, Emma." He showed it in his voice. "I'm too old to keep going like this."

"What does that make me?"

"All I want is a paycheck and a fucking rare steak."

"Well, not all of us are willing to give up on everything that matters to us."

James waited for the sting of the accusation to depart before going on. "Have you heard anything—"

"No," she shook her head. "Nothing." She lost herself in thought for a moment and then returned. "I've been really busy with the club." She spread her arms to indicate their immense surroundings. "How long has he been hiding?"

"In the sewers? Not sure." They stood in silence for a while.

"Where have *you* been hiding?" Her question took James by surprise.

Caught, he conceded. "Berlin. New York before that," he added, stifling a laugh.

"Why?" The question she'd been waiting to ask for over a decade. She'd sharpened it specifically for this occasion, poised it for the hunter's heart, and found flesh.

James melted all at once. "Emma..."

"Why didn't you come back?"

Her words turned to frost in his ears. The hunter felt them drift over him from the top down, hardening his veins as they coasted towards his chest. Shuddering, he shed his lover's mantle and restored the stony skin of his namesake. "It's complicated." The bluntness of his answer seemed to satisfy as much as injure her. "It wasn't because of you."

"The *hunt*," she guessed, mocking him with a click of her tongue.

"Are you sure you haven't heard—"

"Yes," she asserted once more, cutting him off. With a little more tact, she repeated, "Yes," and the room descended once more into dead air.

The fish at the walls watched the scene unfold, undisturbed by the goings-on. From their calm realm of water, everything seemed less than horrible.

"There was something," she began, still thinking.

"Yeah?" The hunter tapped a finger against his glass, hanging on every word.

Her eyes fled to the ground. "In Manchester. Some people have gone missing."

"Manchester? Like what, how'd they go missing?"

"I don't know!" she exploded as her eyes struck him. The room's temperature seemed to drop in answer to her rage.

James leered at her, considering his options. "I can go if you want me to."

"No," she railed without hesitation. "It's been ten years. I don't know why, but I waited for almost all of that time."

"I'm sorry," he said immediately, lowering his defenses a notch. "I didn't mean to break your trust. Things got bad. I had to run. I couldn't come back west."

She shook her head and flooded her lungs with air. "When you

64

called, I thought—"

"Yeah, I apologize." He tried to find her eyes, but her gaze had gone back to the floor, to her mat. She attempted to reclaim her calm. "When I heard your voice…" he discarded his present thought, determined to do what he'd come to do. "I should have thought to tell you that I was coming here for work."

"Mmhmm," she agreed. Her eyes were beginning to well up. "It's all right."

The hunter lost his nerve, at once. "Manchester, then?" he shrugged, preparing to leave.

"Yes," the once lover, now informant said as he approached her with his glass. It was still mostly full. As he handed her the water, he felt something carnal emerge from her, a thought through her eyes and into his. He heard, unmistakably, as clear as if she'd spoken it aloud, *No.*

"Hmm?" he mumbled. "Did you say something?"

She looked at him in similar confusion. "No," she said, as he heard a simultaneous *Yes* emanate from her mind.

"Emma," he began, his doubt rising. "Are you lying to me?"

"No," from her. *Yes!* from her. He chose to believe the inward response.

She saw him react to her deceit, saw the disbelief lurch into his face, and her eyes widened. "Can you hold this?" She handed him her glass.

"Why are you lying to me?" he interrogated her, his hands tightening around the two glasses of water.

She drew her hands into her sleeves and behind her back, listing towards the fish in one of her tanks. "Jim," she said, shaking.

"Why?"

The elf turned to face him. "Casey told me to."

The hunter's heart seized. His mind struggled to comprehend what his soul had already deciphered. "He's a Cultist." Emily did not respond. "He's insane. He's dangerous."

"That's funny," she replied, "since between the two of you he's the only one who hasn't hurt me." The arraignment silenced him outright. "What do we know about the Cult?" She struggled to place confidence in her words. "What do we *really* know?"

James hesitated to respond. "You have to tell me where he is so I can put him down." She met his demand with a cold and impudent stare.

"James, I love you," her voice twisted out of her, "but I will kill you if I have to."

He flinched, motivated by a sickening combination of instinct and revulsion. "What?"

"I worked for twenty years to do what Casey has done for me in a matter of months." The elf stood and stared him down, an unnatural fury creeping from behind what had moments ago been quiet, green eyes. "All the money. All the resources. Integration."

"Do you even hear yourself?" The hunter felt his senses dull but could do nothing to refocus his attention.

"Do you believe in anything anymore? Where's your passion, James? Are you even capable of it?" The hunter took the blows as best he could as she picked apart his old wounds, but he could not suffer this injury.

"Stop," he snarled. "Ten years is a long time. If you'd been through what I've been through, it'd feel a whole lot longer."

"It's been tough all over," she growled back as a tear bled down her flushed cheek. "Thank God it'll be done soon."

"Emma!" he shouted in one last attempt to bring her back to him. "This is not you." He edged towards her. "This isn't *you*." She recoiled as he drew close, assuming a fighting stance. "What's wrong with you?"

"Geoff!" she shrieked. "Nigel!" No response came from the stairwell. "No one. I have to carry the burden myself. Always."

She pulled her hands from behind her back and James immediately saw the sapphire glowing on her hand. His eyes narrowed as he considered what she could be casting. All too quickly it struck him as he loosened his grip on the glasses in his hands.

He glanced down and saw the cups emptying, twin torrents of water rushing towards his face. The two streams hit him like a helix battering ram with all the force of a well-placed punch—one he could not shrug off. When the water cleared, he was choking and coughing on the ground, struggling to stand, the shattered glasses beneath him.

"Leave," the elf droned, "like you do."

"No," he sputtered, still clearing his windpipe. "Don't trust Casey. You don't have to trust me, but don't trust him."

"He's the only person—"

"He'll kill you." And all at once the hunter sprang from the ground. Emily's calm waned in the shadow of her fear and her sapphire dimmed. "I won't let him kill you." His voice softened. "Not you."

A roar split the air as the music outside cut out. After a moment, their ears could make out the unclouded chaos. They heard shouting, gunshots, and fire rising over an alarm.

"No," was all Emily could think to say.

James considered his vulnerability in this situation just in time to hear the door behind him burst open from the force of someone's heel. He heard them enter: one, two, three, with murder in mind. Emily only shivered.

"Before you shoot," he said, still facing away, "just—" A spiteful shot rang from each gun, three bullets right into his back. He sank to the floor without another word.

Emily backed away, half by instinct, and questioned her assailants. "Casey sent you?" Her eyes watered in anticipation of their response.

"No," the man in the lead murmured. He spoke without emotion or intention as he stepped over the hunter's body.

James struggled to breathe without revealing that he was still alive, his lungs constricted in his bulletproof vest and his options limited.

"Who?" Emily asked, connecting to her sapphire as she backpedaled.

"Vaos." The lead assassin trained his pistol on her. Emily brought water crashing through the aquariums just as James sprang back to life.

Two of the gunmen turned to fire wildly at the cascading waters on either side. These the hunter raised and silenced in a single motion. Their necks lifted with all the ease of dolls' heads and snapped with the right movement. The remaining gunman fired twice at the elf, but her legendary elementality stood up to the challenge. She pulled water from her left and right, crossing two streams between herself and the attacker like whips. Both bullets softened in the water and veered off course. Before he could make the choice to fire again, Emily criss-crossed the streams like scythes. Each one took a femoral artery.

The wounded man dropped his weapon, fell to his knees, and looked up, pleading for a moment as if he'd remembered something. Something distant. Emily brought her streams back in a final scissor, severing the thick blood vessels on either side of his neck and stifling anything in the way of memory. He toppled over in a gurgling mess of blood and water as the elf uncrossed her arms and let her element splash to the ground.

The hunter and huntress crouched over their quarries in a frozen instant, their backs heaving as their lungs growled. James glanced at one of his legs, noting a shallow laceration—the by-product of a vengeful elf.

"Sorry," she said, panting.

"An inch more 'sorry' and I bleed out," he scolded her.

"Sorry," she snapped again. Then, softly, "For everything."

"You have nothing to be sorry about." James unbuttoned his shirt and tore open his armor, allowing for a sudden influx of oxygen. Gradually, his thinking cleared. "Can we go out those windows?"

"You can," she answered, shaking off a little anxiety. "If you want to risk the drop."

"Why, where you going?" More gunshots rang out from the dance hall. He could make out the screaming quite clearly now. A dozen deaths at the least, Earther and Mythopian alike. Chaos: the lifeblood of the Cult.

"If he's going to burn down my nightclub, he's sure as fuck not getting away without a scratch." She started towards the door, pulling several hundred gallons of water behind her. "You coming?"

James looked down to his feet where a number of fish flopped for air, now quite concerned with the events outside of their aquatic world. They reminded him of a certain initiate. "Yeah," he replied and followed her out. They rushed down the stairs in a shin-deep cascade of water, opening the second door into a maze of panic.

"Geoff!" Emily flew at once to the aid of one of her guards who lay dying on the ground. Meanwhile, the hunter gazed upon the building before them being consumed by flames while a mass of squeaking patrons clogged the few narrow exits. The fire lurched across the ceiling above, threatening to race down the walls.

"You wanna do something about the fire?" he shouted to his accomplice, insensitive to her circumstances. He took one look at the fallen elf with three bullet wounds in his gut and shrank from her glare.

"In the ways of the old, wisdom." The guard seemed appreciative of her parting words. "In the ways of the young, beauty." He tried nodding, too far gone to mirror the sayings, as was the custom. "In the ways of those to come, serenity," she whispered, and kissed him on his forehead. "Good night," she finished.

"Good mourning," he echoed before passing. Emily then turned to the water leaking down the stairs and set about quenching the blaze.

James stepped down onto the dance floor, finding countless bodies that had been shot, stabbed, burned, or trampled to death, wondering all the while what purpose a Cultist would have for killing these innocents in particular. There was no mistaking it, though: Casey was here. The hunter glanced at a smoldering corpse, that of a human. The area where he stood had been scorched both precisely and ruthlessly. Now soldered into the man's hand was a knife.

James was in no condition to take the fiend on.

He turned to see Emily at work putting out the fire, but it had already spread too much for her to handle on her own. Almost all of her brethren had fallen. The elves that remained, he ascertained, were outside. "Emma, we have to go."

She ignored him, continuing to fight the walls of fire that spread around them. He tried again to get her attention, but it was in vain. Frustrated, he snatched her by the arm, pulled her from her feet, and began dragging her from the club. He shouldered his way through the thinning crowd at the exit, wary of other gunmen and, most of all, the pyromaniac at large. He moved with utter disregard for the safety of anyone but himself and his charge. "Robert!" he shouted, nearing the outside. "Robert Fletcher!" His mammoth voice barely reached above the din.

At last he penetrated through to the outside, the street already teeming with firefighters and police plowing through veils of snow to help the innocent and apprehend the guilty. In this uproar of souls, though, the distinction was as blurry as it could be. He worked to remain undetected as he pulled Emily through the swarming white and black. The elf spoke not a word. Once they had cleared the chaos, he pressed her against a wall and barked, "Tell me what I need to know about him."

She responded only with tears.

"Emma!" he howled loud enough to draw attention from the

bystanders still watching the burning club.

When she sank into his chest, he ceased his assault and held still. Exhausted, with smoke and sirens around them and a thousand questions to be answered, she asked him, "Why did you leave?"

He could not understand her words under her sobs or above the panic, but he knew what she had asked all the same. "Why didn't you?" he asked, an excuse in place of the real answer.

"I love you," she told him. The declaration, however familiar, felt empty. "But I could never keep up with you." He looked around, defiant, at the streets and the city and the madness. "You're always on the hunt. Obsessed with it."

"This is it," he assured her and looked into her eyes. They were green and quiet again. "The last hunt. This is the last time."

She laughed, inspired by anything but humor. "You have passion. So much of it. But it's not for me. And it's not up to you." She buried her head in his chest again.

James felt a pang of something primal, a feral premonition that incited his adrenaline. "I'll take you to Mythic. You'll be safe there." Without an explanation, he felt the need to wrap his arms around her, to safeguard her from impending harm. When she shook her head in response, his heart turned black with worry. She gripped him as tightly as she could, knowing that he could take it, and then she moved away.

The hunter watched a spray of red jet from between her ribs.

She did not react with surprise. She simply let herself slump against the weathered brick behind her. The crowd nearby turned and responded with screams and panicked movement, fleeing over one another.

Turning, James caught the assailant in a deathly glare. It was not Casey, not the name pulsing in his skull, not the prey he wanted...but a knife left from his coat before he could arrive at that conclusion. It shot into the gunman's neck, robbing him of his last breath as he pointed his smoking gun at the hunter. His penultimate round clipped the thread from James' shoulder. The final shot leapt into the sky. Then the killer collapsed before the fire blossoming out of Tranquility. The hectic retreat of the bystanders had devolved into a full scramble. Only the hunter stood fast, his kill set in his eyes.

"Jim!" He heard Robert shout.

Good, he thought, *he's safe*. Then he moved in silence to Emily.

He caught the elf in his arms as she slid down the wall, and he waited for something—anything—to leave her lips. After an interminable moment, he heard a name tear from her lips. "Antony's." He saw an image of a bar with a band playing music in a haunting red glow. He heard a flash of sound—jazz—and he saw a man clad in black, a cigarette in his mouth. He could smell the fire. He could taste the smoke. The memory shifted so that he could see the name of the jazz club as if he were standing right outside its entrance.

"We met there," he heard her murmur. "On a Tuesday."

Emily's voice persisted for a ghost of a second. It was nothing but a quiet rasp. Then it faded along with her. He watched her emerald eyes pale, still shedding tears.

He began, "In the ways of the old, wisdom," and blood seeped from her parted lips.

"James."

"In the ways of the young, beauty," and he kissed her.

"James!"

"In the ways of those to come, serenity," and he closed her eyes. "Good night," he said after a moment, receiving no response.

"James," the initiate's call came bounding through his thoughts, an alarm to wake him from his lamentation.

"Robert," the hunter answered, numb. He turned and saw him doubled over like an animal, fear-struck. "What?" he asked, wiping the blood from his mouth. Robert turned a shaking hand skyward to the rooftop of the building opposite.

Immediately, the hunter saw a man—a powerful man, although he could not make out his features. He beheld only a silhouette, a black shade behind a screen of snow and ash. And though he was engulfed in shadow, James could distinguish as lucidly as a waking dream a lit cigarette in his mouth. It watched him like the small, red eye of a god until Casey Aduro turned and crept back into the darkness.

Part II
On Trapping

Chapter Twelve
The Dreamer

While the rest of the city slept, forgetting the horrors of the evening, James struggled to wrest even an ounce of respite from his nightmares.

He woke with all the horror of a child in darkness, already blinking away the apparitions. He remembered gargoyles, always gargoyles, and the endless labyrinth below. His mind kept taking him there, night after night, deeper into the dark. He refused to sleep long enough to see what was at the base of the hollow.

He took stock of his surroundings, examining his hotel room. A low lamplight emanated from one corner. He saw Robert reading in the other bed, enraptured by the tome of Mythopian lore on his lap. James counted the seconds to his nearest weapon, listened for footsteps in the hallway, then settled back into the sheets.

"You're still here."

"Aye." The initiate yawned.

"*Why* are you still here?" The hunter mopped sweat from his face and turned over in bed.

"Eh," he replied and shrugged. "We didn't make too many friends tonight. Figured I'd stick with you."

His comment led James to check the clock on the nightstand. It was barely past midnight.

"You have a place to live though, right?"

"Well, I had a place out in the country. Little cottage. Sold it not too long ago. You can't sleep?" he asked, diverting the conversation.

"Jetlagged," the hunter deflected.

"Berlin's not that far," he countered.

He scowled. "What about you?"

"Hell of a day." He closed the book and squirmed down under his covers. "Don't really feel up to a nap just yet."

"I haven't slept in a while."

"Sounds about right. You've been running all over since you got here."

James grunted in reply, tossing over again. "I really need some sleep before the raid."

Twenty hours. Less than a day from now he'd be stalking the ex-courier, now Cultist pyromancer Casey through London. If he was truly a creature of habit, he'd appear in Antony's Jazz Club for a drink sometime in the evening. He'd sit on the bank of his usual watering hole along with the other oblivious animals, unaware that there were lions on his flank.

They'd examined the bar, they'd drawn up the battle plans, and they'd made arrangements. Walter Brimford's campaign was in motion. They had more than enough muscle with a private military company lending twenty-four guns to the cause—Mythic's 'Knights of Raforia.' Couriers usually led the charge. In this scenario, however, with an ancient on the loose and everything at stake, Walter had made the decision to make the capture—or more likely the kill—himself.

"Find the eye," he'd instructed the hunter in private without a hint of a smile on his face, "or kill Casey. Whichever comes first, the other must come immediately hence."

And so, James had sharpened his blades, checked and rechecked every strap that was still intact inside his coat, and steeled himself for the encounter. The only thing left to do was sleep. There came the difficulty.

He could already feel the shades creeping across his retinas the second he closed his eyes. His second attempt at sleep was doomed to fail. It wasn't fear that kept him awake, not an abject dread of what was to come in his dreams, but rather a quiet apprehension knowing that they were not just dreams. They were visions.

The things he saw were not phantoms. What he felt was no illusion. Wherever and whenever his mind took him, his experiences were palpable. The darkness around him warped the very instant he slipped from his present reality. Falling water whispered into his ears from a distance. He saw the low light of a lantern, but his vision was blurry and dim. He tasted blood, smelled gore, and most intensely he felt a great, molten agony melting through his gut.

He came to clutching at his stomach, retching as if he'd been impaled. Until he was certain that he was whole, he held his hand to the future wound and heaved. Robert watched him with something between terror and pity.

"What are you reading?" he surrendered to his guest.

Robert hesitated, still waiting for the hunter to calm down. "Your book."

"Yeah," he acknowledged, "what part?"

"The part where you fought the werewolf in Paris."

"The what?" he stood quickly, inviting a painful head rush before steadying his lungs.

"There's a story here…" He leafed back a few pages. "It says: 'The following is a firsthand account of hunters in action, James McCrary the *Stoneslayer* and…' something '*the Shadow*' something something 'hunting a' lycan-something 'in the French capital in the autumn of 1984'. Pretty amazing stuff, brother."

The hunter sighed and shook his head. "It wasn't a werewolf," he corrected, stretching. "It was a lycanthrope."

The Scotsman looked perplexed. "Isn't that what a lycanthrope *is*?"

James laughed. "A lycanthrope is already full wolf. Just a…" he considered how to phrase it, "I guess a really big wolf. Really smart." He looked to see if Robert understood. "A werewolf is the lycanthrope before he turns completely. Still stands upright and shit."

Robert shrugged. "They don't turn back after the full moon?"

"When they get bitten, they go through a transformation period where they sort of fluctuate based on the moon. After a while, though, they stay the same, physically. Takes years."

"Whoa."

"Supposedly they regain some of their sentience or whatever on full moons, I dunno. I killed it on a new moon, so I never really found out."

"You've had a pretty eventful life, there, haven't you?" Robert couldn't help but chuckle.

"You could say that."

"How'd you get your start doing all this?"

James inhaled as if to speak, but he hesitated. Instead, he mumbled something indiscernible and lay back down.

"Oh, now, don't give me this 'my past is too dark' shite. You wanna play that game, you don't know who you're up against."

James rolled to face him. "Who's that?"

The initiate nodded and licked his lips. "Alcoholic father," he said, jamming his thumb into his chest. "I know that's the cheap shot, but might as well, right?"

The hunter, not to be outdone, sighed and took his stab. "I never knew my biological parents, but—"

"Oh, going for the one-two punch, eh?" Robert interrupted.

James mimed pointing a gun to his head. "Alcoholic foster mother."

"All right, moving on up the ladder, then." He cleared his throat. "Mother did herself in when I was a boy." He smiled with a perverse sense of pride. "Six. Right in the room next to mine."

"Violent or passive?"

"Would you call a revolver passive?"

"Mm." He paused for a moment, unsure of whether this game was worth continuing. After a few seconds, though: "Foster father jumped off a bridge. Kind of half and half."

"You ever see the body?"

"Yeah," he responded emphatically.

"Oh, that's the kicker."

"Mmhmm," the hunter agreed with the same twisted satisfaction.

"Let's see. Alcoholic father beat me on many occasions. Couldn't get away because he said he'd beat my sister if I ever left."

"Oh," said the hunter, impressed. "How old was she?"

"Four."

"Oooh."

"And *she* ran away a few years after that, never heard from her again."

"Damn."

"Damn right, damn. Loved that little girl."

"Umm," James fumbled for another tale of heartache. "I'm out. You win."

"Horseshite."

"No, yeah, your past was pretty black, man." James turned back over under a blanket of white. "Congrats."

"Come on, you don't just start hunting dragons after your da takes a dip and your mum starts drink driving." The Scotsman offset his words with a cheery enthusiasm that was as infectious as it was appalling. "That's not how the world works."

The room went dead and still. His face unseen, the hunter stared forward and away as far as he could see.

After a few moments spent waiting on him, Robert's confidence flagged. "Sorry, brother." He moved the tome to the nightstand and clicked off the lamp in the corner. "It was a stupid game." Again, he waited for reassurance, finding none in James' silence. "I'm gonna head over to Mythic, see if there's anything else I can do over there. You need cab fare?" He waited one last time for an answer. "Right, then. Good luck tomorrow." He grabbed his coat and moved towards the door.

"I killed a few guys." His confession stopped Robert mid-step. "Before. Not good guys, but…not really bad enough to deserve it. Spent a few days in jail, then a guy shows up. Big, huge guy. Dwarf. Says he can get me out. Says he wants to 'put that killer instinct to use.' And I did." The hunter faced him with a granite expression. "The first guy I ever killed, I didn't really mean to. It was like a joke how easy it was. I guess, if anything, I was born into it. I didn't start hunting because anyone forced me to. It was a nice excuse, but…I did it because I liked it. I liked the way it felt to kill and I wanted to keep doing it as long as I could." He turned back over and prepared to sleep.

He could feel Robert's eyes scraping at him. They were not judgmental. He was a sheep seeking comfort, burrowing into him. Robert understood so much and so little about the man he'd met less than a day ago, but was for whatever reason determined to vindicate him.

"You do good out there," he assured him. "Hunters." He tapped himself on the hand, lost in conflicting thoughts, then took a sharp breath. "My wife was killed by a gargoyle," he said, and the hunter's stony façade turned to clay. "Little over a year ago. That's how I was initiated. A hunter was tracking it. Managed to stop it before it got to me. Not her, though." He went to leave again.

"You win," James told him, smiling with sad eyes.

"Let's just call it a draw," the initiate called from the door, his voice cracking. "No one wins."

As the door shut, the hunter felt the night caving in around him. If he wanted to sleep, if he wanted to rest up for the fight of his life that was now so near, he'd have to give in to his visions. Whatever it was that he did not want to see would take place regardless. It was always inevitable.

James let the shadows rip his body through the void of consciousness into the realm of sleep. He felt his mind ease into the cooling embrace of the dream. He felt his body relax and his muscles revitalize. He felt everything muddy and fade for one final moment, but he found no rest.

As sleep claimed him, he awoke in another time. The pain in his belly had returned, almost too sharp to feel. Something lava-hot was pinning him to a cold wall of stone. He rolled his head to the side, watched as a shadow lunged. He heard gunshots, saw the black figure stagger, and witnessed the gunman collapse with a hole-riddled chest, quivering and smiling a stupid smile all the way to the ground.

Robert.

* * * *

"James."

The hunter leapt with unprecedented celerity. He had knives in hand and the intruder thrust against a wall before Robert could shut the door behind him. He spoke not a word, holding Yin against the initiate's neck for a solid three seconds before relaxing. He stumbled back to the bed, panting.

The Scotsman, though, held his timid stance. He spoke as if at gunpoint. "Michelle is missing."

Chapter Thirteen
The Abductor

"Don't touch that," the hunter warned him. His voice rattled out of him gruff and weak.

"What is it?" Robert examined the splotch of white gunk on the hallway floor from a safe distance.

James let himself into Michelle's apartment and took in the flat in a matter of seconds. Bedroom, dresser, bathroom, counter, fridge, table, table, armchair, done. He reached out with the rest of his senses. Empty. Michelle lived more simply than he'd anticipated, but such an existence was not uncommon for a Mythopian. He turned back to see the initiate hunkered over the puddle of gargoyle saliva and strained for an explanation.

"I don't know the scientific name for it," James began, "but you don't want to touch it."

"You know what it came from, though?" He leaned closer to the goop. "Who took her?"

"Yeah, probably," the hunter announced and went to check the bathroom.

"What happens if I touch it?" Robert reached his hand out just short of the substance.

"Burns like hell," James warned him from the bathroom.

"Then what?" he grimaced.

"Burns like hell some more."

Robert stood upright, still studying the mess. Then he felt something spatter on his shoulder. He turned to face the silver stain on the hallway ceiling just in time for another drip to fall directly onto his forehead.

"Fack," he gasped. "Jim! Jim!" He pawed the mucus from his face, spreading it to both hands. It stung with a sensational cold that sent him sprawling to the ground.

"You touch it?" the hunter asked, emerging from the flat.

"It's on my face!" the Scotsman shrieked, rolling into the puddle. "Get it off me. Get—" His fortune turned again as another globule of gargoyle saliva dropped into his open mouth.

"Robert," the hunter said, attempting to steady the flailing, gagging, sobbing initiate. "Robert," he tried again. The victim rolled to his feet and spat onto the ground. All the while he scrubbed at his face with his coat sleeves.

"Is it off?" he wheezed, standing still for a moment. "Did I get it?"

The hunter stared him down for another few seconds. His face was smeared with grey. "You're all right." He extended his hand in a show of faith and let some of the cool saliva spill out onto his outstretched palm.

"Christ almighty, Jimmy, you scared the piss outta me." He spat again for good measure. "What was all that?"

The hunter shook it from his hand. "Gargoyle spit."

"Why isn't it burning us?"

James shrugged, still piecing it together himself. "It's just a baby."

"Bloody great. Got gobs of baby gargoyle all over." He kicked the puddle in a huff. "What's that mean?"

"I think a baby gargoyle took Michelle." For once, the hunter was as confused as his comrade. The uncertainty rang in his tone.

Robert stood silent for a moment before asking, flabbergasted, "Why?"

They doubled back into the flat, desperate for answers. "Check the bathroom, see if I missed anything." James, meanwhile, surveyed the room for anything in the way of an explanation.

The gargoyle had likely never crossed the threshold into her apartment, judging by the state of the living room. Michelle hadn't offered any resistance, but a reader wouldn't have been able to do much against a gargoyle. With no sign of struggle, though, the question became why, exactly, had the creature targeted her? Hunger would have led to a messier apartment, as would anger. What kind of adolescent gargoyle had the presence of mind to abduct someone? Or the audacity?

According to Robert, she hadn't reported anything to Mythic. Her work had her on daylong shifts. With the news of Casey's discovery, she'd only gone home briefly to prepare for an even longer stay. Her return to headquarters was hours overdue. Walter's duties had him preoccupied, and Xiang was similarly indisposed. The task of finding her, then, fell to the resident hunter. Despite the situation, James looked to the analog clock on Michelle's wall and wondered why, with the immense responsibility of apprehending the most dangerous man on the island, he'd been awoken after a few measly hours of sleep.

"Oh!" Robert's exultation preceded the sound of splintering glass. "Jimbo!"

"Robert," he yawned and shuffled to the bathroom where his accomplice had shattered the mirror.

"Look at that." He gestured towards the cavity where the mirror had stood only moments before. "Secret hollow."

James' eyes widened in spite of him. The hole in the wall held a number of items: a revolver, a fold of bills, passports, and a slew of documents. "You really have to break it?"

"You think I'll get seven years bad luck?"

"You'd be lucky to live that long." Only after the remark did the gravity of his joke strike him. James shoved the dark thoughts aside and stretched out his hand. The initiate obliged him with the papers and took the gun for himself. "You don't know how to use a gun."

"Course I do," he lied. The hunter stared him down. "Yes, I know how to use one," Robert repeated. "I do." His ally's gaze was unwavering. "Fine." He replaced the pistol and stepped past James into the bedroom. "You're gonna get me killed, brother."

The hunter believed the opposite. Shrugging off the attack with more than a twinge of discomfort, he skimmed through the folders. Inside each one he found a photograph and a stack of records. He instantly identified Xiang the courier, Walter the executor, and Michelle the reader followed by a number of other Mythic employees. Thomas Bailey, the mercenary leading the operation against Casey; Alvin O'Hare, Mythic's private pilot; even Robert had his own file. There was only one key member missing—the hunter.

"What are those?" Robert asked from the foot of Michelle's bed.

"Files." James completed the circuit and set down the dossiers. "On everyone at Mythic."

"Good thing the gargoyle didn't get his hands on those, eh?"

"This is a challenge," the hunter said in an undertone.

"What was that?"

"He's calling me out."

"Come on, James," the initiate cajoled.

James slipped from the apartment and down the hallway towards an open window at the end. The duckling followed behind him.

"You gonna tell me what you just figured out?"

A tenant from a neighboring room opened his door and stepped out into the fray. "You girls wanna keep it down?" he railed with a scratchy voice. "It's six in the fucking morning."

The initiate stopped to address him, flashing the pilfered pistol that he'd tucked inside his jacket. "Back inside." The diminutive, balding man took one look at his adversary before complying and retreating into his home.

Reaching the window, James cracked it open, welcoming a swallow of frigid air, and ran his hands along the edges. He found exactly what he was looking for: claw marks. He briefly judged the tracks before arriving at the conclusion that this was a sizeable brute for its age.

Robert appeared next to him and looked out across the twilit landscape, checking each and every snowflake for clues. "He took her out this window?" James nodded. Robert glowered. "Come on," he roared. "Where are you, you git?" He felt at once another splash on the back of his head. "More of this gob shite!" His hand shot out to wipe the mess away before he twisted round and turned to stone.

"Stoneslayer." The hunter looked up, as well, at the grey fiend perched above them. "The grove. Sunrise." The beast was large—*very* large. By no means an infant.

"Where's Michelle?" the initiate demanded, his face still pale.

The gargoyle let its mucus seep down onto the two of them. They warded it off with outreached hands. "Come. Then we talk."

They pulled back into the hallway just as Michelle's abductor dropped down across the length of the building and arced into the sky. They stood watching it thrash its way through the night until the flurries covered its trail, but James knew where it was headed.

"Get to Mythic. Let them know what's going on. I'll take care of it."

Robert scoffed. "I'm helping, brother. I have to save her." The solidity in his eyes set firmly above his pallid cheeks echoed his resolve.

Reluctant as he was to put Robert at risk, James was more concerned about the emotional stability of the beast he'd aggravated. A misstep in accepting the challenge—a moment late—could spell death for more than just Michelle.

"All right."

Chapter Fourteen
The Challenge

The ground crunched as he marched through the previous night's snowfall. It was very soft and very slippery. James emerged into the glade with all the pretense of a proud warrior stepping into an arena. Just another day in gladiatorial garb. His coat was tightened around him, strewn with every blade he could carry. He wore a knit cap that covered his ears, thick black leather gloves, heavy canvas pants, and even thicker boots. The moment he came in sight of the clearing, however, his pervasive conviction dissipated. He may as well have been naked.

He moved with determination but not confidence. His heels drove down with something other than bravado. He felt an unfamiliar feeling—something he seldom allowed himself to experience, the last thing he needed to distract him on such a crucial day. The hunter felt, in spite of his grandest efforts, fear.

He slid to the center of the wooded coliseum, stumbling through the fog and stillness of English winter, fixated on the figure he perceived to be there. He saw, to his amazement, a man standing in a long, black duster.

He wore a sword slung over his back, a red hourglass that warned predators, promising feral retribution for any approach. James saw heat whirling around his shoulders even from a distance, an invisible aura that ascended from him as if he were smoldering.

James whispered, "Casey," too afraid to draw the man's attention.

"Jim," Robert said behind him, drawing his focus back to the tree line. "This yours?" He indicated a single knife protruding from the trunk of an oak.

He only nodded in response. When he turned back to confront his nemesis, he saw an empty space. Cold mist and night terrors. "I'm hallucinating."

"You what?" The initiate came towards him.

"I'm seeing…" He considered his words then his thoughts before them. "I'm imagining things."

"Well, that's not good."

"No," the hunter laughed. He heard the rushing wind of beating wings above the forest. "It's not."

Before them, morning gave birth to the sun. It was just bright enough for James to see the first six gargoyles touching down in front of him. It was just silent enough for him to hear the dozen landing behind him. It was just static enough for him to feel the adrenaline ramp up and his eyes start to shake.

"We keep our words, James McCrary." The gargoyle from the apartment ambled over to him from behind. He recognized it by the gristle tone in its voice. "Your associate."

He distinguished two sets of breath: the deep, easy in and out of the beast he'd need to destroy soon and the shallow, erratic gasps of its captive as it forced Michelle to the ground.

"Are you okay?" James turned to examine her. She seemed bruised but not bloodied, injured only from the flight and kidnapping. She was in little danger relative to the hunter and understood as much.

"I'm fine," she managed, still shaky. Robert came to her from the fog—followed by another pair of gargoyles—and knelt to help her to her feet. The abductor grumbled and shoved him onto his back.

"Explain," it barked to the reader.

She took a moment to steady herself. "These are the children of the gargoyle you captured."

"Not children," the demon roared. Michelle did not flinch. "Tell him what to do."

"You fight the firstborn," her voice shook, "then the second, then the third…" she trailed off.

"Until I kill all of you," the hunter asserted.

"Until we are satisfied," the gargoyle corrected him, moving to his front. It was noticeably smaller than the one he'd captured, though still dangerous. He glanced around and completed his count: twenty altogether. He'd fought in more dire situations but with much more energy. And much more sleep.

He stepped away from the fiend to prepare himself. "Robert, Michelle, get out of here."

"No," one of the gargoyles contested. "They stay. Watch you die." Its cohorts growled in approval. "Once you are dead and our father is free, we will let the woman go."

Robert crept over to Michelle and pulled her up, slowly so as not to enrage the swarm of gargoyles that had begun circling them. They formed a ring—the stage for the spectacle, the altar for the divine huntress, the moon, still shining through the fog from overhead. The noncombatants moved to the edge, leaving the hunter alone with his first opponent.

The firstborn had long surpassed its father in size. It outclassed its progenitor even on bended knee. The hunter measured it from toe to tail in a matter of moments. "For your crimes against all gargoyles," it spat, as engrossed in rhetoric as its haughty forebear, "you fall."

The beast, in all likelihood, was fully aware when it charged. It was probably conscious of its movement right up until the moment its target disappeared—a blur of black and white—to its side. James leapt atop the beast like a gryphon tamer, wrapped his legs around its arms, and bound his bicep across its throat. The firstborn struggled to move its arms, though that was a useless exercise. It beat its wings to no effect; the hunter was sitting above them. It lashed its tail against his back, once, twice, three times with the speed and force of a bullwhip, but after a moment it fell, unconscious or dead, into the snow.

Its silence stripped the sound from the air.

James pulled himself from atop the carcass, dragging a long, thin knife from the inside of his coat. "And…"

The secondborn howled and launched, betraying its approach. The knife in the hunter's grip twisted, flipped, and shot through the air, lodging itself in the roof of the brute's mouth. It fumbled at the dagger for a few fleeting moments before its body struck the surface of the earth. It writhed like a snake severed from its head.

Save for the spine-wrenching sound of a demon gargling ichor and steel, the hollow remained quiet. The circle of gargoyles froze in unison, a single body and mind astounded by what it beheld. The calm persisted for quite a while until the third and fourthborn stepped into the arena.

The hunter drew Yin and Yang from their sheaths, bared his shining metal fangs, and circled around the ring with the other two bodies. He had no objections to their advance. He just wondered why only two had come.

"You got em, Jim!" Robert called from the sideline, invigorated by the blood sport.

James twirled his daggers to limber his wrists and muttered, "Come with it, then."

They struck on either side in pincer formation, each with a distinct set of attacks. They clawed and whipped simultaneously so that their assaults left little room for error. The hunter contorted like a gymnast, content to evade their blows, and dove through the single clearing they allowed. He planted on one fist, rolled to his shoulder and then to his feet before turning to face them.

The gargoyles spun, primed for another approach, before the fourthborn reacted to the indescribable pain in its tail. It cocked its head to the side, roaring, to see the limb lacking. Its ghastly grey eyes found the remainder of the appendage squirming in the snow between it and its opponent. Frenzied, the beast flew ahead of its ally and engaged the hunter in singular combat. He danced around its claws, under the remnant of its tail, and met its snapping jaws with a surgical stab that penetrated through to its brain.

He threw the animal to obstruct its sibling's advance, but the thirdborn swatted the corpse aside without a thought. Its claws came in the shape of a bite, wide and unwavering. James passed under its arms with a shiv to its side, but the beast triumphed, for the moment. The cusp of its devil wing tensed, retracted, and slashed across the hunter's back with enough momentum to drive him to the ground.

The demon, too, reeled to its knees, wounded and dismayed. It struck the beast as incredible that a human could force steel through stoneskin with a glancing blow, or that one could take a full set of tail lashes without flinching, or that a human was fast enough to dodge the strikes of two gargoyles at once. "They say you are inhuman," the creature moaned. It saw the hunter stand as if untouched and prep a pair of throwing knives. It saw the shadow of death standing behind him. "They are wrong." The thirdborn bore down on all fours and spat silver. The hunter crouched and spat blood.

The gargoyle darted after its prey, took one knife to the shoulder, then one to the chest. It did not falter as it closed the gap. James stepped forwards to catch the beast's claws a moment too early. The thirdborn leapt into the sky five feet above its target and came crashing down. Yang found its heart, but not before the hunter felt the full force of the gargoyle's descent. He collapsed under the weight of its dead body.

By the time he'd climbed to his feet, the boundaries of the ring had begun to thin. Three fresh bodies stood in the center of the arena. The fifthborn—the abductor—stepped up to speak.

"You do not fight us like you fought our father." It seemed as disgusted as it was offended. "Trapped like a dog."

The hunter wrenched his blade from the corpse of his latest kill. "Our fight was fair."

"Then please," the abductor considered its statement with an air of superiority, "extend us the same courtesy." The fifthborn was a tribunal, demanding recompense from a seat of indignation. Its request was more a mandate than a plea.

James hesitated. "With him it was one on one."

The fifthborn spat. "We fight as one."

Reluctantly and regrettably, the hunter sheathed his daggers.

Robert stuttered. "Jim?"

He removed his coat, and the knives along with it.

"What are you doing?"

He tossed the bundle aside.

"Are you out of your fucking mind?"

The hunter flinched at the cold. The blood seeping from his back congealed and denied him mobility. He rolled his shoulders and grimaced from the pain.

"You three," he said, and pointed out the combatants, "and that's it."

"Agreed," the abductor growled with duplicitous intent.

James' adrenaline began to climax. His heart pumped blood with the strength of a jet engine, inflating every inch of his body. He felt, in spite of the cold, all the warmth of a hissing flame. Then he saw, in spite of himself, a sword-bearing serpent in the periphery of his vision.

"No," he reminded himself, ever-vigilant as the abductor and its brethren crouched. Just to be sure, though, he moved his head to regard the black specter. Casey stood in the shadows, a statue concealed in the fog of war and consciousness. When he turned his face upwards it was blank; a sheet of empty skin. "Am I dreaming?" James wondered. The gargoyles answered him.

The hunter went down hard into the snow. He hadn't any knowledge of what had happened or how he should recover. He sprang up just in time to catch a tail in the shoulder and was struck back against the ground. The abductor leapt with claws and fangs poised. James could do nothing to stop it.

His pushing, pressing, punching blood slowed the action to a crawl. He watched the demon come at him for eons, its jowls twisted into a malevolent grin. He was aware that even if he brought his arms up to defend himself, he'd only meet the beast's hands as they wrapped around his throat. He failed to register defeat, could not acknowledge death. He simply sat and waited.

So blank was his mind that he did not hear the cock of the gun behind him. He heard it fire like a distant whisper. The impact, however, met his senses with all the volume of a dragon's roar. The bullet hammered the gargoyle's skin, bending its breast inward and shattering two of its ribs. Its arms dropped and the demon went down.

"Robert," the hunter murmured, turning to the initiate who stood with smoking gun in hand and a look of desperation in his eyes. The gargoyles catapulted into cries of upheaval. Their caterwaul accompanied a torrent of insults as they encircled the hunter and his companions. "What did you do?" he continued as the Scotsman lowered his weapon.

The wounded gargoyle stood after a moment, laughing and coughing up bile. It held its chest in pain but was far from death. "Guns," it growled, "always guns. You mongrels lack the honor necessary for combat." It approached the initiate with a stony smile and vengeance in its heart. Michelle raced between them.

"No," Robert gasped, his eyes feverish.

"He's an initiate," she defended him with her arms stretched wide. "It wasn't—" The gargoyle swatted her aside before she could finish.

"Olivia!" Robert brought the gun back up and fired again. The gargoyle ducked the shot with minimal effort and tore the pistol from his grip. In another instant, it had lifted him off the ground by his neck.

The hunter reacted on instinct alone, flying from the surface of the ground. The gargoyle's wings were outstretched, but if he could leap over them and get the demon into a lock, he could free Robert and strangle the beast in a single movement. He planted his foot to jump onto its back and met with a startling discovery. The beast's wings retracted and it turned more quickly than the hunter could have anticipated. The next sensation he felt was that of the gargoyle planting a single talon against his chest.

James hit the ground, pinned under the mammoth strength of his opponent, with no leverage whatsoever to work with.

The gargoyle briefly regarded its foes: the initiate choking in its grip, the reader panting on the forest floor, and the illustrious hunter trapped beneath its foot. It chortled.

"James McCrary the Stoneslayer, Michelle Reid the Dreamwalker, and the Gargoyle Gunner, all in one fell swoop." The abductor's allies rallied behind it with barks, shouts, and roars of triumph. "With this, Mythic will know the power of the gargoyle. We will not be hunted into extinction," it snarled, spitting silver at the initiate.

The hunter watched its saliva spatter harmlessly against Robert's skin. It hit him suddenly, surrounded by baying beasts and in the face of sure death. "You're his daughter," he realized aloud. The creature looked at him, irritated. "You're a girl."

The gargoyle hissed, baring her fangs. "And all the same I conquered you." She loosened her grip on Robert and tightened her talon until the hunter could feel his ribcage begin to buckle.

"Stop," Michelle commanded as she stood. Her shout seemed to hush some of the horde. She moved to the abductor, her face paralyzed in disbelief and indignation. "You're female?" The abductor grunted in response. "Do you realize what you're doing? Do you realize how rare that is?"

Michelle looked to the other gargoyles to see if any of them grasped her meaning. "Do you understand that your species is going extinct because of how few females are born?" The abductor stayed silent, perplexed. "And you're out fighting *hunters*?" she demanded, striking the beast in the leg. She turned to face the coven. "I don't care who your father is or how much you want revenge. You're killing yourselves with this!"

The gargoyles leered at her as if she were mad, all of them silent now.

"The chances of a gargoyle being born female are less than one percent. Do you understand that?" They continued to gawk. "Mythic isn't driving you to extinction. We don't have to. You're killing *yourselves* by letting queens go out and fight like this. Let go of him," she said, pointing to Robert. "Let go of both of them."

The young queen refused. "You have no voice here, reader."

"Let them go," she repeated, "or I will have you killed."

The abductor laughed. Her comrades followed suit. They devolved back into a muddle of howls and growls. In the uproar, they couldn't hear their deaths approaching.

Michelle held up her arm. "I don't want to do this," she said, obviously sincere. She held the ruin of a species in one hand.

"Do what you must," the abductor taunted her, "as will we." She saw in the feeble human merely a last-ditch attempt at survival.

The reader sighed. The gargoyle watched her as she dropped her arm and completed the signal, her laughter fading like a dream. She saw, in an instant, the face of a woman shifting from bravado to callous remorse. "You've doomed your race," she said to the young queen right before the end came.

The creature tensed as she heard the crackle of ice on the edge of the glade, too loud for any animal to have caused. She smelled the stench of men smiling as they watched her. She felt the same dog-like fear her father had experienced two nights ago.

"No..." she whispered. The first round cut her short. Her limbs went rigid as the bullet entered through her jaw and pitched upwards through her brainstem. Her claws slackened an instant later, releasing both her prey.

The remaining gargoyles had a fraction of a second to react before the humans hit the ground and the bulletstorm ensued.

Gunfire erupted through the glade, catching most of the demons in its wake. The rounds that glanced bruised them, the bullets that deflected merely scratched them, but the shots that struck them dead-on penetrated their bodies and sent them either into the throes of death or hydrostatic shock. Some of them leapt to fly, but the hail of gunfire brought them down, too. Each mercenary had expended the bulk of his magazine before the riflemen swept from the cover of the forest into the glade. They moved swiftly and softly, the dozen of them stepping with the volume of a single man. Their weapons discharged in a second salvo, a coup de grâce for all of the hopeless beasts that still bayed and slithered in the snow. Within seconds, the entire expanse stank from the black and grey viscera that melted the snow.

"Watch the gobs," the commander reminded his men before lowering his rifle. "Michelle?" The reader raised herself timorously from the blood-moist earth, watching Robert and James do the same. "All right, love?"

"Sweet as a nut," she replied, standing. She looked over the carnage and shuddered. "Thank you, Thom."

"No worries," the commander said, pulling his scarf from over his mouth and smiling. Thomas Bailey stood at one hundred eighty-five centimeters, impressive for an Earther. He sported a thick, blonde beard and a thicker neck. Even by Mythopian standards he and his troops were particularly virile. They'd been bred, it seemed, for combat. They wore arctic camouflage and carried assault rifles. They were efficient, disciplined, and well-equipped enough to conquer even mythical obstacles.

James, having regained his senses, approached the commander. His mind was still reeling from the chaos and the pain in his chest. "You found us. How?"

Bailey nodded to Michelle. "Some useful tricks you Mythopians have, telepathing from across the city."

James' jaw dropped as he scrutinized Michelle.

"They call me the Dreamwalker for a reason," she asserted.

"Thank God for readers, eh?" the commander laughed.

"Sir," one of the mercenaries called from a distance, "one slipped through."

"Bugger." He departed to instruct his men. "Radio second team, tell them to keep watch on the north edge. We still have clean-up here. Eight minutes, gents. Can't be late for the night's festivities."

The hunter caught sight of Robert still standing in the midst of the fallen gargoyles, petrified. He couldn't determine if it was the shock of the morning's events or the biting cold that had immobilized him.

"Robert," he began, uncomfortable in the initiate's pale gaze.

Michelle mirrored his concern. "Is everything all right?"

Suddenly, it struck the hunter that his vision might have come to pass. Without wasting a moment, he stumbled over to the Scotsman, oblivious to the increased difficulty the task brought on. "Were you hit?" He patted the initiate down for bullet wounds, frantic, sure that he would find injury. All the while Robert stared at him, slack-jawed, unable to speak.

The initiate was fine. It was the hunter who stood in death's shadow.

"Oh, God," Michelle spoke from behind him. He heard horror in her voice. As the adrenaline faded from his veins at long last, pain came rushing to him in its place.

He staved it off for a moment, reaching his hand around to his back to find it engraved by the myriad scratches and lashings of the struggle. He looked down and saw himself standing in a pool of deep-red blood quite distinct from the grey gore that still seeped from the gargoyles' many carcasses. He turned and saw a trail of the claret leading all over the forest floor and wondered just how long he'd been bleeding to death.

By the time the pain reached him in full force, he'd lost too much blood to cry out. He sank down onto his haunches and then onto his back, soaking in the red and the white and the grey, dreaming of the past.

Chapter Fifteen
The Dwarf

He remembered the first time he'd held daggers in his hands. He almost didn't notice the weight. He moved them like feathers, the quills of a poet penning horrid lyrics wherever he went. All that he wrote, he wrote in red.

He remembered the first man he'd assaulted with tempered steel. He could still recall the words he'd chosen as the blades floated over his victim's neck. A sword in hand, the dwarf had struck right then high. His swings fell slow but deadly.

He remembered his surroundings—the empty office building, half-built on the edge of the city, dark enough that the single lantern illuminating the site could not be seen from outside, bare enough that even the rain outdoors underscored the struggle, hollow enough that their grunts echoed through several stories, isolated enough that no one would come looking for a pair of men locked in combat.

He reacted adroitly, a natural. The entire engagement lasted mere moments. As he poised his fangs for the first time, body aching to spill blood, he spoke like a child full of wonder in a twisted classroom. "This is where I kill you," he said, irresolute.

"Yes," the dwarf returned, body stiff and eyes fixated on the boy now towering above him. His words held not an ounce of fear. "This is where you kill me."

James smiled and pulled his knives back. "Cool." He extended a hand to help the red-haired titan to his feet.

"Very cool," the dwarf beamed and tore him down to the ground next to him. The boy collapsed without even attempting to balance himself. "Unless you do something stupid like that."

The two warriors laughed.

"I'd never help the other guy up. Kill or be killed, right?"

"No," the dwarf corrected him, standing. "There has to be honor." The boy wavered. "There always has to be honor."

"Don't matter if you're dead," James contested, rolling to his knees.

"That's *exactly* when it matters. You don't want to be remembered for being a coward."

The boy moved to a wall and leaned against it, defiant. "How are you a coward if you're the one who wins?"

"Cowards win all the time. They're good at it. That's all they care about. And if they can't win, they run away so that they won't lose."

"But," the boy's face wrinkled, "you said it was cowardly *not* to run."

"I—" the dwarf hesitated. "Well, it can be. It can also be cowardly *to* run." One look at the young man's rising eyebrows convinced him to abandon the rhetoric. "Never mind. Just—" He fumbled for a takeaway. "Don't be so quick to judge that which you do not understand." Satisfied with his trite point, he concluded, "And that's all I wanted to teach you today."

James shook his head, laughing. "You say some dumb shit sometimes, Ooie."

The dwarf glared at him. "Thanks, James."

Uwe Löwe was an earnest hunter, if a tad dim. He was certainly a peculiar dwarf. He did his utmost to rely not only on brute strength—of which he had plenty to spare—but his intellect as well. It was a work in progress. At six foot four inches, though, his size delivered him from even the most dire of situations whenever his meager cunning failed him.

He was broad-jawed with crimson hair and near-black eyes. His facial features seemed swollen, as if bruised. His cheeks appeared vacant, lacking the luxurious facial hair typical of his kind. His height drew him enough unwanted attention without a chest-length beard complementing it, though. Instead, a thin layer of rust-colored scruff lined the reaches of his frame. He cut the rest of his hair short.

James McCrary was, at the time, his exact opposite. Dark brown skin, shaggy hair, light brown eyes, more than a foot shorter. On his upper lip was a feeble attempt at a first moustache. He had no more fuzz on his chin than a peach. His body was slender, his face regal. His muscles were smaller than those of most young men his age but operated at a higher level. He bench-pressed two hundred fifty pounds without issue.

His mind was pliant but still muddled with unhealthy aspirations and delusions of grandeur. He longed for glory, to be feared and loved at the same time. A shadow of the Stoneslayer resided within him even from adolescence, and the hunger was there all along. He preferred violence as a means of resolving issues and understood that he was gifted enough to wield it well. Uwe was uncertain how long he'd be able to control the boy's impulses. Still, James was far from amoral. He seemed to truly wish to use his vice to help the world at large, and Uwe was determined to guide him however far his path might stretch.

"I have to go," the dwarf mentioned, apprehensive.

"Oh," James said. His eyes sank.

Rainfall filled the chasm of silence between them.

"I think there are a few gargoyles nesting in Central Park. I have to get them to move. It's going to take...well, anyhow, I should get you back home."

"Right," the boy mumbled and began to gather up his belongings.

Uwe watched him pack together food and clothes, tuck his brand new pair of throwing knives into the bottom of his duffel bag, and seal it shut.

"You want to come along? Get a feel for it?"

The boy looked up from his things, intrigued and perplexed all at once. His eyes glowed with something between animal and human curiosity. "Go with you?"

The dwarf laughed. "Should be pretty safe," he lied. "I don't see why not."

"Yeah," he replied, still dazzled, "that sounds..." He winced for a moment, noticing that his eyes were beginning to sting, and cleared his throat. "That'd be cool."

"We just have to call your mother."

He nodded, still skeptical. Then he grabbed the lantern from the floor and suddenly realized something. "We get to go in your squad car?"

Uwe sneered at him. "You don't have a squad car when you're a detective," he asserted. "It's just a car."

"It got a siren?"

"Yes," the dwarf conceded.

"Squad car."

"Police vehicle," he reprimanded.

"Can we *use* the siren?"

Uwe shook his head and started towards the stairwell. "Yes, I want the entire NYPD to know that I hunt monsters while I'm off the job." His voice echoed up from the floor below. "Jesus, kid."

James stopped short of the stairs and gazed down the unlit corridor to the bottom. His stomach growled. His heart lurched. He heard his teacher trample onto the first floor and moved to follow him down, down, down into the dark.

* * * *

The hunter's eyes opened to an uproar unfolding above him. He peered through a film of mist and a blaze of white, but even so he made out the shapes of a number of familiar individuals. He could hear them: Walter, Michelle, and Robert at the least, arguing over blood. Whoever else was present chose to remain silent.

"I'll do it!" Walter screamed. "Take mine. Take mine." He felt the executor slide next to the bed.

Pinned on his back, he could only see the white ceiling of Mythic's private hospital ward. A bunker bereft of windows and stocked with machinery and artificial light, it was anything but soothing. They kept saying, "Hold on, James. Hold on. Hold on. Hold on." Trapped under the lights and the shouts and the burning wounds all over his body, he found himself wishing they'd leave him to die.

In the tumult, he turned to his bedside and identified another one of the room's inhabitants.

"Ooie?" he spoke aloud. The name rang hollow, atrophied from disuse.

The dwarf lifted his head. "James," he answered, smiling, but sank his head back down a moment later.

"Long time."

"Yeah," he said with a cruel smile. "I heard you were hunting an ancient, though. Knew I had to come up. Flew all the way from hell to get here."

"You came to help me?"

"Sure, why not?" Uwe kept staring out over him in the direction of Walter's voice as the executor tapped a vein for the procedure. "Seems like you've got plenty of help already, though."

"I'm doing this alone," he protested.

"A hunter through and through."

"I could still use some advice. For fighting an ancient."

His old mentor shot him a look. "What, cause I've done it before?"

"Yeah," James pleaded.

"I couldn't beat him. Not sure what advice I could give."

"You shouldn't have been alone," James encouraged him. "I should've helped you. We could've won."

Uwe's eyes fell back to the ground. "Thing is, you can't go in expecting victory. But you can't go in with any fear. And I know you've got some." James swallowed hard. "The man I fought…" The dwarf met the hunter's gaze. "I was terrified. He was the most powerful man I'd ever met. But I knew I couldn't be afraid of him. I knew that if I let any fear into my heart, it'd be over. It takes a lot of passion to go to the end without fear."

"Why shouldn't I be afraid?" James defended himself. "I can't win like this."

Uwe stood and moved to his side. "Lesson of the day: *you* don't always have to be the one to win." With that, the dwarf turned and started out of the ward.

"You're leaving?"

"I gotta go see a horse about a man," he answered without turning back.

"That's still not funny," James called out.

"Was it ever?" Uwe mused and left.

There was a strange pressure bubbling up in the hunter's veins. He felt the executor's arteries supplementing his, and his heart seemed to lap up the new blood gratefully. Even with the transfusion, though, his strength had disappeared. He closed his eyes for what he perceived as only an instant, but when he reopened them the room was silent.

Chapter Sixteen
The Ancient

An interview with Casey from when Walter hired him. I thought you might want to read up on the bloke before you hunt him.
- Robert

James removed the makeshift bookmark and opened the tome the initiate had brought for him. He checked the beds on his right and saw Walter, asleep but alive, resting atop one of them. The farthest bed was vacant. He imagined that both the courier and the initiate under Casey's direction were currently under Xiang's ruthless scrutiny.

Looking back to the tome, he noted that the top of the page read 'Interview #1' and was dated 9 March, 1993.

Walter Brimford: Welcome to London, Casey.

Casey Aduro: Thank you very much.

W: Please be seated. I know this is an interview, but I've no need for any pretense of formality. Our business is difficult enough without us wasting energy keeping up appearances.

C: I agree. [laughs] Sorry, I was told that you were old-fashioned. You're not really what I expected.

W: [laughs] I'm old-fashioned in a different way. How are you enjoying England?

C: Not a huge fan of the weather. It's supposed to be spring.

W: That's the UK.

C: Yeah, it's fine with me, just makes it a bit of a [expletive deleted] to cast.

W: Right. Would you care to remind me about your background in elementality?

C: I studied elementary fire under Tadashi Sato in Tokyo.

W: Not much. Bit of a shame for such a skilled hunter to go uninstructed like that.

C: I can cast.

W: I usually prefer my couriers to be a little more diverse...to have a little more formal training.

C: Formal training. Yeah, breathing under a waterfall for half a year was fun. I admit the stomping was actually helpful. I definitely fit Eastern styles better than anything else I've tried. For me, though, the real training was hunting zhulong on Kyushu.

W: I'm well aware of your exploits.

C: What you've heard from Mythic and the reports. You can't write into a report that you tackled one into an active volcano and lived to tell about it.

W: I did hear about that, actually. At Mt. Aso, was it? Sato told me all about the incident.

C: *What about the thing with Hotaru?*

W: *[laughs] Oh, I heard about that, too. Hotaru's the reason you're sitting in that chair right now.*

C: *She was a real [expletive deleted]. She was, though. They don't make them like her anymore.*

W: *We don't have nearly as many as we did a while ago.*

C: *So I've heard.*

W: *Have you had experience with any golds or greens?*

C: *Yeah. They're different, but not too much worse. Almost easier if you can catch them mid-breath. Quick little [expletive deleted].*

W: *What about blues and whites?*

C: *I've killed the whole rainbow. Only thing about ice dragons is that they roost up high and they always live in the cold. You try casting fire below zero.*

W: *What languages do you speak, Mr. Aduro?*

C: *English.*

W: *Honestly? You didn't pick up any Japanese?*

C: *What's that saying? 'A naked sword speaks every language.'*

W: *I can certainly understand that. What about martial arts?*

C: *Kenjutsu, Kendo, and Iaido as far as weapons.*

W: You do favor the Eastern styles. But Sato would have you caned if he saw your sword on your back and not on your hip.

C: It's conspicuous either way. More of a let-your-flag-fly approach.

W: I'm sure. Hand-to-hand? Firearms?

C: A little easier to conceal. Aikido? I don't know. I tried everything they'd teach me, but I honestly don't use my hands much. Pretty good with a handgun, I'd say.

W: Well-rounded. Good.

C: If you don't mind me asking, who else are you looking at for this position?

W: I don't mind, but I can't divulge much of anything. I can tell you that a certain native of Liverpool is under consideration.

C: You know about him, then.

W: I know the two of you did some work together while you were in Los Angeles.

C: Back before I could cast worth a [expletive deleted].

W: Aduro and Jones, the terrible twosome. When's the last you worked with him?

C: We tracked down Solomon the Great.

W: Impressive.

C: I'm sure he thought so.

W: Do you regret not being the one to take his bounty?

C: For the money?

W: For the glory. They say all of Europe shook when he died.

C: Must have been some [expletive deleted] fight.

W: Must have. I wonder if he found it ironic that it was an ancient who found him. Adure's heir, no less.

C: Hmm.

W: It's not the kind of detail that goes unnoticed in this sort of operation, Casey.

C: If you know I'm an ancient, you also know that it's a very bad time to be one.

W: No one's accusing you of anything. If anything, your heritage is an asset.

C: I don't want you taking me on just because I'm an ancient. I have more to offer than saving you money on gems. And I don't want any special treatment.

W: The treatment that put you through school in Tokyo? The treatment that's paid for every expense in your life?

C: That treatment. Yes.

W: You have a special gift, Casey.

C: That's the kind of thing you hear before they put you in shock therapy.

W: Casting any of the elements without a gem? Seems like it'd be worth it. To be free from constraints. To have all that power.

C: Sato told you. Almost took it to the grave.

W: [pause] Have you had any visions?

C: No. I get headaches.

W: What happens when you dream?

C: I typically wake up.

W: It's not as if there's a protocol for this type of thing. How many ancients do you think we've come across since Mythic was established?

C: I know how many.

W: And how many have stayed in the open? You have to understand why we're taking a keen interest in what you do. How you do it. Your power is an asset to anyone trying to do good for Mythopians. For the world.

C: Thing about that is, I've got the next couple centuries to waste my time helping the whole Mythic circlejerk.

W: Then what is it you're looking for now?

C: A fix.

W: For what, might I ask?

C: I've been hunting everywhere on the planet. Since I was twelve. Doesn't that seem strange? That I've made a life killing innocent people?

The Infidelitous Earth

W: You think all the dragons you've killed were innocent?

C: Maybe. Aside from all the people they had to kill because we're forcing them into holes and murdering their children for flying in daylight.

W: It's necessary.

C: It's eugenics.

W: I can't give you absolution.

C: I don't want absolution.

W: You want integration.

C: I want progress. I want to feel like something is happening. Can you imagine living a hundred years watching mankind crawl after a goal it could be sprinting towards?

W: Or dragged to. Integration is impossible at the moment. Believe me. I've been around long enough to watch people of every race and religion treated like inferior beings, but we've come along. It is the nature of this world to subjugate the minority. It's no different with dwarves or elves. It's just a matter of time. At the very least, you will see change in your lifetime.

C: I can do better. I'll make change.

W: How would you start?

C: The people of this world have no respect for life. No loyalty to the living. No passion for existing. There's a word I've been dreaming of. This, this infidelitous Earth. Mythopians were born here, but we have to force it to sustain us because it doesn't want us anymore. Not the way we are, anyway. Changing the world is tantamount to changing the people in it. That's what I want to do. I want to inspire people and make them live again.

W: I'd like to help you achieve that. You're not the only one who'd like to see the world change before he dies.

C: [pause] You were right about what you said before.

W: Which was?

C: You're old-fashioned in a very different way.

The instant he closed the tome, James noticed a pair of sunken eyes watching him from the next bed over.

"How do you feel?" Walter murmured.

"I'm alive."

"And awake."

"We'll see for how much longer."

"Long enough to do the damn thing."

James smirked. "Why did you save me?"

"You'd have preferred that I let you die?" The executor attempted to shrug, searching for an explanation he seemed unsure of himself.

"What if I'd died anyway?"

"What if you'd gotten an infection? You would've died even *with* all my blood. We'd both be out." He paused. "Don't want to live?" The hunter's silence answered him. "You're my hunter. Do your job. I'm not paying you to die before Casey does. And money's no good if you're dead."

James looked down to the tome, still mired in the words of his enemy. "I don't know about this guy."

Walter lifted himself, groaning, into a sitting position before regarding the hunter with his full attention. His trademark grin was nowhere to be found. "He's strong, a born soldier, but by no means invincible."

"When I read this interview, I didn't see a soldier. I saw a zealot."

The executor smirked. "Zealots don't scare me. I understand zealots.

They're sacrificing themselves for their greater good. Maybe not my greater good or yours, but it's greater for someone. What scares the hell out of me is a psychopath. Someone who goes against the grain, not to get to heaven, not to get power, not to get anything. Just to taste the madness. Animals do that. Animals and demons."

"So which of those are we dealing with?"

"Just a man." Walter sighed and lay back down. "Nothing more."

James leafed past the interview to see if he could extract any more information from the text. He stopped a few pages later. After Casey's interviews and a few blank pages, the tome ended, flipping shut.

"That's it." He stared in agitation, almost expecting the book to speak more volumes.

"I've told you everything you need to know about Casey. The rest is up to you."

Then I guess we're out of luck, he thought but did not say.

"Do me a favor."

"Yes, sir."

Walter smiled, an impish grin fit for a jester. "Get your arse out of that bed. Take my key, go down to B2, and tell Xiang to come see me right away. And you get ready to end this."

"Yes, sir."

"Good boy."

The hunter caught sight of the clock on the far end of the ward. Seven o'clock. The operation would go into action at nine.

As he moved to leave, Walter girded him with his words: "There's nothing to be afraid of. You have this. There are no gods anymore, James. Solomon the Great has been dead five years."

"Dead and buried," agreed the hunter.

Chapter Seventeen
The Calm

The instant James stepped into the first room on B2 he met the stench of a poorly kept dungeon. The chamber was organized like the backroom of a circus, dimly lit with a catalog of cages stationed around the perimeter. Held in the first on his left was the infamous Gerard Jones.

His face was bruised and battered, more a pulp than a visage. Still, he smiled through a catastrophe of purple and red, even with some of his teeth missing, and even in the wake of their recent duel. "Heard you got a nasty scratch, mate," he said with a laugh.

James turned his attention from the barely recognizable inmate and pressed on into the center of the room. Xiang stood over a sobbing, fiery-haired initiate with a pair of electrodes in hand.

"That's kinda redundant," the hunter offered.

"That's what I told him," the ex-courier snickered from the corner.

"You'd think he'd be less of a windbag without his emerald," Xiang observed.

"Hardy har," Gerard retaliated before subsiding.

Smiling, Xiang continued, "Walter send you?"

"He wants to see you."

The lightning elementalist turned off his torture device and grabbed a rag to wipe the blood from his knuckles. "This one knows nothing," he said, nudging his victim with one foot. "I think one of us gave him a concussion."

"And Jones?"

"Believe it or not, he knows when to shut up." He finished cleaning his hands and moved to the elevator hallway. "James," he considered, slowing, "if you can help it, bring Casey in alive. The Cult is what's important."

James examined the initiate once his torturer had left. "That's some convenient memory loss." He struck the whimpering mass with his boot.

"Come on, now," Gerard beseeched him. "We've been through that already." The hunter ignored him and kicked the initiate again. "Come off it, already." One more blow sent him over the edge. "He's not faking it!"

"What makes you say that?" The hunter appeared in front of his cage in a flash.

Shocked, the ex-courier reeled to the back of his enclosure, silent. James lingered at the edge of the cage until he responded. "He's brainwashed."

James took a moment to process the information. "You brainwashed him?"

"Wasn't me."

"Who was it?"

"Who knows?"

"*Someone* knows."

Gerard almost answered before he laughed and sat down, defeated. "Don't waste your time with initiates. Don't waste your time with *me*. Only Casey knows what's going to happen next."

"Then I guess I'll ask him myself," James retorted and opened the door into the hallway.

"I'll be sure to send your family flowers," the prisoner murmured from the floor.

James locked the dungeon behind him and strode down the corridor as if reborn—a veritable phoenix. Though his injuries continued to accumulate, his vitals remained extraordinary, his mind continued to clear, and his spirit was ready for the task that lay ahead.

He emerged from the elevator into the lobby to behold the staging ground for Walter Brimford's final campaign.

Bailey's men paraded around the room in full uniform, fitted with rifles and pistols and body armor. Some even carried flameproof riot shields. Thomas stood center stage, orchestrating the operation in a dress shirt and slacks.

"That's what you're going with?" the hunter asked as he approached.

The commander seemed surprised when he turned. "Look who it is." The mercenaries erupted into applause. "Our fearless leader."

James stepped into the circle of cheering soldiers, silent, and the bedlam died down around him.

"Few words, maybe?" Bailey muttered from beside him.

"Why?" he demanded, perplexed.

"You're taking Walt's place, right?"

James grunted and looked around to see the twenty-three expectant young men watching him. They were eager, perhaps too much so. He wondered how many of them had ever engaged an elementalist before. Aside from that, he wondered how many of them it would take to put Casey down.

Lastly, he wondered what it would take to incite them to victory. What would it take to motivate himself, for that matter? The answer came to him as he inhaled to speak.

"The Cult of the Apocalypse has committed more murders than the Nazis and Communists combined. They had that record beat before Germany or Russia even existed. They don't fight for territory; they've got territory in every country on Earth. They don't fight for survival; to them, death is a victory. They fight to end all life. Everywhere. Forever.

"And a lieutenant of this genocidal cult is planning something here in London. If you need more motivation than that…we're fighting for our survival, because at the end of the day that's all any animal can do. We're hunters. We kill to our last breath."

James looked again to the commander as the troops stood in awe of his ethos. He repeated his previous question. "Why aren't you in gear?"

"I'm coming inside with you," Thomas reassured him. "We can't set up outside until Casey's in the club. I come in with you, wait for him to have a drink, give the word, and we bring the hammer down on this Nazi fuck once and for all. Yeah?" He pulled a coat on to conceal his holstered sidearm and continued, "Now ideally, we detain the prick inside to minimize civilian whatever-the-fuck, but in the likely event that he attempts to escape, we've got the front and rear exits covered. If he gets past that, we'll have to double back a few blocks south. There's a multistory car park there overlooking the Thames. If we can get him there, he'll have no place left to run. Unless he wants to have a swim in Deptford Creek," he laughed. "Sound good?"

"Yeah," said the hunter, "sounds good." He considered the likelihood of the most powerful man in London running from a fight and discarded the notion.

"Right, then." Bailey moved to join his men. "Pack it in, gents. Time to kill an ancient."

Michelle and Robert sat in the corner of the lobby by the reception desk, watching the goings-on. James noticed the two at length and moved to join them.

"You're both still here?" he asked.

Michelle shrugged. "Until Casey is dealt with, it's the safest place. I doubt it will take long," she added, smiling.

"Michelle..." he started.

"No," she interrupted him. "I know—"

"Thank you," he continued, undeterred.

The reader stood. "You're not the only one risking his life all the time," she remarked.

"Time to do it again."

"You're heading out, brother?" Robert asked, already red-eyed and on his feet.

"That's right, brother." James held out his hand. The initiate ignored his handshake and threw his arms around the hunter's massive frame, squeezing him as tightly as an Earther could manage.

"You be careful, now, Jimothy," he told him, blubbering.

"Will do." He waited until the Scotsman loosened his grip to pull away.

"Phew," Robert heaved, wiping his eyes. "I could use a drink."

Michelle jumped at the suggestion. "Oh, we'll be doing more than drinking." She produced a tiny, orange bottle and rattled the pills inside. "Walter does keep a lovely Bordeaux in his office, though." The Scotsman gaped at her as if the two had just become soulmates.

"I'll hail the lift," he tittered, leaving Michelle and the hunter alone by the desk.

The reader watched James, her eyes narrowed in quiet discernment. He looked back at her with a similar expression but an opposite intent.

"You're a good hunter," she told him after a moment. "You can do this."

"If I were as good a hunter as you are a reader, we'd already be done with this."

She took a step towards him, now closer than a mere acquaintance would stand, gauging his reaction. The hunter stood fast.

"You're not as easy to read as you think."

"I try not to be too legible."

"I'd kiss you," she sighed, "if it weren't for the woman that's always on your mind." He laughed, embarrassed. "Are you blushing?"

"How can you even tell?" he mocked her.

"Do you miss her?" the reader asked, her question razor-sharp. It cut deeper than any blade.

"Always."

Michelle nodded and backed away, her eyes to the floor. In the next moment, she stepped forwards and embraced him.

"You should give Robert a chance," he advised her as they parted. "He's a decent guy."

"I don't date married men," she contested. "Certainly not initiates."

"He's a widower," James informed her and turned to leave.

She stood in a stupor for several seconds before starting towards the elevator.

James McCrary steeled himself for the impending battle. He went over his inventory in his mind. Ideally, he'd have more to rely on in such a vital conflict, but his arsenal had run thin over the last few days. For a fight like this, in addition to Yin and Yang he'd ordinarily have two KA-BARs, two butterfly knives, a parrying dagger, a ballistic knife, and a skinning knife along with twelve throwing knives, twelve feet of wire rope, zip ties, a full set of abseiling gear, and a net. He had with him few to none of those items.

He did not forsake, however, his coat which would undoubtedly prove instrumental. Blood-drenched and tattered though it was, it was absolutely essential. The black dragon molt that lined it had protected him from pyromancers' flames before. Hopefully the material could withstand Casey's, as well. Aside from that, he had Yin, Yang, enough throwing knives to keep Casey from casting with impunity, and the two USMC-issue KA-BARs just in case. In spite of it all, though, he was invigorated. Even hours away from bloodshed he could feel the adrenaline in his body coaxing him into a characteristic trance.

He felt the moon fill as he stepped outside into the dark and the cold. Looking up, he saw the celestial huntress' smile widening as if she could not contain herself. She had a front row seat to the spectacle that would soon play out beneath her.

"Watch this," he admonished, hoping to sate her once and for all.

Thomas Bailey moved to his side and stifled a shiver.

"You ready?"

Chapter Eighteen
The Hunter's Fangs

En route to his destiny, James polished his weapons with long, smooth strokes. A ritual. Yin and Yang shined white in the glow of each passing streetlamp. He reflected for a moment on the blades' history, how he'd come to possess such potent tools of destruction. It was unsettling, at least to him, how iconic they'd become. The razor edges were a household name amongst gargoyles, fables told by Mythopians, maledictions uttered by their victims. The only more famous twins were the two moons which cycled nightly above the Mythopian skyline. Of course, the blades had achieved their mythos from past owners.

Nasir was the first. A chief combatant in the War of the Falling Sun, he bore the blades with cunning and daring and brought the corrupted city of Ponsithia crumbling to the ground. There in the depths the weapons atrophied until they were recovered with the city's reclamation. They were then reforged and wielded by Lord Wallis. After his death, the blades were passed on to his son. And his.

Soon thereafter, the swords made their way to Tonita, and again their form was altered to suit the purposes of Aldous the Rose, a master assassin. After he was captured and killed, the weapons were auctioned and purchased by Sundos II, the Lord of Legend. He recognized for the first time in some generations the daggers' lineage and restored them to their original cut.

With each retooling, Yin and Yang were adapted to a new sinister calling, but each owner echoed their darker purpose. Nasir, aided by the blades, nearly took the life of the valiant Aias. Now the blades would be loosed upon an ancient once again.

It was as if this was the reason the blades had been born. All swords drink blood, but only Yin and Yang clamored for it. The blood of an ancient, though, was their most dire dessert. It was the blood they'd never tasted but had always craved—Casey's.

James could feel the malice in them, the selfsame intention that ran from his heart in waves of red. He remembered with open eyes the ceremony with which he'd received them. They were wicked weapons. Uwe could not have thought otherwise.

"Open them."

James remembered letting the light into his gaze and seeing before him a crossed pair of blades. He was not a hunter yet, but after this ritual he would be.

"Swords?" The neophyte baulked at Yin, then at Yang—still sheathed and safe and silent—before looking up to Uwe.

"Not quite swords, not quite daggers." The dwarf stretched his hands out farther, pressing the gifts into his hold. "They're closer to kukri blades."

"I don't know how to use swords," James responded and lifted the blades to gauge their weight and feel.

"Well, you said you were having range issues. I thought a new weapon might help you out. Besides, you're due for a little variety." He smiled. "You're a hunter now. You're one of us."

The newly anointed's thoughts went first to the handgun under his shoulder, then to the daggers lining his back. "I'm fine against anything that flinches at a bullet." He shrugged.

"And gargoyles?" the dwarf contended.

He sighed. "Have been giving me trouble."

"Those blades are meaner than they look," Uwe suggested, casting him a sidelong glance. "Trust me."

Intrigued, James drew out the first blade and a tremor resounded in his breast. Yin, curved like an iron smile, greeted him with frigid glee.

"They're twin blades, James," Uwe rushed him.

James waved him off and took out Yang to match. Together, the two seemed almost joyful. He saw in the weapons an animate quality like the lilting of a flower. The thought made him ill.

"Those blades have quite a history," Uwe went on, sensing his discomfort. "A lot of blood between them."

"I can tell." James watched them dance as they twisted in his grasp, bouncing light and dazzling him with the illusion of life. He jolted up to Uwe. "Did you use them?"

The dwarf turned solemn, nodding. "Many times."

"Are they named?"

"Oh, yes." James awaited a more satisfying answer. "Oh," the dwarf stumbled, "I don't know their names. Well, not their real names," he corrected himself, "just what they meant." Then, after a moment, "They are known as Life and Death."

"Who names a sword 'Life?'" The young man laughed.

"Someone," Uwe scolded him, "who knows the true power of violence. The power to preserve as well as to destroy. Or save through destruction," he preached, tripping over his tongue, "or destroy through salvation."

James, still getting acquainted with the new blades, pretended to follow his words, responding only with a shallow dip of his head. "Yin and Yang," he continued before turning to his mentor. "Like some Bruce Lee shit. Balance."

Uwe's eyebrows lifted, indicating perplexion. "They're not attached to their titles," he assured his apprentice, "only their profession."

"Yin, Death, whoever, has this scar here." He held one of the blades up and showed Uwe the fault.

"It's been there since I got it," the dwarf replied, raising one shoulder in a half-shrug.

"I'm not complaining," James said, shaking his head. "I dig it. These are real weapons."

"Anything that can take a life is a real weapon."

"This is the kind of thing that will get me respect," he explained.

"As if anyone has any reason to respect you."

The young man shot him a scowl.

Uwe swallowed hard and went on: "You'll come into your own one day." He paused, affirming the statement in his head. "You'll do some incredible things. I'm sure of it."

"Fuck that," James exclaimed, shattering the gravity of Uwe's praise. "I just want to kill some dragons, get paid, and get out."

The dwarf's jaw tensed. "I'm sure."

"Ooie," James continued, "thank you, man." He glanced down at the blades. "This means a lot."

Uwe only stared at him with an obsidian gaze. Seventeen years old and already the boy was a titan. He was brash, he was foolish, he was inexperienced, and he'd be hunting drakes and gargoyles within the year. His body had grown, but his mind still seemed the same. James was still the adolescent boy he'd saved from imprisonment, delivered from mediocrity, and brought into excellence. In combat, he had all the prowess of an elven knight, the might of a battle-hardened dwarf, and the heroism of all his human forebears combined. He thought like a boy, but a bright one. In spite of all his virtues, though, he was missing an unplaceable quality essential to his survival.

Was he ready?

Uwe snapped to attention at the sight of James beginning to sheath the blades. "No!" he growled and dashed to tear them from his hands. "I know what you're missing," he said, having secured Yin and Yang. "These blades have a certain contract attached to them. They must never be put away without first drawing blood." Without warning, he brought Yang across his left wrist and Yin across his right. The flesh billowed claret, the mark of a dwarf, unprecedentedly profuse bleeding that slowed after only a few seconds.

Yin and Yang sang in delight, no longer refracting light but still and dark with deep-red blood. Uwe sheathed them and handed the sopping cases to his apprentice. "But never your own," he went on.

"Won't they rust?" James panted, still shocked by the spectacle.

"Not these. No, not these."

The young hunter claimed to understand with a single nod.

"You understand? This is about loyalty to the hunt. The only way you will survive is if there is nothing you value more than your own life...to be willing to destroy everything else."

"I understand."

"Everything, James. Just like I've taught you."

"Everything," he repeated.

Everything.

James winced. Superstition had no place in his aesthetic. Yin and Yang sat before him, squirming with anticipation, but they'd be fed soon enough. Besides, he had no blood to impart but his own.

He slid each blade into its proper place and could almost hear them crying in protest. Now, deep in his hunter's trance, he hushed them, knowing well that they'd be ravenous just in time for Casey.

Then he'd prove his loyalty. Tonight. In this last, glorious hunt.

Chapter Nineteen
Casey

There was something unsettling about the denizens gathered for a night of music in the cool, red glow of the jazz club. Calm poured from the brass and the bass and the soft rap of the drummer, sedating everyone in the building but James. His heart prowled in his chest, sending a growl of chemical alertness through his bones every second. Everything had to be perfect. Everyone had to be ready. Each and every inch of the club had to be inspected and pulled apart for all of the tactical advantages it could impart.

He'd gone over the building countless times in the last half hour. The bar, the bathrooms, the kitchen, the stage, the cigarette smoke in the air, as well as the positions and occupants of every table and every standing observer that would stand between him and a clean kill.

"You're on edge, mate," Bailey whispered, appearing from over his shoulder. "You need to take a drink and relax before this all kicks off." He moved back to his table at the far end of the club.

He was right. Even now, with his chest heaving and his blood burning, James McCrary the Stoneslayer had let someone get close enough to whisper into his ear without noticing them. He glanced over his shoulder and reevaluated everyone sitting behind him, identifying potential threats—Casey could have initiates lying in wait wherever he went.

The madness of his speculation soon overwhelmed him. He got up from the table and marched over to the bar.

"Whisky, neat," he requested, leaning against the countertop. "And for the love of God, bring me a steak." His nerves eased even before he took the drink to his lips.

"Sorry," the bartender said, "we don't serve any steaks." The look the hunter returned could have killed a man. "Would you like to see a menu?"

"I'd like to see a steak."

"I could ask if—"

"Steak," James repeated and poured more whisky down his throat.

The barkeep held fast for a solid moment. He then asked, "Are you police?"

James flinched, resenting the suggestion. "No." After some internal conjecture he asked, "Why?"

"Cause you look like one."

"No, I mean why would a cop be here?"

"What, cops can't like jazz?" The hunter's face did not shift, but its lingering provoked a less caustic response—at least in the bartender's eyes. "They'd be looking into the arsonist who comes here."

"Casey."

The bartender breathed out, now more than willing to divulge his concerns. "Guy comes in here all the time with a fucking sword bragging about all the fires he's started. He was in here last night, drunk off his ass, talking about how he did the bit downtown at that club, skulking around the kitchen and all that." He whirled around before continuing, "We've been calling the cops on him for weeks. Nothing." He shrugged and turned to serve another patron.

His revelations sent James' mind spiraling through possibilities. Then, at that very moment, he saw him.

It struck him at a strange enough time that he'd never seen a picture of the once-courier he'd been commissioned to apprehend. James had previously perceived him only as a shadow, a glimmer of imagination and speculation. Yet there he was, Casey Aduro, striding up before him into the center of the room, identical to his visions. His gait unmistakably suggested that he was a killer, a hunter, and a beast of a man.

He sat at an empty table with his back to the hunter before James could make out his face, watching the band perform. His unkempt golden hair dropped to his shoulders as he slumped into his chair. He wore a black duster light enough that he did not have to remove it indoors. Fastened across his back was a long, red sheath poised like a scorpion's tail. James dreaded the blade that slept inside its casing.

He saw, despite the attitude he'd always maintained, not an object of prey but a fellow predator. He'd ventured out to claim a sheep only to find a wolf in its place.

Suddenly, Casey howled and applauded, joined by the other patrons at the close of the band's song. He called the trumpeter by name, received a candid response, and shared a laugh with him. James felt as though he were dreaming.

He rebounded from his daze and locked eyes with Bailey at his table. He dared not speak a word. The commander motioned for him to remain seated then muttered something into the lapel of his coat and settled back into his seat, smiling.

The band began their next song.

James took a sip of whisky.

Casey pulled a cigarette from his coat pocket.

He held his fingers around the tip, and in an instant, it sprang into flame. Content, he took a long, luxurious drag, pulling the flame inward before exhaling. The smoke rose around him in a halo, melding with that of the other guests'.

The music turned fierce. The tempo quickened, the volume intensified, and the musicians livened. The club's entire dynamic shifted in seconds. A few couples moved to dance before the stage. An ordinary man would see a bustle of vivacity and excitement. James saw only obstacles.

He watched Casey's head sway back and forth with the bass. His movement was smooth and solid. It never faltered. The hunter swallowed hard, imagining the fluidity of his sword. He watched him ignite another cigarette without the aid of a match or lighter. His ruby was nowhere in sight, but Casey clearly didn't need one; he was an ancient. He took a single pull while the bassist dove into a solo, then he stood.

The club came to stillness, an audience to the Cultist's incumbent performance. He caught even the musicians' attention. He turned but did not meet the hunter's eyes. He saw him without seeing him, felt him in the static and the dark.

The hunter felt time idle as he watched the predator prepare.

His thin lips curled upwards as he flashed a smile. His face was clean-shaven. His eyes burned blue like fire.

The percussionist joined the bassist on a pair of drums, punctuating the hunt's commencement. James could feel the beat in lockstep with his heart which now catapulted blood into every reach of his mind, yet he did nothing.

He watched Casey without blinking, already locked into the duel. Neither stirred. James did not see Bailey move to draw his pistol in the corner. Only Casey did. James did not hear Bailey click the safety off his gun. Only Casey did.

Onstage, the brass prepared to join the rest of the ensemble.

Casey felt a shudder in the pit of his stomach and muttered something to himself. James only watched.

Then the Cultist's arms flew out like dragon wings, summoning a wave of bursting, crashing, purging fire. It rolled around him, isolating the front half of the club. James brought his coat up reflexively and, when he lowered it, Casey had vanished.

"He's out the side!" Bailey roared over the scorching, screams, and patrons scrambling for the exits. The commander motioned to the door he'd used.

Standing between the hunter and his opponent, however, was a wall of fire.

"Head to the parking garage!" he shouted back and bundled his jacket around himself. With it secured around his head and hands, he charged through the flames. He emerged on the other side unburned, unsinged, untouched. For the moment, he was grateful that he had such a useful tool.

He hurtled through the exit, shattering the hinges, and surfaced in the alley behind the club. He instantly caught sight of the five mercs who lay dead or dying on the pavement. Their shields had done nothing against the flames. "Casey," he commanded them, apathetic to their condition, focused only on the hunt. One of the five, still smoking from his encounter with the Cultist, raised a shaking hand to the fire escape on the opposite wall.

He heard the clatter of boots on metal. Looking up, he caught a glimpse of Casey as he disappeared onto the rooftop.

James tore onto the fire escape with Olympian grace. He ascended with abject disregard for his human limitations. He vaulted up the stairs at incomprehensible speed. By the time he reached the roof, though, it was done.

He appeared in time to see Casey fire a single pistol round into the last mercenary's head. Finished, he leapt onto the next rooftop with all the prowess of a great cat, ignoring the hunter completely. James raced along the roof, counting the gunmen—one, two, three—as he ran. Eight of the twenty-three mercenaries had already been dealt with.

He rolled upon impact with the second roof and drew a throwing knife. The blade jetted out like a bullet—a bullet which Casey detected. He turned from the other end of the roof for a single instant to see the projectile hurtling towards him. One small step to his left and he evaded it without incident. He was fast. Very fast.

The ancient lifted his pistol before the hunter could draw another knife, firing precisely and decisively. He watched the round strike James in the chest before he turned and leapt onto the next building.

James went down to one knee, cursing. There was a reason he'd fired at his body and not his head. The hunter cycled back through the mercenaries he'd already found dead and counted the causes of death. Three to fire and four headshots, only one still alive. Which meant that Casey wanted *him* alive.

He recovered from the shot and bolted back onto his feet, tearing open the second bulletproof vest he'd ruined that week. He'd been careless. By all accounts, he'd just cheated death for what might be the last time. His next move would have to be as decisive as Casey's. He readied more throwing knives and bounded onto the third roof. The Cultist was only halfway over.

James' eyes darted to the next roof over and saw, in a moment of relief, that it was too far to jump even for a Mythopian—even for an ancient. This time, there could be no escape.

His first knife whirled towards Casey's legs. The second he aimed straight at his head. The ancient pivoted and dodged each in turn. The third, however, he did not anticipate. The hunter's hidden blade shot forth and struck the Cultist square in the arm that held the gun.

He reeled from the pain.

James ripped Yin and Yang from his coat and charged ahead full speed, but his prey wasn't ready to face him. Casey turned tail and sprinted for the clearing between buildings, knowing full well that he couldn't make the jump. Instead, he went straight down into the alley.

"No!" James shouted and continued his rush. He was at an advantage for the moment. The second Casey put more distance between them, he'd lose his edge. He reached the end of the rooftop and peered down to see the Cultist sliding into the street on the downspout of a rain gutter.

Turning again to face him with a taunting smile, the Cultist pulled the throwing knife from his arm, saluted James, and tore down the street. The hunter's heart continued to slow. Based on his current heading, the Cultist would bypass the car park outright. Without wasting another moment, he sheathed his blades and leapt after him. He touched down and pursued the Cultist along the pavement at a lion's pace, dashing past the pedestrians his eyes and ears ignored, but they could not ignore Casey.

"Can you feel it?" his voice rattled. "James?" Thin, a wisp of a flame, searing to the ear. "That's not adrenaline in your veins." Casey turned mid-stride with a shark's grin, his hands outstretched. From his open palms leapt a wave of destruction.

The hunter girded himself against the blaze and emerged intact. In the corner of his eye, though, he saw a bystander smitten with fire. Over the deafening cries of the baying cattle he commanded, "Call an ambulance!" knowing full well the futility. Even beneath his heat shield he'd felt the flames gnash at his skin.

The street was in an uproar now. He could hear it all, shouting and scrambling and shots in the distance coming near him. The bullets meant for Casey streaked past him instead, scarcely missing his larger frame. He cursed the mercenaries at the end of the street firing at their target with blatant disregard for any collateral damage they incurred, but only as it applied to him. Their fervor fed his momentum as it did Casey's. The chaos tasted sweet to the both of them.

The ancient swept forth, ignored their gunfire as if their weapons were toys, and freed his howling weapon from its cage. Before James could reach him, the katana struck forth and returned, sated, to its sheath. Now the ancient was moving to an alley perpendicular to the street.

The hunter recollected the layout of the remaining mercenaries, and the memory sent a flicker of glee over his vicious features. Casey tore into the alley with his gun lowered, his sword still, and a maleficent grin upon his face.

"It's over, Casey." Commander Bailey knelt at the opposite end of the alley with pistol primed, backed by four riflemen. Each had the ancient sighted and their safeties switched off. James emerged into the backstreet with Yin in his right hand and a throwing knife in his left. Casey was cornered. "On your knees," the commander warned him. His target stood motionless in response. The beast's resolve unsettled all of them. "Casey," Thomas repeated, and his apprehension broke through in his tone.

Casey laughed and moved forwards. One step. Two steps. Three steps. All without inciting a single shot.

The hunter thought to act, but why should he? How long would the mercenaries wait before they fired? Even an ancient couldn't face a firing squad head-on. Bailey thought likewise, saving his pistol rounds in case the skirmisher slipped through their initial salvo. All the same, his mind shook like a child in winter. His men should have fired three steps ago, he thought just as the ancient made a fourth stride and pointed up above them.

They stood as phantoms poised over a cemetery, haunting the alley. Casey's initiates pressed their guns down into the passage and every eye below went to them. The hunter's heart limpened. The mercenaries pointed their guns skywards. Bailey gasped.

"Go!" he shouted and emptied his gun into the air. His men followed suit. Casey dashed through the alley, an apparition, and James flew after him, but the soldiers spent their focus on the gunmen overhead. They didn't think to fire a single round at the fire elementalist until he stood only a meter away. The commander brought his gun to bear. Casey's sword descended with the certainty of a scorpion's sting and split his arm apart.

Bailey's outcry peeled his soldiers back as he gripped his wounded limb upon reflex. Only then did they manage to break their attention from the initiates already retreating from the edge of the rooftops. The first mercenary to train his gun back onto the ancient had a sword hilt thrust into his jaw. Casey blew flame onto the second. The shower of cinders—a cone the width of a feather—shot across his face and blinded him. A single sword stroke sufficed for the last two. Then he heard the whistling of an approaching projectile and reacted as quickly as only he could do.

The dagger glanced off his sword, striking with much more force than he'd expected. He barely managed to regain his balance before another throwing knife came straight for him. He applauded the hunter's tenacity with a smirk as he dipped out of the alley and back down the street.

James steamed onto the street with a look of madness on his face. The car park was close now, but Bailey and his men had been decimated. One of the mercenaries reeled from the alley and fired at Casey in vain. Their quarry sprinted to the opposite sidewalk alongside cars and pedestrians, preventing any sure shots. The rounds struck around him, shattering windows, puncturing metal, denting stone. Some even met with flesh...just not his.

There was only one option for the hunter now. If he could drive the Cultist into the parking structure and hold him long enough, the remainder of the mercenaries could catch up to them. James counted them off in his head. At least two full squads would make the rendezvous in a few minutes' time. All he had to do was get Casey there.

As he pursued him, invigorated by his action plan, and still bursting with adrenaline, a smile made its way across James' lips. He could hear the ancient meters ahead of him, panting. He could feel himself gaining on the weary animal. Casey turned again to see him coming, and his earlier glee was nowhere to be seen.

James had removed all other options and he knew it. The mercenaries had the other side of the street covered. The buildings on this end had no climbable surfaces. Their back exits emptied into the Thames. At last, James heard the English sirens creep up from behind, and a sadistic calm settled over him. His eyes began to shiver in their sockets. Yin and Yang snarled like drakehounds, begging for release.

There was nowhere left to run.

Casey tore into the car park and James followed.

Casey Aduro vaulted over the concrete boundaries onto the second level and James McCrary bore down on his tail.

Casey Aduro, the Flamestorm, servant of Vaos and the Cult of the Apocalypse, leapt at length to the structure's roof, and James McCrary, the Stoneslayer, was close enough to grip his collar.

Then Casey stopped and turned, lifting his gun and turning the Stoneslayer's blood into sand.

James' eyes ran over the environment in a panic. There were no cars on the uppermost level and no other objects to give him cover. He counted the light posts dotting the terrain. The closest was a three-second sprint away. He saw to his left the downwards ramp where the mercenaries would soon arrive. He perceived the outer wall of the structure behind Casey. Over the side was a branch of the River Thames, too shallow to leap into from this height, with another building beyond that which was too far for even him to reach. The last thing he noted was the smile that had slipped back across the ancient's face in all the sloping shadows, even without him noticing.

"I've waited a long time for this." Casey savored the moment with a deep, inward breath and, when he exhaled, smoke streamed from his lips. "Worth it. Just for that look you've got right now."

The hunter closed his gaping mouth and clenched his jaw.

"I get it. I do." He laughed. "You're a hunter. You want to live. You would do anything right now to survive. Sometimes, though, there's nothing you *can* do."

He gripped the pistol. Pulled the trigger. Two clicks, but nothing else.

The hunter exhaled steam, his jaw releasing. His hands were shaking too much for him to make an attack.

"You knew that was empty," he remarked, panting.

Casey beamed as he holstered the weapon. "Honestly? No. I didn't." His smile broadened. "Neither did you. Apparently."

"You wanna fuck with me?" The hunter's eyes were wide, filled with fear, filled with confusion.

"Killing you is not ideal to my plan. I want to keep that plan the way it is." His words fell still and dry. "You keep fucking it up, though, I might have to work you in. So here's how I've got it set up: You turn around. Get a plane back to the States—God knows we both miss em. You crawl into a hole and wait for this to run its course, and I can wire you two million dollars by New Year's. That's it."

The hunter steadied as he stood with eyes locked on his prey. Home. Home and two million dollars were all he could think of in that moment.

"You know it's the safest deal. You have to think about where your loyalties lie. With this?" He spread his arms and they swallowed the world. Home, two million dollars, and the Cultist uprising were what James thought of in the next moment. Still, he stayed silent. "You can't hunt forever. It's what Uwe would tell you to do." The name sent lightning up his back. He wondered, for an instant, if the action he took was his choice or that of his subconscious. All the same, he did not question it when Yin and Yang appeared before him.

The Cultist flowed into a battle stance. "Come on," he roared, his sword hand hovering over his back. "The last thing I want is to have to kill you."

The hunter trembled with anger. "I bet you said that to Emma." He could barely utter the name without charging.

The words sank into Casey's flesh with all the impact of an arrow lodged in the center of his chest. "I—" He thought to defend himself then looked up into his opponent's eyes. "I would've killed you a hundred times before I touched a hair on her."

"No," James railed. "Apparently."

"No," Casey erupted. "I tried to save her. I did everything I could." His body began to smolder. "I did everything."

"And stabbed her in the back," the hunter muttered in response.

"No." His hands burst afire. The flames spread up his sleeves but consumed neither cloth nor carcass, and in amongst the crackling Casey rebuked him. "I loved her. More than you ever did." He hurled his words like coals, but they stung with cold.

"Loved her?" The hunter laughed, red-eyed. "You killed her." He could feel it now; more power than he'd experienced in a decade. He could not hold himself back from the fray.

"You think you could've saved her? You would've what, taken her to Mythic? Do you have any idea what they do to defects there?" he cried from conflagration. James' mind wandered to thoughts of Xiang in the basement, of the brainwashed initiate. "I didn't send those initiates. I went there to stop them." Casey's tone warped. He drew his katana from its sheath and wrapped the hilt in glowing heat. "When I find out who sent them, trust me, I'll kill them whether they're a Cultist or not."

"I don't believe you." James readied his weapons.

Casey's fire subsided as he reclaimed his composure. He boiled the moisture from his eyes. "Fuck it. We don't have time for this. Let's see if I can make a believer out of you."

The moon glowed with laughter, all too eager for the ensuing exhibition. Her light was a glint compared to the ancient's flame. He commanded it with body and breath aligned, stepping forwards and wide and shooting one arm out to the side. It followed like an invocation, mirroring his form, and dove after the hunter.

James spun into the lining of his coat, digging into the shroud until the moment he felt the heat pass over him. Then he sprang from the covering and saw the Cultist smiling brighter than the moon itself. With his breathing tied to the flames, Casey could not speak, but his spirit lashed out with fiery maledictions. The hunter caught a hint of an utterance before he ducked to evade the ancient's next cast. It arced above his head and curled the hairs on the back of his neck.

He winced, but his adrenaline limited that reaction. His mind and body were separate now. The one conducted and the other played his savage symphony without protest. Yin and Yang lurched in perfect form, but Casey's Stinger was poised to counter. Before the hunter could blink the blade had warded off his initial assault. It was all he could do to avoid the riposte that followed. He granted ground to his opponent, now wary of the weapon's reach, but could not prevent Casey from casting at a distance.

Ordinarily, an elementalist would betray his casts with a trace of color beneath the clothing or a glowing gem held in plain sight, but Casey offered nothing in the way of a precursor. His fire came without warning, bitter and brutal.

He summoned one wave that James deflected with his coat. A second swell instantly followed. The hunter sidestepped but took a shadow of the heat across his exposed skin. Still steaming, he turned and saw a third surge rippling through the air. His countenance fell.

Casey watched the hunter dive forwards under the fire, turning his mantle to the scorching heat, and laughed as he rolled to a melee stance. "More?" he started to say but was interrupted. James' hidden knives shot from his sleeves. The left KA-BAR he didn't bother to aim, but he had a target in mind for the right.

The blade left him like a curse and caught Casey unprepared. He maneuvered to one side, felt a cold bite on his cheek, and blood furrowing across his face. With that, the two were locked in close combat.

"Good!" he barked as he warded off Yin when the hunter streaked by. "What else ya got?" he beckoned as Yang approached.

James ignored him. He placed all his focus into the spacing of their skirmish. Too wide a berth and Casey would cast his fire unimpeded. Too little room and Stinger bore an advantage. Just out of reach, he could move in to strike and move out to dodge. One, two, three, four, two, two, three, four. Their styles melded into a single song. By the sixth measure neither had gained an edge, but at that very moment the hunter's trump card came storming through the car park. He sensed them, distant but determined, and broke away from his adversary.

"That's it," he said at last and wiped the sweat from his forehead.

Casey took the reprieve to stifle the cut on his cheek. "I guess it is." He could hear them too, now, perhaps three or four floors down. He sheathed his sword.

"You can still live," James reminded him, returning his blades.

"Thanks for the concern." He hesitated, examining the hunter for a moment before drawing a cigarette from his coat pocket. "I'm sorry about Emily." The hunter's ears perked up. "I am. I didn't want her to die. I loved her as much as you did." He lit the cigarette with a whisper and took a single, satisfying drag.

"Those'll kill you," James joked.

"Everybody's got something that makes them feel alive," Casey reasoned, "even if it kills them."

"Hand over the Eye and I can keep you alive."

Casey turned. "What the hell are you talking about?"

The hunter shifted, losing patience. "Give back what you stole from Mythic."

"Ah," he sighed. "Is that what he told you?"

"What?" asked James, wary.

"Your employer's not who he seems," he said, floating to the far side of the roof. "You think he's after me to save the city? To cover his ass? You've got a lot to learn about this world." He peered out over the river and looked upon the Earth with contempt. "Goodbye, James." The mercenaries were at the final ramp. "Maybe I'll see you and Emily in a better world," he mused from the darkness.

James thought to stop the Cultist, but his impulses lay silent. He saw oblivion over the edge of the roof and decided that Casey could embrace it of his own volition.

The mercenaries stampeded onto the roof with weapons hot. "On the ground!" some of them yapped. They steeled their minds, knelt, and took aim.

Casey did not turn.

James examined him once more, striving to understand why he would not admit defeat in the twilight of his life. Why resist? "Casey!" he shouted after him, cowing the vengeful mercenaries into silence. "It's over. Please. Let it be over." He wanted immensely for the Cultist to face him. He hungered for his prey's final façade—for a frown, a scowl, even neutrality. Anything but a smile, the twisted expression that conveyed to him everything contrary to a hunter's desires. Not victory, but deadlock. Like the moon, unappeasable, mired blindly in its course night after night. Like a hunter. "Why are you smiling at me?"

It dawned on James far too late to make a difference.

Casey's arms spread wide like the ebon wings of a vanquished drake, conjuring a wall of flame that split his attackers in two. Behind the impassable column, the mercenaries fired mindlessly, loosed dogs with the blood of a fox in their path. Ahead, James tore to the ground, sheepish.

He peered upwards and saw Casey standing on the edge of the roof with a smile rivaling the sun's. He rocketed from the structure atop a plume of fire that accelerated him to an incredible height. As his soaring reached an apex, the flames dissipated and he landed soundly on the next rooftop.

James clambered to the rim of the car park. The image that awaited him was exactly as he expected. Casey was scrutinizing him from a distance, his cigarette glowing and his hand extended as if in welcome. It occurred to James that he was preparing to cast.

He saw the brilliance of it now.

The glorious chase, tunneling his senses and barring his mind from any adequate evaluation of his opponent. The odds stacked against him, James had overestimated his enemy, although not nearly enough. He was shivering now.

He recalled the cars positioned in the lower levels, the innocuous white vans—bombs—and regarded Casey's choice of element.

The Cultist was laughing again. He held three fingers aloft, prepared now to seal his promise to the reckless hunter.

James saw the irony of the situation. He'd always considered Casey to be another predator. He'd simply never conceived of himself as prey. Yet there he stood, ensnared in Casey's pitfall in the sky, trapped like a rat.

The ancient snapped his fingers and the bottom levels of the building churned to life. The fire warped steel and stone and splintered pillars. The force rode up all the way to the roof to paralyze everyone but James.

He knew that it was the nature of the hunter to always resist defeat by another, even if it meant defeating oneself. He could not win, but he would not lose. Loyalty to the hunt was about survival only.

Strengthening his spirit, James gripped the lip of the rooftop and vaulted into the aether. He couldn't see the moon or Casey laughing at his frenzied action. He thought that he could hear the one, though. He could smell fire from the crumbling edifice as it consumed him. He could taste the ash, soot, and debris filling his lungs. The river below offered no consolation.

He struck with concussive enormity and all was oblivion.

Part III
On Hunting

Chapter Twenty
The Hunters

Sheol. Hades. The Covered Hall. Ever portrayed in neutrality and monotony. Yet the grey distance they impart is in some ways greater than the rapture of Rapture, the ecstasy of Elysium, or the virtue of Valhalla. The ignorance they allow, the separation from self, the bliss of illusion, amnesia. So thought James McCrary when he visited—if only for a while—Death. It was not the first time and would not be the last.

Upon drifting back from the realm of Death, he felt the excruciating sensation of his lungs churning fluid and wished at once to return to the waters of Lethe. His bodily members paralyzed by cold and his airway constricted by water, his mind flashed red, purple, and black before his closed eyes. In the darkness of the River Thames, he saw the face of a man. His consciousness shuddered and, in an instant, he was home.

* * * *

"James?" he heard from sleep. The first murmur seemed gentle, warm, and protective. "Are you joking?" it turned mean. "Wake up, you bastard." He felt the sharp pain of a kick to his shin and sprang up, fists clenched.

His eyes opened to the sight of a colossal man standing a head above him, red hair tinged with grey. The hunter's demeanor softened. "Ooie!" His arms opened and wrapped around his mentor.

"Good to see you, boy." Uwe embraced him before pulling away with an outstretched hand. The two gripped forearms and met eye to eye before the dwarf spoke again. "So you come all the way to Zurich for a hunt jetlagged?"

James maintained his fierce smile for a moment before voicing his retort. "I see you started going grey since last time."

"Really?" Uwe's face reddened. "Straight to the old jokes."

"How old *are* you, Ooie? Ninety? A hundred?"

"I'm half that, and you know it." He laughed and added, "Thanks for the dentures on my fiftieth, by the way. It was a riot to open that in front of company."

"The dentures? Not the diapers?" Uwe delivered a harsh look. "Huh. Must've got lost in the mail."

"I'm so glad humans live longer than dwarves. You'll have *decades* to regret all of that abuse when I'm gone."

"Come on, you're not out yet, old man. And look at me." The young hunter stepped back, flexing. "Not even thirty, baby."

James was doubtless beginning to hit his stride. No longer the thin prodigy of Mythopian youth, his physique now reflected his capabilities. He could bench press a quarter of a ton without straining. He was confident that he could do twice that but dared not attract the attention such a feat would incur. He'd been hunting now for ten years. He hadn't seen Uwe in six.

"You are..." Uwe bit his lip and searched for words to express his approval, "almost where I thought you'd be five years ago."

"Fuck you," James replied, chuckled, and relaxed his muscles. "Good to see you, man. I missed you."

"Yeah, yeah," the old Mythopian grumbled. "You ready to go to work?"

"Serious?" He raised an eyebrow. "I've been on a plane for more than a day. Haven't done any real work since May. Haven't fed Yin and Yang in months." He beamed. "I'm dying to kill something."

Uwe grimaced. "Poor choice of words," he said and grabbed one of his bags. "Welcome to Switzerland, Herr McCrary. Gehen wir dann," he said, smiling, "in den Schlund des Kultes."

Outside the airport, Zurich still slept, rooted in placidity. The air swirled, vacuous and cool. The two hunters could hear the hum of the winter wind but no more apart from the trudging of their boots.

James awaited an explanation as they moved away from the

terminal, still sporting nothing but a naive smile. January, however, encouraged solemnity and the elder hunter obliged. "All right, then." He watched the heat pass from his lungs with a sigh. "They found him."

His apprentice tensed, either from cold, anxiety, or both. "The yeti?" he sniggered.

Uwe held stern. His eyes saw farther than the path before him. "Solomon the Great."

James nodded as he shivered and swallowed hard. "This is the big one, then." He laughed again, weaker this time, and stared at Uwe. "We're ready for it."

"We are."

At length, they reached the town car parked away from the terminal. As the dwarf unlocked it, James strode over to the passenger side and set his hands upon the roof. "So, where to?"

"We," Uwe began, shooting him a sly glance, "are going to see a horse about a man."

"I don't know what that means," James admitted. The dwarf's face remained twisted in a clownish leer. "Are you having a stroke?"

"Don't worry about it," came Uwe's reply as he plopped into the car and started the engine. "Check our gear. Pick out something pretty."

The hunters exchanged looks as James ducked inside. He dove into the back and lifted an enormous handgun. "Oh, Ooie, you remembered."

"Mmhmm, .50 caliber, just for you. Maybe now you'll know how to give a decent gift."

"You know, a lindworm ate my last one."

"Ah," the dwarf said, wincing. "I can see why you didn't want it back."

He ran through the rest of the assortment. "I want the SPAS," he asserted, hefting the combat shotgun into the front seat.

"Pah," Uwe scolded the boy with a slap to the wrist, almost veering off the road. "That's Leoma. She's my baby."

"Yeah? What's your baby got for dragonscales?"

"Armor piercing, flash, exploding, and my personal favorite—" he reached into his coat pocket and produced a few shells, "Dragon's Breath."

"Ha," remarked James, rolling his eyes.

"What did you bring that can take down a dragon?" he asked, defensive.

James opened one of his bags and brought out a band of throwing knives, brandishing them for a moment before tossing the roll into the back. He did the same with the next two dozen blades.

"When Mythic says they'll get your full arsenal through customs, you take it seriously, don't you?"

The blade-wielding aficionado ignored him. "You wanna see what's gonna take down a dragon?" He moved to unbutton his coat.

"I get it," Uwe said with a sigh, "you have muscles now. Congratulations. Welcome to the club."

While his old teacher poked fun, James pulled out the amulet he'd been hiding under four layers of clothing. At a glance, it seemed innocuous enough. Without the gemstone, it appeared to be nothing but an ordinary gold chain. The garnet the size of a cherry tomato, however, held incredible significance for those aware of the stone's properties.

"Where did you get that?" the dwarf questioned him, astounded. "Is that where all your money's gone?"

"You know where my money went," he rattled.

"Don't snap at me. I was the first to tell you not to invest in First National Mattress." Uwe regretted the easy barb and nudged the boy. "You find the guys?"

"Yeah."

"But not the money." He watched the hunter scowling at the dashboard. "Look, I don't distrust your common sense, just your good nature." James laughed. "Kind of a waste, though, right?"

His young friend's expression turned into a scowl. "Just watch me cast."

"It's your money, Herr Millionär."

"Yeah," he scoffed, "I'm just made of money these days. You think I didn't spend myself even further under Aaron's thumb just getting here?"

"Aaron's a heartless bastard, but he takes care of his hunters. You said you hadn't had much work lately," Uwe probed.

The first sunray struck from behind the eastern ridges, catching James unaware. He blinked at first, adjusting to the light flickering between the buildings. The cityscape's beauty appeared to him in a flourish. He considered, for a moment, what life might be like in such a place before answering, "I've been busy. I met someone."

"About damn time," his friend laughed, pulling down the sun visor to shield his eyes. "I was starting to think that hunting had ruined you for love." James smiled in kind. "What's his name?"

A swift jab to his shoulder made Uwe regret the remark. "I think I'm in love, Ooie."

Already cramped in the compact vehicle, the dwarf tried in vain to nurse the pain in his arm. "I think you broke it." He glanced over to his companion who seemed lost in the river that ran alongside them. "Yeah, you might be." Seeing that James was still ignoring him, he threw a pair of snapping fingers in front of the lovestruck fool's face. James rebounded from his dreamstate as if he'd actually been asleep. "Listen, son, you may have already learned this in Paris, but there's no place for love on a hunt."

The hunter returned an absent stare.

"Jesus," Uwe cursed, realizing he'd yet to learn the lesson. "I'm just saying Sartre knew it. You do, too, somewhere in you. A man needs complete and total focus on a hunt. You rely on your most carnal instincts." He looked to make sure that James was still following him. "Now, love is a wonderful thing. It makes you feel..." he fumbled for words he hadn't known in years. "Tingly? Warm and complete—"

"Well..."

"That's not what you want when you're elbow-deep in dragonfrost!"

"I—"

"You need that cold, boy. That bite that presses you onward. You need the rage that comes only when you're close enough to Death to smell his cologne. You need the hopelessness that comes when you're all alone with him. Cause when you have that, all you care about is the kill." The novice hunter now hushed, the dwarf sank his fangs into every word. "That's all that matters. And that's all that should matter. The blade in your hand, the man you want on it, and that bitter end."

James gave him a single nod. "You want me to be loyal to the hunt."

"If you could save the girl you love or kill the beast you hate, the true hunter sees only one choice. Now, this bounty pays more than every one you've ever collected. More than you ever imagined a single sword stroke could bring you. I've fronted us the top-shelf equipment and you don't even have to pay me back. Just promise me loyalty."

Unsure, James opened his mouth to speak but stopped short.

The car rolled to a sudden stop as Uwe's gaze bore down upon his. "Loyalty, James." His voice blackened. "We kill to our last breath."

The dwarf extended a hand and, as the human took it, the two exchanged silent vows. Somewhat satisfied, Uwe sighed and pulled back onto the road.

"There's an SG in the trunk with your name on it. Vests, grenades, climbing gear. This is gonna be a hell of a fight."

"We're going out in the alps…" James posited, more a question than a statement.

Uwe laughed. "We're going wherever the hunt takes us."

The hunt took them south, out of the capital and towards the mountains. The sun had climbed high by the time they reached the Swiss Alps, but now the clouds suffocated it beneath a great expanse of grey haze. Snowfall sifted from the sky, checkering the air with patterns of crystal flakes, each reflecting whatever light could crawl past the clouds. Snow brought even more silence to the dismal landscape.

Uwe wheeled the car off the main road at the sight of a distant farm. It sat a ways into the fields alongside the highway but warranted a visit nonetheless. James followed him through the ice up to the barn across from the farmhouse. As the dwarf slid open the structure's large door, the two were assaulted in every sense by the farm's inhabitants. The warmth that swept across their bundled faces was welcome. So too were the cheery, accompanying bleats. What deterred the hunters was the stench that hit them harder than any other sensation.

"What, are we getting bait?" James gagged.

Uwe pulled his scarf from his mouth. Then he gathered air through his nostrils, and the sound of dislodging mucus made the younger hunter's teeth itch. Relieved, the revolting dwarf held out a hand to one of the baying lambs that had surrounded them.

James closed the barn door behind them, repeating his inquiry. "What are we doing here?" He studied the man standing before him caressing a sheep like a long-lost lover.

"Feel that." His smile was two miles wide.

Slowly, his accomplice moved to stroke one of the wooly scalps. He understood, if only a little, the peace such an action could bring. Even so, he felt out of place amongst such docile creatures. "Yeah?" he prodded after a moment's petting. "And?"

"No," the dwarf cooed, sensing that he had not understood. "James," he spoke gently, "you mean to tell me you've never *felt* an animal?"

His mouth opened as if to reply, but James found himself completely nonplussed.

"What else did I forget to teach you?" He squatted down and pressed his brow against the lamb's.

"I don't get it," James said, feeling like he was on the wrong end of a bad joke.

"Oh, James, you've never felt anything like it." Uwe looked up from his emotional connection with endearing eyes. "You've never felt anything until you've been inside one of these little guys."

James' eyes widened. "What the fuck?"

"No, no, no!" Uwe exclaimed and leapt up. "I mean..." his forehead wrinkled as he pondered. "Melding with them. Reading their minds."

"Oh," James sighed relief. He and his old mentor stood in an uncomfortable silence for a thirty-minute moment. "You can do that?"

"With sentients, you sense the conscious—or the subconscious, if you dig deep enough. Even memories." His tone took on an ethereal edge towards the end of his explanation before reverting back. "Arcane though the art may be, it's much simpler with animals. With them, it's all in one big pile. What you see and hear when you read a sheep's mind is just that: their whole mind." He turned back to his lamb. "One big abstract—ignorant, oblivious happiness or complete, crippling anxiety. They don't feel anything halfway." He gestured for James to give it a go. "Try it."

The hunter turned to one of the smaller members of the flock and set his eyes against its. He had by no means mastered telepathy, but he always found it to be easier with eye contact. His consciousness seized for a moment before contact was reached. He'd done it before with Earthers, humans who sometimes didn't even bother guarding their outermost thoughts. He'd gleaned names, attitudes, and motives from prey, from friends, from lovers. A quick jab with the part of his brain that afforded him his sixth primary sense and he could lash out and touch the mind of anyone else in close proximity.

It felt, ordinarily, like intercepting a radio station with a weak signal. Visually, it was like watching someone from beneath the water's surface. With the lamb, however, his mind's eye and ear were useless.

He heard nothing. He felt his hearing dull as if it had been taken from him. The sheep did not think in words, only in sounds and smells and images. It appeared to his sight as if a great, shapeless mass had appeared before him. He could not decide if it was due to the animal's lack of development or if this was truly how the beast saw him. Nonetheless, here was James: a warm, grey blob before him and before the lamb, standing neutral and indifferent.

And yet the creature had all the emotions of one who'd known eons. It was at once calm and excited and timid and ecstatic and captivated and unafraid and bold and feeble and trusting and apathetic and curious and reserved and peaceful and energetic and young-bodied and old-souled and happy! So very happy. And the next moment, the feeling changed completely.

James withdrew, more apprehensive than when he had approached, and looked to Uwe for instruction.

The dwarf only smiled. "These are happy animals. Carefree." He cradled his lamb like a watchful shepherd. "Or maybe careless. I could draw a knife and that feeling would not change in the slightest." He held his hand around the sheep's throat, balancing on the precipice of betrayal. "Until the very moment I bleed this lamb dry, he will always feel safe with me." Upon hearing his own words, Uwe took on a look of surprise. "For some reason."

James felt ill at ease. His body quaked in spite of the barn's warmth. He felt the heat in his eyes, red and watery. "Why are we here?"

His smile fading into a resolute and shapeless form, Uwe released his lamb. "I find it amazing that no matter how old we both get, I still feel like I have the world to teach you."

"And you'll never stop trying, will you?"

"Come on. I meant what I said before. I don't have *decades* left anymore. Hunters do everything in their power to survive, even if the only way they can do so is through their legacy."

They visited three more farms before noon. The goats, horses, cows, and sheep all reflected the same animal tranquility. A short while after, they came across a small dairy farm tucked within the pines.

"The air is different here," Uwe noted.

"Colder," added James.

"I can already feel what we're looking for."

Here, in this pocket of rigid white and dead air, the world burned with turmoil. The hunters sensed it in the stillness. Every falling flake sounded with the fury of cannon fire. The wind whisked mayhem through the trees. As the hunters stole into the estate, the farmstead dipped down into a set of knolls where the cows had been set to pasture. In ice.

"Who the hell puts cattle out in the Alps in winter?" James' brow furrowed, shadowing indignation rather than confusion. He tore down through the vale and into the huddle of animals. The beasts stood in a tight pack, vying to warm themselves. There were a dozen at the least. Up on the opposite end of the dell, a second set of bellows could be heard. The majority of the herd was still held indoors and in safety. So why these individuals had been sent to face a frozen death he could not understand but did not appreciate nevertheless.

"Feel them," Uwe beckoned, descending into the mass with heavy features.

James was reluctant. He knew by his teacher's tone that he would not enjoy whatever impulses their minds held. Uwe's eyes pressed him on, though, and he submitted.

In an instant, the cow he melded with bayed and cried and ran from the group. In the milliseconds he held with its consciousness, he made out a great shadow lurching over the earth. In that moment, there was only fear. Terror and fright and panic and distress and anxiety and uproar and neurosis and danger, all whipping him, all inciting each other, redoubling their mirror emotions ten, twenty, a hundredfold until his every sense beheld utter black and cold.

The young hunter writhed to the ground, setting his enraged eyes on the reckless dwarf who'd brought such pain upon him.

"I'm sorry," came the uninvited reply. "You've felt dragonfear before. It's a special kind of dread. It's not imagined. It's the mind's response to the mental signal that an adult dragon can emit."

James tried to respond, to rail against his mistrusted ally, but was still paralyzed by his secondhand horror.

"Drakes like the ones you've fought don't have it nearly as refined as Solomon does. I wanted you to feel his dragonfear so that it won't cripple you later." Uwe spoke with all the pretense of a caring guardian. "Do you understand?"

The young man nodded, still struggling to speak.

"I am very sorry. Animals experience the fear without resistance. What you felt was the highest intensity possible."

James dug his fingernails into his palms to steady his frame. He halted the quivering and brought his mind back under his reins. "I've felt worse," he growled and climbed to his feet. He hadn't, not really, but he would.

"I knew you were strong enough," the dwarf beamed. "Now we're ready."

With a deep inhalation, James rolled his neck and stretched his hands.

"Feeding an adult dragon is a monumental endeavor. You can only import so much livestock before you raise suspicion from Mythic. In order to supplement the beast, you have to grow meat for it yourself."

James nodded, on the same page now. Before he could impart his opinion, however, there came a shout from the top of the dell.

Both hunters twitched, turning towards the source of the commotion. Having sighted the coated civilian at the top of the hills, they squinted to make out the form of a large gun in his hands. The man shouted again, barely discernible, down into the valley.

"Swiss German," Uwe scowled, detracting his attention. "Disgusting. Did you catch that?"

"I got 'schiessen'," James reported, alarmed. "We really need to hear anything else?"

"Yeah, I heard it too," the dwarf frowned.

The man with the gun shouted a third time. He stressed each and every syllable but placed a particular amount on the threatening verb in question.

146

"I'll handle this. Entschuldigung!" Uwe began, doing his best to appear as harmless as possible. "Wir wollten Ihnen keine Angst einjagen. Wir sind nur Bergsteiger." His hands raised and his teeth bared in apology, he played the part quite well. The farmer eased his grip on the rifle. "Wir haben Ihre Kühe—"

In the next instant, the man hefted his weapon level with their heads. James saw his impulse at once and reacted.

Following a seamless movement he'd performed hundreds of times before, the hunter drove his boot into the snow. The impact sent a shudder through his skeleton. At the same time, he drew power from the garnet still tied around his neck. The gem imparted to him a feel for all of the world around him. Dislodged by his forceful footfall, the earth was poised to obey—he need only command it.

In the final step of the maneuver, he brought his forward arm skyward, and the soil followed suit. The ground split apart with the sound of an avalanche, and the rock beneath them rumbled up in a large, thin sheet half a second before the farmer shot twice down into the valley.

The first shot splashed against the rock face, throwing a few thick chunks into the air. The second cleared the haunch of one of the cows, sending the herd into panic.

"Damn," Uwe marveled, crouching under the makeshift bulwark. "Nice wall."

James took to his knees. "Nice handling," he countered.

"Can you cut me a path over to the car?" The dwarf flinched as his side of the boulder erupted into debris.

"Yeah, yeah," the younger hunter replied offhandedly and gathered his focus for the next cast. He suspended his hands as if he were a puppeteer, pulled his fingers deep into his palms, and widened his feet. The garnet glowed amber brown through the folds of his clothes as James shot, striking the air in front of him. Then the earth rippled up in a jetty, providing an outlet across the glen.

"You call that a wall?" Uwe scoffed at the shallow ridge.

"What, you don't think that can take a bullet?" James came back, panting.

The dwarf started before another shot rang out onto the top of the boulder and showered them with dirt. "Fine," he surrendered and charged along the rock rampart. The wall did little to hide his movement, and the farmer had the altitude to halt his advance. He fired a round at the dwarf, dismayed when the shot clipped the wall instead of his target. "Jesus fuck!" Uwe roared, diving to the ground. "Cover!"

James was ahead of him. He spun from behind the rock wall with his handgun drawn and zeroed in on the farmer. He was at least as confident in his gunmanship as he was in his elementality. He discharged the weapon and the slug smashed into their assailant's shoulder, knocking him to the ground. James drank in the hit through gritted teeth, enjoying it for a moment too long. A bullet came pounding through the air and shattered part of the rocky wall just over his head. He reeled back into cover and cursed.

"Two more," he called over a brief lull between shots. The farmer's allies had likely come from the house after they heard the gunfire. Suppressing them would require a little more tact than firing a pistol at this range. Understanding this, the young hunter rolled from under the boulder once more and fired two shots, unchecked, towards the top of the hill. As expected, the fire at least drove the attackers back. He looked to see what progress Uwe had made, but the dwarf had vanished.

Another half dozen shots made quick work of his earthen barrier. He groaned and conjured another wall in front of the original.

"Ooie?" he cried across the frozen battlefield. More gunshots drowned his plea in lead and fire. No reply came from the road. "All right," he grunted at last and turned to face his wall. He holstered his sidearm and gripped the barrier with elemental force. After a few seconds, he could feel the entire structure fragmenting. The hunter threw his shoulders back and apart, ripping the wall to shreds. The shards held steady in the air, dangling at his direction. He saw shots come from his flanks, deflecting off the myriad pieces of debris that surrounded him. They were circling now; he'd acted just in time. His grace period, however, was gone. "Down, Ooie!" James' arms flew out and the stones dispersed in every direction in the form of a hailstorm.

The rocks took cows to the ground, exploded into the earth to throw up flurries of snow and dust, and collided with the gunmen that were surrounding him without enough force to drive the life from their bones.

What was more important, however, was the cover that the scattering snow would bring him. James took less than a second to retrieve his pistol and race up towards the farmhouse.

Before the snow had cleared, he was at the top.

His last four shots all met with flesh, crippling one man and ending another. He heard a command given in German and emerged from the icy vapor to see the remaining forces take to the house. In the next instant, he saw a pair of arms jerk from red snow, a firearm aimed at his chest.

The hunter reached instinctively for a knife, stopping short when he realized that he had none on him. The impetus to charge his foe came almost immediately after, but still too late. The first and only round screamed forwards and grazed James' side.

The man corrected his aim, lining up his next shot, uttering a curse beneath his labored breath when the earth around him dispersed and swallowed him whole.

Behind the man who'd been buried alive stood Uwe, wide-legged with a garnet glowing on one finger. The dwarf shot James a judgmental look. "Really? Couldn't think to cast?"

"I froze up a little," he admitted defensively.

"Give a man a magic amulet and he bum-rushes a man with a gun."

"Four in the house," he deflected, listening for movement.

Uwe nodded. "They're setting up for a breach." He tossed a bulletproof vest to his partner and tapped the one he'd already slipped on. "You first, or me?"

James shook his head, dropped the vest to the ground, and turned to face the farmhouse. It was relatively small: two stories with only a few rooms on each floor. His garnet hummed to life and he felt another floor below ground. "Bad foundation," he revealed before assuming a warrior's stance.

The strength came to him in waves. The radius of his influence upon the earth increased with each passing moment. In a few seconds, he could feel the entire farmstead through the soles of his feet. Uwe watched him shut his eyes slowly, the lids fluttering from the tension. To hold so much matter in his mind required incomprehensible concentration. Manipulating it would require ten times that.

The earth elementalist's arms flexed. The blood vessels beneath his skin swelled and bulged. His fingers shook. Inside the house, he heard a shout and knew that he had no time left. He stretched his right hand high into the air, the limb straining with the immense weight, but even so he held fast. And now, with teeth grinding against one another, both legs quivering, he struck down with colossal magnitude.

He felt the slab of rock beneath the farmhouse shatter at one end. The wall on the right side bent, buckled, and finally broke, calling the rest of the structure down along with it. The entire building tilted towards the weak edge before the framework fell apart and the opposite side came down as well.

A blanket of dust and debris rushed around the two hunters, caking their closed eyes and lips with dirt, stifling their nostrils. They coughed amidst the cacophony of snapping beams until the house settled in a heap and winter retook the scene with silence.

Uwe whirled the dust away with a cast and struggled to compose himself. Beside him, James knelt with considerable fatigue. "Well done."

"Thanks," he wheezed.

"I think that commotion served more than one purpose," the dwarf added.

James followed Uwe's line of sight to the southern skyline. Even without the frigid air he would have frozen just as quickly.

The beast's size was, even at this distance, demoralizing. Its wings spread and contracted like the sails of a warship. Dark, azure skin encapsulated all the hatred, the fury, and the power of a fully-grown dragon. Solomon the Great.

Like his father Dorian before him, the drake was a titan among his kind. The demon bore off short of the farm so that it never came within earshot or weapon range of the hunters, but its gargantuan golden eyes detected them with all the precision of a hawk's gaze. It could see them shivering five kilometers away, but they could not see the glee twinkling in the beast's eyes.

Solomon turned again to regard them, and for the moment it appeared that he would make an approach.

Uwe sprang from the dragonfear first and shook James from it with a cry. "Come with it, then!" He ripped the shotgun from his back. "Vaos dies in the white hills of Europe today."

The novice hunter replaced the magazine in his pistol and steeled himself for the encounter. The epinephrine in his system doubled in dose, numbing the pain in his torso and reinforcing his stare. He knew that a diving dragon could close this kind of distance in under a minute. He wasted no time in his preparation.

Then, without warning, the monster veered and circled back again. Solomon wasn't charging them; he was taunting them.

His roar rolled across the sky. Its force dislodged the snow from the surrounding peaks. The cows went into a frenzy again, fleeing over the corpses of their dead as far as they could within the fences of the farm while the human and the dwarf stood resolute in the face of destruction.

With that, the dragon vanished into the folds of white covering the mountain range, his challenge soundly issued.

Uwe looked to his apprentice without words. His expression was all but complete bloodlust.

James recognized it instantly. "We've done this before," he said. He wasn't referring to the hunt.

"He's waking." The sound came as if from Uwe's mouth, but it wasn't his voice. It was feminine, but firm.

"Smelling salts," said another voice—a different voice—as the dwarf's mouth opened and closed.

"Go on home, James." Uwe this time. "You've fought this fight already."

He hadn't a chance of piecing together the illusion while still in a dreamstate. The realization struck him, however, as he awoke. He left the vision begrudgingly, fighting against the waking world as best he could. That last hunt five years ago was the closest thing to home he could remember.

Chapter Twenty-One
The Prince

"Do you know," crawled the grisly voice before the hunter, "who I am?" His tone betrayed a sinister cunning.

James wheezed, expelling ammonia from his nostrils. His lungs ached, although they had somehow been cleared of water. He felt concrete on his knees, his hands bound behind his back, and a forceful hand on his shoulder. He could also sense a number of others present in the room. Then he opened his eyes and beheld the image of his savior.

He knew at once the name of the leather-clad man, but he held onto it for a moment until the figure grinned and blew a sheet of smoke from his lips. The ruby earring on his long, pointed right ear glowed faintly. The left ear was missing almost entirely.

"Faolan Ashtongue," James managed, coughing again before steadying himself. "The banished prince."

The elf's smile widened. "I actually like the title," he muttered, rubbing one of the myriad scars on his face. "It has a certain…piquancy to it." He snapped his teeth together.

Though he hadn't yet noticed, James had been grimacing since he'd first sighted the loathsome creature sitting before him on a throne shaped like a tacky armchair. The one missing feature would have been tolerable on its own, but every other aspect of the prince's person warranted distaste. There was a gash on the side of his mouth (his father's sword), a mark on one eye that split the eyebrow into two halves and blackened the cornea (a Cultist's dagger), a permanent disfigurement on one cheekbone

152

(a Salamancian's mace), a break in his nose that had healed incorrectly (an old ally's fist), scars on his chin, brow, temples, neck, jaw, and cheek (burns, bruises, and blade strokes from opponents too numerous for even him to remember), and a severe burn on one corner of his head that restricted the growth of any hair in that region (the flame of a renegade mage). The only fortune in his misfortune was that the last wound usually detracted attention from the rest of his mangled visage.

Through sheer happenstance, the prince had never had access to healers following any of his major injuries. Eventually, he began to reject the healing of his wounds outright, adopting the scars as trophies. Few could admit to forgetting the face of Faolan the Prince. This occurred to him as a strength even though he knew that most saw it as a shortcoming. Still, initial reactions always amused him.

"Beauty in the ways of the young," he offered. "The elven creed most adhered to." The comment brought James' attention back center stage. "I apologize for my appearance. Elves are notorious aesthetes, and my bloodline especially is known for its matchless appeal." He and the other elves laughed. "When my younger sister was born, my dear mother did not survive the travail. It is said that she stole her beauty away from the queen and took her life along with it. Few could deny the former." For approval, he looked to the man on his right who wore formal Earther dress and a sword at his belt. The elf agreed without much coaxing. "Some, however, would say that even as she aged she continued to sap the beauty from those around her. I like to think I'm victim of such a phenomenon," he concluded, ending his yarn in jest. Again, the whole of his guard shared a laugh with him.

James peeked around, given the pause of the moment's fun, to find that he'd come to in the middle of a warehouse. His dripping clothes and common sense told him that they weren't far from the water. Faolan's guard was made up of about a dozen elves, mostly women like the comely sentinel still forcing him to kneel. Until he could confirm otherwise, he was under the assumption that he was in danger, although he did not feel that way. In order to have an audience with him, his captors had first saved his life. That fact convinced him that he didn't have to worry just yet.

As James pondered the situation, the banished prince intervened on his behalf: "I'm sure you have a host of questions in light of recent events. Namely, how your heart's still beating. You're probably wondering how it is you survived your fall from grace. Hell of a stunt. You'd have to be an earthshaper to survive that fall on land. You're probably also curious about how the vision behind you plucked you from the River Thames, drained the water from your lungs, pulled the debris from your body, saved you from acute hypothermia—"

"I'm more interested in why Ciric elves are helping Mythic."

"Ah," the elf declared, raising his only unscathed eyebrow, "I couldn't care any less than I already do about what Mythic does until they keep me from capturing one of the most dangerous men in history."

The hunter considered his words with surprise. "You're talking about Casey Aduro."

"Fuck the puppet," Faolan blurted, discarding his formal veneer for a moment. "I'm looking for the man holding his strings."

James' eyes softened.

"Casey is only a lieutenant in the Cult of the Apocalypse," the prince explained. "Ancient or not, he doesn't have the information needed to quell the Cult's present activities on Earth. I do know that he is taking orders from someone higher up. And how in the hell do you get higher up than an ancient?"

The potential of a ringleader even more sinister than Casey was as unsettling as it was confusing. "I thought that Solomon the Great was the leader of the Cult."

"There's no evidence to support that claim. Some dwarf killed him years ago, and the organization's still at full tilt. Every so often they dangle some doddering dragon in front of Mythic so they can slay it and say the Cult is dead for a while longer. Cutting the tail off a beast with a thousand heads."

James squirmed, still kneeling. "So, you're trying to stop the Cult...why not work with Mythic? Put your theory to the test?"

Faolan leaned forwards in his seat. "You knew who I was, so I assumed you understood the relationship between the Cult and the royal elves." He studied the hunter's expression for confirmation. "No?" he asked, shaking his head in disgust.

"Not completely." He didn't like feeling patronized.

The prince scowled. "What do they teach you people before they put knives in your hands and send you after psychopaths? I don't have time to go through two centuries of history with you. Just—" he sighed smoke on the hunter and rubbed his eyes before going on. "The Cult wants me captured for the same reason Cire wants me dead. I and my father are privy to information that is essential to their suicidal interests. Casey's hunted me ever since I arrived on Earth and has gotten damned close to finding me since then. If I let Mythic know where I am, they'd want to protect me and end up selling me out to the Cult by accident. That, or they'd ship me off to the homeland for a royal execution and collect a banished prince's ransom. Point is: it's too large an organization to keep untainted. That's why I stay separate with my own trusted guard. Why I let Casey get close. Because the closer he gets, the better look I get at that puppet master of his. Once I have a clear line of sight, I can end the Cult once and for all."

James only blinked, impressed with the finality of the elf's plot until he realized that Mythic had just served as an obstacle.

Faolan recognized the telltale sign of enlightenment. "Yes, there it is. I intended to use your manhunt this evening as a distraction. While Casey obliterated you and your coalition, my guard was setting up to strike and solve your problem in one deft blow. Until you idiots decided to blow yourselves to nothing."

"You..." James rejected the notion at first, then again before considering what Faolan was suggesting. "You knew about the bombs?" The hunter bounded to his feet and the rope around his wrists snapped. Before anyone under his speed could stop him, he had one hand clasped around the prince's neck.

"You didn't?" Faolan rasped, windpipe stifled by the hunter's grip. "They were your explosives."

In the next instant, James had six sets of steel pressed against him. In the corners of the warehouse, he heard six gun slides pull back and clack forwards. He released his hold on the treacherous royal, pushing past his attackers into open space. The elves lowered their weapons at the prince's sudden command.

"You think I'd use bombs against a fire elementalist? That's just asking for a farce. That trap had Mythic's incompetence stamped all over it."

"It wasn't us," the hunter panted. He shook his head, staggered by the puzzle. "We..." He considered explaining Walter's secondary objective then thought better of it. "We were looking for something else. If we killed Casey and blew up any evidence he had on him, we'd never find it. I saw him snap his fingers. Casey set it off."

"Maybe," Faolan conceded, "but I saw the blast. It's easier to set off plastic explosives with an electrical charge. The flame you'd need to detonate them would be near impossible to cast at that distance."

James lashed back at the prince as a suspect. "Who else would detonate the bombs with me and Casey both still inside?"

"Oh, you know I wouldn't have done it. You're both too valuable to me to throw away." The bite in his statement hid beneath the charity of his intent. When James looked up at him, he knew he'd exonerated himself. "I might actually be able to use you for this next part. The Cult is planning something besides apprehending me, and I know someone who might have an idea."

James laughed in disbelief. "You already found him."

"My agents," Faolan announced, "detected an unwelcome visitor in our lovely metropolis some weeks ago." He could tell that he'd piqued the hunter's interest. He regretted that his next revelation would not please him: "It was a mandor."

The hunter's eyes bolted back to the makeshift throne. "There's a mandor in London?" He couldn't stop the horror from dominating his expression. "What kind?"

"Rest assured, it's a larva. Anything bigger and I'd have fled to South America weeks ago." Even this fact did not console James.

"Last time I checked, a larva could kill just as quick as a nymph."

"You won't be fighting it, James." His volume hushed the room. "I underestimated Casey. I admit that. The direct approach is clearly not the best way. He has employed this mandor to indoctrinate an army of Cultists from Earther stock, and he's been very successful thus far, I'd say. His men attacked a nightclub, killed dozens, and then withdrew back into society with their memories altered. Untraceable. They were there tonight in case he needed them." James accepted his words with a deeper understanding than he let on. He knew this to be the brainwasher Gerard had spoken of. "He sent them after my soldiers tonight, otherwise we could have saved you the near-death experience. A few Londoners with guns can do wonders in combat with the element of surprise in their arsenal." He bent forwards, as though even his closest subjects could not be trusted with the rest of the information. "If we can penetrate this level of the Cult's hierarchy, we can not only disrupt the mandor's control of these initiates but also find out where, when, and how Casey intends to act next."

James' expression turned baleful. "I can't sneak past a mandor without giving away my identity. I don't have that kind of mental training."

"Few masters of the mental arts can best a mandor larva. I daresay none at all can overcome a nymph." He let the assertion sink into the hunter's confidence before overlapping it. "There is, however, a way to deceive even the most brilliant mind." The prince smiled insidiously. "Their technique is designed to shed light on every conscious aspect of a man's mind. The more you think, the tighter the grip they have on you. But even a mandor can't access the memories of an amnesiac."

The hunter twitched and glanced behind him, half-expecting an elf to be on approach with a club. "And you can simulate amnesia?"

Faolan's smile evolved into a full cackle. "Are you familiar with the concept of dreamwalking?" The phrase more than caught the hunter's ear. "A form of hypnosis. Some call it *true* hypnosis. Taking mental suggestion to the end of the spectrum. Allow me to implant my consciousness into yours. As long as I keep my distance, the mandor will not sense me. I will fabricate an entirely new mind for him to read. With your active intentions and memories shrouded, you will appear to be only a lowly initiate seeking the solace of the Cult."

The simplicity of his plan was impressive, if a little insane. Still, James hesitated to allow the prince that sort of access. "I don't need someone else taking up space in my head," he insisted. "I've got enough to think about. Just make me forget everything. Then I can go in without worrying."

"No," Faolan protested. "You won't be able to carry out the mission without either direction or your own memories. If I wiped them away, they would not return." In spite of how dire he made it seem, the option was not altogether unappealing to the hunter. "If I remain in your mind, I will only suppress the subconscious, allowing you to function normally. Meanwhile, I will feed you instructions when the time is right, be able to perceive the information you are given—what, you really don't want another man inside you?" the prince smirked.

"There are things in my mind that I don't ever want to relive," James railed. "And things I don't want anyone else seeing." His tone was absolute.

The elf laughed. "A hunter with a shadowy past. Such a cliché." He shook his head. "Almost as bad as the banished prince, wouldn't you say?" he addressed his guard.

"Yeah, but a little less pathetic."

Faolan's countenance soured. "I won't be able to see your memories. It's as simple as me putting a lock on that room in your mind. If *you* did it, the mandor would see you standing in front of the door. With me there, it will be as if the door never existed."

James considered the proposal again for a moment, reluctant as ever, but saw no other recourse.

"Will you be able to see my dreams?"

The prince scoffed. "Have you ever tried to watch someone else's dream? It's as hopelessly cryptic as the deepest hallucination anyone could endure."

He could not trust Faolan absolutely, but James knew this to be the best method of approach. Having lost the element of surprise themselves, Mythic would need a new tactic to inflict any injury upon Casey. He took in a deep breath. "Do it."

Anticipating the hunter's acceptance, Faolan lurched forwards onto his feet and took James' head into his hands. "Don't blink."

The elf's eyes opened as wide as black holes, one dark and damaged, the other brown and pure. The latter was widely considered to be the only true remnant of his familial beauty. Through it, the prince poured his soul. There was no ethereal sensation, no numbing effect. James could sense the prince outside of himself and then, suddenly, could not sense him at all.

Faolan's body went limp and started to fall backwards to the ground. Two members of the guard flew to catch him, scooping him up into their arms.

"Faolan?" James questioned the carcass.

Right here, James.

He jolted upright. He felt the prince's words like something entirely different from speech. They emanated from within him rather than elsewhere. It was a sensation that was impossible to become accustomed to.

"Can you hear him?" one of the elves asked to verify the success of the maneuver.

After a moment, James responded, uncertain, "Yes."

I'll try to keep the whispers to a minimum. They have been known to drive men mad.

"Good," another sentinel sighed. "We'll keep his body near you to facilitate a return should the need arise."

See that it's done, Muirgel.

James did not deign to repeat the command to her. "So, where is the mandor?" He was all too eager to complete the task at hand.

"We've yet to determine where he is based," Muirgel reported. "We have a survey area as far out as the coast, but if—"

"That's all right," he answered, his mind galloping now. "I know someone who knows."

Chapter Twenty-Two
The Prisoner

"A long shot by any stretch of the imagination," Walter Brimford murmured. Michelle and James followed him from his office to the lift and watched his trembling finger press the call button.

"We're all exhausted," the hunter comforted him, "but we don't have any better options."

The executor turned and confirmed James' statement. In the last few hours he'd become a ghost of a man. His lupine eyes sagged into his cheeks, purple rings forming underneath. They flicked from person to person, unsteady and unchecked. He clasped his hands as firmly as he could, but they shook in spite of the effort. "No," he managed through dry lips. "I suppose not."

He'd lost his private military. Its commander was unconscious in a hospital miles away, his wound too grievous for their meager medicine. Even with professional care, though, it might be years before Bailey held a weapon again, if ever.

"How will you defeat the mandor if you can find it?" Michelle asked. "You can't even guard against a human."

"I can guard against you," the hunter claimed, "and I can guard against a mandor."

Taking offense at his bluff, the reader dipped into his skull to prove a point. Her shock was palpable as she came up against a mental block unlike anything she'd ever encountered. "How on Earth…?"

"I don't plan on fighting the mandor. If I can just gain his trust, I can learn all I need to know about Casey." Now, with his plan fully illuminated, the group came to realize just how difficult it would be. "I know it won't be enough to simply block my memories," James went on. "I have to look like I've got completely different ones."

Walter stepped onto the elevator as it arrived and sighed. "James, I am overjoyed that you managed to escape the car park unscathed. Overjoyed. Astounded. But outsmarting a mandor? That might be too difficult even for you."

Here came the tricky part. Faolan maintained that the success of his operation hinged upon his anonymity. At the same time, James still needed Mythic's trust to complete his mission. Convincing them that he was equipped to handle a mandor without outside assistance would take some doing.

He heard Faolan laugh inside of his head. *Oh, that's good.*

"I realized a while ago that I had trouble guarding. It was interfering with some of my jobs." He steadied himself for the final sell: "So I had a reader in Berlin erase my memories and replace them."

Michelle's countenance twisted in confusion. "But you would lose everything you had before then."

"Normally," the hunter conceded. "He layered it so that the memories are only masked temporarily."

The reader's doubts gave way to curiosity. "You want me to try and repeat the ritual?"

James smiled, seeing that she had taken the bait. "The amnesia comes back whenever I hear a certain phrase." Cueing his mental passenger, the hunter produced a slip of paper with a single phrase written on it.

The reader and executor crowded around the bewitching writing, fascinated by the novelty of such a procedure. Each read the carefully selected quotation with mute excitement. It was Uwe's favorite verse: "Der Rest ist Schweigen."

Walter began the words aloud, stumbling through the German just as James hushed him with a finger over his mouth. "If I hear the whole thing," he cautioned them, "my memory won't come back for a while." Michelle shot Walter a harsh glare while the hunter folded the paper and handed it to her without explanation. "It's been years since I've gotten to see Hamlet in German," he reflected, sealing the phony story with half-truths.

"Then we read this just before you meet the mandor… and your memory will return after it already trusts you," Michelle beamed.

"Outstanding," said Walter, slumping against the elevator wall. "It's worth the attempt."

"It'll have to be."

You've got them now, came Faolan's smoky whisper.

"All I have to do is get Gerard to talk."

Few would describe James McCrary as a murderous man. He committed many murders, yes, but these crimes were—at least to him—justified. Cold blooded assassination was against his nature. His veins were warm, sometimes fiery, rarely temperate, but as he entered the secret prison hidden away beneath Mythic, its inhabitants detected in him a baser purpose. The hunter was no novice in the art of torture.

Michelle faded back to linger in the hallway and shut the dungeon door behind her.

"Well, spank my arse and call me Mary," Gerard cackled. "How the hell did you manage that?" The elder gargoyle lifted its head from its chest, studying the intruder before settling back into a heap. The fiery-haired initiate sprang up at once and took to the bars of his cage, dough-faced and panting.

James eyed him first, unsure of what state of mind the minion had arrived at. Even less certain of the hunter's intentions, the man remained silent lest he be tormented a second time.

"Seriously," Gerard yapped, demanding attention, "how is it that you're still alive?" James moved to his cage as if to engage him but said nothing. "What, you offer him your firstborn?" He elicited no response. "He give you a deal?" he tried again.

Facing the prisoner, shadows masked the hunter's expression. The only light in the room of cages drifted from a fixture in the center of the ceiling. Gerard could hear his lungs, slow and smooth and soft—a tiger's murmur. Aside from that, he couldn't discern a thing. Soon, though, he heard jangling and caught the glint of metal at the lock of his cage.

A smile stole across his discolored face as the gate swiveled out. A swarm of explanations swam through his thoughts as he took a first cautious step out from his hollow.

"Take me to the mandor," the hunter ordered him with a liquid gentleness.

Gerard only sighed, crestfallen, and took another step out into the room. "I see," he muttered. "I thought maybe you'd switched sides. But you still can't help me." His arm launched like a piston, his palm flexed and poised straight for James' solar plexus. One move, one strike, one hit would bring even this titan to his knees. The attack was perfect, its execution flawless. With a decade to rehearse it, he could not have performed it more exactly.

James seemed to warp through the air as he rotated. To even the ex-courier's eyes it appeared as if he'd disappeared. "What—" and in the next quarter of an instant he felt the impact of a shuttle launch meet his gut. At the turn of the same moment, he crumbled down to the concrete and heaved as if he might vomit, hacking into the dank air.

Squatting over his gagging carcass, James reminded him, "I asked you a favor. Now it's a demand. When you catch your breath, I want you to have a better answer for me or I'ma start cracking ribs one at a time." He could hear the initiate shaking in the corner of the room. "Where is the mandor?"

He stood in a cacophony of Gerard's coughs, the gargoyle's wheezing, and the initiate's whimpers for several seconds before the prisoner attempted a response.

"You should kill me quickly." He paused, stumbling within his own words. "I don't know a damned thing about where the mandor is." The hunter let him cough up the rest of his defense. "Just end it," he spat. "That's the best you can do for me."

James' stony outlook veiled his concern. If Gerard didn't have the information he needed, he would have no other alternative. "Nobody ever gets the chance you have now," he offered, pressing his desperation under his voice. "To redeem themselves. Even Cultists have compassion."

Gerard managed to scoff through the pain. "Open your eyes." He stared up at his dominator with stalwart dedication. Complete loyalty, or something close to it, filled his eyes. "I've seen men of Mythic do much worse than Cultists."

The accusation caught James unaware. "I have, too." He stood, never removing his gaze from his target, resolved to break him. This stare, though, he had not seen in some time. Likewise, Gerard had only encountered the gaze that the hunter held once before—in Casey.

"Michelle," James called out to the hall. His purpose was unmistakable. He heard the reader fumble to unlatch the steel door and shuffle inside with the hunter's trump card in hand. Gerard paid close attention to the small, glass vial as she slipped it to his tormentor with a look of disgust.

Without so much as a whisper, she looked to the man on the floor of the dungeon, crossed herself, and departed.

Any semblance of Gerard's sangfroid left alongside the reader. His eyes darted to the exit, to the vial, then to James in an instant.

"You know what this is?" James leaned down once more and held the bottle out over him.

"I don't know," came the captive's hushed answer.

"No. No you do not."

"I don't know anything," he reiterated with a bit more bass in his voice.

"Gerard Jones doesn't know gargoyle blood when he sees it?"

A burst of air fell from his lips. "Gargoyle blood is black." He indicated the sanguine tint of his tormentor's vial.

James sneered. "Only when it's fresh."

Gerard shot a look to the gargoyle on the other side of the room. The beast's head was raised, its full attention on the exchange playing out before it. The black eyes bored into him, imparting quiet delight. They did not move. They did not blink. They only consumed the sight around them. Deep inside, though, Gerard thought he beheld a glimmer of a smile hidden somewhere below the demon's tenebrous gaze.

"I don't. Know. Anything." His utterance was never more emphatic than now.

"You know why gargoyles have stone skin?" James was smiling now. Not an ounce of adrenaline heated his blood. It ran in frigid rivers from his brain to his heart and back again, feeding him with Gerard's fear. "It's to keep this from seeping out their veins. It's not like acid, though. It's smarter than that. It goes straight through the skin, through the muscle, all the way to the nerve. And then," he said, unscrewing the bottle, "then you feel pain like no man should ever feel."

"I don't know!" he shouted.

"Fresh blood is the kind that makes men scream out loud. When it sits, though... this is the kind that makes your soul scream."

The prisoner jarred, attempting to stand. His movement was met with a boot pressed hard into his chest, knocking another wave of life from his lungs. Even without the air behind them, though, the hunter could still make out his tired words: "I. Don't. Know."

"Aged gargoyle blood will stay in your system for years. It's a pain you will never get used to. When you think it's unbearable, it will raise the threshold in your brain to heights you can't imagine." James pinned Gerard's head to the floor and tipped the bottle, tempting gravity with its horrific contents.

"I don't know," the courier moaned as he stared up into the vial's teetering mouth. "I don't know!" he screamed, beseeching him. The same fatigued reply to the same question that plagued him. Where was the mandor? The creature was everywhere, it seemed. In the empty eyes of Casey's initiates, sheep in wolves' clothing. In the intent of the Cult itself, machinations to which even Casey was not privy. In the single drop of dark ichor that threatened to drop directly into Gerard's gaping eye. "N-no," he stammered. "No!" he barked.

"Stop this," the gargoyle snarled, holding itself upright.

The hunter's bottle tilted back as if he'd been expecting an interjection. His eyes, though, betrayed his surprise. Gerard was still hyperventilating, unsure of what had occurred. After a moment's respite, he too gawked at the gargoyle.

"The pain from red gargoyle blood can kill any man." The figure lurched forwards until its iron restraints snapped taut. "But you are a killer, then, aren't you?"

The hunter stayed silent, unwilling to accept his words as praise or condemnation until he could determine the monster's motive. "I do what I have to to survive. Always."

"Loyalty to the hunt," the beast recited. "It is a creed we taught the hunters long ago." James was shocked, for a second. He moved to recover his façade. The creature went on: "Understand that gargoyles still live by these customs." It let its head fall to one side in observation of the hunter's features to see if he followed. Satisfied with the survey, it continued, "I have fought Mythic for years to protect my heritage, my progeny. All that a hunter can preserve of himself."

James' thoughts flew to the gargoyle's slaughtered young, buried in shallow snow in the countryside. He did not let his apprehension show through.

"I agreed to aid Casey Aduro only when he promised me that he would protect my coven," the beast admitted without remorse.

"The Cult doesn't care about your children. They'll die with everyone else if they ever get their way."

The gargoyle nodded. "And so I task you with the conservation of my race." It took a firm hold of its chains and gripped them with ancient vigor. "My daughter is the first matriarch my line has seen in thirty years. If she is destroyed, my blood will vanish from the world forever. Surely you understand the pains a father must take to protect his brood," the patriarch entreated him. The hunter stood fast, unsure of how to respond. "Promise me this, and I will tell you where the mandor resides."

James' eyes lit up. The prospect of victory intoxicated him. "You know?" his words left him in a whisper.

In spite of his injuries, the gargoyle managed a smirk in the face of his adversity. "There is a church in Surrey near to the border of Sussex. Atop the building rests a damnable artifact—a gargoyle—in repulsive likeness." The beast released its hold on its bindings and settled back against the wall. "You will find the mandor there tomorrow, seducing lesser men like a rouged harlot." In its final address, the gargoyle did not deign to look at its captor. "When the demon is dead, promise me that my daughter will be let alone."

James could no longer maintain the rigidity of his blood. He felt his heart lift up with a sudden burst of energy. The sap that boiled through him set his soul afire. "You have my word," he said, hands shaking from excitement. "No harm will come to your daughter." He thought to promise the gargoyle freedom as well but stopped short, realizing that this would only serve to shatter their trust. Even so, he saw the figure nod from the shadows, content. "What's your name?" the hunter asked. The request surprised even him. When it hesitated, he went on to explain, "I've never learned a gargoyle's name."

"Volodymyr Sewick," he told him. "My daughter is Kalyna."

The familiarity of their names disturbed James. He'd half anticipated demonic monikers. Here, though, he found that the gargoyles were more human than he'd ever realized.

"Tell her Volod has sent her a guardian in his place, and my children will trust you."

James bowed and went to leave. Upon turning, he noticed Gerard still recovering on the dungeon floor. He glanced at the vial in his hand.

In a flash, Gerard sensed his impulse and flinched in response, but to no avail. With a sudden jerk, the hunter dashed the contents of the vial across the prisoner's face.

Gerard bayed like a lamb at the sensation, scratching the material from his skin, feeling at once the adverse effects, smelling instantly the familiar aroma. He snapped to stillness as James lifted him by his collar and shoved him into his cell. Even as the door locked shut, he did not make a move.

Slowly, apprehensively, he touched his tongue to his sopping fingers and cried out, enraged, "Wine?!"

The modest torture artist did not stay to revel in his trickery. He'd left the room before the courier could hurl any insults.

"You bloody wretch!" the ape thundered from his pen.

Resigned on his haunches, Volodymyr watched the dungeon door close, watched Gerard rub the Bordeaux from his face, and saw the initiate smiling on the other side of the room, his fear caged if only for the moment. The gargoyle laughed to himself.

Chapter Twenty-Three
The Brother

Despite nearly drowning, surviving the collapse of a building, minor burns and cuts, a gunshot to the chest, and the psychological weight of having a man living inside his mind, James did not find himself sleepy by the time he had traveled back to his hotel room. He'd returned primarily to address the man he knew would still be camped out there. His ally. His friend.

"Robert."

The Scotsman sprang from a chair with what could have been grace had it not been for the product of his clumsiness and grogginess, so he toppled onto his face instead.

"You stupid git," the initiate laughed, lifting himself up from the ground.

"Michelle already called you," he observed.

"You should've called me first," Robert exclaimed, half offended. The other half of him couldn't hold the appearance of anger and, in another moment, had him extending his arms out wide.

James rolled his eyes and accepted the hug before shoving his affectionate accomplice aside and making straight for his belongings.

"Good to see you, too," Robert chided him. He fell backward onto his bed, leering at him until the hunter produced a bottle of whisky.

"Want a drink?" James crooned.

"Oh, Jimmerson, you do care." He rolled onto his feet with the poise of a gymnast and snatched up the liquor just as deftly.

"You're not still feeling the wine you and Michelle had, are you?"

Robert snickered. "Lass can handle her depressants. And sedatives, for that matter." He took two glasses from the cabinet opposite the beds and filled them both to the rim. "Had to tap out halfway through."

"Still thirsty, then?" the hunter confirmed.

"Oh, you have no idea." Robert handed him a glass and threw his back with a staggering gulp. He started work on glass number two right away. "I think I've aged thirty years over the last two days. Lady friend gets kidnapped..." he took a drink, "gargoyle tries to kill me..." and another, "employer almost dies from giving up half his blood—"

James stayed his hand. "If we make this into a drinking game, this isn't gonna be a good night for us."

"Well," the Scotsman shrugged, "got to bait out the positive karma somehow or other."

The hunter agreed and raised a glass to his companion. Following the toast, he took an inaugural swig, pulled off his coat and boots, and sat back against his headboard. "What did your wife think about that?" he wondered with a sidelong glance.

Robert's drink caught in his throat. James couldn't tell if he'd struck on a painful or pleasant memory. "You kidding?" he coughed. "Who do you think I learned it from?"

Relieved, James joined him in a laugh and settled into silence.

"What about yours, brother?" the initiate prodded.

"Not married."

"No girlfriend?"

"Nope."

"Never?"

"Nah," the hunter parried.

Robert did his best impression of a James McCrary stare down. "Come on, now," he teased. "You're a hunter. You've never set upon some unsuspecting doe?"

"A lot of the time," James admitted, "it's too easy to enjoy it." He laughed to himself, recalling one experience in particular. "When you can kick the shit out of any five guys in the bar without putting down your drink," he boasted, lifting his glass again, "you tend to turn heads."

"Oh, I know exactly what you mean," Robert giggled, rolling his eyes.

"But," he went on, "it's the quality women that make it tough. The ones that want something more out of you." He cleared the lump in his throat. "It's hard enough when your job takes you to a new continent every couple of months, but when you can't tell them why you're leaving or what you really do, you can't expect them to trust you. And then you can never trust them."

"But you've been close to something like that," Robert remarked, grinning like a schoolgirl. "You've definitely been in love, Jamie-boy."

"You gonna settle on a nickname?"

"Haven't found one that feels right yet."

James sighed, caught in a smile, and gave in. "Three times." Robert sat up with crossed legs, his head bobbing from one side to the other. The sight alone was almost enough to dissuade James from continuing, but he did so in spite of it. "I met Emma in Manchester when I was twenty. Fresh out of training. She was gorgeous, smart, and powerful, and she was the first girl I met who felt more alone in the world than I did."

Robert only nodded in response, understanding the hunter's narrative the way that few had ever had the chance to. There was a certain poignancy in the brevity of the account. It reflected well the true nature of the relationship.

"When I'd hunted enough—made a name for myself—I was gonna come back here so we could be together."

"Instead…?"

"Instead I got obsessed with finding a lycanthrope in France and fell in love with another hunter."

"Oh, this is promising," Robert mused with saucer eyes, arms buckled around his knees.

"Daphne Sartre." The hunter could do nothing to mask the emotions tied to the memory of his former lover.

"I didn't know black people blushed," the initiate cackled.

James was too lost in his recollection to notice the comment. "Daphne was…" He glided through his thoughts for an appropriate phrasing. "Our relationship was very feral." The mention drew his pulse up even more. "The night we finally killed that wolf, boy…"

"All right, all right," Robert cut him short. "I'm a romantic, not a pervert."

The hunter's phantom sensations soon subsided as he continued the story. "They used to call her Sartre the Shadow. I didn't get it until she walked out the morning after the hunt." His words fell with the tone of timeworn disappointment. "She was a hunter in the purest sense. She lived for it. Couldn't live without it."

"Where is she now?"

"Who knows?" The hunter shrugged. "That night was the last I ever heard about her."

"Did she just leave you? Did you try and stay with her?"

James handed him an empty glass, hoping for a refill. "Being with Daphne made me realize I didn't want to hunt forever. She'd been doing it her whole life. She was addicted. She couldn't make me love it like she did."

"Interesting," Robert said, passing him a topped-up glass.

"I went back to Emma, ignored job offers, tried to settle into Earther life and realized I didn't have a choice anymore whether I wanted the hunt or not. I belonged to it. I left Emma after a few months and didn't speak to her again."

"So…there was someone else?" The hope rang from Robert's throat in a warm melody. "Emma wasn't the last woman you fell in love with."

The look he detected on the hunter's face was a sorrowful smile—an expression that held all the joy of promise and all the pain of impossibility.

"I worked in a few places before I went home to New York for a couple hunts. I shot some elven serial killer in the street, got his bounty, and met her in a grocery store the same day," he laughed, half-mad, juggling his two loves in his head. "Diana."

The name lilted out with all the majesty of a choir. It echoed like a timeless title bereft of a family name without any other context, and all the same it reflected enough beauty to bring a tear to Robert's eye. James sat stiffly. His eyes welled but did not leak. He wouldn't let them.

"She was… it." Each word took him an eternity to orchestrate, as if in retelling her glory he was writing a masterwork of amorous poetry. "I found her buying—" he stuttered at the realization that the memory had faded. "Tomatoes? Peppers? She was making lunch for friends, a family recipe." James stopped, discovering something about the experience. "I don't remember that conversation," he blurted and laughed more wildly than before. Robert smiled along with him. "I had dinner with her and, without tricking her, without impressing her…there wasn't a thing we couldn't talk about. And without her knowing a thing about me, she understood every piece of me there was to know." The hunter pressed his forehead into his hand, rambling now, and rattled off the details of her personage that he knew would bring him to tears if he lingered on them.

"She had green eyes. I never met a girl with eyes green like hers, not even Emma. It made me think, I don't know, it reminded me of my mother. She died when I was two weeks old, but I could…I could see her in Diana." His voice fell to a whisper upon repeating her name. It was too much for his psyche to shoulder, but he came up to meet Robert's gaze with stony eyes intact, unclouded.

"And you didn't marry that right away?" the Scot growled, indignant. The hunter returned a guilty stare. "I married Olive as soon as I could afford a ring. And it was a shite ring."

"I tried," James staved him off, raising his shoulders. "I did." He polished off the remainder of his glass in silence. "I didn't have any money, and I owed Mythic a debt. Still do. I didn't have a place to live between hunts. I didn't have a bank account. I never paid taxes. I didn't even still have a social security number. Convincing her that I wasn't a criminal took long enough and she was living tight enough already without me dragging her down into my troubles. I couldn't support the two of us and still make her the world she deserved. I almost could, but…things got more complicated." He hesitated at the mention of the issue. "So I left. Like I do."

Robert felt as though he should have gasped at the revelation, but he remained quiet. James paused again for a split second. "There was a job," he explained, "that would've taken care of everything. I never would've had to hunt again. But it was all fucked up. I fucked it up. And I never saw her again after that."

"I can't believe it," Robert said after a moment of stillness. His drinking glass had made its way to the nightstand, untouched for several minutes now. "When was that?" he demanded.

"I left her five years ago," James confessed, and each year hung on his heart with the weight of a lodestone.

"And you haven't seen her since," the initiate confirmed.

"Finding Casey is the only way I can make things right," he said half to Robert, half to himself. "I can take care of her forever with that kind of money. If she'll forgive me. If she even remembers me." James knocked back a nearly-full tumbler and, when he'd finished, set the glass aside.

"I'll be damned. All this time you've had everyone fooled." James grumbled in response and rolled over onto his side, away from the nosy initiate. "James McCrary, the famous hunter, the bloodthirsty warrior, just trying to get home."

James lay still and silent and sorry.

"One thing I don't understand, though, is why you didn't just go back after you failed the one hunt?"

Had he not the patience, the hunter would have cursed Robert to his face. His mind was returning now to the dark, to the cold, to a memory.

"Night, brother," he posed instead.

"Night, James." Robert watched him for a moment and then turned off the lights.

James dreamed a frightful dream.

Chapter Twenty-Four
The Dragon

"Dream on your own time, Jim," Uwe murmured, effectively rousing him from his ethereal reverie. They had a need for secrecy.

Surreptitious in their ascent, he and Uwe exchanged only instructions. No platitudes, no jokes, no words spoken aloud. Here was the dwarf in rarest austerity, ravished by the hunt. His disposition stood as a barrier, a crag, a weapon, and a way of life all at once. The garnet on his finger glowed soft in sepia light through his thick gloves, illuminating the shaded cliff in a warm yet chilling tone. At his behest, the rocks in his hold solidified and they made their way up a wall of sheer ice and stone to Solomon's roost.

After hours hushed in the shadow of the mountain, James could feel his ire slipping. The bloodlust that fueled the hunt was falling from him down, down, down the mountain, deep into the dark. He had no doubt that it would return but was anxious to ease his body's craving for adrenaline, so he looked up mere meters to Uwe. The dwarf climbed without hesitation, without error, and without words. His old friend's resolve redoubled his own and he too clawed at the white rock face pockmarked with black earth, pulling himself onwards into the heavens.

Around them, the air currents rampaged in protest as if called by the Grand Cultist himself. The crosswinds bore from the mountain's crest down into the valley below, tearing at the hunters' covered faces and tugging them down with the weight of the skies. Even fully bundled and well-equipped as they were to reach the summit, the mountaineers shivered and bowed their heads to the sudden storm. What horrid force was this that aided the dragonlord? Aeolus enraged appeared to be at their necks and the invisible enemy showed no signs of letting up.

Through the wailing winds the demon passed by once more, the third time that hour. The minor light of the dwarf's ring dissipated and the men attached to the rocky wall held fast and faint and flat against it. There came the dragon's roar, as earth-shattering as the first cry, and then the beast soared above the chasm and off into the distance. Solomon's cursory search did not reveal the hunters, but his screech rumbled across the high ridges and drove billows of snow and rock rolling from the peaks.

Without so much as a whisper, the elder hunter slammed his palm into the crag and his ring hummed to life. Eight tons of avalanche poured down towards them. Uwe stretched out his free hand and the earth above them followed his form, sloping and diverting the hulking, crashing ice down around them. James watched it fall with numbed senses, discarding the near-death experience from his thoughts after a few seconds. The trifle was nowhere near the cataclysm he'd need to reinvigorate his spirit, but that would come soon.

The hunters watched Solomon set down beyond the neighboring mountain and began their climb again. They understood that the dragon did not wish to see them frozen in the white pits beneath his alpine lair, that he was only guiding them. Taunting them. Inciting them. Their efforts only increased as a result.

Though the younger hunter had not felt his hands since noon, he commanded them with a physical intelligence that few in the world possessed. They gripped with all tenacity and no tact, the fingers either spread wide or wrapped around the given surface. Rock after rock, handhold after handhold, he fumbled skywards in search of the beast.

They carried abseiling gear. They carried modern armor, weapons, ammunition, and camping supplies. Tied to each hunter's back was a rucksack that multiplied his weight and made the journey that much more treacherous. At the height of their climb they were nearly inverted, clutching a ceiling of frost with feet and fingers just to keep from falling. Their packs dangled straight down, an extra hundred pounds apiece, while they kicked at the thin scarp and dug their toes up into the earth.

James let out his first sound in hours. He groaned as his hands strained to support his weight. Blood caked on his rigid digits and rime gnashed at his boots, but he was so near now that the arctic anesthesia dulled him to the pain. He looked ahead and saw Uwe already lifting himself to the relative safety of the overhang. He felt himself slipping, but the elder hunter would not let him fall. Not when he was so close.

Through the whirling white, Uwe's hand appeared over the ledge. James marshaled the rest of his strength, took hold of it, and the dwarf lifted him up onto the precipice. Though the man's face was covered, he could see jet eyes contrasting the silver shadows all about. In those eyes was all the warmth the young man needed to stir his soul, but even still he awaited the fire that would drive him to the kill.

He nodded to the dwarf in thanks before looking to the cavern directly across from where they'd landed. There the serpent lay in waiting. It would have been a shame to keep him that way. So they accepted Solomon's long-standing invitation and crossed the threshold into his lair.

The mountain chamber was massive; a throne room the size of a palace and fit for a king just as large. Its master, though, did not appear. James took advantage of the extra time and studied the battleground. The walls were slick and steep, worn bare and vertical by years, decades, maybe centuries of nitrogenous breaths. Outside, the temperature had been unbearable, but here the chill pierced his chest and wrapped around his heart. A ghostly vapor lined the firm ground—the unmistakable mark of a frost dragon's dwelling. It was not potent enough to freeze like the drake's breath, but scraped at their ankles all the same.

High above, the icy walls converged into a glassy dome thick enough to hold the vault intact but translucent enough to cast hushed, azure light down into the air. As clouds swept past the sun, the refracted daylight wavered across the walls in waves of brilliance, suspending the scene in a submarine simulacrum. At the far end of the room the ground was raised, a frozen altar and a bed for the lordly drake. This unnatural dais, though, represented true fear for the hunters, for even if the dragon needed only half of the bed, it would have to be gargantuan.

James could feel it now. The trembling in his eyes, the pulsing within his breast, the burning of his blood. He pulled the cloth from around his mouth and inhaled the cold. It thawed inside his lungs and melted against his throat. This was the apex of the hunt. This was his animal destiny. This was euphoria.

"Solomon!" the hunter erupted. His call bounced off the blue edges of the chamber and roared forth from the mouth of the cave.

Uwe tore the shotgun from his back, James his rifle. As the two turned, the demon set down upon the ledge with full force and turned the ground to glass.

It was a sight beyond all that which either hunter had ever beheld. His eyes burned a tawny yellow, braziers atop a fortress of plate. His scales were a Stygian shade of blue, matte and impregnable. His head hung broad and rugged from a thick tower of a neck. A quartet of grey horns twisted above and alongside the dense skull, framing the horrific jaws that opened and closed like a portcullis. Deep arches of bony slate protected his throat and reached to his belly, overlapping and nullifying all but the most forceful of sieges. When Solomon stretched the tattered webbing between his lofty digits, the wings extended to the top of the cave's entrance. With his body alone he blocked an opening that would have permitted passage to a jetliner.

So here he'd trapped the hunters, but only in this space could they hope to combat him on equal ground. Without flight, their element *could* best him. They could win, but only if this devil didn't destroy them first.

"They said they would send an army against me," Solomon thundered. The derision rang through his jaws and into their ears as clearly as through a smile.

"They kept their promise," Uwe called up to him.

"A dwarf and a nigger do not an army make," the beast returned.

James started, on the brink of firing, but Uwe's raised arm halted him. "He'll try and taunt you," his mentor counseled him. "Keep the lust, but hold the temper."

Solomon's throat rumbled. "I thank you, though, for bringing this bit of nostalgia with you." He scrutinized the young man with ravenous intent, reflecting in his crystalline shrine on his migrant youth. "It has been centuries since I hunted your kind."

Raising his weapon, James chose to keep the peace. Losing his composure would strip from him the balance necessary for his elementality. The moment the dragon saw that temperament shift, he would strike and the hunter would not have the earth to protect him. He let the rage boil up and settle in his heart, far from the faculties that reigned over his body.

"I long for those days to return," he chortled. "Hunting on the islands, taskmasters releasing you into the fields like cattle, prime for slaughter. A young drake's dream." His black tongue flicked out into the air and recoiled. The young hunter's agitation doubled.

"Steady," the dwarf chanted and activated his garnet.

Steady, James repeated to himself and did the same.

"And now you'll die like the filth that spawned you should have, trapped like a beast. After all this time." James started to speak but caught himself, releasing a cool, pensive sigh instead. "You will not die proud like a hunter. I will consume you like the slave you are."

"You're gonna die hungry," James boomed.

"They feed me with chaos, boy," the serpent snarled. The hunters caught the craving in his voice. Both sensed the tail tensing behind him like a scythe. "I will never go hungry."

The cavern flared into havoc faster than the hunters could blink. They saw, in a flash of movement, the dark blue whip descending—a thunderstrike upon them—and all was chaos.

The hunters split, the drake reared and retched ice into the hollow. James dove and drove a barrier of rock against the torrent. It shattered and sent splinters of stone streaking through the sky. The mammoth's claw poised just above, the hunter sprinted aside and the shock brought him to his knees. The air cleared just enough for him to hear the other firing into the demon's armored carcass. He turned to the dwarf, but Solomon's tail lashed back and swept over their heads, striking the anterior wall and crumbling the enclosure down around them. The rolling rocks stopped just short of James as he reached one arm out and lifted the other to fire once, twice, thrice. The bullets splashed against the beast, and while the spattering blood sprang out, the whirring mist and dirt were all around and he could not see the result.

"Flash!" he cried over the tumult.

"Flash!" he heard echoed back.

The dragon wheeled around to face him and he heard the telltale heave before the ripple of frost. The earth before him buckled, lifted, and finally held rigid. Solomon tore the wall to shreds with his head still cocked, his breath speeding unmitigated across the floor. The hunter fell back with his garnet still aglow. The rocks came fleeting to him like a blanket, but the chill was too fierce to resist.

James lay shivering beneath a layer of ice and earth, his eyes dry from the cold. Stunned by the flashfrost, he saw as if in a dream or a nightmare the demon leap over him with its jaws parted, and he wondered if this was Death come to greet him. And so he shut his eyes.

In the next instant, a brilliant, burning light exploded into the monster's left eye, a dazzling *bang!* accompanying it.

The young hunter opened his eyes blind, deaf, and frozen, but he knew that the dragon was the same.

Solomon shrieked a ghastly cry and catapulted his skull into the ground, grinding it like a plow across the earth, doing what he could to alleviate the burning, blinding agony.

In a rush of thought, the dwarf saw his accomplice in the monster's path as it thrashed, and he called out a pillar of stone to impede the beast. As Solomon collided against the column in full force, he reeled his skull back into the air and turned his unmarred eye upon Uwe.

"Blind on the left!" he shouted to the grounded hunter across from him as he warded off another tail swipe.

James coughed nitrogen from his cracking throat and lurched up, noticing all at once that his rifle had fallen somewhere beneath the debris. Where it lay in the rubble he could not determine with anything in the way of celerity. Even if he were able to locate it, the dragonbreath might have rendered the gun entirely inert, so he went for his sidearm with its seven shots and sought to make good use of them. Though his index finger was numb, he discharged a round that deflected off the demon's horns, another that sank into its haunch, and another that struck it dead in its spine…but where was the weakness? Where the frailty? He'd hardly bruised it in the head. The beast was a city unto itself, affording no breach except—

"Ooie!" he clamored in a voice hoarse from the hoarfrost, holstering his pistol. "Dragon's Breath."

The dwarf was presently engaged. Thus far he'd raised half a dozen walls against the drake's relentless onslaught. Each took the same effort as overturning a car, but each was ruined with a half-aimed swing of the dragon's immense claws. The beast's nitrogen could be diverted, but the frost scalded the dwarf even when the fumes were far away. A plume of ice a meter away was cold enough to brand him. Uwe had already been marked in this manner four times, and Solomon was still toying with his prey.

James' eyes narrowed. He freed Yin and Yang from the linings of his coat in practiced motion. The starving sabers unhinged from their master's grip, twirled once, and then he charged. Just short of the dragon, the ground beneath him softened and shot up, vaulting him into the sky. The hunter came down on the dragon's neck with Herculean vigor and sank his fangs deep down into the flesh.

Solomon bellowed and rattled his neck with all his strength, shaking the hunter away, but James had the beast's full attention now. The drake made his way to his quarry, ignoring a salvo of shotgun blasts at his back. A growl rocked the cavern.

Mired in his gaze, the hunter stood without looking away and hoped to God and the moon and all other deities that Uwe could deliver. There was hunger in Solomon's stare; James had the same look whenever he hunted, himself. The beast would seek to appease that craving above all else. Rime seeped from his nostrils. Saliva too foul to freeze dripped from his jowls. With each step, the drake shook a gallon of blood from his scales. Solomon was close now, but the hunter stood fast.

And there the dragonlord's maw opened, the breach in the city's walls, and before him stepped the dwarf with his special shot, and into the Cultist's craw he fired Dragon's Breath. The round burst into a jet of flame, burning the fleshy innards the beast had displayed and sending him into a frenzy.

With wings spread to full length, Solomon rose onto his hind legs and roared. Now and only now could they strike to full effect.

"Together!" James barked. The hunters moved in perfect synchronicity. Each took a wide stance and lifted his forward arm, sending his reach racing to the ceiling high above. There they groped for rock amidst the icy arches overhead, anything to bring down upon their raging foe. The instant they found it they struck, bringing their arms down in the selfsame motion, and their might splashed forth along the stone in a fissure. The fracture ran between Solomon's back legs, up the wall and across the dome, and split the heavens into pieces and there, dead in the center, shards of ice fell in a shower that buried the dragon in seconds.

The clouds were still gathering above, but the hunters' haphazard renovation allowed the sun into the hollow. A pillar of light shone down into the cavern, illuminating all that they had wrought. The two panted from the performance, admiring their handiwork and hurrying to replenish their stamina. If Solomon emerged from the rubble, he would rise with all the ire of eternity. He did not disappoint.

The monster ascended from its rocky tomb without so much as a stutter. He was upon them in an instant. James crossed to the demon's right to draw its functioning eye, but the beast did not take the bait this time. It gagged steam and blood and frost all at once, and the assortment converged on the dwarf in an unholy triad. Uwe conjured a wall, but even this barrier could not weather the ice. Then the dragon lashed his tail in rapid succession against the wall behind Uwe and, upon the final strike, the wall came toppling down in a landslide.

The dwarf sent a burst of energy through one boulder, dashing it to pebbles. The second he warded away with another motion, but upon sighting the third—a rock twice the size of the others—a shudder ran through his heart. He twisted his feet even deeper into the earth and raised his hand to strike...and Solomon broke his stance with the mere flapping of his wings.

All of this in the time it took James to empty the rest of his gun. He saw his mentor throw his arms above his head in a last-ditch attempt to save himself. The young accomplice reacted as quickly as his body would allow, lighting his garnet, planting his feet, and throwing every bit of elemental force he could at the avalanche. He'd smash it, he'd shatter it, he'd obliterate it if he could only reach it in time.

The stone, though, fell without incident, and an instant later James' will passed over it and into the far wall, sending an earthquake across the other end of the cave. The ground and ceiling shuddered. Even Solomon wavered from the force. Had that colossal energy reached the rock in time, it would have split it into dust.

James reached one arm out after Uwe, his eyes tearing over the rubble, finding nothing. A low thump turned his focus to the dragonlord as Solomon stepped towards him. With an empty pistol, no rifle, and no energy left to spend, he thought at once to run, knowing that he would not make it far. Besides that, he was determined to maintain his loyalty—to Uwe and to the hunt. He stifled the unfamiliar quake in his heart as Solomon approached. The dragonfear kindled within him and the black began to tighten around his eyes.

"Valiant finish," the beast wheezed aloud. "Just as my breath was thinning." James' countenance sank at the revelation. Without his frost, the hunters could have ended the fight with relative ease. "Don't worry, I've at least half a dozen still in me."

"We could've handled them."

"Perhaps. Perhaps not. It is the actuality that kills."

The man and the dragon stood in iron deadlock for several moments. The wind outside and their breaths within were all the sound in the world.

"Serve me," the demon said at length, "and you will live to see the end."

"I'm nobody's slave," the hunter rebuked him.

The dragon seemed to shrink away at his response. His one tawny orb gazed out across his shattered paradise. "We are all slaves to something, James." The sound of his name rattled the hunter to his core, deeper than even the cold could reach. "You think that the hunt frees you, but it shackles you to the fear of death. You will not be free until you can go in peace." His words were absolute, the basest truths he could present. "I offer it to you to be free. To go in peace, with honor."

The hunter considered his proposal for a moment. The urge to flee rose up again, but he kept on suppressing it until it came again with a familiar sensation and coaxed him towards the cave's entrance. His face lit up.

"I'll go," he answered the dragonlord with sudden inspiration. Then he turned and ran.

Solomon staggered, nearly hesitating to disgorge a wave of ice across the cave. James turned and brought a jagged mound of earth up to meet it. The stone and ice collided and crackled, and in the next instant the hunter sent the rock sprawling to bits. The dragon turned his skull downwards to deflect the stonestorm and charged headlong after him.

"You cannot escape fate, boy!" he roared after him as they neared the entrance.

"No," murmured the predator, "you can't."

There was very little room to run on the ledge outside of the cave. Rather than leap to his demise, the hunter turned to face his foe directly. Solomon stood at his lair's entrance. With his left eye still blind, he did not see the dwarf waiting in ambush on that shadowed side.

Uwe trained his shotgun carefully on the devil's mangled skull and waited.

"Last words?" James offered.

"Be quick with it," Solomon replied.

"Poor choice," he thought aloud as the other hunter pulled the trigger.

Uwe's shotgun slug was an unstoppable force. It met the soft surface of the dragonlord's unseeing eye and penetrated straight through to the bone. The beast's body did all it could to protect itself, but at this range, with this bore, it could do very little. The bone folded then snapped and eventually bent straight into the brain. He did not feel the vengeance of an indignant god or the justice of a mob. When Solomon the Great's end finally came after so many centuries, he did not feel anything at all.

At first the almost-carcass seized so that he stood up on his hind legs and clawed at his chest as if to tear out his own heart. After a few lumbering moments, though, he fell in a great, hulking heap and his head slammed down onto the bone-white precipice.

Uwe heaved a sigh at last and shouldered his gun. "For a moment there, I thought you might not bait him."

"I didn't know you were doing it," the hunter defended himself. "I was supposed to hear you reloading that far away?"

"No," the dwarf complained, "but you were at least supposed to run."

"So you were counting on me being a pussy."

"Your words," Uwe chuckled.

"Yeah," James laughed, his glee rushing out through his eyes, "but we did it."

The two turned and regarded their monumental kill. The dragon did not look peaceful in sleep. He looked beset by evils, forever unable to rest. It disturbed the younger hunter, if only for a moment, while it took the triumphant smile straight from Uwe's face.

"Mr. Holub will be waiting for us down the mountain," he said, his usual disposition restored. "Let's get a move on." The elder hunter procured his pack and pulled a set of chains from the ruck. After a moment, he looked up at James. "Well?" he asked, and his tone turned harsh all at once, "What are you sleeping there for?"

James felt the dream begin to fade.

"Get going!"

* * * *

The hunter awoke in his hotel room without fanfare, without rest. Robert was still asleep, and he was alone with his thoughts.

He checked the clock by the bed and surmised that the car would be there for him soon. Until then, he sat up with Uwe's image looming in his memories and Solomon's eye seared into his.

Chapter Twenty-Five
The Pilot

En route to the church near the coast Volodymyr had described, James found himself transfixed not by the task at hand but by the curious new member of the Mythic crew. The company's private chauffeur, Alvin O'Hare, was by no means limited to piloting aircraft, but up until then the hunter had not encountered him on any of his tours of London. He was not new to Mythic, but his hunts rarely brought him in contact with the company personnel. He wondered why this frail, old man had been chosen to assist him in this particular instance.

Even as Michelle debriefed him on the finer points of their operation, his focus lay elsewhere. "Mr. O'Hare is our shooter," she interjected from his side after a while. She didn't even have to read him to determine his curiosity. She hoped that he'd be less transparent later on.

James looked first to the reader then to the front of the car where Alvin peered from the rearview mirror. The hunter mouthed a soundless *oh* and nodded to the driver. Alvin tipped his cap and then stared straight ahead again. "A sniper?" he asked Michelle under his breath, still dubious.

"My appearance is my greatest asset," came the old man's doddering voice, so gentle that the hunter thought the words might be his last. He turned again to Michelle.

She smiled. "You see a man like Alvin walking in a crowd after a shooting and no one jumps to him as a suspect. Ever."

"But—" James stammered. He could not believe, for all his effort, that the tender soul in the front seat could take a life with such nonchalance. "You seem so innocent."

"I've nothing against you or the young miss," Alvin noted. "Why would I be anything but pleasant?"

Michelle beamed in twisted admiration for the death-dealing senior. James moved his focus from her back to his new ally and examined him once again. Upon a second glance, the man appeared even worse than before. His pallid face was speckled with age, spots almost hidden under the folds of his flesh. His eyes were vibrant, if sullen, but couldn't be the hawk-like mainstays of a sharpshooter. The loose skin on his neck shook when he spoke, and the rest of him trembled when he kept silent. It looked like some plucked fowl had stretched its neck up through his suit and now stared beady-eyed down the road ahead. The hair that formed the half-halo on his crown and the push broom moustache over his lips was dove-white. The former was wispy and poorly managed, the latter groomed and pulled up alongside his polite smile.

Alvin watched James study him in the mirror and his smile stretched up to the wrinkles by his eyes. "The first time I killed a man was in South Africa." The hunter raised an eyebrow, dubious of the circumstances. "The Boer War. February. 1900." James swallowed his astonishment. "And in the Great War, and again in the second World War in the RAF…" he reminisced fondly over the events. "I would have served in the Falklands, but my apparent age raised some suspicions. That's when Mythic first found me and how I learned that I was a Mythopian."

"You were…" James delayed to manage the numbers in his head, "over a hundred before you started wondering how you could still fight wars?"

"No, I never wondered," he said, still grinning. "I aged the same as others, but when my companions began to pass on, I simply didn't. I didn't die. For all the flak I took, for all the bullets, I simply didn't die." It was clear that the man took great satisfaction in his seeming immortality. "I've worked with Walter since then. Young ones have come and passed, but I still haven't."

The hunter couldn't help but be charmed by the centenarian's bravado. He certainly had the ego of a sniper.

"I still don't get why I haven't met or heard about you until now."

"Mr. O'Hare made a special request to drive you today. He—"

"I wanted to meet you as soon as possible, in light of last night's events." Alvin interrupted Michelle. She quieted out of consideration. Seeing that he'd piqued James' curiosity, he continued, "I thought you'd been killed, which would have spelled disaster for all of us. You see, I kept company with our former courier. I daresay we were good friends. He often came to me mornings still plagued by nightmarish visions, portends of the future—the kind ancients are cursed with. Often, they were too brief to be intelligible, but occasionally they revealed secrets." The driver's quiet eyes hypnotized James. "He told me shortly before he defected that I would die protecting a hunter. That he'd be the one to do it."

Michelle stirred at the mention of the augury. Her brow wrinkled, her lips pursed, and her attention shifted to the man in front of her. "Is Walter aware of this?"

"Of course he is," Alvin cooed, assuaging her unease. "How else could we know when Casey intends to act?"

"I thought you were friends," James intervened, refocusing the conversation.

"Well, he killed me before we met." Off of their silence, he went on: "It was a dream he had long ago, but more than a dream. When an ancient dreams he doesn't see the future. He lives it. He killed a man pointing a gun at him for reasons he couldn't possibly understand. He killed me. Then his mind returned to the present, he met me years later, and I suppose he felt guilty for having murdered me already. Time must be quite strange for those who don't experience it linearly like the rest of us."

"That's crazy," said James.

"I'm inclined to agree."

"But ancients' visions aren't completely accurate," he continued. "They can change."

Alvin sighed, eyes stuck on the endless road before him. "For Casey, it already happened. This will come to pass, like as not. For all our sakes, it must."

James fell against the back of his seat, guilt-ridden. Michelle glanced at him as if he'd committed the murder himself. The spindly trees on their side of the road started to curve up over the roadway, darkening the day with a web of leafless branches. Shortly, they began to sense that the church was near.

"It's not as if I'll go without a fight," the driver addressed Michelle, "but I've learned to let my enemies come to me." The soldier's hardness escaped for a brief instance. "When Fate finds me, I'll deal with him accordingly."

Michelle dismissed the banal assurance with a scoff and darted her eyes to the window. "You're taking me back to London when we leave James." Her tone reflected her resolve. "I'll come back with Xiang tonight to wait for him."

"That's quite all right with me," the old man tittered as sweetly as a fawn. "Que sera, sera."

The utterance restored the reader's focus just as they approached the church. Alvin stopped short of the hidden drive to allow Michelle and James their parting words. Before he saw the hunter off, though, he saw fit to mention a more pressing detail of his intentions.

"There's a reason his vision *needs* to come true." James had already exited the vehicle but leaned into the front seat to receive Alvin's final pronouncement. Michelle idled on the other side of the car with her arms folded, unwilling to weather the old man's superstition. "Something I learned from my conversations with Casey." It unsettled James to have the name thrown about with such coolness, but he listened nonetheless. "If an ancient's vision is derailed, his visions subsequent to that one change entirely." Now the driver leaned to his ally and emphasized a crucial memory: "The last time I spoke to him, we deciphered a dream that we determined to be his incumbent death. I *have* to die to ensure that he comes with me. It's the only way to guarantee victory." With that, the old man nodded to the hunter with a knowing smile and the two broke off from each other. "It was nice to have met you, James."

"You too, Alvin."

Michelle glowered from over the top of the car. James lifted his shoulders and almost spoke, but she cut in front of him. "Are you ready?" she asked, retracting her anger.

Are you? Faolan queried from within.

I almost forgot you were in there, James thought.

I chose to grant you some peace and quiet. You've had an eventful few hours, the prince jeered. *Must have been quite the nightmare that woke you at four in the morning.*

The hunter ignored him and responded to Michelle in the affirmative. "I'm ready."

"I'll do everything I can to help you if problems arise, but I have to keep my distance."

My guard will remain nearby in the event of an emergency. They can respond in minutes.

"There won't be any emergencies," the hunter said aloud.

"Right, then," the reader sighed. She was beginning to think that staying where they were any longer might prove dangerous. "Be safe," she entreated him. "Stay alive." He did not like seeing so much worry darkening her face. "We'll do everything we can."

I'll be with you all the way, but if it comes to blood, be ready. The moment you regain your senses you may already be in danger, so when you see the light, come out swinging. James heard Faolan's words as Michelle opened her mouth to speak.

"Der Rest ist Schweigen."

James felt his consciousness warp like a ship swallowed up by a great storm. He lost control of his faculties for an instant. His knees buckled and he fell to the snow. There was only the black expanse of oblivion. Somehow, during the ritual, a smile made its way across his unconscious face.

When he awoke, though, he was not the hunter James McCrary. The frightened child that sprang from the snow could hardly even compare to the Stoneslayer. The newborn looked over his moist overcoat and felt the urge to scream.

"Are you all right, sweet?" he heard a woman ask.

The dark-haired, brown-eyed doll that rushed to him seemed at once terrified and bereaved.

"What happened?" he spat, his inflection wavering as if he'd never spoken a word. He chewed the air in his mouth in distaste, displeased by what had just left it, and tried again with a different question. "Where am

I?" It was much better this time, but still lacking the force of his former person.

"We're at the church," his anonymous caretaker explained. "The man at the Grey Gargoyle gave you that card? You wanted to come here?" She hoped her words would take root.

Though he still shook, the man in James' coat agreed, somehow sure that these facts were correct, and turned to walk the dreary trek to the church. After a few pathetic steps, he looked back and saw that the woman was not following him. "You're not coming?" he mewled.

"Oh," she deflected, "no, dear. I have to go back to London."

"Oh, okay," he muttered, dejected.

"But I'll be back," she promised.

"Okay," he echoed. He watched the nameless woman get into her car then watched the vehicle pull back onto the main road and steam away. He stood for some time in the cold, then, petrified and unsure of what to do, where he was, *why* he was, or even *who* he was. But he knew he'd rather not be alone at that moment.

Are you ready? rattled something inside him. He should have been startled, but he wasn't. He thought to the inner voice that he was, in fact, ready and awaited a response.

It's all right. I'm with you. Let's go inside. The voice was so sure and benign that it had to be his own mind spurring him on. He couldn't remember ever hearing it speak to him in such a way but appreciated the company he imparted to himself. The James that wasn't drove his hands into his coat pockets and sloshed through the snow.

As he neared the church, he gawked up at the large structure, a temple built of stone and secrets. Gothic in nature but simple in its design, the granite walls led up to a vaulting roof with a single bell tower at the east end. Overlooking the ecclesiastical architecture from the tower was a rocky figure—a gargoyle—modeled like a fiend. It seemed almost animate in its detail, but at the same time felt out of place above such a holy place.

The man couldn't remember ever having entered a church. He wasn't confident that he would be welcome. He felt somehow immoral stepping up onto the portico, but his mind kept on reassuring him, *it's all right, it's all right, it's all right*, and he felt compelled to believe it. The voice that spoke from his soul sustained him. It gave him comfort. It gave him purpose. It gave him faith.

It's all right. It's all right. It's all right.

Everything was all right.

Chapter Twenty-Six
The Priest

An almost overwhelming warmth washed over the man as he entered the church atrium. A pillar obstructed the view of the nave from the entrance, and an endless line of candles wrapped around the walls. He began at first to remove his coat, but the inner being encouraged him to keep it fastened, so he decided that he would endure the heat. Still, the garment hung heavy around his shoulders and prodded him in his ribs so that he winced as he edged around the column. He extended his ear to catch any service that might be in progress and found himself relieved as he rounded the corner and saw that no ceremony had begun as of yet.

The candles extended into this main room as well, around the pews and aisles and up the pulpit with the raised altar at the east end of the building. They illuminated the temple in a hellish red. The man was distracted, for a time, by the feat of so many lit candles. He wondered how a church could afford such impractical lighting. His musings only waned when he realized with a shudder in his heart that he was not the only visitor.

It seemed smaller inside, yet he felt so distant from the other members of the unholy congregation. Here towards the back was a man sitting, hands clasped around a silver crucifix, eyes closed, entreating some invisible spirit in the sky. The ritual struck the newcomer as archaic. He tried not to act on this observation, though, for on the other side three others did the same. He performed a cursory count, identifying eight besides himself. Some were hovering at the walls, others sitting in the pews, all awkward, unbelonging. At the fore, however, he noticed a visitor on the raised bema conversing with a woman draped in regal, white robes hemmed with gold. She also wore a violet stole around her neck. The novelty of the clergywoman took the man's attention only briefly, however. The priest saw him and smiled; the man felt his lungs shrink from the connection.

It's all right. It's all right. It's all right.

He turned away, catching the eyes of the man praying at the back, who in turn nodded to him. He smiled for the first time he could remember doing so. The muscles quivered in response to the attempt, as if atrophied. The prayerful man scowled at the display, gradually returning a half-hearted grin. The man with the awkward smile rubbed the back of his neck and moved to sit with his new acquaintance.

"Hey," he managed, despite his nervousness.

"Hullo," the godly man acknowledged his greeting and gestured to the priest up at the altar. "You heard of her before?"

The man's eyes flickered to the priest and back, lest he invite another stare. He shook his head.

"Gene," the man said, remembering his manners, and extended his hand.

The other took his hand and inhaled to speak but could think of no name to give. He held Gene's hand for two seconds too long before the name reached him in a wave of inspiration. "Theo," he yielded excitedly, thinking that it was a very fine name to give.

"How'd you hear about the meeting, Theo?"

"The same way as everyone else," he responded in a bout of slyness that surprised him.

Gene moved his tongue around in his cheek and nodded. "I talked to a few others," he claimed. "We all spoke to the man with the umbrella. All had the same dream. All saw the same church."

Theo bobbed his head, astounded. The memory was faint, but…no, it was clear now. The man with the black umbrella. The church foreshadowed in a strange dream. "Why are you here?" he thought to ask his newfound friend.

"Why do you think?" Gene leaned in and rested his arms on the pew in front of him. "Did Umbrella-man show you what he could do?" he laughed. "Yeah. I'm here for some of that."

Theo laughed along with his friend but found himself confused by the answer. He could not recall any particular demonstration by the man with the black umbrella, only that the man in question existed, had handed him a card at the Grey Gargoyle, and that he'd gone to bed that night with a vision of a dream directing him to this very church. Beyond that, he couldn't recall a thing. Slowly, though, he was beginning to understand with the help of his new friend. "Yeah," the pious Gene repeated. "We're all here for *that*."

Up ahead, they saw the priest end her exchange and direct her guest to sit. Next, she took the podium. The congregation sat up with anticipation and dread, and her dulcet benedictions fell with the charm of a sweet, perfumed flower.

"Welcome. Each and every one of you. My name is Lumina Benedictus." Her light voice tickled with the softness of a feather but rang out with the clarity of a bell. "From the bottom of my heart I say to you, you are all more welcome here than you have been anyplace else." Her smile shone with a brightness befitting a cherub. Her golden, curling locks reflected like brilliance. A pair of piercing eyes embodied the heavens in her gaze, and her freckled cheeks completed the perfect visage which brought a smile to the face of each and every visitor, man and woman alike. Even Theo was enthralled. He could not escape the attraction he felt towards her. Something between love and lust stirred within him. Hot blood bubbled from his heart. All the same, he did not trust her. He did not trust that face.

"Not one of you is quite sure why the man with the umbrella led you here. Or how. I sense that." Some of the guests chuckled in agreement. "Some of you feel uncomfortable in this setting, some outright afraid, but this place accepts you all. Lion," she said, eyeing some of the guests, "or lamb," and she looked to Theo with angelic deviance. "Here in this place you can begin the transformation that you all so earnestly seek. You can reclaim the power that was taken from you when you learned this world was not yours alone. If you're willing to give something in return."

"Ah," came a sudden outcry from the south wall. "This where you ask for the handouts?" A thin shadow of a man moved forwards in his protest, looking to the others for support. "Dip into our pockets?" His censure upset the congregation.

"No, Mr. Templeton," she sang, cooling the room's agitation. "The demand is not for money." The man at the wall shrank back, frightened. Unbeknownst to the rest of the audience, he had never told her his name. "I ask only for the same thing God asks of us all. Fidelity."

Theo felt dizzy for a moment. When he regained his senses, he found himself standing in the pew, mouth agape in unexplainable awe of the prophetess before him. Gene laughed at the sight of his neighbor standing like some raptured imbecile and yanked him back down into his seat.

Benedictus giggled at the display as well, motioning to the stuporous gentleman in the rear. "Yes," she repeated, "faith. If you can give me that, you'll have found a place in this world where you can belong. When you've achieved this, when you understand your place here, you will have ownership over the Earth in ways you've never imagined."

"I want to belong," Theo said. "I want to belong."

Gene eyed him as he continued to watch the altar.

"Tell us where we belong," gasped a restless girl across from Gene and Theo. She bit her jagged nails, her hair was unkempt, her eyes sunken gorges.

"Poor dear," Lumina tutted. "How long has it been since your last fix, Ruella?"

The haggard girl stuttered up in surprise. She twitched for a moment before responding, "Few days."

"Truly I say to you, after today you will never use again." Hope blossomed across the young girl's face like never before.

Gene took in the event with disdain. "What is this?" he nudged Theo. "Narcos not-Anonymous?"

"No, Gene," the priest waved a maternal finger, "this is a place for healing." He snapped to attention. Rebounding from her disciplinary stature, Lumina gave him a forgiving smile. "This world has hurt us. Turned its back on us. It has no love for any of us anymore. Here is where we learn how to reshape it and make it ours again." Evidently, the homily proved too rosy for the rotund man in front of them. He stood and blocked the line of sight between the penitent Gene and the spirited

Lumina before shuffling to the exit. "Excuse me, Shaun," Benedictus called out after him. "You haven't heard what I have to say."

Now thoroughly perturbed, the large gentleman turned and threw his hands up at the priest. "We get it," he spat. "You know our names."

"I've figured out much more than that," she countered, "but feel free to leave. That vodka won't finish itself."

After another display of derision, the man somehow recovered his confidence and turned again to leave.

"Do be sure to watch that second step at your flat, the one that's been giving you trouble. I'd hate for you to slip." The man stammered, exposed. "Isn't that what the police thought? How Mr. Joyce died? Or did you push him?" Theo recognized at once in the man an animal panic he'd seen somewhere before. "Was it because he found out about you and Mary? Or because you didn't want to share your new plaything any longer?" The cornered vermin looked up to the pulpit and opened his mouth to defend himself. "Don't answer. I already know. It's immaterial."

"Who the fuck are you?"

"You've been lied to," Lumina informed the congregation as Shaun stumbled up to the bema. "You are not alone here. You have never been alone. Mankind has stolen the Earth from every other creature that deserves it by right of birth."

The man fell on hands and knees and beseeched her, "What are you?"

"I am a mandor," the priest proclaimed. Not a single eye turned from her as she stepped down from the altar. "A creature akin to a snake in likeness and, historically, in cruelty." A single laugh sounded from Mr. Templeton in the back, quieted with but a glare.

"She's not serious," Gene muttered.

"I am told that I, personally, am descended from Medusa," Lumina revealed. "We've been called naga, succubi, and lamias. The Greeks called us Gorgons, for we are indeed dreadful." The sentiment caused her to laugh; she did so alone. "I try to ignore the semantics," she told Gene and Theo. When she looked to the woman across from them, she saw that the poor girl had raised her hands over her eyes, and she smirked at the effort. "Don't worry, you won't turn to stone. That whole story is taken out of context."

Gene raised an anxious hand from the back. "Who says you look anything like a snake? You look human enough to me." Theo nodded at his friend's question in support.

Lumina found the inquisition quite amusing. "The human mind sees what it wants to see," she explained, coming towards them in a slow and sloppy serpentine stride. "You can't hear my footsteps because I have no legs and the ears are a bit harder to fool."

Theo watched her movement, noting the soundless steps drifting from side to side. Wonder welled up within him. His confidence was returning from unknown realms. Something inside compelled him to pry, and so he did. "Can we see you?" he requested.

The priestess smiled, overjoyed, and reached her hand out to the young parishioner. "Don't be afraid."

It's all right.

At first touch, he felt the cold he'd come inside to escape. The hand was hard, the fingers unnaturally slim. As she pulled him from the pew, he felt her claws dig into him and he trembled, but he did not speak. The others watched the spectacle in low murmurs, a rhythmic mantra that underscored the grand revelation. Her eyes did not flicker as they beheld him in all his childish fascination. Then she placed his hand behind her body and he felt near the ground—where there should have been nothing—a thick, smooth tail.

He only blinked, but when he looked up he saw Lumina as she was. The muted auburn skin, squamous like that of a massive snake. The lithe tail that led up to a broadening trunk, bereft of legs but with lengthy, alien arms. The head itself fit perfectly with the creature's elegant design, a royal cresting V a touch darker than the body with no features aside from a pair of slit nostrils and a pair of golden eyes that had not ever and did not ever and would not ever blink.

Even in the face of this monstrosity, Theo's inner calm soothed him. The look of shock stenciled into his expression assured each member of the congregation that they did not wish to see the creature as it should be seen. The mandor, however, would no longer extend the courtesy. With a thought, she dropped all pretense of humanity from her appearance, and the instant each visitor shut their eyes and opened them again they were met with the gruesome vision.

Lumina watched Theo with outward neutrality, not a single emotion showing on her inflexible face. Had she the advantage of conveying emotion physically through her tireless eyes or rigid jaw, or if she could somehow tense the nonexistent muscles over her crest ever so slightly, she would have expressed appreciation for his meager contribution to the "confession" portion of the meeting. Instead, she looked to him for a few blank and stressful moments before winding about-face and gliding back to the pulpit through the shrieks and gasps and horrified stares of her enlightened flock.

Her motion was so seamless and swift that it came as no surprise they hadn't detected any incongruities in the pace before. Gene glanced to his right as Theo sat back down. The blood was gone from the older man's face, sucked away by the succubus' sudden unmasking. Something told Theo that Gene was not here for some of *that*.

Benedictus collected herself at the podium and the parishioners took the time to acclimate to the sight of the serpent looming over the altar. The perversity of the image refused to leave Theo's thoughts.

"Now you know the truth," she announced to them, mindspeaking as she had been up until that very point, only now her features did not shift with her speech. "Any of you who wish to leave may do so now without penalty, knowing that I've ruined you for this world." Instantly, four of the visitors shook to their feet. Their bodies made all the noise that their throats could not as they dashed towards the exit. Lumina looked upon them without surprise as they departed. "Understand, however," she warned those who remained, "that from this point forward, the penalty for desertion is death."

With the added caution, Theo lifted up onto his feet. He felt the reverent Gene clutching at his coat, imploring him with his sheepish eyes not to abandon him. Likewise, the voice inside tried to soothe him, saying, *It's all right. It's all right. It's all right.* So he retook his place in the pew, much to Lumina's delight.

The Gorgoness took stock of her freshly-culled herd. There were five of them in all now, still scattered across the church. The addict, Ruella; the murderer, Shaun; the malcontent, Mr. Templeton; the saintly Gene; and Theo.

"You five," she enticed them, "will inherit so much in the world to come."

"What world?" Gene managed to ask, emboldened by the thinned audience.

"I have two separate promises for two separate kinds of people," the mandor went on. "For those who have faith and believe in a higher power, don't you feel that it has abandoned us?" When Theo glanced around, he saw Ruella nodding with red eyes, Shaun agreeing with a remorseful soul, and Gene concurring with a raised hand. "We've found a way to rouse that negligent god from his sleep. We are an order that believes salvation will come only through destruction. When the waking god sees what we have done, what merciful being would not restore life to the righteous souls perished in the flood?" A light sound escaped from Gene's lips. He implicitly understood the call. "For you we promise amnesty. You will aid us from the light and receive the blessings of the world rebuilt." Still, Theo saw that Mr. Templeton was unconvinced. It was clear that the gaunt figure had no desire for redemption.

Benedictus began again: "For those of you in search of power, you have that assurance instead." Mr. Templeton's attention turned once more to the platform. "You are the martyrs of our cause. Not only will you witness the atrocities, you will carry them out. You will preside over what remains of this realm with fire and steel until the end comes."

"And then?" Mr. Templeton asked.

"At the end, you will receive at least rest, at most everlasting damnation for your crimes." As the others recoiled from the malediction, Mr. Templeton stood fast. "You'll burn in hell. If you believe in such a thing." He nodded in solemn understanding of the agreement and finally took a seat in the pews. Lumina nodded to him. "Choose now," she commanded.

"I want the light," Shaun said, standing. Ruella echoed his sentiment.

"Give me the power," Mr. Templeton growled from the back.

Moments later, Gene stood and said the same. Not even the promise of destruction could turn him from his goal. "The power."

"And you?" the mandor targeted Theo, upset that she still could not extract a name from him. His mind whirled in a thick fog, polluted by fear and uncertainty, obscuring what lay beyond his most immediate thoughts. Thoughts of his life, thoughts of surviving, thoughts of doing whatever it took to stay alive.

The choice, then, was clear to him. His soul was too steep a price to pay for power alone. He began to speak of the light, just as the voice within him stayed his throat. *Only martyrs,* it whispered, *will learn the secrets. Only power will give us what we want.* Dazed by the thought, the man recoiled. *It's all right,* it promised. *It's all right. It's all right.* But he understood that it would most certainly not be all right. "The light," he replied at last. He felt his inner self churning against the words, protesting from his gut, but knew he'd made the right choice.

"No," Lumina said to him as if correcting a child, "you will receive the power."

Theo thought at once to object, but how could he challenge a monster he barely understood? Still, he felt the outward ache in his belly subside when he did not dissent further.

"What is your name?" the mandor asked when her attempts to learn it failed again.

The voice within gave him a family name to speak along with his given name as he moved to answer. "Theo Redmunn," he recited.

Even through her fixed features Theo could sense surprise in the priest's reaction.

"Theo Redmunn?" Lumina asked to confirm. He only nodded. "Your name is an anagram..." the creature noted, as entertained as she was incredulous. A second glance, though, showed no malice behind the moniker. "You are a rare man, Theo," she remarked, abandoning the suspicion. "Whether your aim is to reach the light or the darkness, your path will be the same. Only the recollection of the journey will differ." Theo reconciled himself to his assigned destiny, knowing no other recourse. By now, though, the others were boisterous.

"What next?" Gene pressed. The others mirrored his enthusiasm.

"Now comes the fun part," a voice materialized from the atrium. All eyes descended upon the man now entering the cursed temple: an intruder with dusty hair, a black coat, and a long, red sword on his back.

Theo felt acid creeping up into his throat. Something inside him growled from the depths of his consciousness, begging to be loosed. He waited for his inner voice to reassure him. He pleaded for the inside-him to tell him that it was all right, but the comfort did not come. It lay silent.

"Ah, the prodigious son returns," Lumina called from the pulpit.

"You mean prodigal," the man in the black coat replied, lighting a cigarette and skulking, at length, towards the altar.

"Not you, no," the priest digressed. "I try not to get bogged down in semantics."

"Says the woman with the four-digit IQ," he mocked her.

"Quiet, Casey."

An infectious fright stole over Theo like a disease at the mention of the man's name. He felt the unmistakable suspicion that he'd seen him before, but Casey did not turn to examine the churchgoers as he approached Lumina up ahead, and the trepidatious man in the back felt that it would be best not to draw his attention.

"This," Lumina announced to her disciples, "is one of our brothers in arms. A martyr. The most powerful man you will ever know." Casey shrugged off her accolades, turning over his shoulders to the pitiable flock and blowing smoke down at his feet.

"I didn't come here to meet your sheep," he hissed, stepping up to the pulpit. In spite of his apprehension, Theo strained to hear the dialogue between the two dark figures. "I want to know if he's the one who planted the bombs."

"Gerard?" the mandor asked.

"You know who." Theo's inner voice swelled in his chest, waiting.

"I've not heard of any bombs." She pulled away, her face and mind unreadable.

Casey could only pretend to see the evidence in her eyes. "I think our friend is closer than we thought."

"Well, that's good news."

"It might be."

"You came to satisfy curiosity?" Lumina scoffed.

"I did. Were you the one who sent the men to Tranquility?"

For a long time, the two did not break from one another. In time, though, the mandor wheeled away and regarded her audience.

"I'm afraid our ceremony will have to be expedited," Lumina snapped at them with abrupt severity. "You will learn more later on, but for now, conversion is essential."

"Did you hear me?" Casey rebuked her.

"If you're asking if I ordered her dead, the answer is no. If you're asking if I intended for her to die, the answer is no. If you're asking if her death concerns me at all, the answer is an emphatic no." From below the altar, Theo watched the man in black almost stagger back. "You didn't want her converted. You understood what that might mean for her later on. I'm not assigning you blame. I'm giving you an explanation."

"Oh," was all Casey said.

"We have a responsibility that far outweighs the life of a single person. You need to remember that." The congregation watched their leader with newfound veneration as the man before her crumpled back on his heels. "Now to the matter at hand. We wanted new members; here they are. There is promise in them," the priest exclaimed. "One in particular. The dark-skinned man in the back."

The discovery shook Casey into a rigid posture. He looked over the crowd and fixated his gaze upon Gene and Theo. "The black guy or the Indian?"

"Stand, Theo." The man sat petrified in the pew in spite of her command, trapped...helpless...calm.

It's all right. It's all right. It's all right.

His stance relaxed as Casey stalked closer, and he moved onto his feet.

The man with the mournful blue eyes saw at once something familiar to him, but there was no confidence in this creature he beheld. "What's your name?" Casey asked him.

"Theo," he replied, and the softness of his voice seemed to rattle Casey as much as it intrigued him.

"He may have Mythopian blood," Lumina maneuvered behind them.

"Oh, I don't doubt it," Casey said, never removing his eyes from the hunter masquerading as just an ordinary man. "Go ahead and convert them," he said brusquely and tore back to the atrium. Before he reached the exit, he stopped to deliver one final word to his accomplice. "You're right," he told her. "It was my fault."

"Good boy," she chided him. "We all pay for our mistakes."

She heard Casey laugh as he went.

"Now," Lumina mused, watching him go, "we must understand what is at stake." The congregation sat and gawked under her pulpit. "This world won't go lightly."

Chapter Twenty-Seven
The Sacrifice

"Vaos was a dragon that lived over a hundred years ago, a great black titan renowned for his legendary blue flame." Lumina now moved freely between the pews as she delivered her sacrilegious sermon. The livestock she lectured lapped the words from her red hands. "He believed that the most basic inclination of sentient beings was a desire to destroy. You will engage in a foul form of destruction today, but first you must understand why it is we seek to preserve through our evils." She passed before Shaun the murderer and placed her claw atop his bare scalp. "You know that death can be dealt unjustly. Only through death, however, can we truly hope for impartial judgment."

"Kill them all and let God sort em out," Mr. Templeton mused.

"Semantics," the mandor scoffed, "in so many words."

"How does that work if you don't believe in God?" he laughed.

"If you don't believe in a higher power, then the path you've chosen can yield no consequences worse than death. So long as you live, you will know no suffering."

Mr. Templeton seemed contented by the concept, but Gene shifted in his seat. "And if you do?" he exhorted her.

"Then it is a grand sacrifice you make. You may seek glory, but you must understand that in the world to come, the martyrs will be cursed like devils if we are remembered at all. Your only reward is the knowledge that you extorted paradise from a god too selfish to relinquish it."

"Is it worth it?" Theo asked from beside him.

"It will be," she claimed, bowing her head.

"You keep mentioning," came Ruella's mousy, fragmented speech, "that we're going to end the world. How is that possible?"

And here the mandor retook the stage, moving at a snail's speed. "There have been men who have tried in the past. The first of note was a dwarf, Keiser Thunderfist, who lived far away from here." She found herself amused by how timidly they accepted her words, given the rest of the day's revelations. In time, the wonders of Mythopia would fail to faze them, but for now each new piece of information might raise as many concerns as it addressed.

"He was an elementalist, a man with the power to control nature, who had reign over lightning. He was the first of our order to attempt mundicide, and though his efforts were laughable in retrospect, he showed us that killing off all life is simpler than we think." The parishioners were dubious in spite of her words. "All things are possible through faith," she admonished them. She turned on them without warning, eyes aflame and swirling like storms. "The faith that you all still withhold from me." The sweetness had departed from her voice completely. In its place was the seductive timbre of the serpent.

"Ruella," the siren called out with sudden saccharine tones, "do you not wish to shed the burden of this world? It holds nothing for you."

The addict felt herself resisting at first, for a fleeting moment. Then the girl stood, speechless, and ambled to the pulpit, her eyes caught in the glowing golden webs that refused to blink. "I want to forget," she said.

"Yes," the mandor hissed. "Oblivion: the refuge of the meek." The others bore witness to the haunting ritual with static amazement. "Come smiling to me, child. It will feed your eyes with malice." Over time, the junkie's tremors subsided. She stood erect and still, and somehow unafraid.

When she turned, the other disciples expected to see a zombie, some doe-eyed marionette with a stenciled smile. Instead, they saw Ruella warm-faced and lucid with all the darkness of her heart locked away by the mandor's mercy. "Incredible," she wept.

"Absolution," Lumina preached. "Purgation of all blame." She glanced at Shaun. "Salvation. I would shoulder it all, freeze in a dozen hells if it meant that you might find peace."

The burly man needed no further persuasion. He strode to the podium in seconds and surrendered himself to the mandor. She swept over him and the others at once. Even the Earthers could detect her filling their thoughts. Had they not been assured death only minutes ago for anything less than complete loyalty, some of the recruits might have objected to the intrusion, but given the limited options of this opiate or death, they did not hesitate to yield.

"Power," Mr. Templeton reminded her with a pointed finger before he relented.

Gene checked his friend's expression before submitting with a smile. "This is it," he gasped.

Theo looked only to himself. *It's all right*, came the voice within. *It's all right. It's all right. It's all right.*

And he too gave his mind.

He felt at once the mystic balm pass over his face, seeping back behind his eyes, and he became drunk with joy. He and Gene rose and shambled up onto the bema where the others were already worshipping around Lumina.

The mandor ran her reptilian eyes across them once more before slithering from the pedestal. Mute from the cerebral opium, the disciples only stared as she moved down the transept.

"Come, children," she commanded and revealed a hidden stairway leading down to some hellish understory. "Now we kill."

The neophytes appeared unshaken by the dark task at hand. They plodded after the mental breadcrumbs the temptress left in her wake. As if caught in the stranglehold of some crimson star, they followed deep down into the glowing pit.

It was colder in this quiet chamber, the air stiller. The only light within was flame. Here below, the candles were arranged in a sparser pattern so that even in the constricted dungeon Theo had to lean forwards into the center of the room to discover the final rite constrained in chains against a black altar: an elf.

The man controlled his movements as best he could. Splayed naked on the platform, his eyes dilated as he shivered from the chill he'd endured for two nights and two days. The eyes fled with the elf's pleading spirit across the faces of all the visitors, importuning them with squeals. He bellowed like a proper lamb through a rag bound around his mouth until he came at last to Theo.

Although the man stood in arrant apathy, he heard a new voice come from within him, replete with deep sorrow, saying, *Not this. Not this. No.* And another sensation, one he could not identify, sprang from inside like a demon straining to overthrow his faculties. And this voice recited, *Leon.*

"This man is an enemy to our cause," the mandor alleged, unseen. The disciples encircled the dais under Lumina's coaxing and, while the elf looked to Theo with unwarranted hope, the mandor appeared from the shadows with a dagger. The weapon twisted in her grotesque hold, absorbing the radiance around it rather than reflecting it. "He must be removed." The kris wavered like a withered branch, a harbinger of death to all who beheld it, and the disciples were dazzled by its shape.

"Death comes to all, regardless of might or measure. It is the final test of the living to suffer Her black embrace."

They applauded and tittered as Lumina twirled the dagger and made a single, shallow incision in the elf's chest. The prisoner made no murmur, but held fast with his eyes still resting on the man standing to his assailant's left. Between Theo and the mandor, though, stood Gene and Mr. Templeton. Lumina extended the blade to the former so that the ritual could proceed, but in spite of her grasp, for all the haze in his mind, the angelic Gene hesitated. The Cultist, however, had no patience for disobedience.

"This man will die today with or without your contribution," she reminded him. Gene opposed her eyes with a forgotten fervor, something lost far below her control of his mind, but the smoldering emblems which did not blink kept constant hold of him. His body began to tense with the pressure of her domination until he felt that his entire frame was stone. "You will join him," she warned. "Accept the power." She released him and thrust the misshapen knife into his hands. The man took a reckless grip on the dagger and jabbed the blade into the elf's side. When he saw what his red hand had wrought and heard the muffled scream gush from the elf's mouth, he smiled.

"This world is ending quickly. We offer our adversaries the blow of mercy that they might be shown further forgiveness in the world to come."

Mr. Templeton freed the knife from Gene's grasp and repeated the abuse, twisting the weapon with barbarous lunacy. He raised it for a second strike, but the matron stopped him. "No," she scolded. "The deathblow belongs to Theo." Even in perfect obedience, a splotch of spite stained the sadist's face. He handed over the dagger as if abandoning a part of himself, regarding the other disciple with a venomous leer.

"The martyrs are men resigned to condemnation. This burden they share. It is too great to carry alone."

Theo accepted the kris with indifference, noting the surprising familiarity of the grip, but the grapple taking place within him made him hesitate. He felt the inner him denying the reality of the event, refusing support. He felt the other voice, too, a stronger, more grounded spirit than the first, but heard the words only as indistinct murmurs in his subconscious.

Lumina sensed the turmoil within him with ease, yet on the surface there was nothing. No thought to impede the impulse, no guilt to choke back the strike. "End this," she chanted. The command moved Theo's clenched fist up into the air, but still he did not attack. "Time will only betray you. Kill him now," she repeated, and at last he heard his soul's vital sanction: *It's all right. It's all right. It's all right. Everything is all right.*

He could see nothing wrong with killing the elf. This man was his enemy. *Their* enemy. He simply had to die. And why shouldn't he be the one to do it? Who was he to deny Lumina? Theo Redmunn considered for a fraction of a second all that he had ever been and all that he had ever desired, and the emptiness of the introspection shook him. Who was he to do this? Who was he?

"Kill him," came Benedictus' voice once more, this time with weight, "and let the water of Vaos redeem him. Kill him, Theo."

He ignored both her and the voice within that was still saying, *It's all right. It's all right. It's all right.* The other voice, tearing at the seams of his mental falsehood, he allowed to breathe at last. It grew, swelled, and filled him from his core. *Kill her*, he heard it think, as if the intention had risen from his soul. *Kill her*, it said again, stronger this time.

"Kill him."

The echo of the second voice rebounded, saying, *She's got you. She's got you, James!* Upon hearing his true name, the hunter stirred. *Wake up*, it roared, but Faolan echoed, *It's all right*, as the puppet Theo pulled his dagger back to strike. The hunter had no choice but to force Theo and Faolan into nothingness.

The blade shot forth with all the swiftness of a serpent strike, poised not for Leon but for Lumina. The hunter held the mandor in his vision as tightly as he could—a folly, for as he neared the witch's heart, his rushing hand jerked to a stop and Lumina's indecipherable face withdrew into the darkness.

"I see you, James." She could hold him still only as long as her tenuous grip on Theo persisted. After only an instant, the hunter's momentum carried him forwards onto his knees, but the mandor was nowhere to be found.

Then, from twilight, the black priestess spoke, and the hunter felt her words pollute him in a litany of curses. "The demon hunter come to kill me," she jeered. "You will not leave this place alive." In that moment, he knew that she was affecting him. Though she could not control him, her influence lapped at his senses. "This man is an enemy to our cause," she vowed from shadow, and the other disciples drank in the words. "Destroy him."

They turned on him without question as he stood. The savage Mr. Templeton snarled and James felt the cry assail his ears with hyperbolic intensity. The steps they took to strike him, the scuffling sounds of their feet grinding into the stone, all of it sounded and resounded with the volume of gunfire. Amidst the thunderous sensations as the disciples came from all sides, the hunter realized that the threshold of his senses had been altered. He did not relish the pain that was to come.

Shaun came first with a clenched hand while the hunter was still deafened, and he felt the straight glance off his chin as if he were made of glass. The hit that would not have staggered him under ordinary circumstances now sent him reeling backwards in agony. Each and every sense he possessed fired with such hypersensitivity that the girl who leapt onto his back fell with the weight of a war hammer, and her gnawing at his neck singed like fire. Gene's claws flogged his skin, and Mr. Templeton strangled him with the grip of a god.

Shouting curses, the hunter sliced the choking acolyte away, and Mr. Templeton went sprawling to the ground. He tore the imp from his shoulders, threw her at Shaun, and the two fell motionless in a heap. Then Gene set upon him with mortality in his eyes, and the hunter reacted only as his instincts allowed. The wildfire bubbling from the other man's belly scalded him, but as he pulled the knife and pushed the initiate away, the contrite Gene collapsed with the ruins of humanity in his eyes.

James rested for just a few seconds in the sudden stillness. Though his body and ears felt relief, his eyes still consumed everything around him, insatiable orbs that fed him figures where there were none, phantoms where only static lingered, fear where only darkness lived. When he closed his eyes, even the blackness overwhelmed him.

Soon, though, the pain began to subside, and the mandor's second strategy settled over him—that of analgesia. Caught in a dark underworld, the hunter stumbled forwards, his senses dulled to nothing. Through the veil of the narcoma he saw Mr. Templeton leaning against the ground, his face sopping red before the blood faded to black in James' muted vision. The disciple looked to him with anger but lay rooted to the ground. His mouth moved but imparted no sound that James could perceive. He shouted but made no noise. Soon, he faded from the hunter's misty eyes altogether so that he never learned the curses Mr. Templeton spat.

James pawed at his scalp, rebuking his brain for the senselessness it provided him. Here in this prison of black mist and white noise he stood for a brief eon before lurching back to see the injured elf still lying on the dais. He tried to comfort him, tried to reassure him, but could not be sure that the words ever left his lips. Though he saw the elf's form quite clearly, it appeared too dark to make out the features on his face, so neither did he know if Leon spoke. All he heard was the hushed crackling within his head, and all he saw was the all-consuming darkness of the world.

He peered at his hands, inches from his eyes, and they appeared to be miles away, wrapped in sable silence, but through the dusk he saw a dagger that bore the blood of innocent men caked even to its hilt, and the half-sight restored the heat to his heart. James McCrary cast the kris aside, reached into his coat, and Yin and Yang awoke with muted wails.

In his anesthesia, James could hear only the blades. Their cry sounded without impediment, their aim indisputable, and the hunter listened when they chose to address him not with soothing banalities but baneful sooth. *Kill her*, came the call, like a prophecy already fulfilled in the hell-bent brown eyes that gazed up a shrouded set of stairs towards the church.

Chapter Twenty-Eight
The Mandor

Lumina Benedictus was not born with that name. She, like all others of her kind, was born nameless. So she remained while she lived among her own. Owing to this idiosyncrasy, those outside of mandorian culture took up the practice, over time, of addressing each individual mandor as 'Nameless'. Likewise, when the mandors refused to christen their homeland, the other nations began to refer to it simply as the Nameless. The rest of their culture became colored in this strange praxis in the same way. The mystique of anonymity served to augment the already immense strength the mandors derived from their intellect. Through the wonder brought to them by curious outsiders, through stoicism, through study, and through discipline, the nameless tribe cultivated a peerless hierarchy of military, agricultural, and economic geniuses.

Yet the company of such prodigies and the promise of total prosperity proved too romantic for some, and so many individuals moved to reject the utopia of the Nameless, choosing instead to weather the lesser world, exiled, in search of truth. However, the mandors that pursued hedonism found humanoid pleasures too somatic, and the mandors that sought comfort in religion could rarely accept it, owing to their philosophical upbringing and their ingrained skepticism. Spurned by their people and disunited from anyone who might understand them, these rogue mandors looked almost unfailingly to the allure of power. Here they found rage, jealousy, hatred, and all the facets of man that their own culture had been built to overcome. These poisons corrupted their minds, twisted their intentions, and transformed them into something beyond humanity and beyond the nameless nature of the mandor.

Thus existed the priest, Benedictus, as she lay coiled in wait within the empty church with venom boiling beneath her scales. All the emotion that lay illegible on her face gurgled in her limbs—the twitching, trembling claws that clutched a spear with such raw panic that they made her palms bleed.

Lumina had never believed in God. She had believed once in love, when she'd left the Nameless. Not for her mate, whom she'd matched minutes after birth, the man imprinted in her mind with a chemical touch that should have prevented either mandor from ever loving another, but for a human. The love she felt was real, by common standards, but was a trifle in comparison to that inimitable physical and mental connection that was a mandor's birthbond. Of course that love, like all else in her life, had failed, and she had learned like many before her of the ephemerality of all things beautiful and hideous. So it was that she could not possibly ever believe in God or any other notion of eternity. She found, though, a certain solace in the transience of life and love, the thought that anything *could* end, that everything *would* end, and that all things could *be* ended.

It occurred to her, in a moment of depraved clarity, that the world itself must share a similar fate, and if the world was to die, its death should be swift, decisive, and soon. This parsimony, however misguided, struck her as an act of mercy upon the universe, though it was drowned in the malice of a creature too tortured to long for the future. For Lumina, the chemical release ushered in by wanton destruction was an opium too potent to discard, and so she would embrace it until the sweet end.

Now, however, in the throes of her rage, the mandor beheld something she had never seen before, and the discovery stilled her shaking all at once. The latch forced open, she watched the hunter—still masked in her mental smokescreen—stumble from the shadows of the crypt below and saw not a man but a deity. Here, surrounded by the icons of earthly religion, she witnessed for the first time something so powerful and unexplainable that she could only describe it as divine.

Then the deity's arms spread, revealing his daggers, and she realized that she did not have time for doubt. The instant she attacked, he would see her. The moment she struck, so would he. Beyond that, even the mandor could not see.

James crept forwards, drawn through the haze by the dull scent of blood. The static droning in his ears was louder now. The illusion was climbing and he was getting close. The mandor had not fled, and this matter would not be settled while both of them still lived. The hunter took stable steps and monotonous gasps of air. Though he could not hear them rising from his lungs, he could still sense the change in pressure. Only in this way could he determine that he was still breathing. He felt the slow pulse of his heart while he walked, the only remaining signal of his continued existence: in, out, up, down, balancing on the precipice of the storm, until all at once the candles crackled around him, the light pierced his eyes, the warmth enwrapped him like dragonbreath, and the copper beast took flight.

The burst of sensation muddied his reaction, but James still sprang sideways with practiced poise. The spear came at an angle, trailing after him as he dodged. The priestess was no novice. James evaded the follow-up and returned with his long-awaited first strike, a chance to end the engagement there and then, and felt his heart explode with energy as Yin plunged deep, deep into her breast. The blade was there. He was sure of it. Implanted at most inches from whatever black heart the priestess-demoness possessed, and yet she struck again.

The wound did not slow her movement; she still threw her attacks with lightning intensity. Lumina's body whipped left and right as she leapt, momentum sprawling through her arms and sending motion rocketing through her glaive as it danced through the air as if on strings. The hunter did battle more with the massive weapon than with her, dodging each strike at close range, reaching for the dagger still hanging from her chest all the while. Soon, snarling, he switched Yang to his other hand and adopted a stronger stance to begin the brawl anew.

Benedictus howled with her eyes alone. Inoculated from all pain by adrenaline even more potent than his, she shrugged off attacks with godly resilience. Meanwhile, the hunter received a single laceration on his shoulder that sent him roaring back. His blood could do nothing to dull the agony Lumina's mind underscored. All the same, he preferred this melodramatic nightmare to the stupor in which the priestess had trapped him before. To feel something—anything—was better than to die.

After rejoining the melee, James saw his opponent flinch from a feint on his right, so he threw his caution aside. In the half-moment between blows, he gripped the mandor's spear with both hands and tore at the weapon with all his might. Lumina, expecting no such strength from a human, almost lost hold of the javelin. Her characteristic intelligence, however, did not preclude a brawn to match. When she let the blade fall upon the hunter, he pushed back. When he determined that she might wrest the weapon from him, he pulled. When she felt her grip loosen, the mandor whirled her tail around his legs and brought them both crashing to the ground.

In seconds, the serpent had herself looped about the hunter's body. He felt her tighten around him but did not relinquish the spear, so she choked the air from his lungs. The hunter listened to his bones bending and the creature's swollen muscles straining, but he would not submit. Even as her blood poured onto him like hot pitch, he would not submit. Not in the face of death.

"Death comes for all, demon hunter," she told him. "Even you."

James could not speak. Veins were filling at his neck, the blood trapped in every vessel. His eyes bulged.

"Even gods die."

James summoned strength beyond what he knew he possessed. He commanded his body with every neural prompt he could think of, bolstered it with all the epinephrine he could produce. Here at the apex of dying he felt the bliss of asphyxia, all the peace of eternity here at his fingertips if he would only let go, but he reasoned that eternity would be there to greet him for a long time to come. He felt no need to go to it with such urgency.

The moment the mandor felt her body begin to uncoil, her yellow eyes dimmed. There, within them, lurked fear. The hunter slid an arm from the chokehold just as the creature constricted again, stayed her spear with one hand, and with the other ripped Yin from her lung. Lumina gasped a horrid gasp and writhed.

Her tail came hurtling down as he rolled onto his feet, still lightheaded. He caught sight of the frenzied limb crashing through a pew as he redded out. By the time the blood had cleared from his eyes, the beast was rushing again.

Life seeped crimson from her wound, but even an injury as grievous as this would not bring closure to the duel. Where across this looming husk he should strike next, the hunter could not ascertain, so he instead sidestepped and felt the shock as Lumina's polearm smashed through the wooden benches. James used the pews while they lasted to gain the high ground, and in seconds had made another series of cuts along the mandor's arms and trunk, though none bled like the gash in her breast. Still, the priest came at him constantly, without mercy, slashing, striking, splintering everything, until he drew her back across the hallowed temple up to the bema, leapt to the level ground below, turned, and stood defiant in the wake of sure destruction.

A sound shot from the mandor—a sort of half-cackle—and he saw the pus leaking from her maw, a putrid yellow ichor that echoed the same death he saw above him. He realized, all at once, that the monster was already undone. He'd killed her. When the chemicals in her blood no longer fueled her corpse, she would succumb to that first wound and fall dead. Upon seeing this, he relaxed and let his blades fall to his sides.

"Stop," he panted. "It's over."

Lumina wheezed, speeding her heartbeat in order to maintain her chemical anesthesia. "I will hold my bloodlust until you, too, are sated with death."

"There's no point to it," the hunter reasoned. "Just die."

"*Just* die?" The mandor sputtered, struggling to stay upright. "The grandest endeavor of any living thing. I will not see it through without pageantry."

"It's not too late to make peace," he deflected.

"It's never too late for peace. That is why Death is there."

"You can still redeem yourself. Tell me what Casey is planning."

Again, Lumina seemed amused. "Redemption is a panacea only for the unenlightened." Seeing a certain light in the hunter's eyes, she went on, "A cure that you yourself seek." Her eyes shone against the dark. "I cannot best you in the conscious world," she conceded, "but a nightmare can kill just as quickly as a knife."

James felt his senses dull at once, seized by the demon's reckless eyes. Although his senses remained, the church and his surroundings descended again into darkness and the beast herself began to change.

"Who is it that drives you to absolution?" she pressed. Though her body did not move, he felt her eyes drifting nearer across space until they were upon him, then within him, tearing through his soul. "Who is it that you fear more than Death? More than all life could wreak? This incubus that follows you even into the light?" Without warning, Lumina's shape twisted and contorted until she was human once again. The form she bore looked at once familiar and ambiguous—murky, even—until the hunter's memories solidified and he saw his father standing there in front of him.

Though not his father by blood, the man had an uncanny likeness to the boy whom he had loved, but he was scrawny and old, a victim of time and its devices. The fire welled up in his eyes only when he saw his fostered son and departed whenever the two were separated. His presence now brought fear into the hunter's heart, not because he feared for the man's safety—a quick drop and the water's surface had quenched that concern long ago—but for the uncertainty surrounding the encounter.

After a pregnant pause, the apparition said faintly, "James." It was the selfsame voice that the hunter's memory had recorded and locked away in an unreachable mental crypt, never to be recalled but by some fateful moment such as this. James smiled. The old man smiled. Then he vanished without another word with the exact suddenness that he had decades earlier.

In his place stood his wife, James' abrasive foster mother, fat and slothful with tangled hair and a damp, round face saturated by malaise. Her spongy fingers pointed at him.

"You killed him," she accused in that haggard, rolling sickness of hers that passed for a voice. "Takin care of you," she railed, swept up in the inebriating arms of her only true comfort. He smelled the liquor on her tongue, more pungent than it could have been in reality, churning with Lumina's blood and sweat and bile. "Workin himself to death and takin care of you, that's all he ever did. Never had time for me or no one else. Just you." Her black eyes accused him even more harshly than her black lips. "You worked that man to death." But these assaults, even after so long, did little to affect the stonelike man who stood before the bema. Here, beneath the stage of his life's own tragedy, he did not flinch. He'd dealt with the pain of this scene long ago.

Seeing this, Lumina catapulted forwards in his mind. It was not long before she discovered another object of woe for the hunter. Her name was Diana, and the illusion itself was perfect. James struggled not to reach out to her, so clear were her viridescent eyes, so real her wavy brown hair, so soft her rosy cheeks. And she smiled! Here in front of him, in spite of all he'd done, she smiled.

The mandor snatched the vision away as quickly as she'd brought it on, resenting the hope it brought to him. Where was the fear? Where was the dismal cold that would send her adversary spiraling into his own animal panic? She shifted at once to a source she knew would invoke such an emotion. Casey Aduro roared to life on the platform in a blaze of brilliant flame, his sword drawn and fire swirling about him, completely prepared to strike. But if Lumina chose to assault James with this spectre, the hunter would be ready. He rolled Yin and Yang in his wrists and stood unyielding. He'd fought Casey before, and when the time came he'd be able to do it again.

Benedictus was in disbelief. What being could incite more dread than the man whom even she feared? Her eyes sprinted over James' bared soul, searching for anything stronger to assault him with but finding nothing. The hunter feared none of his past enemies as greatly as Casey, and the latter terror was not great enough to press him into the shadows.

But, the mandor discovered with a happy shudder, there was indeed fear in this man. Perhaps not of a single man or beast, but James McCrary had felt, at one time, immense and incalculable terror. When Lumina brought the shade to light, alarm bounded across the hunter's face in a wave of phobic recognition.

Now before him stood his mentor, Uwe Löwe, the triumphant titan towing the head of Solomon the Great.

"What happened that day that brought you to your knees?" the mandor beckoned, anticipation rattling in her tone. "What horrors did the

Stoneslayer witness?"

James remained silent in the wake of her interrogation. He stood frozen as though he were there, back in the Swiss mountains. His eyes did not move from the callous man who now peered into his soul without speaking. Without moving. Without blinking. No trick of the mandor—this was his complete recollection of that day. As James began to fall into the depths of his memory, he saw the dwarf approach him, arms raised, as Lumina attacked.

He dodged instinctively as deftly as he could, but his motion was slowed by the impending dream he could not escape. The waking nightmare that took hold of him as the mandor struck again, again, again, again. He could not see her now. His body acted on its own, dodging, ducking, dipping, diving. He could feel the inertia of his evasion for but a moment longer. How he kept fighting he could not be sure, for his mind was still fixed rigidly on the unflinching eyes of Uwe Löwe.

Chapter Twenty-Nine
Uwe

The hunter's breaths fell heavily, in this world and the other, as he dragged the colossal dragon's severed skull through the snow. They'd been pulling Solomon's final remains across the icy hillside for hours now. The effort had left a trail of dark red blood from here to the mountain's peak like a scar upon the massive rock. Even now it still bled, so before them stretched the vast expanse of frigid white, behind them the stench of the fallen drake, and between them only sparse words as they trekked until the dwarf moved to the heaving man walking alongside him.

"Here," Uwe offered, taking the irons from him, "let me." With a muted grunt, the great hunter took on the burden and began hauling the head across the plain. "It's too much to carry alone." The words left him, hollow, out into the air.

"You should've brought more chains," James suggested, looking back at the trophy as he wound down.

"Honestly?" Uwe strained, glancing at the load, "I didn't think he'd be that big." The two descended again into quiet, a stillness softened by the drag of Solomon's skull, the shaking chains, the steady wind, and the tender snowfall.

The lull unsettled Uwe. Without the hunt to occupy his thoughts, he now preferred conversation. The past few hours had been brutal. In light of this, after a while he reached for a topic he knew would enliven James so that his accomplice would speak while he drudged through slippery powder.

"Tell me," he said, panting already, "about this girl of yours." He felt the other hunter awaken like a sudden flame.

"You serious?" James asked.

Uwe returned a sly glance. "We're not...on the hunt...anymore."

"You sure you don't want me to keep carrying that?" he volunteered.

"Just let me get a rhythm going," the dwarf wheezed. "Tell me about the girl."

"Nothing much to tell." James watched his feet. "I didn't really leave her on good terms." Uwe raised an eyebrow, urging him to go on. "I never told her about Mythopia. I didn't bother making up some lie about what I did. I just told her I couldn't talk about it."

"Mm," Uwe murmured.

"But she never questioned it." The young hunter was reminded, shuffling in the snow, how close he'd come to perfection. "She accepted it. As long as I promised her what I was doing was legal, which I guess is a grey area anyway, she didn't ask. And I kept quiet."

"What went wrong?"

Difficulty graced the hunter's words. "She didn't want me to leave. But I did."

"You did...what you had to. Few days...you'll be back...with more money than you could ever need."

The sentiment warmed James' soul. In the earlier turmoil, the thought of a reward had not occurred to him. He'd done it. He was free. "I'll never have to hunt again."

"No," Uwe smiled along with him, their thoughts syncing. "You're a free man. What will you do?"

Again, the notion caught James unaware. "Just..." he pondered for several moments. "Live." His mentor cast a sidelong glance upon the beamish youth beside him. "What about you?"

They were near the end of the ridge now. The snow cut down into a wide gully, flat and surrounded on all sides by steep walls. As the ditch came into view, the hunters spotted a man dressed in a grey overcoat and ushanka standing in the center. From this distance, they could not discern the features of his red face, but he was almost certainly smiling.

221

Uwe dropped the chains and stretched his aching shoulders. "Čeněk Holub. Executor over Eastern Europe. Probably has the checks written up already."

"You didn't answer," James jeered.

The dwarf inhaled deeply for a moment, letting out a long, white sigh. "I'm a hunter. Always have been. Always will be." He thought to add something, but soon realized that he had nothing left to say.

"You can't keep it up much longer," the other hunter said, only half joking.

"Yeah," Uwe conceded, "but I'll keep on until the end." He raised a hand in greeting to Mr. Holub down in the hollow.

James' tone warped as he stabbed his eyes into the dwarf. "That's crazy, Ooie."

"That's passion, James." His mentor retaliated without forethought. "Loyalty. Faith. Call it what you want, it's something only certain men have. They owe it to the world."

"You're saying that I'm not being loyal to the hunt?" he tutted. "Because I don't wanna die fighting?"

Uwe turned away from the man in the ditch. "I'm saying,"—and now he considered his words—"you're not being loyal to your own nature. Because you're not *willing* to die fighting."

"That's bullshit. I'm not gonna put myself at risk just to feed some fucking bloodlust."

"It's not about the lust. It's about going to the end. With purpose. The hunt will find you," the dwarf spat, eyes wild with caution, "whether you keep your eyes on it or not. If you turn your back on this life, it will destroy you."

James watched Uwe, wordless in the wake of endless winter. The wind galloped around them into a crescendo of sound.

"You're powerful, James. More powerful than almost every other man alive. You and those you love will be targeted by men whose measure you can't imagine." The dwarf's declaration was more a prophecy than a warning. "Did you hear what I said just now?" The boy's eyes were on his but looked through him rather than at him. "Passion. Loyalty. Faith. Conviction. You have to believe in something. Even if that something is just you." Without another word, Uwe swallowed hard and slid down into the gully towards Mr. Holub. James spat onto the icy ground, waiting a few moments before following. At some point in the last few minutes, he noticed that the sun had dropped below the mountains all around them. The chill of his bones deepened in the half-light.

"I'm relieved!" Mr. Holub called out as Uwe drew near. "I was beginning to think we'd have to go up after you."

"No such misfortune," came the dwarf's reply. He cleared his throat. "He's sitting up on the ridge," he went on, pointing up past James. "Well, not sitting. More like a headstand." He stuck his chin out like a man on the chopping block.

"A job incredibly well done," Mr. Holub applauded him. He made a motion with one hand and a group of riflemen in arctic camouflage appeared from the opposite edge of the gully. Four soldiers swept over to the skull. "I'm amazed you got it done so quickly."

Uwe raised a shoulder as he watched the men round the hollow. "We work fast."

"So easily."

"We work well."

The weathered man agreed as he saw the second hunter approach. "James McCrary," he remarked, astounded. "I've heard of you."

James bowed his head in greeting.

"There are rumors that you are of ancient blood, Mr. McCrary."

At the very utterance, James' mental world shook violently. Although the players of his memory did not react, the entire artifice shook with cataclysmic shock. Somewhere far off in the present, Lumina recoiled from a truth for which she had not been prepared.

James confirmed Mr. Holub's suspicion with a sly nod. The executor jarred. "When you said you'd have help, Uwe, I think I was picturing a platoon of elementalists going along with you." He scrutinized the young hunter for a moment. "I suppose having an ancient on your side is a step better." James gave a polite laugh. "How long have you known Uwe, James?"

The hunter flinched at the question. "He trained me," he explained, smiling at his friend. "Initiated me," he corrected himself.

"Is that a fact?" the strange man murmured, removing his wool hat.

He scratched the dull brown beneath before replacing the ushanka and looking again to the two of them. "Well, that's a damn shame."

The hunters turned from each other. James saw one of the soldiers behind them signaling Mr. Holub with one hand, sensed movement all around them, felt ice forming in his heart.

Uwe's eyes narrowed. "What is this, Čeněk?" In moments, the company of riflemen had surrounded the hollow. Thirty of them, at least. They held their rifles at the ready. James reached for his sidearm out of instinct but stopped his quivering arm short.

"You tell me, Uwe," Mr. Holub rumbled. "Was it painful killing Solomon? Your leader? To become a traitor twice over?"

"What?" Uwe gasped.

"And this one?" Mr. Holub cried, extending an arm towards James. "What kind of audacity does it take to corrupt an ancient?" He shook his head, shuddering as he backed away from the trapped hunters. "Your ruse is forfeit. The Cult dies today." He raised a hand, and that hand brought thirty-two rifles to bear on the bodies of two men.

"Hand over your weapons."

"Don't do this," the dwarf barked, his hand hovering over his shotgun.

Holub shook his head. "Put your weapons on the ground so that I can hear you out with my ears rather than my nerves."

"Don't do this," Uwe repeated, kept on repeating, while his eyes flashed over his surroundings.

"Uwe?" James scanned his countenance and found the other hunter's stormy glare alarming. He saw at once the animal in his eyes, the old dwarf caught off guard by the hunt he worshipped, ready to dive into it without a thought.

"Let me speak to Aaron," the dwarf reasoned. "What does he know about this?"

"He doesn't need to know. Put them down," the executor commanded.

"I'm not a witch you can burn to indulge your paranoia," the dwarf snarled. "This is not right!" He turned to the other hunter, a different panic washing over him. "Don't hurt him," he begged, but his eyes would not leave the boy. "He hasn't done anything wrong."

"I'm sorry, James," Čeněk lamented, drawing Uwe's fierce eyes back onto him. "I really am, but we can't let one of you fall into their hands." The words fell like an epitaph, inciting in the younger hunter a dread he had not known before that day. Soon enough, Holub was out of earshot.

"All right, boy," Uwe said opposite him, turning to stare Holub down. The gravity in his tone could crush a moon. "We've had worse odds." He drew in air deeply while James pulled his gun. The riflemen trained on them were not novices but expert shooters who wouldn't miss any ounce of flesh that presented itself to them. They were professional killers who dealt with elementalists regularly and accordingly. Expert soldiers who would not yield to anyone but Death.

"Back to back," Uwe instructed, a general in the clutches of ambush. "Block your corners and sides. Suppress your front. We'll shift in your direction." He took in another long, last, pensive breath and poured energy into his garnet. "You ready?"

James was. He couldn't die here. He refused to die here, and his body moved in lockstep with his animal inclination. The adrenaline found him, filled him—every ounce of him—to the point of bursting, and it was out of his control. His hands shook as he held his weapon, and the rattling alerted Uwe to the fact that everything was not as it should be. When the dwarf turned to face his apprentice, he could see down the barrel of the gun.

In that moment, Uwe's face crumbled, the stone expression giving way. James had never seen that look in all his life.

In that moment, he looked to his friend as if the two had never met and could not, for all his efforts, prove to himself otherwise.

In that moment, winter whirled down through the hollow with clamor and discord and cacophony, a dragon's roar in comparison to that endless silence between the hunters.

In that moment, all the mighty dwarf could do was gape in absolute awe of his own naivety.

In the next moment, he whispered to himself and to the wind, "James."

In the moment after, James fired.

A wall erupted from the ground and split them, absorbing the impact of that first shot. Uwe rushed from behind the barrier with his countenance refortified, hefting his shotgun aloft with a bone-shattering cry. The person James watched emerge from that rocky outcrop was not any Uwe he had ever known, so he did not hesitate to wave a flurry of debris between them as the dwarf fired his first shot. Then James fired another two rounds into a veritable squall of earth and ice, and the hunters were upon one another.

James drove Uwe's gun up and away while the dwarf did the same, pressing his pistol towards the sky. In this armed grapple, the older hunter was the first to act. He brought his knee up into James' gut. The young man recoiled, twisting to keep the shotgun pointed away, and slammed his elbow into his opponent's barking face. Before he could capitalize, though, he felt the ground beneath them softening.

Uwe scattered the soil under his feet and tore footing away from him. James, however, planted one palm against the ground, righted himself with a spin, and swept the balance from his adversary. In the next instant, both hunters were on their feet and taking aim once again. Both fired, both dodged, both missed, both lunged for one another again, but the dwarf's swift hand brought out a shortblade to supplement his gun.

Sidestepping the initial slice, James took firm hold of the shotgun—which Uwe could now no longer pump—and the dwarf relinquished the weapon without contest. By the time James had discarded the gun, Uwe was attacking again with every bit of his strength funneling through his blade.

Yang answered the blow, deflecting it, but the reverse strike took James' pistol without incident. Uwe shook his prey's blood onto the previously stainless snow and came again for a second injury, but James' reddened hand released his other blade and they responded with twin howls. Now the three blades whirred in syncopated beats, guided by the warrior-choreographers of this fated dance, a whirlwind of sliding steel and glancing wounds until the white ground beneath each man was no longer pure.

In a flash of blinding darkness as James thrust his dagger forth, he saw not Uwe before him but Lumina, and the mandor cringed from his blade in this reality as Uwe did in his memory. In this waking instant,

James dove from the mandor's spear, brought steel up across her torso, and saw fear dancing in her golden eyes before the illusory memory entangled him once more.

With a bitter grunt, Uwe sustained a shallow cut and reacted with a stomp, a turn, and an arm launched into the air. Alerted by this elemental cue, the ground by James shot up and he narrowly avoided the rising spire of jagged rock. Not to be bested in their element of choice, James solidified his stance and in one, swift movement brought a cluster of rocks streaking from the ground. In his second gesture, just as Uwe steeled himself for the onslaught, James shot his palm out and the stones followed like a row of cannons, launching at meteoric speed toward their target.

Uwe shattered the projectiles into a puff of debris and returned a salvo in like fashion. The rocks drove James back as he deflected and demolished them, and at this distance he could not attack with Yin and Yang, so he unleashed another volley upon Uwe as Uwe did likewise unto him. Most of the slugs of gravel impacted against one another, but some shot forth with such velocity that neither hunter could stop them. Overwhelmed by the battery of debris, each hunter took the blows and staggered to the ground.

In the moment's respite, the bruised combatants lay winded in the red snow.

Around the arena, Holub's vigilant soldiers knelt as the events unfolded below. When the dust settled, Mr. Holub peered from the safety of his icy overhang to see if one or both of them had fallen. An ocean of blood lay between them, more than he thought any one man could produce—but then, they were more than mere men. He expected nothing less of them. Though Uwe bled less from each wound, he had sustained more injuries than his counterpart, so the executor could not determine who had the advantage from his far-away view of the battlefield.

Uwe, though, stood first. James followed suit within seconds, still wheezing steam. The epinephrine rendered him oblivious to the mass of cuts and bruises he'd endured thus far. Aside from the fresh blood that seeped from his brow down into his eyes, he knew nothing of his traumas. He growled like a wild beast when he saw the dwarf draw a dagger with his off hand and begin to charge. The cascade of blood

227

across his body acted as an invitation for the bullish brute. Uwe roared, and James opened his arms as if to embrace him before he bore down, bellowing, and ran out to meet him.

The dwarf ignored the dagger that struck deep into his abdomen just as James ignored the knife that stuck out of his. Even as they tore out the weapons, the two men screamed, blasting air and blood at one another. Their eyes never broke away. They lashed out at each other with arms extended, again, again, again, again, again, again, until all measure of tact had left them. Their calculated movements devolved into savage strikes, motions that knew not the future and its concerns but only this moment, this strike, this kill. Who they were, who they'd been, and who they'd ever be did not matter to either man. Balance was gone and with it any capacity for elementality. The two stumbled around each other, hacking away like something more animal than the basest of beasts.

Suddenly, James saw Lumina and the whole of the church again, a shattered world apart from the illusion, and he managed to stab her once before the nightmare returned.

Uwe's eyes burned, deep and vacuous and black, the way James imagined hell must be. To be trapped in this deadlock, fixated on those indomitable eyes, was exactly how he pictured hell.

The two of them were slowing now. The mutual blood loss gained on them. The ardor their hearts called for their bodies could no longer maintain, so each hunter began to waver as the curtain of Death drew over their performance, but on they fought. They circled, groping and grappling with steel implanted in their flesh until at length Uwe staggered away and back, weak-kneed, and fell.

The titan leaned up, still conscious, as though he might rise again to fight, but his sword fell from his one hand and the grip around his dagger went limp. James struggled to remain upright, begging his body for allegiance as he teetered towards the dwarf. Yin stayed up with what he thought must be its own demonic will, for he did not think that he had the strength to lift it. After an endless shuffle, he fell on one knee beside Uwe, who still lay back on his elbows, and drove the blade into his gut.

The blood came from his parted lips in a gurgle—not a cough— pathetic and repulsive. All the while his eyes did not move from James'. They spoke of mortality, of eternity, and all that was between.

In the instant that followed, they spoke of rage.

The dwarf leapt without warning, retching red, his dagger clutched and poised for the human's throat, gagging, gargling, growling. James did not flinch with anything but exact reprisal. Before the metal could reach his skin, he'd plunged Yang into his oldest friend's chest.

The look that replaced his anger was that of the Uwe he had always known. Stony, stalwart, unflinching, with a neutral smile on his face.

"To the end, James," the hunter heard his mentor sputter. Still, his features did not shift. Softening without warning, James released his grip on Yin and Yang and cradled Uwe as he began to collapse. "Don't let them numb you." His words fell softer than the snow as blood flooded his lung and choked away his voice. "This world. No matter how broken. Faithless. Infidelitous." He shook his head and red overflowed from his lips. "Still worth fighting. Still worth saving."

James crouched over Uwe without speaking. For the rest of his life, he'd never have the words for that moment. He did not weep or look away. He looked into Uwe's black eyes until the end.

Soon, his dream state began to dither as Mr. Holub called down into the hollow. James did not remember what he'd said, though he remembered seeing his hand shoot up to give the command to kill him, even in spite of what he'd done for them.

He remembered the movement of the riflemen all around him. He remembered sensing their intent. He remembered standing, somehow, despite himself, turning his head skyward, and seeing the moon for what seemed like the first time, full and pale and ghostly, a god's eye watching him, seeing his crimes, delighting in his betrayal.

He remembered the fear that came with the epiphany that he must hide himself away from that eye. The rage that came from the realization that he'd never be *able* to hide from it.

He remembered feeling for the mystic strength of elementality. His garnet did not glow. He was an ancient—he didn't need it.

He remembered the earth swallowing him, absorbing the gunfire that sought to end him. He remembered that same earth reaching out and devouring Holub's soldiers, one and all. The entire ridge fell level with the hollow in the quake, leaving him with thirty-three men to dispatch.

He remembered flying through columns of earth like a gargoyle, guided by purpose alone, obliterating every man he came across with detachment. Without Yin or Yang or any firearm, he destroyed them all. By hand. By earth. Until he'd left none alive.

He remembered descending upon Čeněk Holub, having been trapped under fallen rubble in the initial tremor, and he remembered the fool pulling his sidearm on him. He remembered crushing that arm. He remembered taking his throat in one hand, his broken arm in the other, and asking him:

"Who else knows I was here?"

The gnarled man wept with uncertainty, responding only when the hunter tightened his grip. "No one," he bawled.

"What do they know?" Again, he leaned on the man's injuries to elicit a reply.

"They know that Uwe Löwe had help hunting Solomon," Čeněk sobbed. "An ancient. They'll know he didn't kill us all himself," he added, desperate.

James remembered moving away, realizing at that very moment that he could not return home with this crime haunting him. He could not hide from Mythic or from the Cult in plain sight, so he resolved, without hesitation, to head north to the land he knew until his name was safe from suspicion and retribution.

"I'm sorry," Čeněk choked out. James took him in from a distance. "You have to understand. What the ancients can do...can you imagine what the Cult could do with this sort of power?" The executor understood the hunter's need for survival and did not blame him when he began to grip the earth all around them. "Only..." he began and brought the hunter's eyes back to him. "You shouldn't cast." He nodded to himself. "Not as strong as you are. They'll know you're one of them."

James remembered nodding to the executor with red eyes and a heavy heart before he cast one final time and opened up the mountainside to consume them. Uwe Löwe, Čeněk Holub, Solomon, and the soldiers all fell down into the depths to be covered in white innocence until the end of the Earth.

* * * *

Lumina afforded the weary hunter no repose as he rebounded from his mind into all the disarray of reality. The church was in ruins, every wooden structure splintered, the altar shattered, and its matron as ruined as her sacred tomb.

She struck with her glaive as ferociously as she had the last hundred strikes, but somehow the blow came slower than James remembered them. It was weaker. Above all, it was more desperate, for the mandor now fought not some clever hunter, not some powerful warrior, but an ancient. A god among men. A demon she could not hope to defeat.

And because the hunter had grappled with his inner demons as well as this external fiend, he'd dealt Lumina another half-dozen wounds to tax her failing body so that when she struck out, it was not a deathblow falling upon him but a feeble staving off of death.

He avoided the first assault, sliding Yang across one arm, causing her to release the hold on her weapon once and for all. The second lunge missed him, and he slashed the creature's face. Lumina looked, broken, to her attacker. She had nothing left to give.

With her body in such disrepair, her mind also waned. She shook with fear and weakness before her arms reached out one last time, too slow to catch an ancient, too slow to catch a hunter, too slow to catch anything.

James slid beneath her final strike with Yin and Yang streaking alongside one another and brought the blades up to scissor into her jaw. The momentum of the blow carried with such force that he lifted the mandor off the ground and into the air. There she hung suspended like a true martyr, motionless.

Lumina Benedictus was doubtlessly powerful. While she yet lived, he felt her like a parasite in the reaches of his mind, burrowing, squirming, fighting. James found himself smiling, if only in derision. "To the end," he echoed and stared up into the mandor's eyes.

"Had I known you were an ancient," she mindspoke, "I would never have committed such a shameless suicide."

"It's not too late," the hunter quieted her. "What is Casey planning?"

"Fitting," Lumina mused, ignoring him. "Adure and Aias were rivals a century ago. Now their descendants inherit their enmity."

"Tell me," James pleaded, feeling her consciousness begin to slip.

"If I devoted my entire life to a single cause and betrayed it at the very end, what would be the point?" she wondered as much to herself as to the hunter. "A sinner in either faith."

"Casey left you here to die. You could help me kill him."

"Oh, no," she said. "Revenge makes for such a sorry epitaph." Her eyes darted over his for a moment. "Was it worth it for you? Do you think your friend was a Cultist?" she asked. "Uwe?"

James had no response for her.

"To the end, then," she said, and he felt her fade fast.

The hunter panicked. Still holding her body aloft, he panted, refusing to believe that she could pass without redemption and leave his hunt in deadlock again. He began to withdraw his blades before Lumina flickered back to life.

"Parliament," she confessed. "He's going to destroy Parliament."

With that final plea, the hunter tore his blades from the mandor's skull and Lumina fell, lifeless, to the ground. In death, her eyes haunted just as they did in life, glowing golden, tapered like swords, penetrating as far as the soul. Those eyes could feed a man's nightmares for an eternity.

Chapter Thirty
The Pact

It occurred to James as he stood over the mandor's acrid carcass that no more than a few minutes could have passed since he'd first attacked her. All the same, the battle had seemed to last hours, so when she finally fell silent and the needless prying at his brain subsided at last beneath the surface of the warm air, he moved first to sit in one of the smashed pews.

His heart, still racing, ebbed graciously at the rest, and he felt his limbs deaden as in sleep, though he clung to the waking world. The glow from the bordering candles coaxed him into slumber, but the hunter vied to remain alert. He had come out relatively unscathed, although his mental fatigue drained the very thoughts from him. Still, he did not have the energy to address the myriad concerns that had risen around him as the mandor fell, as much as he might need to.

With a long and empty sigh, the hunter glanced to his kill and then upwards, as if the vaulted ceiling would advise him. The structure only echoed his moan back at him, reflecting his exhaustion. This place held no more answers for him, but the figures standing at the rear of the chapel might.

"Rested?" spoke one of them with veiled agitation. The gravel in Faolan's voice betrayed his identity as he approached the hunter from behind. James turned to confirm his suspicion, seeing the incensed prince rushing towards him. "You fucking moron." His tone revolted James as much as his visage.

He stood to defend himself, but the elf drew a dagger to his throat before he could protest.

"You understand there's a specific protocol for removing a consciousness *safely* from your own?" he spat at the vulnerable man before him. "Instead of just expelling him into the goddamn void?" Somewhat satisfied with the emotional release, Faolan returned his knife to a holster along his leather vest and stepped back. "I said you were valuable, not indispensable." He read the stupor on the hunter's face before a twisted smile stole across his own. "Of course," he glanced back at the two members of his guard still standing at the rear, "that was before I learned you were an ancient." He laughed as James' eyes twitched. "Aias' heir."

The hunter's vigor returned without warning. He readied his daggers as if he were still under attack. "How long have you been here?"

Faolan raised his hands in deference. "Long enough to see you kill a mandor. Larva or not, that's damned impressive." James settled, however slightly, upon spying the two sentinels at the exit lifting their sidearms. The prince, however, ignored them. He examined James as if he were discovering a new toy. "You fought through the haze?" he asked.

James nodded.

"And the havoc?"

"Yes."

"Incredible," the prince reveled. "I haven't heard of many people strong enough to do that." After a moment, though, he made the startling connection: "You're the ancient who killed Čeněk Holub." The hunter's eyes widened. "I don't blame you. From what I've heard, the man was a terrible executor. Good in the sense that he loved to *execute*, but..." he shifted his eyes between the hunter's, trying to discern the truth. "I imagine he cried wolf and you only did what came naturally."

James stayed silent, but the prince read the story in the lines of his face.

"Of course, your secret's safe. You're a good man, James. Beast of a man. Noble beast." He placed a hand on the hunter's shoulder, hoping to put him at ease. "Take it from someone who's seen what makes you tick. Muirgel. Ysolt," he signaled to the guards. They holstered their weapons without delay. "See to the prisoner below. And the Cultists." The elves marched past the ancient and the prince to the cellar. "As for you," Faolan winked to his new plaything, "I do want you to appreciate how close you came to killing me today."

"You tried to—"

"Or at least lobotomizing me."

"You—"

"Thankfully, I was lucky enough—"

"You were going to kill Leon!" James cried, defiant.

Faolan gave a flippant shrug. "One life," he explained.

"One life that *I* would have taken. One innocent life."

"What was Holub?" His jab provoked a vicious glare. "Come on, James. You were in the Cult of the Apocalypse for a mere two hours. You know there are no innocent lives." As if in response to the remark, a gunshot rang out in the chamber below. James jarred towards the source while Faolan stood firm. "Had you been able to overcome your own selfish apprehension, we might have learned more about what the Cult intends to do next." Another shot sounded. And another.

"What the hell are you doing?" the hunter railed. He stammered for further words, found none, and stared at the hatch down to the basement as a final blast went out. After a few moments, the opening lifted and the two guards emerged, carrying a wounded elf wrapped in Muirgel's jacket between them.

"He's all right," she reported as they moved across to the nave.

The elven man looked up to regard his saviors. As he sighted James, a modicum of color filled his thin cheeks. "James."

"Leon," the hunter nodded, filled with relief and unease at the same time.

"Now you've saved my sister and myself," he mumbled as the elves helped him down the aisle. Then, to himself, "James McCrary," before the sentinels took him outside.

Upon their departure, the hunter turned his anger onto Faolan once more. "You saw them all get brainwashed, Faolan. They didn't have to die."

The prince scoffed, turning to the altar and the auburn corpse lying alongside it. "They'd find their way back to the Cult some way. They always do." He peered back into James' rocky face. "If it helps you sleep," he postulated, "I'm sure they were just shooting the chains off Leon there." The farfetched theory made him snicker. "The rest of my guard will be along soon to..." he skirted the line between amusing himself and consoling James, "purify them. We'll burn any vestige of the Cult from their bodies. Bury the sin. Leave the wickedness at the bottom of the English Channel." The hunter did not smile. "James, God will sort them out." His last play on words entertained Faolan past his associate's level of comfort.

"I feel like a lot of elves use atheism as an excuse for being assholes."

Faolan emerged from his laughter to address the allegation. "If God exists, he has a sicker sense of humor than I do."

James shook his head, disturbed by the notion.

"You believe in God, James?" the elf asked, shocked.

"Let's get on with the hunt."

"All right, then. Let's."

"With Lumina dead, Casey won't have any initiates to help him attack Westminster. You think he'll call it off?"

"No," Faolan rebutted, "he's more than capable of acting alone. If anything, it will force his hand. He'll strike sooner rather than later, but I'm wondering what reason he could even have for attacking it."

"Integration," the hunter affirmed. "He's gonna force the British government to acknowledge Mythopians."

Faolan's face soured. "The Cult of the Apocalypse is infamous in Mythopia, but Earthers know nothing about it. That secrecy has made them more dangerous here than anywhere else. Why would they want six billion more people to know about them?"

Rattled by the concern, James groped for an explanation. Gaining inspiration from a remembered passage in Walter's tome, his face lit up. "The uprising."

"Impossible." The prince's face darkened.

James nodded, encouraged by his opposite's denial. "This is how it starts."

A moment of silence hung over them as the possibility revealed itself to the banished prince. Preparing for this moment was his life's work, his royal inheritance, and his greatest fear. To come so unexpectedly…

"It will not come to pass," the elf asserted. Even as he spoke, the crimson earring on his good ear began to glow red. "Not before my very eyes. Take me to Walter Brimford."

"And tell him what?"

The resolve showed through Faolan's horrid scars like a beacon through shadow. "I've been hunting Casey, as well. I tracked him to this church, helped you kill the mandor, and now," his impish grin widened as fire leapt to his fingertips. "*Now* we end this farce forevermore." Around them, the candles danced before their lordly master. The flames lifted and lurched, threatening to engulf the church if they escaped their keeper's steady command. "I'll burn this world to the ground before I let the Cult do it. James McCrary," he said, extending his burning hand.

Without thinking, the hunter took hold of the elf's emblazoned arm. The fire swept over his outstretched limbs, but Faolan restrained the heat with virtuosic control. There the men stood in an unspoken pact, beset by red-hot vapors, untouched by the ire of the flame, until the prince drew back and sealed the accord with words.

"Not since Vaos was killed has a Ciric prince fought alongside an ancient. Your forefather and mine."

James responded with a stark smile galvanized by Faolan's intensity. Upon seeing this, the banished prince followed suit and, along with his joy rushed his rage. The candles erupted into life and the fire raced along the walls of the mandor's temple, dousing the church in cleansing flame.

They stood awhile amidst the orange embers of the basilica, still grinning. Faolan rested a smoldering hand on the hunter's shoulder.

"Let's end this," he said.

Part IV
On Killing

Chapter Thirty-One
The Deity

"You realize," Faolan cautioned Xiang as he exited the elevator with the courier's pistol in his face, "that you can't shoot a fire elementalist." Xiang's eyes narrowed. "I can keep the powder from igniting," Faolan explained.

The instant Xiang recognized the man before him, his face blanched with fear. "Faolan Ashtongue—" he started.

"The banished prince," his target interrupted and shouldered his way through the hallway. He could not be prevailed upon to introduce himself to every terror-stricken individual he encountered. Marching into Mythic headquarters with a dozen armed elves, he'd more than startled the reader situated at the front desk. Now, even without his posse, he'd shaken Walter Brimford's right-hand man to his very core. He clicked his tongue against his teeth as he strode by Xiang. He was followed by the hunter who did his best to reassure the courier.

"It's fine," he promised. "He's with me."

Embarrassed, Xiang collected himself and went along with them to the sealed door of Walter's office. "Here," he said, moving to activate the hidden switch.

Faolan stopped him. He'd had enough of his elves visit Mythic to know the headquarters' inner workings. Smiling to himself, he reached into the inner lining of his vest and produced a silver locket adorned with a small diamond. He shook the amulet in Xiang's face as the gem warmed. The courier answered with a scowl while the prince tapped his index fingers together to initiate the electric current. He then ran a hand over the hidden mechanism. The door unlocked, Xiang slid it away, and Walter greeted his guests with outstretched arms.

"You're early," he rasped through his typical grin, acknowledging James in particular. He did not stand to meet them but invited the group in with the warmth of his voice.

James pressed forwards into the room, shrugging. "Had to make up for last night, right?" The sun beamed above the city skyline in spite of the many clouds that marred its rays. Even the tint of the executor's glass wall couldn't hide the light. The hunter drank in the warmth with vampiric hunger. The end of the hunt now in sight, his soul was burning. It needed all the sustenance it could gather.

The executor noted his vitality, much in contrast to his own. "It's a relief to see you in sound body and mind." His delight swept through the room alongside his smile. Despite it, though, James could see that his strength had waned even more since the night before. As he turned to Faolan, Walter's smile subsided. "Now what catastrophe has brought the prince of Cire back to Mythic?"

"Banished prince," Faolan muttered, motioning for James to explain.

"He's been hunting Casey," he announced. "Working opposite us this whole time."

Walter nodded, accepting the information and filling the gaps in his own understanding. "They can't know everything of our operation," he probed the hunter, his brow lowered.

"No." James steadied him, having kept word of the Eye to himself. "But they found the church. He got there just in time to help me kill the mandor."

Walter's head rolled back against his high-backed chair. "Then the infiltration wasn't without complications."

"There were some hiccups..." His eyes flashed to the elf's. "But we found out where Casey's going next."

"You—" The executor's jaw slackened. Before he could regain his faculties, he found himself stumbling to his feet, mouth agape before the hunter who continued to meet and exceed his expectations time and time again. "James!" he clamored. "Well, out with it, then."

"He's going to attack Westminster."

In spite of the gravity of the hunter's words, the executor seemed at first happy about the revelation. After a moment, his misshapen expression hardened into one that indicated not fear or concern but confusion. He opened his mouth to speak as his forehead furrowed in perplexity, but he stopped to consider his thoughts a few seconds longer. Meanwhile, James looked to Faolan with similar puzzlement. Xiang, unfazed by the announcement, leaned against the door with a sigh.

"Brimford," the elf began, attempting to reach him, "you understand what we've just told you?"

"Of course," the executor chided, reeling back into his seat. "But…why?"

"The uprising," James enlightened him. "It's starting."

While he trusted the hunter, although he had the greatest confidence in his abilities, something within Walter made him doubt that this was the fabled insurrection. "This is no uprising," he decided. The others in the room attended his words. "I lived through what I thought was the uprising. In Salamance," he recalled, addressing Faolan. "Years ago. When the uprising comes, not a man alive will have had a moment's warning. I promise you."

The hunter marked the executor's demented look as he made his pronouncement. "What makes you say that?"

A glimmer of uncertainty shone through the old man's countenance. His age manifested for a moment of weakness and dread. In the grip of that instant, he let out a death rattle of a sigh. "The Cult of the Apocalypse thrives on chaos. Vaos paved the way for his uprising by springing from anonymity and bringing every world power to its knees. In seven days, he made the greatest nations in the planet's history utterly helpless, and in that pandemonium, he became a god."

"Yes," Faolan added, moving over to Walter's desk as he spoke, "he used the mayhem of his conquest to cripple any who would oppose him, not because he was a god but because the people made him one, and until he was killed he might as well have been one, but chaos was not his goal. It was his weapon." He caught the executor's eyes for a fleeting second. "Fear was his goal."

"So?" Walter prodded, spurring on the prince's line of thought.

"Casey is an ancient." He made the mistake of looking to James, but he quickly corrected his focus, bringing it back to the executor. "And almost every ancient on record has displayed a clear God complex." He thought to exclude his present company, choosing instead to quiet the impulse. "He's going to do the same thing Vaos did centuries ago. Destroy, divide, and be deified."

James seemed satisfied by the prince's logic, but Walter remained unconvinced. "What do you think, Xiang?" he asked the silent courier idling against the far wall. "You've no opinion on this?"

Xiang made no motion as he answered the executor with his trademark composure. "Fear only helps to control men's hearts. It cannot bring about the end of the world."

"Well said," Walter commented. He let the ensuing silence hang to further discredit James and Faolan's testimony.

"But what if fear's not the only weapon he has?" James asked the prince.

Walter's face softened. "James," he checked him.

Faolan jolted at the mention. "What are you talking about?"

The hunter rushed to take back his words. "I—"

"What weapon?" Faolan went on, shocked that he could have missed so much during his stay in the hunter's mind. "He stole a weapon from Mythic?" He poured over the other men's eyes, desperate for an answer. "The bombs?" he inquired of Walter. His eyes shook but did not shift. "No, it's more valuable than that. More unique. But the only artifact of consequence in Mythic's vaults is..." The prince's throat seemed to sting at the realization.

The executor, seeing the secret surface, answered him before he could say it aloud. "The Eye of Vaos."

Again, the banished prince's destiny darkened in his mind's eye. "Casey Aduro," he thundered, "has the Eye. Of Vaos."

As the elf stood in muted trepidation, James recognized that the prince of Cire might possess more knowledge about the gem than any one of them. Walter, too, came to this conclusion. Unlike the hunter's, though, his eyes did not beg for an explanation.

"I knew I never worked with Mythic for a reason. I told you personally to seal away that abomination years ago." He laughed, tickled by the audacity of it all. "The Eye of Vaos is made up of a very rare substance with *very* unusual properties. The same substance that's in the blood of every ancient." This time he did not keep himself from looking at James. "What gives them their...abilities. For most non-ancients, the Eye is just a useless jewel. For Casey, though..."

"He can use the sixth element?" James cut him short.

The prince seemed confused by the notion. He saw the hunter look to Walter for validation and scoffed. "You're all idiots. You have no idea what's going on here."

The executor planted his hands onto his desk and lifted himself up again. "Nothing, if we can help it."

Faolan watched the addled man, as baffled as the hunter by his sudden frailty. "Walter," he started after the executor, clear and precise with his words, "are there any other gems, artifacts, anything in Mythic's possession that are made up of the same material as the eye?"

"No, Mythic has nothing else like it."

Soothed but not at complete rest, the prince pondered for a moment. "Westminster?" he confirmed with James, who nodded. "The Tower of London's not far from there," he muttered to himself. "We can stop him." His attention came back to the room. "I think I know what Casey's planning," he announced. "I'll need the night to investigate a hunch, but at the very least we know he is going to attack Westminster. And soon."

"Tomorrow," Walter stated, absolute in his assertion. "If he's going to do it, it will be tomorrow. Without fail. We cannot go another day with him loose."

Wrinkling his disfigured forehead, the prince wondered how the executor could be so sure.

"One of his visions we know about," James informed him, sensing his bafflement. "And a gargoyle we captured. They're with him, so if Casey's going all out, we can expect them, too."

"Yes," Walter concurred, "but we'll need every resource at our disposal to repel an ancient and a coven of gargoyles."

Faolan smiled. He'd been waiting for his opportunity to play hero the entire meeting. "My royal guard stands ready to resist the Cult of the Apocalypse." He enjoyed watching the wonder drip down the executor's features. "It is their sworn duty, even above protecting me."

"How many?" Walter asked him.

"Twelve. All top-rate soldiers, skilled in arms both modern and antiquated. Any one of them could contend with Casey, I'm sure."

"For the most part, firearms will be useless against him," the executor reminded them.

"I agree, but for the gargoyles they will do nicely. As for Casey, the three of us." He spoke matter-of-factly, without a hint of jest. "Xiang, James, and I—"

"Four," Walter corrected him.

"Four," the prince quoted, more than a little dubious of the declaration as Walter struggled to stay on his feet. "All powerful. All ready to annihilate him. He doesn't stand a chance."

"Outstanding," Walter gasped as he drifted back down into his chair.

James bowed his head to him. "Vaos dies in the streets of London. Once and for all."

"Xiang?" Faolan petitioned the stagnant courier. "Will you join us?"

"Xiang?" James repeated, extending a hand to him.

Xiang turned his head up to them. "We will end it tomorrow," he admitted and sank back into his original position.

"It's settled, then." Faolan clapped his hands together. "I'll have my guard establish a perimeter around the palace immediately." He turned to leave the room. "I'd advise you to have your men in position by sunrise tomorrow." He hesitated before adding, "What's left of them."

Walter let the pain of the affront show on his face. "And how many have you lost?" he wondered aloud after the elf.

"Not yet enough," Faolan called over his shoulder. He turned to regard James. "When you find yourself in danger at the brink of the abyss, I'll be there to aid you. Aside from that," he added and smiled, "I'll see you when it comes time to kill Casey." With that, Faolan Ashtongue strode to the elevator at the end of the hall to gather his forces.

Alone, the three members of Mythic watched one another in silent anticipation of the day ahead. The hunter's heart shook with ravenous lust while the courier's trembled with anxiety and the executor's tapped with desperation.

"Are we ready for this?" the hunter asked Walter, hoping to break the lull.

In answer, he only sighed. Without speaking, the executor gathered a few papers from his desk into a satchel and lumbered once more onto his feet. "I'm going to the Grey Gargoyle," he announced, hobbling to the lift. He spoke as if the pub would be his final resting place. "I'd like for you both to join me." He turned with his signature smile stretching through the heavy dolor of his heart.

Xiang, even in his stoic indifference, could not refuse the old man's request. "Of course," the courier consented, and James went along as well.

"It's not as if I think I won't survive tomorrow's ordeals," he swore, sensing the charity in the young men's support, "but I'd like for us to enjoy at least one more night all the same."

James laughed with him, though the executor's sudden despondency concerned him. He'd aged a hundred more years in these past few days. A sense of finality lingered in his tone, in everything he said, in each word he uttered. It reminded him of Alvin, and further of Uwe. He shook the memory from his thoughts. Xiang's attention, however, stayed on Walter, and Walter's eyes gazed back down the hallway through the vast pane of glass across his office.

He watched the sun hover in the sky, bereft of concern while the clouds paraded in front of its face. The great, burning star would not set for some time. He saw no poetry in the moment, no deeper meaning in the orb's inevitable descent. He never had. Still, he wondered how it maintained its power, how it could burn through eons of fuel for a thousand thousand lifetimes and never lose its brilliance. And yet it did so without fanfare. It simply sank, day after day, beneath that same horizon as it always had since the Earth had blinked into existence and the sun had risen that first, revolutionary time.

Without turning from the window, he asked the hunter and courier a question which neither of them could answer.

"How long do we burn?"

Chapter Thirty-Two
The Martyr

That night, the moon was asymmetrical, oblong, and incomplete. It looked less like a smile and more like a rock floating above the Earth in sunlight and shadow. James watched it for some time, trying for whatever reason to make out a likeness but finding none in the shapeless mass. That night, it was not as if the moon were smiling. That night, the moon was simply the moon.

As he stood in the cold outside of Robert's pub, forsaking the company of his friends to search for secrets in the sky, James was no closer to settling the rapid fluttering in his chest. It came whenever he gazed upon the moon, night or day. It came whenever he saw it in the sky, in random pictures, in his dreams. The feeling came no matter how the satellite appeared: as a grin, a laugh, an eye. Peace came two nights every lunar month when the body vanished into its pall. Then it became a sickle, a scythe, a smile, jaws opening slowly, inexorably, and closing with the same conceit. During those days, it reminded him of the hunt, life waning while death waxed, always in balance, absolute. The life he bought with Uwe's years ago he owed to the hunt, but one day he would fall under the black shroud he so liked to peer beneath. The moon acted as the herald of this fate.

The hunter stared up at the harbinger, understanding the omen and accepting it, but he refused to flinch until the survivalist pang in his heart receded. That night it did not.

He heard a sudden swell of noise from behind him as the door of the

Grey Gargoyle opened, a jukebox playing the songs of some time-lost pioneers of British rock and the members of Mythic laughing and carrying on in the pub that had been cleared out just for them.

"James," came a light voice. For a second, the hunter connected it to the moon before he recognized Michelle. She had an unmistakable goodness in her voice, a clear desire to help, but when he turned to her he made out a cross expression and remembered how wrathful the reader could be. "Aren't you cold?" she asked, her ire outweighing her concern.

James laughed at the idea. "Warm enough."

"Well, come inside anyway." She folded her arms within the doorway. "Get out of your head for a bit."

Wishing that he could, the hunter closed one eye in a gesture of refusal.

"Come on, then," Michelle repeated. "Last thing we need is you coming down with something." The maternal command chilled him, as much as he expected it of her.

"Guess I should keep an eye on Robert's drinks," he surrendered.

"Actually," she started as he moved by, "he stopped after the first."

James turned to her with astonishment. She smiled back.

When he entered the pub, the temperature did not seem to change much. His blood cooled to match the shift, and the change in condition went unnoticed. Besides, the hunter found the Scotsman who was rounding up another set of drinks behind the bar to be more interesting.

At a table in the middle of the bar sat Xiang, Walter, and Alvin, all wrapped in warm conversation. James heard Michelle bolt the front door behind them and watched Robert bring the beverages over to the group. He set one down for the courier, executor, and the reader as she took a seat. The liquor, it appeared, had calmed Walter's earlier tremors. He found a strained peace under its influence and invited another beverage.

"How about you, brother?" Robert lifted a glass of whisky to him.

The hunter only shook his head. He did not want to rely on alcohol to calm his body. Though his heart's upheaval proved exhausting, the possibility that a single drink might impair his senses the following day was even more unsettling. The last time he'd contended with Casey, one drink had allowed the other ancient to match his speed with ease. This time he'd need his full focus, all of his speed, and every last bit of strength he could conjure.

"Water," he suggested. The initiate gave him an approving nod. While the others chattered, James watched him toss the glass of whisky out behind the bar. Moments later, Robert approached him with two cups of fresh water. "You're not drinking, either?"

"I'm a good bartender," he defended himself. "I'm not always drinking. It's just that when pyromaniacs and killers are running about with guns and swords, it can get a bit overwhelming."

"You're a terrible Scot," James remarked.

"Yeah?" he marveled, his eyebrows high. "Well, you're a worse black. I haven't seen you steal a thing since I met you."

"What are you talking about?" the hunter sneered. "We stole a letter off a guy I almost killed."

"Hmm," the initiate mused, impressed, before his expression turned to one of troubled puzzlement. "We have the worst arguments."

"We do," James chuckled. Inspired by the moment, he raised his glass. "To strange arguments."

"Aye," agreed the Scotsman, tipping his glass.

"Bad luck," Walter tolled, watching the ritual from the table. The pub grew still. "It's bad luck to toast with water," he warned them. The other guests sat restless until the executor smirked and proceeded, "But it's good luck to toast with friends." He lifted his drink. As the tension in the room dissipated, he concluded, "To friends!" Everyone followed suit, repeating the salute. Then Walter nodded to Robert as he and the hunter sat down.

"Uh," the barkeep stammered, caught off guard, "I liked yours best."

"Come on," Michelle encouraged while James nudged him.

"All right, then. Jimmy says I should act more Scottish, so…" He cleared his throat. "Slainte mhor agus a h-uile—"

"Not *that* Scottish," James interjected.

"Fine, fine." He rolled his eyes and prepared another. "May the best ye've ever seen be the worst ye'll ever see. May a wee mouse ne'er leave your pantry with a teardrop in its wee eye; May ye always be jist as happy as we wish ye always to be…and may ye always have at least one Earth to call home, if not two." He and the guests tipped their drinks.

"Very nice touch," Michelle praised him, backed by the others.

"Mythopia is as much your home as it is ours."

"Hear, hear," Walter reiterated.

Robert absorbed the sentiment with an unprecedented smile. It comforted him more than he thought it would have. He started to thank them but felt a more effusive response welling up in his throat. "Michelle?" he gestured to the reader, choking down his emotion.

"Oh," the reader giggled, understanding the trend but resenting the attention. She took a moment to imagine a decent toast then looked up to see everyone fixated on her. "I can hear all of you," she chastised them. The others detracted their eyes, laughing. After another few seconds, she lifted her head and shrugged. "To the mind," she conceded. "Clear as day when you're above the surface, but black as night underneath."

"Appropriate," Alvin O'Hare mused from the next seat at the table. Knowing himself to be a man of few words, he delivered a simple toast, saying, "To life," and his meager laconism had all the significance of one hundred years of words. The group met his glass in silence, took their respective drinks, and smiled at the old man.

Soon, though, all eyes fell on Xiang. He'd scarcely spoken for the duration of the evening. He did seem more lively than in less casual settings, but if the pilot was laconic, then the courier was altogether mute. As if to challenge Alvin's brevity, he only lifted his glass into the air. The others did the same, he nodded, and he downed the rest of his drink.

"Guess some of you need new drinks already?" the attentive pub owner asked. Walter and Xiang held up their glasses. Alvin had emptied his as well but chose to abstain from another round. He smacked his lips before requesting a cup of water. "Right," Robert answered and turned back to the bar.

In the brief instant he faced the windowed front door, his eye caught something in the dark outside which it refused to ignore. Even as he moved it lingered. The signal, however, did not reach him until the mass outside shifted, raised a hand, and rapped on the glass.

Xiang lurched to his feet with his pistol drawn before the initiate could freeze. He understood that he would not be able to see the figure in any detail from his vantage but did not intend to leave whatever it was with that advantage for long.

"Wait!" Michelle shrieked as she heard the safety click off of his gun. She delayed his trigger finger for but a moment.

"Stop," Walter declared, but Xiang had already trained his gun on the interloper in front of the pub.

Only James moved fast enough to stop him. The hunter swept across the ground with a single surging step and threw his arms over the courier's. Xiang felt his weapon drop and released his hold on the trigger lest he invite some misfire, and James tore the gun from him as the knock came again, louder this time.

"Look," Michelle went on, having been afforded a little extra time. She could feel the man's familiar mind from a distance. "Thomas!" she called out as she moved to the door. "You're absolutely mental." She tumbled the lock and ripped the door open. In from the cold stepped Commander Bailey in a navy blue dress shirt stained with scarlet as well as a pair of black slacks. The only detail different from his uniform was the telling sling he wore on his butchered right arm.

"Bailey," the executor reeled, more astonished than outraged. "What the hell are you doing?"

"Doped-up fool," Xiang remarked, the irony lost on him, before snatching his gun back from the hunter.

"You should be in hospital," Michelle scolded, securing the door.

"Just got out of hospital," the pale-faced commander smirked. "Checked out early with some complimentary medication."

"You almost lost your arm," she reprimanded him further, approaching the man as he stumbled over to the bar.

"Oh, it's pretty much lost," he reported. "Completely lost. Can't even feel it." In a moment of staged grief, he cried out, "I lost my shooting arm!" The others softened at the mention. "And I don't mean guns," he snickered, recoiling from the façade.

"You're delirious." The executor forced him to sit.

"Like a fox," the wounded soldier responded. "What are we drinking to? Hopefully finding the bastard who did this."

"He's attacking Westminster tomorrow," Walter informed the mercenary, feeling obligated to tell him.

"Good," Bailey came back. "Meds will have worn off by then." He nodded to himself, still figuring out the details in his head. "I'll be good to go."

"Are you serious?" asked Walter. "You think you're fighting? In this state?"

Bailey's tone dropped. "And you are?" He pressed his good hand against the table and sank his eyes into Walter's. "You owe me this one. Someone's gonna pay for what happened last night."

"You'll hurt more than you'll help," James interrupted.

The mercenary turned upon him with canine tenacity. "I saved your arse, McCrary. Last night I watched that car park fall and saw good men falling with it, but I'm still alive. I can still shoot a gun. I can still kill a man. You can't take a day off when the world might end tomorrow." James glanced from Bailey to Walter, shaking his head. The executor agreed with him without moving or speaking, but the soldier could still sense their aversion. "He has to pay."

"We'll handle it," Walter promised.

"He has to—"

"He will."

"For them!"

"I know."

"For every..."

"I set the bombs," said Walter.

James almost missed the confession. The rest of the room turned to the executor even later. Not a single one could voice their confusion in the moment that followed before Bailey spoke up.

"You what?" he asked.

"The bombs were mine," he repeated. His eyes were too heavy with guilt to lift to the wronged commander. "Commissioned some of your men to plant them. Set them off myself."

James unleashed his mind and it darted past the facts and over the gaps in logic. "But you weren't..." He looked to Michelle and Robert, realizing that neither of them could vouch for the executor's whereabouts the night before.

The hunter's instincts moved his hand to Walter's throat before his reason could catch up. It wouldn't have stopped him, in any case. He tore the executor from his seat, launching the table aside, and pinned him against the bar. His eyes bore down with murderous intent, his grip tightened, and he felt half a dozen arms jerk him from his target.

"James, no!" Robert cried, dashing behind the bar to catch his eye while the courier, reader, and pilot pulled at him. Nothing could stop the beast at that moment until James felt a chunk of metal press against his neck and heard the safety click off Xiang's gun. Still holding Walter's eyes in his, the hunter released him, staggered back, and fumbled for a chair, still panting.

Xiang kept his gun drawn while he helped Walter to his feet, but the others stood at a distance in light of the man's revelation. The executor collapsed into the chair opposite the hunter and caught his breath as well.

"Can you forgive me?" he panted, but the hunter's eyes would never stop condemning him. He switched tactics: "Can you blame me?"

"You tried to kill him," Michelle said, rallying to the hunter's side.

"Casey," he defended himself. "It should've killed Casey." He turned to James. "You'd give your life to stop him?" He took the silence as an affirmation. "How is this different?"

"You didn't give him a choice." Robert moved to stand with the two of them, Bailey close behind.

Only Alvin stood neutral between the two groups. With arms raised, the pilot attempted to reclaim the peace. "What we have here," he interpreted, "is not a division of intents." James turned to him with disbelief but trusted the man enough to hear him out. "I don't condone the forcing of a soldier's sacrifice. I've seen it countless times and it's sickened me in every instance, but we have a job to do. That job is to keep this city and this world safe from men who want to kill you for nothing."

Though the hunter and his defenders understood the urgency of their mission, they could not reconcile themselves to the thought of trusting Walter Brimford ever again.

"And what about the ones that did die?" Bailey petitioned. The pain of the betrayal penetrated every ounce of his medication. "They died for nothing."

"Not as long as we're here," Alvin was quick to answer. "He'll answer for what he's done," he said, looking to the executor. "In time. Until then, we owe it to the fallen to complete their mission."

"We are Mythic," Walter intruded. His guilt unloaded, he stood with newfound strength. "We are the Knights of Rafor." James stood to match him, dwarfing him in size. "We stop the Cult at any cost."

"We stop Casey tomorrow," the hunter agreed at length, "but when this is all done, I hope they hire me to hunt you."

"Anything for a pound," he dismissed him in reply.

"Or a fix," added Xiang.

"You're not innocent of this," Michelle reminded the courier.

He smiled, spreading his arms in challenge. "I haven't been innocent a day in my life." His derision of the reader drew the hunter toward him like a moth to flame.

"Why would you help him?" James barked.

"Following orders," he deflected.

The hunter wouldn't accept the dodge. "Are you that much of a goddamn lunatic?"

A squall sprung across the courier's face. "Call me crazy," he spat, resenting the allegation and ambling towards him. "I've tortured dozens, killed more, and I get my thanks in cash. I'll never wear medals. They'll never write about me. Of course, I seem crazy. I'd *have* to be crazy to martyr myself for a world of fucking ungratefuls!" he shouted as he shoved his finger into James' chest.

"Enough of this," Alvin intervened, separating the two. "Xiang. Walter. I'll take you both back. We have a lot of work to do." He hurried the two of them towards the door, but James called out after them.

"You think you're a martyr?" he asked with a very different thought creeping from the back of his heart.

"I know I am," Xiang said without turning. He and the executor exited without any other hindrance.

The hunter, though, hustled after them, the feeling still lingering in his gut. "Walter," he said, emerging into the cold. The others watched him from inside, wary of his rage, but the weather and his intent calmed his blood. He saw Xiang waiting a ways down the empty street and turned so that only the executor could hear him. "You set the bombs," he confirmed.

"Yes," he said, almost apologetic. "I did what I thought I had to."

"You and Xiang went to detonate them," he went on, piecing the narrative together.

"Xiang drove me," he admitted, "but I went myself to do it."

"Casey knew," the hunter explained to him. He couldn't have seen the story more clearly. "How did Casey know?"

The executor followed his logic an instant behind him. He glanced to the street corner, saw Xiang idling there, and turned back to James. "Come to my office at ten sharp. We've additional matters." With that, he went to join the courier.

When the hunter turned back to the pub, the others had already gathered their things to leave. Michelle came outside just behind Alvin.

"James," the pilot said with a nod, rushing to catch up to his passengers. Thinking better of the hasty exit, he turned and added, "I won't let them out of my sight."

"Thank you," James returned, nodding to the old man as he backed away.

"It's been a pleasure." He tipped his hat and took his leave.

The reader pulled the hunter's sleeve from behind him and did not hesitate to embrace him as he wheeled about-face. "I'm sorry," she comforted him. "I can't believe we let this happen. It was right in front of us."

He couldn't disagree but preferred to keep his eyes forward in the wake of the night's events. "It's not the worst thing that's ever happened to me."

She laughed. "I don't doubt it." When she pulled away, her hair fell over her eyes, but he could still see the tears spilling. "Why are we so broken?" she mused, fighting the emotion with a grin.

James brushed the hair from her face and returned the smile. "Still worth saving." He shrugged.

"You're right," she said. "You can save us. I believe in you." The show of faith dazzled the hunter as she lingered close to him. Soon, though, Robert helped Thomas out of the pub and broke the moment. Michelle and James looked to regard the Scotsman and his patient.

"I lied," said Bailey, wiggling his injured arm. "I can feel it. I feel it real bad."

"We should do something before…you know," Robert warned her.

"Right." She stepped away from James to help the injured commander. "I'll take care of him. The two of you need to rest. James," she called as they moved up the pavement, "I'll see you soon." He smiled, confident in the assertion. The hunter waved to them as they left before ducking back into the Gargoyle with Robert.

Inside, the initiate had righted the flipped table but was still working on sweeping up the broken glass they'd ignored. As he retrieved a broom, he saw James sink into the nearest chair. "How ya feel, there, Jimily? You all right?"

The hunter shrugged. "That's it," he stated.

"What's it?" Robert moved to him.

"That's the last time I'll see all of you alive," came the dour response.

"I know you want revenge, brother, but you may have to wait a while."

"Fuck Walter. I don't have time for him right now. I'm talking about everyone else."

"Well, thanks for your enthusiasm," the barkeep conceded, grabbing his jacket. "Guess you're saying what everyone else was thinking."

"No," James corrected him. "I'm saying what I *know*." He locked the initiate's eyes within his own. "Robert, do not come after me tomorrow. At any point. Don't do it."

He tried to chuckle away the hunter's severity, choking instead. "I'm not daft. I don't think I'd help you by putting my life on the line."

"Yeah?" James parried his defense, rolled to his feet, and reached his hand into the Scotsman's coat. When he withdrew his hand, it clutched a pistol. Robert stared at him, wide-eyed. "Who keeps giving you this?" he quipped.

"Hey, I saved you once with it, yeah?" He raised his eyebrows in defiance. "I'll do it again."

"No," he grumbled. "No. Robert, if you try and save me with this again, you're gonna get shot four times in the chest."

"Four times? Bit counterproductive, your whole method of being protective."

"No," he snapped. "I'm saying someone else will do it."

"What?" the initiate critiqued him. "You're trying to...I'm confused."

James shoved him backwards and thought of a new mode of attack.

257

"Some Mythopians can read minds. Some Mythopians can read dreams. *Some* Mythopians can see the future in their dreams."

"You saw me get shot in a dream?" Robert asked as his face filled with doubt.

The hunter sighed and nodded.

"Normal Mythopians don't see the future," the initiate observed, piecing the information together in his head. The discovery pulled his eyelids wide open. "You're an ancient?"

James jerked. Of all the obscure things Robert could possibly know about Mythopians, of course he was well-informed about the qualities of ancients.

"Who else dies?" he demanded. "Walter?"

"Robert—"

"Xiang?"

"Rob—"

"Michelle?"

"No one else dies." He considered the statement. "I don't know. But you don't have to die as long as you don't try and follow me."

"Okay," he agreed, still reeling from the revelation. "Why didn't you tell me you were an ancient?"

"Long story," he explained. "Just do me a favor?"

"Name it."

"Don't tell anyone else."

"Because…?"

"There was an ancient a while back that Mythic suspected of being a Cultist," he remarked. "They tried to have him killed. And they'll keep trying as long as they have any suspicion." It dawned on the hunter that Robert's mind might not be the safest place for this knowledge. "Just don't think about it. They'll read it off of you."

"No worries," Robert assured him and mimed buttoning his lips. After a moment's thought, he gestured buttoning his forehead as well.

James hung his head and sighed again.

"You know what?" the initiate began. "You should get to sleep. You might dream of something that will help you tomorrow." He seemed elated at the potential.

The hunter, though, understood the dread of the future.

"What do you usually see in the visions?"

He turned to the door. "Gargoyles."

* * * *

Always gargoyles.

Uwe had told him once, early on, that a hunter who dreamt of anything but the hunt was a poor excuse for a hunter. If so, then James McCrary was an *extraordinary* hunter.

He felt them near, the great, grey beasts, heard them calling to him. The Stoneslayer. He was back in the black car, taking another leg of a drive that had taken a dozen dreams. Then he arrived at the entrance to their nest, a segment of the sewer torn apart by stone claws and hidden there in the depths of the city. His final arena. The hunting ground of his dreams.

Then he knew this city to be London, and he knew this place to be his destiny.

In a blink, he'd traversed the cavern, down into the dark where only the gargs could see and where their dreary eyes lusted after him. Then deeper into the waterworks, where the black became overwhelming, before he discovered a man standing in the hollow with a red sword slung across his back.

Casey turned, stupefied, as if in a dream.

"You," he gasped, startled like an animal. "Are you dreaming, too?"

James shook from something between apprehension and delight before responding. "Yes."

"You can really see me?" the Cultist questioned him, unable to mask his excitement.

James said only, "Yes."

"So you're an ancient." He smiled. "I've never dreamed with someone else before. I didn't even know there were other ancients here." Then he pulled back the sleeve of his coat. In one hand, he held a great black gem, the Eye of Vaos, in the other a twisted black dagger. On his arm, he displayed a row of incisions all carved into his skin, nine in total. "I started making these cuts," he explained, "one for every year I've been dreaming." He laughed, impressed that his plan had worked. "I only remember making it up to three, so that means it's 1997. Six years after I went to sleep. Smart, huh?"

"That's not bad," James admitted, "but it's still '96 for a couple more weeks."

"Fuck," he said, looking back at his scars like a wristwatch. "Still. This is as far as I've ever dreamed," he confessed.

"Me too." Strange as the circumstance was, the hunter felt governed by decorum. "James," he said, and extended his hand.

"Casey," he replied as he moved through the dark. As he raised his hand, though, his eyes met the knife in his grip. "Oh," he said.

James lowered his hand. "Yeah."

"That's too bad." He lowered his. "We can't change what we see."

"Yeah."

Without another word, the Cultist started stepping back into the black, out of sight. "Well, it was nice meeting you, James."

"You too."

"All right," he said. As he did, the air began to burn around him. "I'll see you around."

Chapter Thirty-Three
The Traitor

To survive as a hunter, an animal must maintain his senses. More than any kind of fighter, a hunter relies upon foresight. Every animal depends on its ability to detect danger before it appears. James' feral instinct sent a premonition over his skin as the Mythic tower pulled his lift into the sky, and he knew more definitively than ever what was to come.

Treachery. He'd seen it before, felt its sting both imagined and actual. The parents who abandoned him, the friends who gossiped about him, the employers who cheated him, the lovers who fled; even a body can betray its master.

When the doors opened and Xiang's handgun greeted him in the hallway, he knew what he could expect.

The courier darted his head to the side, perturbed. "You're late." He holstered the weapon, swiveled around, and started down the corridor. "This is not the day to be late."

The hunter ignored his advice and trailed him into Walter's office as the other man triggered the doors apart. His focus bore so tightly on the courier that he did not hear the elevator being called back immediately behind him.

"You wanted me?" he asked the executor slumped behind the desk.

"Yes," he managed, lurching forwards onto his elbows. The red circles under his eyes bulged, moist like the rest of his dark face. He struggled to breathe through his mouth. "You've been to Westminster already?"

James nodded, eyeing him with visible concern. "I stopped by."

"And?" he waved him on.

"Faolan and his people are in place. Michelle's canvassing minds." He peeked at Xiang as the courier leaned into their exchange. "Nothing so far."

"We'll run mental at this pace," Walter laughed. The laugh became a cough. The cough became a retch. The retch almost pulled him from his chair.

"Walter." The hunter moved to his side, but Xiang reached him first, helping him back against his chair.

"It's nothing," the executor spat between fits. As he settled, he shook his head, wary of the lie. "It's nothing," he tried again. Then he turned his head up to James. "It won't take long. If it does, though, I might not make it that far."

"Won't take long," the hunter assured him.

"I suppose," he replied, shifting his dry eyes to Xiang. "I didn't ask you here for peace of mind."

The courier flinched, wondering if he'd directed the comment at him.

"I figured," James answered, stealing the attention away.

"You're ready, then?" The hunter made no movement, his impulse coiled in his breast. "Xiang," Walter started, and the steely courier stared him down with his arms folded. "You should get to the palace. Provide an extra set of eyes." The suggestion cemented him even more. As the moment rolled over the room, the hunter and the executor exchanged brief looks before the latter blurted out, "Go." Walter's eyebrows burned white over his eyes. "So that we can end this."

Xiang bowed and turned to leave, but the hunter barred his path. When his head came up, he jerked to avoid running into James altogether. His face turned to clay the instant he saw the blades come streaking out of the hunter's coat.

"You're done, Xiang," James murmured, holding Yin and Yang at his sides.

"I'm not sure I know what's happening," the courier said, stepping back. He watched the hunter's eyes narrow as he reached for his sidearm then heard the paralyzing click of a gun behind him. He turned to the executor. Walter's arms braced his gun level with Xiang's chest. "So it ends," the courier conceded. "How?"

"You've been trying to get away from me for days now," he observed. "At every mention of a job, you were the one trying to slip off into the shadows. After every discovery, every revelation, who was trying to run off?" The courier snickered as he listened. "So why now, when there's real work to be done, are you so hell-bent on staying right by my side? Because Casey had two couriers." Xiang's face dropped into a sideward and monstrous glance. "Did he send you to kill me?"

"To manage you," the betrayer responded. "Why would we kill you? We're not done with you yet."

James took in a breath that tightened both his grip and his jaw.

"You came to us so young," Walter sighed. "When did they have time to turn you?"

"They never turned me," he protested. "I've made my own decisions."

"And you've decided to be a monster," James chimed in.

"This room is full of monsters," he proclaimed, moving his hand over his pistol. "I'm the least of them."

"Don't," Walter stammered.

"Are you going to tell him?" the traitor-courier asked Walter. "Or did you plan on shooting me before it got out?"

"Don't turn this on me," he warned him. "I'll answer for what I've done, but the penalty for aiding the Cult can be no less severe."

Xiang looked to the hunter. "He's dying for a reason, you know. He's in withdrawal." He could see the hunter wavering as he turned to the executor for an answer. In that moment, Xiang made his move. As he'd anticipated, neither of the other monsters tried to stop him even as he pulled his gun and pointed it straight back at his old master.

"Put it down," James ordered him, bringing his focus back to the fore. Whatever other wrongs Walter had committed would have to wait for as long as their tenuous alliance remained.

"I'm sorry, Walter," came the courier's calculated speech, "but you are too weak for this." His taunt invited the emphatic shift of the executor's pistol from his chest to his head, at which he only smiled.

"Too pathetic to face the world on your own power. Too soft to even notice when your own gun has been disabled."

Neither the hunter nor the executor flinched.

"No, I noticed," Walter informed him, "which is why I swapped our guns last night." The announcement vacuumed the smug look off Xiang's face. Walter took up a weary grin in his stead. The courier pulled his weapon's trigger to no effect.

"Really?" James said from behind him, causing him to turn. "You thought that was a bluff? You're fast, Xiang, but you don't know about subtlety."

"What do you know about subtlety?" he barked, dropping his sabotaged gun to the ground and stuffing his hands into his pockets.

"I know that necklace better not start glowing or I'll shove it through your chest."

"You know nothing, you animal," he spat, still fumbling. "You kill and fight and kill with no style, no form, no code. You are not a hunter. You are a beast."

"Watch it, now," James cautioned him.

"Fight me like a man," he went on, wiping one hand across his nose with a snort. "Like you love to do."

James leaned in close now, close enough that he felt the courier's desperate snorts reel up to his face, just to reply: "No." He stepped to the side. "Shoot his ass, Walter."

"What is Casey planning?" the executor interrogated him instead. "You might survive this day yet," he continued after a considerable gap.

"Come on, fucker," James coaxed him, but the courier stood fast. His right hand pawed at his nostrils and his left hand dangled at his side.

"What?" Walter pleaded, struggling to conjure meaning from his silence. "What are you doing? What are you doing?!"

"It's over."

"You're finished."

"Come on."

"Just tell us."

"Come out with it."

"Tell me, please," Walter begged him, lowering his gun. "What are you waiting for?"

James saw Xiang turn, saw his teeth flash white, felt a shudder. "Why are you smiling at me?"

The answer arrived in a moment of providence as the elevator doors down the corridor scraped apart. James stepped towards the hallway to receive the intruder. The executor knew that there wasn't another free soul in the building who could be under his command. The shock showed in the sudden looseness of his flesh. The hunter, too, stood awestruck, but the echoes of his nightmares and the mettle of his heart fortified him against the moment, that very moment when Casey Aduro stepped out into the light.

Walter did not wait a moment longer before he raised his gun back up to Xiang and crushed the trigger. The gun did not fire, and his hand began to shake. As Casey marched towards them, Xiang slipped his off hand from his pocket and waved the glowing ruby ring that was now wrapped around one of his fingers.

"Casey instructed me a little for such an emergency," the courier boasted.

"Can't fire without fire, can you Walt?" the true fire elementalist called from the hallway. He entered the room with another shadow behind him, and James cursed when he identified the battered legend, Gerard Jones.

"How did—"

"Made a little prison break," Casey saved him the trouble. "Xiang was nice enough to leave a key under the mat. Thought about bringing the gargoyle up here, but...." He drew a handgun from his jacket and winked at the hunter. "Need a ride later. Put those away," he used the pistol to gesture at Yin and Yang. "We're all friends here. You too, Walt," he warned the executor as he made his way towards the old man.

Somewhere between Casey's entrance and his approach Walter had found his breath. He choked the air down into his lungs and managed with what he could gather, "You're not supposed to be here."

"Where'd you think I'd be?" Casey laughed. "Buckingham Palace?" Xiang scoffed alongside him, still snuffling, and ripped Walter's gun away from him. "I didn't trust Lumina because she was smart," he said, eyeing James. "I trusted her because she was faithful. You can't buy that kind of loyalty." After a beat, he smiled. "But you know that."

Inside his chest, the hunter's heart gasped for blood, just like every sheet of metal tucked into his coat and boots roaring for release. Outside, his knuckles were white against brown skin. His blood swayed him towards sure suicide while his mind kept him silent and still. At the moment, though, he had never felt such an irresistible drive to hunt.

"I should've killed you," James lashed at Jones before restraining his rage.

"Come off it," the bruised ex-captive censured as he chambered a round. "Like you—"

"Now," his leader hushed him, "you're the only one I need, Walt, and you know what I came for."

"I don't," the unsteady executor scowled. Casey discredited him with a smile, but Walter held fast. "What could you want? You have all the power you could ask for."

"The other half," he said and waited. Then, "Where is the Eye of Vaos?" He saw an inkling of a clue in James' sudden turn.

"You have it," the hunter stammered. He could barely hear the words leave his lips.

Casey's determination collapsed into pity. "You really have no idea what's going on, do you?" He pressed the muzzle of his gun against the hunter's neck as gently as a kiss and glared at Walter. "Tell me." In the ensuing calm, James considered a maneuver. If he could move fast enough, could react quickly enough, he could turn Xiang and Gerard into an advantage. If he accounted for the difference in his enemies' speeds, he could—

The Cultist proved that he would not leave time for hesitation. James felt the gunmetal lift from his skin, and before any other synapse could fire his ears registered a shot. His head snapped around so that he could see Walter, body motionless, sinking to the ground like a statue. The instant his right leg collided with the ground, the executor bellowed, the sound filling the room like no gunshot ever could, and his hands clapped onto his thigh.

The blood burst out before his scream did, and Casey tore towards him at comparable speed. He lifted him by the collar, smashed him into the desk, and shoved the pistol through the executor's trembling hands until the gun's muzzle settled into the hole it had made.

"Now," the maniac hissed as steam rose from the wound, "you have a few minutes of consciousness left—listen to me," he silenced Walter as he began to protest. "If this happens before I get what I want, I will burn this building to ashes." He twisted the gun in further to curtail the next complaint. "And I won't have to burn London. When the rest of Mythic learns what happened here, they'll do that for me. So you will walk to the elevator with me, and I'll try not to make you lose any more blood."

Walter bobbed his head at the offer, mouth agape. Casey ripped the weapon from his leg and placed it back into his jacket before pulling the mewling man onto his feet. Opposite him, Gerard stood fast but stiff while Xiang jittered. The purple of Gerard's face had faded. When James glanced at the two couriers, their eyes latched onto his and would not let go for all the horror in their periphery. Even as the executor hobbled between them, mute from pain, they stayed still. Xiang's eyes bubbled from his face, red and wild and ready.

Soon Casey stood on the edge of the room while his charge worked his way towards the lift. "I know you can get away from this," he counseled the hunter. "I don't know how, but we both know that you can." Xiang's discomfort warped into confusion as he looked to his commander. "If you follow me, though, you already know what happens next: I kill you." He tapped the sword slung over his back. "I don't want to. I'll have to." He met Xiang's gaze and shot him a conciliatory glance.

"We can't change what we see," the hunter reminded him.

Turning back to James, he mused, "Always worth a try."

Gerard, Xiang, and James watched him disappear into the lift with Walter blanched and leaning against the wall. "Jame—," the fragile wight attempted before the doors trapped him in and a thick enmity vanished from the room.

"What he said..." Xiang started, noticeably less anxious, before rethinking his words. "You can't take on the two of us. It's not possible."

James agreed, at least on a basic level. Yet he too had leapt to the time beyond this. He knew that this was not the end of his story. He was destined to leave here, to survive in spite of the couriers. How, though, he could not see. The hunter in him could not have cared less.

He called Yin and Yang to his hands, and though he did so at a leisurely pace, neither courier fired.

267

"You can't," Xiang reiterated. "You cannot." He took firm aim at James' head.

"You know who wins in a grapple, right?"

"You're not an elementalist," he barked.

"I'm a hunter."

"You're a fool."

"I have to go to the end," James murmured. Xiang had to tilt his head forward to hear. "You can try to kill me," he taunted him, "but I'll never die."

"We'll see," Xiang snapped.

Then James spoke the words of his mentor, the selfsame credo he'd always used to begin his hunt, an invocation of valor, an invitation to the bloodlust—a pact. A pact to go to the end with passion, with loyalty, or with faith, however near that end might be.

"Come with it, then."

Xiang braced his arm to fire but was not so tunneled that he did not detect the abrupt shift to his left. Even without turning he knew that Gerard's gun had changed targets. He blinked, his mind sputtered, and he spat every curse he knew. "And why in Vaos' name are you doing this?"

"If I see that ring glow, I'll shoot it off." The legend himself peeked over at James as the hunter's head tilted to one side. "I've known Casey my whole life. He knew too much about me not to use me. They've...they've got my mum!" he cried. Through the busted lips and swollen face, Gerard managed a smile. "But we're through all that, now."

James nodded and raised his fangs. "You and me, then?"

"Bloody yes already," the triple agent griped.

"Then there are two questions before we commence," Xiang announced. "Have you ever deflected a bullet with those knives?" he petitioned James, who grinned in answer. "And you," he proceeded with Gerard. "Did you think that Casey would trust you with a real gun?"

At the mention, Gerard faltered. That was all Xiang required. A pulse, a wave, a particle, was all he was as he blinked to Gerard's side. His gun whipped into place as if it were magnetized, set square against the other traitor's chest. Any ordinary opponent would have fallen right then, but Gerard was, after all, a legend.

More by luck than any other attribute, he bent his body away from the first shot. The second rasped by him. Before the third, James had joined the fray.

Xiang sensed him coming and knew that he was faster, but he did not imagine that Yin could dance as quickly as it did. A song of steel sent the Cultist's weapon sprawling away in a shower of red, but he preferred doing battle without it. Before the hunter could strike again, he'd already sprung into the air.

His legs coiled and whipped, and James winced at the speed of his motion. Even in exhibition with his spine electrified Xiang had not moved this fast. He whirled in a black dervish and each foot caught a different target. James and Gerard both dropped to the floor.

"Don't let him cast!" the latter shrieked, sighting the diamond on Xiang's neck gaining light.

James didn't need the reminder. He bolted at the courier, but even his speed was insufficient. He could stop Xiang from casting outward, but not from casting inward. The lightning elementalist's hands clapped together in a crackle of energy, and he became faster than anything the hunter had ever seen.

Yin and Yang rushed at complementary angles. Only a contortionist could have moved between them—that or the fastest man alive. Xiang's open palms sailed more quickly than a drake in a crosswind. He deflected both arms with one bloodied hand and, with the other, caught an elbow, driving the limb above the hunter's head. Yang vanished before James could blink. In the time his eyes fluttered open, he counted three hits to his chest. Gerard interrupted the fourth.

The legend's emerald in full glow, he ran one hand over the other and a gale shot across the room, plucking the two combatants from their feet. Xiang and James combined split Walter's desk in two before they rolled to their feet.

"Watch the wind," James commanded, stepping into a feint. He'd fought the courier before, knew his style, knew his speed, but Xiang's reactions bordered on prophetic. His synapses fired at near instant speed, but the impulses appeared to preempt James' every action. His blade met air, his fist met palm, and his chin met another jab before Gerard split them apart again. Xiang leapt up immediately, smiling his way to his feet. His hands flowed over one another, inviting a current of silver-blue energy to ripple between his fingers.

"I said watch it!" James railed.

"And I said—" Gerard gritted his teeth as he pulled another torrent of air across the room. The courier danced alongside the column of wind, losing his grasp on the charge but not his concentration. "Don't—" Another blast dodged. "Let—" The third he ducked. "Him—" The fourth ripped a bookshelf to litter. "Cast!" Xiang leapt over the fifth and smashed his palms together, dispersing the electricity altogether. Then the wave ran down his wrist and to his fingertips before he sensed a throwing knife streaking towards his arm and he recoiled.

His hand went skyward, and a bolt of lightning shrieked up towards the ceiling, bursting the arches apart. Debris floated down alongside volumes of ancient books and the leaves of the ruined shelves and made the room into a snow globe of paper and ash.

"Jesus!" James shouted as the courier dove to the ground and started another cast. Rather than allow him to freecast another bolt, the hunter opted to loose a pair of throwing knives across the room. One was necessary to move Xiang, but he needed two to break the elementalist's charge. As Xiang cursed and his diamond darkened, James shot three more knives from his coat and not a one came close to its mark. "The fuck?" he griped, watching the courier flash towards him in spite of the rain of knives.

"You taking the piss?" Gerard wheezed, struggling to keep his emerald aglow. "You having a laugh?" He threw another futile blast at Xiang. "You've never seen a shocker on coke?"

The circumstances of their bout solidified for James just in time for him to dip under Xiang's first serenade of strikes. A few measures in, however, the courier's feet joined the treble of his fists. James felt pain blast through his gut and face but could not hope to have identified the exact source. His adversary rose before him in a crescendo and hammered him down across the floor.

Gerard, though, could close the distance just as quickly with a favorable wind on his side. He sped across the room with a windstorm in his wake, pulling shreds of books and splintered wood into a tunnel behind him, and threw a straight with the strength of a monsoon. The courier caught it without even turning. In the seconds that followed, a stinging surge barreled into the aeromancer's arm amidst a wave of electricity and Gerard convulsed to the ground. While he fell, Xiang saw the hunter climb to his feet with three daggers in each hand.

"Get up." He thrust the flaps of his coat to his sides, baring the rows of knives within. "I need you for this one." With that, he circled around Xiang to cover the exit.

The haughty courier watched a trembling Gerard hobble across the floor to the hunter, and he took another bump of cocaine. "Let's see what you've got." He took a stance, cracked his knuckles, and sparks danced from his fingertips.

His acid tongue tightened the hunter's grip on his knives, but it did not stagger his focus. "You ever try to dodge seventeen knives in six seconds?" he challenged him.

"Not on purpose," he laughed. "Certainly not with the wind behind them, but I'll manage."

"No," James corrected him, and pointed to Gerard while his eyes sank into Xiang's. "The wind is for the paper," he explained, and stretched his wrists.

Xiang's red nostrils flared. Gerard's emerald lit his cresting smile. He stepped forwards alongside the hunter as the courier stepped back and the air between the two parties erupted upwards into chaos. There, behind the curtain of leaflets, notes, records, and pages, Xiang stood blind and startled. On the other side, James McCrary unloaded a hail of daggers.

His eyes counted them jetting through the haze of paper, but he could not see them all. The knives took sheets hostage and continued hurtling towards Xiang, at his arm, his cheek, now his chest. The lightning elementalist could dodge any attack that he could sense, but he couldn't see or hear anything but a howling tempest of white. Backpedaling and bobbing through the office-turned-storm, he suffered paper cuts and dagger cuts and took a knife in one leg before flipping backwards over the rubble of Walter's desk and righting himself in time to watch the madness settle.

The hunter towered, arms still extended, and checked his true target looming just behind the courier. Xiang turned to regard the pane of glass and saw a dozen daggers jutting from the tempered surface. Cracks extended from each puncture like bloodless veins in neat webs, encircling the courier like a net. "One more," James admonished his emerald-toting accomplice, and Gerard was happy to oblige.

"Cheers, mate," he whispered, throwing his arms forward.

The air snaked out from under his hands in whirlwinds converging from either side of their target, driving the courier flush against the glass. The window fragmented in response but did not shatter. Xiang fell from his crystal seine without an ounce of pain, despite the knife still planted in one of his thighs. It could not distract him from the energy forming in his hands. In fact, taking the brunt of the blast had afforded him all the time he needed to charge it, so rather than pull the blade from his leg, he poured his anger into the palm of his hand and lashed out the contents.

Gerard and James broke opposite of one another, wincing from the heat of the bolt as it seared a hole into the far wall. Xiang took no time at all to refill his store of electricity and launch another flash of lightning at the hunter. He ducked, and in his stead the shelving above him burst into flame, sending splinters of wood fanning down over him. Gerard strained for the energy to draw more wind but could not conjure another breath before Xiang shot a thread of thundering energy back at him. Meanwhile, his opposite hand dealt James another flare, but this bolt seemed thinner and weaker. His power pool was fading.

James and his ally continued circling the room towards Xiang while he traded them ground for more lightning, but he could feel it dimming. He abandoned his attempt to recharge as the hunter approached him with one fang drawn. Behind him, he could sense Gerard closing, closing, and he let him rush with brazen tempo. A second before James met him, Xiang's hands sparked to life. His right went forward and his left went back, but only the hunter could dodge the bolt from the blue. While he dove, Gerard reeled forwards with a cry and then fell silent.

Yin retaliated, blazing across the hunter's body, but Xiang hadn't lost enough speed for it to catch him. When the fang sank into the office window, James didn't bother retrieving it. His hands were already moving to meet the grasp of his opponent, and Xiang invited the attack. Even with one leg wounded, he was the elementalist. When he took the hunter's hulking hands in his own, a smile broke across his face. James strained, and his heart sent adrenaline bleeding down his brow. Xiang smirked. The hunter grunted through pursed lips while the courier's diamond warmed.

"You know who wins in a grapple, right?" he asked.

James had his answer. In the twist of his boot, in his sudden shift in direction, he turned his push into a pull and Xiang's footing into an afterthought. In that moment, his electric mind held not a single thought—perhaps emotion, perhaps shock—before his back slammed down onto the ground and he felt his spine quake. Then the hunter lifted him by one leg, using the protruding dagger like a handle, and pitched him against the web of breaking glass. His impact connected the fractures and the glass appeared to bend outward. Before gravity could act, James whirled around, drove his heel into the courier's gut, and Xiang burst through the window with the sound of a thunderclap.

He flailed in the first instant, a child in water, before the girth of his situation reached him and he fell alongside the Mythic building towards the inviting but inhospitable ground below. When James' eyes struck him three stories down, he looked away.

Then Xiang fell one hundred fifty meters like a hunter, thinking of nothing but how to survive.

If he gathered a strong enough charge, he thought, invoking his diamond, he could repel the metal around him or cling to the building, slowing his descent. He'd heard of elementalists magnetizing themselves to walls in order to climb them. He could teach himself the technique. He had enough time. By the tenth story, he'd become convinced that he had plenty of time.

And if he didn't, he'd go to the end with conviction, knowing that he'd done all he could. Knowing what he'd done, though, was the thought that made his heart itch.

Some part of his body felt the ground coming up below him, alerted him to its proximity, sent a frigid jolt up his broken back. He cursed it in a whisper, scorning the Earth, damning the world he'd tried to save. It had rejected him much like the last and like any other world would have. He wondered in that infinite, final instant if the next world would live up to its promise.

"Aduro. What have we done?"

* * * *

James turned away before Xiang stopped falling, though his ears picked up confirmation of the courier's death all the same. His attention lay with the man shuddering on the floor of Walter's office, clutching at his chest.

He tried to pull his arms away, seeing a smoldering stain where the lightning had fused his clothes to his torso, but Gerard batted him away. "Don't play nurse, you git," he stuttered. "Casey never took the Eye, but he does have something. Something he needs the Eye in order to use. We have to finish this mess of a fight."

James backed away from the trembling bundle and turned to the glass, then he glanced to the fang in his hand. He'd managed to save it before the blade went the way of the ex-courier. The weapon called, more than anything, to be reunited with its other half still languishing across the room. With both blades in tow, though, the hunter and his fangs were in full accord with their next goal.

James McCrary had survived as long as he had by preempting danger. Speeding through it when it couldn't be avoided, but more often than not embracing it altogether. He had no intention of preventing any more violence. Until Casey Aduro was dead, there was nothing else in the world that could sate him. He would not betray his passion, his profession, his faith, until the hunt was over.

Chapter Thirty-Four
Walter

By now, the executor's face had grown paler than his hair. His tongue bobbed and smacked on the inside of his dry lips which spoke of nothing but his frailty. The sick eyes sunken in his head followed after Casey as he headed out into the basement hallway of the Mythic tower.

"Stop." The word spilled out low and wilted. "Casey, stop this." Walter toppled forwards between the lift's doors and the panels slid in to crush him. After each effort, they parted, regathered, and then pressed against his torso again. "Casey," he called out, but the Cultist stood deaf to his complaints, disappearing into the chamber at the end of the corridor and leaving the elevator to chew the old man.

Wincing, he took in a few sharp breaths before lurching forwards onto his belly. After another set of stabilizing gasps, he removed his hands from the bullet wound on his thigh. The pain flowed in as the blood flowed out and stopped his lungs outright. Letting the injured leg rotate onto the floor, Walter issued a scraping groan. The bullet was still inside him, killing him with the mercy of a devil, slow and slow and slower every minute, but until it did he had a duty to fulfill. He slapped his bloodied hands against the cement and dragged his carcass out of the lift's steel jaws.

He left a trail behind him, an epitaph in red, proof that he had not yielded, but the writing grew thicker and darker with every inch he struggled. Soon, the copper scent drifting from his palms threatened to turn his stomach against him so that the man-turned-slug halted halfway down the hall in a putrid heap. In need of rest, he managed to shift to his side and replace his hands on his wound but had not seen a moment's respite before Casey emerged through the hall door.

"Here. Let me," is all he said as he took hold of the executor's arm and dragged him into the main chamber. Walter writhed on his back and locked his focus on the man standing over him. His eyes were red, his face was neutral, but his voice could melt a glacier away. "You're an idiot, Walter." He knelt over the dying man and produced a ruby and a flask. "Drink," he instructed him, pressing the container to his mouth. Walter jumped at the sight of the ruby and accepted the water like an infant, then he recoiled at the bitter taste of gin. "Drink," Casey reiterated, driving the liquor down his throat.

"The bullet," Walter spat and coughed, "it didn't go through."

Casey pulled the canteen away. "I know."

With that, the executor felt a volcanic surge of pain in his leg—an intruding object, searing heat, brutal pressure, then nothing but the sting of fire and the stench of sizzling flesh. What started as a roar in his breast became a gasp by the time it reached the surface. Then, for several seconds, Walter Brimford stared up to the ceiling, open-mouthed, and did not think he'd ever draw in air again.

He did, though, just as the ancient stood and flung the bullet aside. He left the ruby and the canteen before hurrying to a large door on one side of the chamber.

"Casey," Walter tried again, clutching at the gem.

"You'll bleed out if you don't cauterize it. Not gonna do it for you." With the executor's key in tow, he swung the heavy door open and vanished into the hidden chamber.

Walter sank his head back against the floor with the hole in him somewhat mended, considering the pain that would come from welding the wound shut. "You're not like them." His voice held firmer now. "They're murderers." He listened for a response from the secret room but could only hear the Cultist rummaging.

He stood in a vault that, for decades, only Mythic executors had entered. Its contents were valued at being in the billions. The weapons, relics, and information within exceeded comprehension. He now had the breadth of eternity in his arsenal. "You could take any single item in there and sell it for millions. Hundreds of millions. You won't because you know you're worth more than that. You believe in something." He heard a scoff from within. "Like Emily Galloway did." The sifting ceased. "Are you a murderer, Casey? You murdered *her*."

"It wasn't me," Casey told him from within the vault. Walter heard something unfamiliar in the utterance, a pain uncharacteristic of the great ancient, and saw an opportunity to strike.

"Emily is gone. You can still realize her dream. You can make integration happen without all this bloodshed. Without the Cult."

Casey emerged from the dark with a torchlight floating in his palm. "You still think this is about integration."

Walter's eyes softened. "What?"

"That's not what this is about." He disappeared back into the vault. "If I *freed* the hidden races of the Earth," he spoke from the shadow, "what would I accomplish? If I released them into this world, they would inherit all the prejudice out there. People would turn their hate loose on them like dogs. Hunt them through the street. Through the wilderness. Through the portals. Fuck, Walter...*we* hunt them, and they're the ones we're supposed to protect." He came at last across the treasure he'd been hunting, and Walter could hear his smile like a laugh breaking through the black. "This world is the problem," he declared, returning to the circular chamber with a great, black gem resting in his palm. "O monstrous world! Take note, o world, to be direct and honest is not safe. Not here—not in this world. An infidelitous Earth that chokes the hope from everyone who believes in it."

With the Eye of Vaos in hand, he reached into his coat and pulled an ancient dagger from its sleep.

The ivory hilt shamed the incandescent light and the pale cement around it. Its bone hue shone truer than any other white in the world. Like the Eye, the thick blade was dark in color, wavering between violet and black. It curved in on itself like the claw of a dragon, a fierce scythe, the Talon of Vaos.

Walter rolled onto hands and knees. "When you took that from me—"

"I know it's been hard without it."

"You have no idea."

"It's almost over," Casey hushed him. "You didn't last long with just one of them. You won't last long without either. I hope casting without a gem was worth poisoning yourself."

"Please. Just one more taste."

"Soon," Casey promised before sliding the weapon into his coat and starting towards the exit.

"What are you doing?" the executor demanded as his old pupil approached the edge of the chamber. "Casey…" he rattled when the Cultist ignored him. "Stop." Walter settled onto his haunches. He couldn't stop him any other way. Now the executor would turn executioner and reclaim his progeny in fire.

Walter summoned a titanic fury. The power flowed into him from the air he pulled in through his nostrils, supported by the feeble legs that refused to buckle as he stood. What he tapped into felt very similar to skimming a fountain. The water he came up with burned red-orange in his chest.

"I should have been stronger," he thought before he threw his arms forward and two fists launched twin cylinders of fire. The flames screamed, erupting to cover the doorway and hose the surrounding wall. The charring skin he smelled was his own, his knuckles blistering raw from the heat. The inferno blocked his vision from anything but his wildfire. All sound, all sight, all smell, all sense was fire. For six seconds he delivered his scorching sentence onto the Cultist. He held the cast until the burst had peeled his hands almost to the bone and he fell back again, depleted.

His flames parted against the now-black walls and revealed not death but tragedy all the same.

Casey did not look back as he drifted towards the lift. When he entered, he cast his eyes down the long corridor and saw the defeated old man crying. The pain of his body was a candle to the pain of his inadequacy. That much seemed clear.

Walter's eyes were red, his face wrinkled and tattered with tears.

Casey's eyes were red. His face was neutral.

But then, just as the elevator doors bit shut, air flooded into him through his mouth.

Chapter Thirty-Five
The Stoneslayer

"I had a dream like this," James thought to himself aloud, wondering why Alvin was waiting for him outside of Mythic with a town car. "The man in the black car." He envisioned what came next.

"I'm sure you did." The driver leaned against the passenger side wrapped in black with a cigarette in hand. He cast his gaze like a shadow south across the clouds. Without coaxing, the hunter checked the glass-covered pavement nearby and darted to the large, white tarp pinned down over human remains.

"Did he take something from you?" O'Hare speculated, still set on the sky.

James peeled back the covering and his jaw tightened at the sight of the frigid pulp that had once been a man. "Walter is down in one of the lower levels," he answered, squeezing his hand into the mess of the dead courier's pockets in search of a key. "He needs help."

"Walter is dead." The hunter turned a glare upon Alvin as he withdrew a handful of slop. "We haven't the time to mourn. Casey left minutes ago on that gargoyle you captured."

"He killed him."

"Immaterial," he emphasized with a raised finger. "Though the cause of death may have been Walter's lingering illness, our goal remains the same—apprehend Casey." James shook the gore from his glove while Alvin went on: "Two things we know happen today. I die, and you and he meet one last time. Now, Death I don't mind putting off, but let's not keep Fate waiting."

"We don't know where Casey is. We have no idea where he is in this entire fucking city. At least Walter could've—"

"You know that wasn't a dream."

At first, he sounded sinister before James soothed away his apprehension over the white-haired chauffeur. Alvin couldn't be one of them. "I don't."

"James, we needn't waste any more time. I know you."

"I couldn't get anything out of Xiang."

"You know because you've seen it in your dreams." The same instant the hunter went silent, his hands flashed to Yin and Yang. "I'm not a Cultist," the old man smiled, his neck shaking over his scarf. "I told you about Casey's vision of me, that I'd die protecting a hunter. That was half of it." Somehow, Alvin's solidity and the smile stretching across his face put James at ease. "He told me that I'd die protecting a hunter and an ancient."

The hunter's hands fell from his blades.

"You've seen where he's going, in visions, in sleep." James had seen it. "Those weren't dreams. They were experiences you've already lived through, your mind skipping through time. You know precisely where he is." He knew where. "Fate will guide us where we're destined to go. Now, tell me—where are we headed?" And so he told him.

And now Alvin opened the door for him and he stepped inside. The limousine growled to life and peeled off into the snowy road. James described the streets and statues and stadiums he'd never seen before, and yet they fell into place before him like a well-ordered picture in an artist's mind, but the strokes on the canvas darkened in time.

"I'm dreaming," he uttered, shaking his reality from its hinges. He didn't recognize where he was or who he was with. The things he saw terrified him.

First, the man with eyes like a skeleton ferrying him in the black car.

Second, he glanced up and saw, too, the moon waxing like his blood, opening like his heart, a sleeping eye watching him as he embarked on the hunt. Even in the sun's presence it would not stop watching him. He felt like howling at it, pouncing on it, tearing it apart until, after they had crossed a bridge, a colossal structure closed up over it and left him and the chauffeur alone with the sun at their backs.

Third, James stepped out of the car and the cold fell onto him like a net. He and the driver looked up to the building in front of which they'd stopped: a car park that towered six stories above them. He baulked at the familiarity of the setting but still did not understand what was happening until they arrived at the entrance and James returned to his present consciousness.

"Here we are."

Far from the garage, tucked in a small canal, was a scar gouged into the stone by a host of vicious beasts. He knew what kind. They waited for him deep within their hollow, as did Fate. Vaos was there, too, in some respect, the old god's malice inhabiting a twisted human vessel. Vaos was here, buried under the grey bones of London, waiting in its black breast with winged parasites clutching to its walls, lapping up the city's blood to prepare for the Stoneslayer.

After taking a moment to gather himself, James examined the area, reaffirming his training, studying the bridge above the canal and the gates that hid it away, wondering how no one could have spotted this. He imagined how many had died to keep this pit hidden. Then he eyed Alvin.

"I'm going in alone."

"I am resigned to my destiny, James. Nothing that happens to me today will be anyone's fault. It is simply the way of the world."

"I need you for something more important," he stated, re-checking his gear a final time. "I need someone to finish Casey. If I can only wing him, I need someone to make sure that he doesn't live."

Alvin considered this. "You'll go alone for now," he conceded. "Faolan and the others will come. You are not alone in this."

The hunter laughed and bared his metal fangs before stepping a foot into the burrow. "Thanks." Yin and Yang rested quietly in his hands, focus matching their anticipation.

"It's an honor to have met you, James McCrary," Alvin O'Hare told him with finality and held up his assault. "How a man can be lucky enough to befriend two ancients, only Fate knows." With that, the driver tipped his cap and shuffled back towards the car. He peeked over his shoulder to see the hunter steal away into the depths.

Fifth came the tunnels. He'd wandered most of the way through them in dreams, but only in bits. Now, as he traveled the bulk of the labyrinth, he began to truly appreciate the darkness. Not continuous or fluid like water but rough and disjointed, the shadows of a hundred bodies draped over him. Colors swirled around the black, flashing to remind him of the sun. He almost forgot to bring out the flashlight tucked inside his coat. The shadows fled from the light and took to the walls arching over the passageway. The walls here looked and smelled decrepit and moist where the gargoyles had gnawed their way through.

He sighted a ledge at the end of the tunnel. Ahead he could hear water flowing—the blue fire of London—and knew that he'd arrived. The ledge overlooked a great circular chamber like a theatre in the round. The edges of the floor, however, did not meet the walls. The gap surrounding the platform dipped down wherever the water flowed, somewhere darker. Standing over the coliseum, James could make out a row of pipes against the opposite wall, almost too small for even a child to crawl through. The cavern's entrance was the only apparent route to this place. To either side of him, the rock sloped down along the edges of the chamber to the central platform, as if this structure had once been hewn for human use. It appeared more like a great hall than a sewage chamber, some secret meeting place sealed away for centuries or longer. Now, James McCrary the Stoneslayer stalked down the ramps as the dark manor's invited guest. He heard them coming the moment he reached the platform.

Sixth: the nightmare's hellish climax. The estate's contracted servants scraping up from beneath him, bubbling up the walls.

He tried to track them with his artificial light but soon gave up. A full coven of gargoyles ordinarily numbered around sixty to seventy. This coven was particularly large.

"Listen to me!" he shouted after them, attempting to overpower the clamor of their claws crunching into the concrete. "The man you're working for can't give you what he promised." The beasts began to spill out onto the platform. While some of them clung to the stone, at least a dozen had entered the arena. "Your patriarch has appointed me guardian over you. Volodymyr Sewick has absolved me." The hunter's déjà vu crept in again as his light hit the face of one of the approaching monsters.

Though he could not have recognized it, this eldest son had seen him once before out in the icy wood, in a glade stained deep with blood.

"My father agreed to spare you if you preserved his daughter alive." The fire in his voice made the hunter's heart boil. "You promised to protect her after you watched her die." As it started to circle, the beast's eyes leapt at him from its skull, even hungrier than the body they inhabited, and the hunter growled in response.

"Where is Volodymyr?"

"Sealing our arrangement with the Flamestorm as we speak," the now-familiar gargoyle hissed. "We have relinquished our claim to our lives. We have asked in return for the head of James McCrary the Stoneslayer." The rest of the coven thundered approval, thrashing their tails against the rocks.

James raised his blades. He understood his greatest disadvantage came not from his enemies' numbers but from the light he was forced to hold in one hand. "I understand your anger," he said in a final attempt to gain leverage. "Let me give myself over to Casey and your father."

The brutes stopped ringing around him as their commander stretched upright in thought. After a moment, he nodded. "Yes." The others faltered. "We will take you to him after we pull you apart."

The demons descended upon him as in a nightmare, but the Stoneslayer fought as in a dream.

His eyes followed his flashlight and his flashlight alone, but all he needed to comprehend fell under its glow. Yang, coupled in the same hand, hacked flesh from the throat of a beast and sent a string of shining sinews spurting across the light. In his opposite grip, Yin delighted in the darkness, ripping through bodies in ways the sun would never condone. When the two fangs met in penumbra, their edges cried out, whistling through gargoyles like a hymn.

Four fell before the dark began to overwhelm him. The shift came in the form of a claw shoved at his chest. He caught the arm attached to it, but the weight behind the limb drove him onto his heels and, with half a dozen behind waiting to mutilate him, James could not afford to fall back. He slipped forwards under the brute's arms and out of its reach— or so he thought—but in all the black and all the cacophony some devil was able to strike him.

He felt its talons tear across his back and he sprawled to the edge of the platform, whirling about to face twenty advancing. He toed the brink of the arena, listened to the wails echoing back from its depths, and sensed that the drop off the side was nothing less than eight meters. Then he flinched from the sting of gargoyle venom leaking down onto him from above and flashed light on a fiend coiled against the wall behind him.

He lost focus for a moment, a folly that might have killed him if something hadn't killed the gargoyle on the wall.

The shot crashed out across the arena high and above the din. James watched the monster's skull burst open before the corpse loosened and fell, clattered against the edge of the platform, and slid into the chasm. James counted ten, twenty, thirty feet before the body smashed against a solid surface. Then he thrust the beam of light onto Alvin O'Hare atop the ledge at the sewer's entrance.

The hundred-year-old sniper nodded once more to him and pulled the breech back on his rifle. To his sides stood twelve elves in full tactical array with swords at their hips and pistols in hand. Even Commander Bailey pointed a gun into the pit. Two other figures stood in the rear, both human. The sight of them sent cinders along the hunter's back. Michelle and Robert toted handguns, the latter of the two looking as determined as he seemed terrified.

From behind Alvin, Faolan Ashtongue slid center and leaned over the railing, unarmed. The fledgling emperor took stock of his kingdom garbed in the traditional Ciric dress of royalty, numbering the denizens of his lovely new catacomb. Each of his subjects watched him with something between reverence and horror. The scar on his mouth made his scowl much viler than it should have been. His face proved even more grotesque than those of the gargoyles. After commanding the coven's attention for a spell, the elf straightened, his army readied their weapons in response, and he delivered his edict unto the masses:

"By order of the Ciric prince, disperse or die."

The people's insurgence sounded with a roar.

Faolan's scar stretched into a smile as the ruby in his ear started smoking. "You have made a handsome choice."

The fire elementalist's stance dropped. He inhaled enough air to rupture a dwarf's lungs. His fist dropped forwards like a hammer, and a single, golden spark screamed down to the center of the arena. The combatants watched the wisp with misguided curiosity before Faolan's hand surged open and the flicker erupted. The ensuing blast doused half a dozen demons and shocked the rest on the platform to their knees.

James winced at the impact but held his ground.

"You heard them!" Commander Bailey barked over the explosion. He led the charge down the hole like Illius himself.

Tickled by his gusto, Faolan snickered and leapt down into the fray. He rolled on impact in a fiery flourish, his robes spinning out from him, and started roasting more gargoyles without another word. James watched the elven sentinels descend with guns and jewels afire— sapphires, rubies, emeralds, and diamonds heralding a tempest of carnage. He heard Alvin's rifle snap, underscored by the rest of the humans' weapons, and felt the gargoyles' bloodlust transcending into the realm of madness.

The hunter's way was lit by the others' lamps, by Faolan's fire, by Ysolt's periodic thunderbolts, but most of all by blood. The silver ichor fountaining through the ring shone like moonlight and guided him step-by-step through the battle. Where he saw blood rain upwards, he stepped and finished the fiends to which it belonged, butchering his way towards his allies until he stood back to back with Faolan.

The prince's flames sent their adversaries into fits of panic. Blazing, flailing, rushing cadavers lit every wall. More demon-like than ever, they directed their seething rage at the hunter, hell-bent on choking him in fiery grips. James met them with his coat raised, repelling the flames and ramming them back to the walls. Soon, he began to distance himself from the trigger-happy royal, considering it more dangerous by his side than almost anywhere else. Having gained some ground, he turned to check on the gunners holed up above.

In a lightning strike, a muzzle flash, and a fireburst he saw it: the singular gargoyle creeping on the stone, poised to take Robert. The hunter never drew a dagger faster in his life. The knife intervened as the creature's wings and arms spread. Michelle and Robert followed the projectile behind them, saw it sink into the gargoyle's jaw, and followed it with three shots each into its skull.

"Watch the walls!" James raged up at them, shaking. His eyes raced to the reader pointing her gun egregiously close to him and he shrank from the gunfire. An instant later, he heard something smack the ground to his side, saw the gargoyle lying heartless, and he shot her an equally dangerous glare.

"No good deed goes unpunished," the reader-turned-mercenary chuckled over the tumult. Just as she did, the hunter's attention swept to a new threat.

Rushing from behind a falling brother, the eldest son came barreling towards him. It lashed sideward as it dashed, catching a sentinel by surprise and goring the elf with a claw before it collided with the hunter. James slid Yin into its chest where the creature's heart should have been, but it continued the charge. He shoved Yang in as well, grating past the sternum, but the beast would not stop. It lifted and drove him down through the gap, down from the others, down, down, down into the dark.

James experienced a sense of vertigo as he started to fall, still rattled by the impact of the last attack. The gargoyle hissed on top of him as the two dropped. The Stoneslayer abandoned Yin and Yang to its chest, flipped a KA-BAR from his boot, and lost it in the beast's neck. It whipped a talon into the wall, grinding away solid stone and slowing their descent enough so that, when the hunter pulled it down below him, it broke his fall completely. He heard its spine splinter and the debris it tore down raining over them. Then he collected himself and wrenched Yin and Yang from the felled gargoyle's rib cage.

The other knife had disappeared into the monster's gullet, so he didn't bother retrieving it. He'd also lost his flashlight in the fall. Standing in the dark of the trench, he peered upwards and heard the battle still at full tilt, although the gunshots now rang out less frequently. He could pick out the sound of the sentinels drawing their swords, their firearms depleted, but he could not be sure how many were still left alive.

He jolted into a crouch as a wave of fire rolled out over the edge above him, and while it lingered he caught sight of a half dozen corpses with him in this segment of the moat. Five were gargoyles. One was an elf. He repeated the elven valediction to himself—the most he could do for her—while he moved around the center pillar in search of a way back up.

"In the ways of the old, wisdom," he preached, and found only more gargoyles dead. "In the ways of the young, beauty," he continued, and the sight of another elf paralyzed his tongue. He pushed ahead, now halfway around the platform. "In the ways of those to come, serenity."

"Muirgel!" Faolan exploded overhead. The next wave of fire resounded like a bomb.

"Good night," James concluded. As he did, he came upon a tunnel, a passageway farther into the black. He couldn't see far in front of him—heard nothing, smelled nothing down this lightless corridor—but he could feel something pulling him with the gravity of the moon.

He wandered into the dark like a beast drawn by blood. It resonated within him somewhere beyond his senses, beyond his body, and beyond his mind. The hole stretched as far as the Earth's belly, it seemed: sometimes up, sometimes down, a portal into the heart of the world. By the end, his vision had faded completely. He'd entered a dream, met another ancient. Then the dream ended and James and Casey squared off at the end of the world.

Where the world ended, its breath came stale and warm from its core, cheek by jowl with a sound like the gnashing of teeth. Up ahead, a lantern hung on one of two immense columns, strewing light throughout the dead-end room. Moisture lingered on the glowing blue walls, glistening. The pair of pillars in the center framed a round set of steps sloping upward to a dark-watered fountain.

On one edge of the fountain, a gargoyle still leaking from torture wounds lapped up the black water like milk. Across from him stood Casey with the Eye of Vaos in one hand and the Talon in the other, grinding the two together like kitchen tools. With every gash the Talon made, a jet of blue sparks sprayed forth, raining into the water cascading from the ceiling. Strike after strike after strike, the glimmering dust sloughed off into the fountain in brilliant, fiery streaks. Then the particles collected in the well, swirled around the base of the fall, and drained off deeper into the ground.

When Casey twisted the Eye, James saw that an entire edge of the black crystal had already been carved off. Still, though, Casey turned the stone like an apple and peeled another layer from its surface. With every cut, something in the hunter stirred: a feral protest, something vibrating in his blood. Casey, too, shook while he skinned the artifact. Every cut pulled more tension to his clenched jaw. Still, he gripped the jewel as he would a fresh kill and bit the flesh away.

Every etch in the Eye brought James' blood further below freezing.

"Do you remember when we met, now?"

"Yes." James watched Casey, unsettled by his actions, then looked to the gargoyle and felt even less sturdy.

"That's destiny," Casey labored under a strained smile. "That's resonance."

The hunter took slow, heavy steps forward. "What is this?"

"This is what's in our veins, James." He took the next slice slow across the stone's face. The sound punctured the air. "This is mageblood." He held out some of the dark powder on his fingertips. "These relics Mythic's been hoarding? They're what *made* us." He pulled his hand back and pocketed both the Eye and the Talon. "Why I can cast fire and you can cast earth without a single stone to help us." He gestured to the fountain. "This is why ancients are ancients."

"What did you do?" he growled with the authority of a dragon.

Casey sighed and turned his head. "I needed the Eye as a source," he started, "but it only reacts with the same material. I needed the Talon first." He watched the hunter's indignation simmer, fascinated and appalled all at once. "Walter kept it a secret from Mythic. Used it with the Eye to become as strong as an ancient. But he was addicted. So when I took it, he needed a lapdog to fetch it for him. It's always been about the mageblood."

"And what do *you* want it for?" he roared. The gargoyle twitched. Casey dropped into a wide stance, all adrenaline, before reclaiming his composure.

"This fountain leads into the city's water supply." The words that followed choked him as they came up. "The mageblood can't be filtered out." James' muscles loosened at the shock. "It's all done."

"Stop," he ordered him.

The Cultist ignored him, ignored himself, and went on. "When people drink the water, most of them will get very sick." The prospect seemed to bother him even more than it did the hunter. Casey saw in the defiant creature's eyes something between disbelief and abomination. He recognized the horror from when he'd given Emily Galloway the same explanation. So, as he continued, he felt the remorse he'd sworn never to face again, yet the gravity of that stare pulled the words from him. "Most of them will be sick forever. Most of the rest will die."

"Then why is he drinking it?" he demanded, watching the gargoyle.

"Those who can stomach it will be like us. But unlike us, they'll be dependent on it. So, after a few years without more, they'll die, too." He felt his voice thin towards the end of his speech. "And that is—" he gestured grandly, ashamed of his own words, "—my master plan."

"Why? The Cult destroys worlds, not cities."

"There's someone in London who I need to meet." Casey turned to face him with red in his eyes. "He only comes out to play when monsters are around." The hunter began sliding towards him like a glacier. "I'm just doing what I'm told. I'm merely a loyal dog, James," he admitted, pleading. "Just like you." He flinched at the tears that escaped one eye before he surrendered and let them fall. "Why can't you understand that?" he laughed. "I'm just a...a wolf. Bred for this. Trained for three things: To obey. To kill. To survive. Just like you."

"They taught me to kill before they taught me to obey."

"Who? Uwe?"

James froze in his glacial pace.

"Uwe tried to teach you loyalty. It's not his fault that you never understood it."

"He wasn't in the Cult."

"You dumb fuckin dog. He told me before he went to Switzerland that he was afraid you'd kill him. He was *afraid*, James," he said to muzzle the hunter, "because he knew you'd do anything to anyone before you let yourself die."

"You're a liar."

"Where did he come from?" the Cultist antagonized him, arms outspread. "Hmm?" The hunter already had his answer. "Where did Uwe Löwe's flight come from before he met you in Zurich?"

"Japan," he relented.

"And you watched him die out there, didn't you?" He read the sin in James' silence, in the way he turned his head away. "Probably left him in the wilderness like some animal," he muttered. "And it wasn't about the Cult. Not believing in them, approving of anything. It was just so that you could survive. So! Tell me, why can't I make you understand why I've done everything I've done? Cause you and me are the same."

James lifted scorched eyes to meet those of the other ancient. Casey identified in them the intention he'd been waiting for. "We're not bad men, just better animals. We've given up faith and love…our humanity. The only loyalty we have is to the hunt." He smiled, baring fangs against his opponent, and tasted salt pouring in from his eyes.

"Then why are we still talking?" the hunter asked, Yin and Yang screaming at his sides.

Casey left his sword sleeping across his back. "So the mageblood has enough time to get to Volod's brain."

James twitched to see the beast standing, water still splashing from his jaws.

Volodymyr Sewick lumbered down from the fountain with every muscle in his body convulsing, scrambling to adapt to the poison filtering into his blood from his bowels. The mageblood already had a hold of him.

His black eyes either saw or did not see. The hunter couldn't be sure, since the orbs had grown a pasty, black film over their pupils. He watched the mageblood leaking from the creature's tear ducts, a brighter silver than any gargoyle had ever wept.

The jaws and arms and legs and wings and tail all shook separate from their master's control, already in withdrawal from the fountain's manna. The movements that were his own appeared entirely uncoordinated, so what effort this monster could possibly make against him, James couldn't guess. Volod blundered forwards, half-blind or bewildered, and his claws started to arc out in attack, but the gargoyle telegraphed his movements well in advance. The hunter thought that he must have another few seconds to prepare…up until the moment the gargoyle snapped to some demonic clarity.

His neurons turned to copper, and the impulses immediately became lithe, lucid, and precise. The slow arms swung shut, and the tail came from behind faster than Solomon the Great's. James almost didn't sidestep in time.

The tail crashed down hard. A grown dragon's fury lay in the length of that dire limb. It recoiled before James could blink and lashed again just as his eyes flickered shut. It broke the bricks under him like glass. All so fast, he didn't detect the back of the monster's claw swinging out. His nerves were only quick enough to register the pain that came with his viscera rupturing inside of him.

The hunter flew into the wall on the other side of the chamber. The collision sent everything he had out of his throat: a gruesome yowl and a soundless screech as he slid onto heels and haunches. Behind him, the mortar he'd dislodged trickled down. Before him, the archdemon Volodymyr rose.

"I know you, James McCrary," he hymned, deep, discordant. "I know what you have *done*!" He spread his arms and wings and eclipsed the lantern light behind him. Then he bore down on the hunter like a falling moon.

His hands danced in the low glow, reaching out to claim the Stoneslayer for all time. The fingers flexed and started to fall upon him, but in that instant the gargoyle's spasms returned, slowing him just enough.

Volodymyr's claws wrapped around the hunter's neck, then went to clutch at the twin blades sticking from either side of his chest before reappearing at James' throat. As they did, the Stoneslayer started to twist Yin and Yang between his ribs. He listened to the ichor filling Volod's lungs, to the stammering, choking bark he spat at him between liquid inhales, smaller and less rhythmic as the demon's roar subsided. When he pulled the daggers out, the beast slumped onto him.

"I'm sorry, Volod. I can't give you what you asked for."

James started to cry out at the sound of Casey's voice before he heard the searing in front of him. He saw the red-hot blade spring from Volod's chest. It pierced the prey and the predator straight through the gargoyle's stomach without resistance. Stinger screeched as loudly as James did when she bit through him. Casey's blade penetrated with all the smoothness of a song, sizzling in their ears. It ran all the way into the rock behind them, pinning the hunter to the wall.

There he dangled on the steaming katana, writhing on the tips of his toes, a trophy held up between living and unliving stone.

When he howled, London shook.

Volodymyr watched him with devilish indifference until the life drained from his body.

Then Casey Aduro stepped back from the wall to see what he had done, and the sight of it made him tremble. He caught James' eyes, wild with rage, panic, and fear, bounding around the room, searching for something, anything, nothing.

"Thank you," he said to the man on the wall, "for killing Lumina." James shot his hands to the length of the sword between his abdomen and the gargoyle's heart. He saw the crimson steam shoot from his fingers and bellowed again. "Emily deserved better. Better than a couple of dogs." Casey circled around to him until he was close enough to feel the animal's breaths pounding down from on high, frenzied but powerful. "This is all we're good for."

He pointed a pistol at his temple—a coup de grâce for a hopeless beast.

Chapter Thirty-Six
Faolan

The banished prince barreled through the tunnels, carrying fire in his hand to light his way. The ruby on his ear burnt red-hot, illuminating a misshapen snarl and eyes that poured over the dark like torches. By now, he'd lost the sounds of battle far behind him, left a lieutenant wounded with her compatriots, and left Mythic to mop up the rest of the coven.

The gargoyles were not the issue here. Somewhere in this labyrinth of sewage, hidden hollows, and secret chambers, their master was waiting to meet Faolan, and Faolan was waiting to meet him.

He stopped at an intersection of passageways, whirling about to number them. The path had already split in two three times before this fork where the roads were seven. A few held a mason's mark, brick and mortar arches carved out by human hands. The rest had been hewn by stone claws.

He cursed and hurled his living torch down the center tunnel. The blaze flowed through the black for a moment before the darkness swallowed it up. Then the elf drew air into his nostrils and threw his hands open. Fire sprang from the skin. Each palm burned hot enough to melt copper, but his mastery of the element warded his flesh from the heat.

He held the fires up to try and see down another hole, but it stretched farther than the sun would show, so he let the flames slip away and paced in thought while the black closed in around him.

"Dark skies, red moons," he sang to himself, humming the rest of the melody. Soon he was sitting between the tunnels, waiting for his prey to call out to him. Just as the old battle hymn resolved, the ground under him shook once and then again as he rose. He heard a shout echo from his right.

His earring energized and the prince blew fire from his mouth to his fingertips, sneered, and tore down the tunnel.

When he found the dead end, the light, the black fountain, Casey, Volodymyr, and James, the gargoyle was already dead. The roars he'd heard flooding the underground made his ear twitch. The sight of James McCrary skewered against the wall made his eyes itch. The smell of man and beast burning only made him bloodthirsty.

"This is all we're good for," the Cultist said, drawing arms.

Watching him approach James, the prince had to push bile from the base of his throat. He almost didn't reach his mind out to the gun in time.

Casey clicked the pistol twice before he realized that another fire elementalist had entered the fray. He gritted his teeth, holstered the weapon, and found Faolan at the mouth of the chamber. His eyes stabbed the prince a hundred times over.

"I'm sorry, James," the banished prince murmured, still fixated on Casey.

He glanced over to the hunter clawing at the hole under his heart then back to Faolan. His eyelids were fluttering now.

"Casey Aduro," he said, "I've come to make a mess of you. I can smell the mageblood from here. So you found something to cut the Eye with." The air around Casey started to warp. The heat on his shoulders made it shimmer. "You've been drinking it." Faolan raised his arms and dropped into a fighting stance.

"I don't need it," he responded, stepping away from the hunter.

"You may be right." Faolan lowered his stance until the air filled his pelvis. He held his hands steady, fists clenched, ready to launch a wave of fire or break one coming in. Then Casey dropped into a stance as well. When he inhaled, Faolan felt the temperature of the room rise. "I can't say I'm not excited to see an ancient's power for myself. Show me what Vaos' fire was like. I'm curious. They say it rivaled the sun."

"They called it 'sunfall'."

"Can you imagine something so hot?" He received no response.

"You won't need to."

Faolan Ashtongue moved with the poise of a dancer, the speed of a thief, the power of a knight, and the purpose of an executioner. He threw fire streaking through the dark with a jab. The first wave opened in a funnel, spread to the breadth of a dragon's skull, and flew to Casey on his right. The second shot—an uppercut, a rolling wind, a wheel—whirled down his left. The third, quick and thin as a red scythe, spun overhead. All in a single breath.

Casey ruptured the first. Too much power in the second. He stepped aside and ducked the third. All the while he held the heat away. Surrounded by fire, he could see the elf leap towards him with a fourth jet shrieking from his sole. The concussion behind this one he needed both hands to block. He crossed his arms in an X and threw them open to divert the fire. Still, the force drove him back on his heels by a meter.

The flames snapped and thundered over their shouts as they engaged. Every burst barked as it sparked from thin air and exploded across the room. Casey let a stone column take the brunt of a cresting flame before firing back a straight. Then two. Then three. Four, five, six. Every punch was strong enough to melt a man's face away.

Faolan skated far from the salvo and returned a continuous spray for as long as he could against the pillar. It hissed away at the moist rock until it was black and dry. The elf stood ready to incinerate anything that moved behind the stone, breaking his posture only to mop the sweat lining his face.

Then he saw a flash of black toss a small, yellow wisp into the air, and he felt his blood thicken in spite of the heat. He raised his hands in defense, cupped them over the spark, drove all his energy into the particle to extinguish it, but could not before it ignited and sent him sprawling across hard stone. Deftly rolling onto his feet, he blindly threw out a wave in an attempt to deter any more bombs, but Casey had already sent one floating after him.

The realization stilled his quaking heart. Then the explosion lit the room in red and orange, yellow and white, and all the beautiful colors in between.

Casey dove through a light rain of dust with flame already in hand, but the elf flanked him before he could even think to adjust. The banished prince threw as many sparks as he could muster—a challenge to the ancient—and the trio of wisps converged on Casey in synchronized spirals. He doused them all just as Faolan thrust open his hands and the chamber fell into black and blue silence for the moment before the ruby earring blazed and its wielder's red battle cry rumbled out.

The fire arced wide to his left, so Casey countered with the same conflagration. When Faolan evaded, he answered with another constant flame, seeing that the Cultist had planted and could not move from his spot. So each elementalist staved off the fire on one side and retaliated on their right, sending limitless energy rocketing off-target. While the heat fizzled past them, their eyes locked on one another, neither one breaking his stance until each man ran out of air.

Even with the power of an ancient, Casey's lungs held only as much as they were trained to. There was only so much in the room to combust. When he'd exhausted the air, his fire surged to a stop, just as Faolan's did.

Perpendicular to the twin blasts, James struggled to breathe. The blood rushed out of him, the air refused to enter, and he felt his eyes bulge as he coughed.

"You see that?" the elf wheezed, pointing at him. "Even ancients can suffocate." He gasped for the oxygen they'd burned out of the air, still trying to hold a casting stance. "But here's where you die, friend." He straightened and stood above the man doubled over across from him. "I don't *need* oxygen to cast." Without so much as a gasp, Faolan shot his hand through the air. A cloud of black soot followed it, springing up from the earth and creeping along the floor. Soaked through with red embers, it wasn't hot enough to burn wood, but it was thick enough to smother a skyline.

The smoke swept over Casey, choking the air away while he struggled to keep the heat from baking his skin. Faolan launched another sheet of soot, heating the breathless air until it produced smoke rather than fire, cooking the stones until they burned black and turned to ash. The cinders billowed around his opponent and trapped him under a deathly shroud of dust.

"This is what happens when they take everything from you." Faolan tightened the miasma over his victim, savoring the congested coughs that issued forth from the black cloud. "When they take your name, take your home, take your face away from you. You learn to do everything with nothing. When my father believed the Cult had turned me, he killed my only son. So when they took my heir away..." he smirked, "I learned to do the same to them." His words choked him more than the smoke did. The heat would have vaporized the tears had they come. "And so they call me—"

"Faolan Ashtongue, the Banished Prince."

The elf flinched at the voice emanating from within the shroud. Casey Aduro spread his arms and stood, and as he did so the smoke blew away from him as gently as it had approached.

"I had to be sure it was you." The prince did not grant him the courtesy of a spoken retort. Instead, he launched both fists and ash mushroomed out over him. Casey waved the back of his hand at the smoke and a gust drove it to the walls. "I didn't think the prince of Cire would be stupid enough to show his face in front of me. But I was really hoping that he would." Faolan blew the smoke from his belly—as much as he could manage—singeing the sides of his mouth for more fuel. A burst of Casey's wind dissolved it. He extended a hand to the prince, an invitation to finish this.

"You cheat," he scoffed, chuckling at his naivety and deriding the Cultist's honor. "Is there an element you don't know?" Casey shrugged, at a loss, and waved him over again. "You can't be serious," he cackled, his voice deepening. "You think you can take me alive? Better men than you have tried."

"There is no better man than me."

"No worse!" he erupted, fanning one hand out at him. The flames that escaped screamed with him, whistling above the wind in the tunnels. They were living embers taking flight against the Cultist. The fire twisted in its path, dancing an aerial in the shape of a phoenix, crashing into Casey with enough strength to push him to the black fountain itself.

Faolan stepped forwards as the energy rushed out of him, still casting as he closed the gap. Ahead, he could see the mageblood radiating in the periphery, sapping up the heat and warming the water a few hundred degrees hotter than it ever should have been as a liquid until it broke from its solvent and the water steamed upwards around the waterfall in columns of white vapor.

The flames dissipated as quickly as they had appeared. Beyond them, Casey stood with one hand outstretched, having repelled the blast, with no patience left on his face. "Keep trying to fight fire with fire," he said. "I'm sure it'll work eventually."

The banished prince did not gasp in the wake of his opponent as his hand shot forth. The only discomfort he showed was a twitch in the mottled skin of his brow where some flesh had once been before someone had burned it away. He knew that the coming fire was hotter than any he had ever felt before.

It fell upon him in a nova, something utterly exquisite to behold.

Moments later, Casey stepped over his body, flames still lingering on his robes and spasms shooting through his frayed nerves. Against his impulse, he quenched the burning regalia and knelt over the elf's face, still covered by shaking hands. He knocked the reddened limbs away, grabbed the ruby earring, and ripped it from the lobe.

He didn't spend another instant attending to his prisoner before he moved back to the much bigger game mounted against the wall. "I'm sorry you've had to suffer so long."

He reached for his gun but noticed the panting hunter lifting a blade. Yin seemed to quiet as Casey clutched James' wrist and pried the weapon out of his hand, tossing it clear across the chamber. Yang, too, hushed as his other hand fell. Still, the hunter's breaths flopped out from his lips as if he were drowning. His eyes hung upon Casey's. They were the only weapon he had left, but their dying gaze was too soft to stop the Cultist.

He wondered how this man had ever been the titan of his nightmares as he retrieved his pistol and heard the click of a gun that was not his.

His sight and weapon lined up with the two assailants in the same instant. He emptied the gun without hesitation. Six bullets left from Casey's end, but only the first five flew anywhere near their targets. The last was thrown off by the single slug that struck his shoulder before Alvin O'Hare went down with a smile on his face. Robert Fletcher stood next to him.

"Got him," the old man sputtered.

"Not you," grunted Casey.

James watched the pilot and initiate fall, numb from his body's last rites, from blood loss, from pain. His eyes only softened more. After the long struggle, his head dropped down and he watched his blood leak out onto Casey's sword.

At the same time, Casey's anger melted the barrel of his gun. He let it drop from his hand, pressed his other against the fresh hole in his shoulder, and darted over to his latest victims. "Not you," he kept saying as he approached. "Not you." Robert let out choked gasps from his mouth. He'd donned a bulletproof vest in preparation for his destiny, but the armor hadn't kept his ribs from breaking. Alvin breathed through the new hole in his throat; he hadn't been nearly as lucky.

The Cultist clapped his free hand over the bullet wound, but most of the sharpshooter's blood had already spurted out onto the ground. Alvin's eyes closed first, then Casey's. The hunter, initiate, and Cultist all groaned from their injuries, but Alvin was silent.

"This is why I have to kill you." Casey stood in mute horror. James tried to lift his head, but his body betrayed him. "This is why men like you have to die." He set his sights back on James and stalked towards him. "You don't understand what it means to be willing to fight for something—for anything—except your own survival. When everyone around you would die just to protect you."

He grasped the hilt of his sword.

"Like Uwe did."

James' eyes opened despite the pain. His neck lifted, his jaw firmed, and air moved to the base of his lungs and back up again in one cleansing wave. His heart filled with blood, not for the thrill of the hunt, but for the love of the man who'd raised him: Uwe Löwe. The detective. The hunter. The man. The dwarf. The mentor. The traitor. The Cultist. The protector. The father. He died defending his progeny—the only selfless way an animal could survive.

Casey pulled Stinger from the wall and, as the blade slid through his core, James' breath filled him all at once.

To the end.

Volod's corpse fell to the one side and left James to support himself before the foe he had never been able to defeat, but the difference now was clear. James McCrary didn't just have something to live for. James McCrary had something to *die* for.

The other ancient poised his sword for a thrust through the heart. The hunter vanished from its path. Casey watched in distilled time as the earth elementalist placed his hand on the bloodied brick behind him. Stinger struck the stone that he had turned to clay a millisecond prior. The blade buried itself almost a meter into the wall before James pulled his nails over the rock and it solidified again, trapping the sword completely.

"No."

Casey bit his tongue, bared his fangs, and freed his hands to blast fire over the hunter just as James pulled a blanket of earth from below. In the next moment, the blanket burst into fragments. Every pebble pulverized the Cultist as he staggered back behind a curtain of flame. He looked up from the assault to behold the Stoneslayer overshadowing him with Yang at the ready and a hand stretched outwards to the walls. He felt the chamber shake from his might. He saw the hole in his opponent's gut go unnoticed.

James smelled the fear on him.

The pillars in the center of the room snapped in two when he crossed his arms. He opened them again and four cylinders of earth crumpled towards his target. Casey rolled from the impact and rushed a ripple of fire at him. James pulled up a barrier of rock between them and, when he did, the Cultist dashed for the chamber's mouth and out into the maze where at least the dark could hide him.

For a moment, James watched as he ran before bolting after him. He had no intention of shying from the lure.

Behind him, the initiate slept away his wounds in an unconscious stupor while Alvin slumbered forever and the banished prince shivered from the pain of his burns. He'd never felt such intense fire, never felt such great quakes. The ancients were unrecognizable, given over to their basest instincts. Still, Faolan smiled, thinking that this must have been the way it had to end, with two dogs grappling at the core of the world.

Chapter Thirty-Seven
James

To be James McCrary in that moment was to forswear humanity. He took up the mantle of the beast in its stead.

Where human fear and anger had resided, an animal hunger trod into the ground. With every step, his boots broke up the earth, compressed the stone, made the tunnel tremble. He charged with Olympian speed while Casey scuttled away from him, turning to slow him with a fireball whenever he could manage.

Where bloodlust had held his features, he wore instead a bestial calm. His eyes glowed golden-brown when the flames snapped at him, then they faded to black when he smothered the embers with rock. His mouth stayed closed, the only fang he needed dangling in his left hand. His nose pulled in the dirt and ash and shot out smoke and thunder.

Where doubt had shackled him, the passion of the hunt freed him. It rewarded the hunter for all his loyalty with the absolution of nature. Each time he tightened his fist, feeling for the faults in the walls of the sewer to tear the bricks apart and shower them over Casey, he had no intent but to kill. Each time Casey moved in to strike, pitched a bursting spark into the darkness or spat a blast of heat along the walls, he exonerated the hunter just as Uwe had. In the dwarf's last breath, when he'd lunged, it was not to kill but to be killed. He'd sacrificed himself so that James would not have to bear the guilt of his death. Now there wasn't a trace of guilt left in the ancient. He had the innocence of a lion, and so nature's impartial justice was his to dispense. Thusly acquitted, the animal blew the sewers apart in his mad dash, unthinking, unfeeling, unyielding.

To be Casey Aduro in that moment was to give up the selfsame claim to human emotions. He knew only the red terror of nature, the sharp panic that sent his blood surging to every muscle he could control and even those which he could not.

He could feel his fear empowering him. The fury that prompted his fire he had never felt burn this hot. This, he thought, was the most power he had ever held and might ever hold. He swiveled on one foot, drove his weight into the ground, lurched his arm out as if to take the hunter's heart, felt the heat sting his fist as it coalesced into a helix of flame and spiraled, shrieking, down the tunnel.

The hunter on his heels swept his arms out to his sides, jerked them back across his chest, and the earth crumbled in between them, burying the blaze. Then he plowed through the barrier, sending a barrage of cobbles crashing at and around the Cultist, and Casey turned tail again, much faster this time.

Any wounds that either man had sustained were of no consequence. There was no middle ground left for them between life and death; Casey would fight to a finale, as would James. Somewhere, a moon watched in daylight. It pried apart the clouds, flashed under bridges and in holes, sensing the hunt and begging the sun to reveal it.

Suddenly, Casey's eye caught the wall ahead as it began to buckle. He dropped into a slide as it imploded and a stream of sewage flooded in after it, blocking the path. He spun around, slipping in the filth, and released a spark down the tunnel. James stopped hard, planted, and slapped a hand onto the brick. He let his energy vibrate through the rock, felt the stone go soft, and watched the mortar puff out in a small radius. When he pulled his hand away, the wall came with it, inviting another rush of water to douse the wisp before it could detonate.

With the hunter's momentum broken, Casey moved into a charge. His shoulder pointed downwards, flaming like a comet, but he kept his eyes up and forward.

James split his feet apart, reached for the ceiling between them, and brought the structure to nothing. It should have crushed his prey, but Casey threw his arm out, the energy popped, and a sphere of hot pressure pulsed from his body. It staved off the debris overhead just as well as it evaporated the water underfoot, and it set the hunter back on his haunches. Casey's dash culminated in an extended hand—a light in the palm—followed by a hose of flame fast enough to outstrip a drake. He had to hold his idle hand to his shoulder just to keep the jet from straying.

The hunter plucked a stalagmite from the ground just in time for the fire to whisk over it. Now, though, Casey could advance.

The flamejet crashed past James on either side, pressing through his fireproof coat, burning his skin. Beneath him, the sewer water bubbled and leapt up in plumes of steam. He crouched down lower in spite of the vapor, reaching his mind out over the ground. Without knowing exactly where Casey stood, he tightened a fist and gripped a patch of rock ahead of him then twisted his heel so that the rock turned to sand. Then he pulled the grains out from under the pyromancer's feet, and the heat washed left of him as his opponent toppled. The hunter saw the conflagration sweep up the wall as far as the ceiling before it winked out, but as Casey struck the ground he let out a bark of flame that curved around the stalagmite where he could see the corner of the hunter's coat. It would hit him. He couldn't have dodged it even with all his speed...had he still been standing there.

A mass of black too quick to notice, Casey glimpsed only the glint of a blade still dripping with gargoyle ichor. The fang flew up and fell towards his heart. He faltered in answering it.

Only the blast of flame he threw desperately to the side could have moved him away fast enough to dodge the strike. The hunter's arm smashed down with enough force to break through the entire wall. James followed it, committed to the attack, and spilled into the cavity hidden beyond while Casey sprawled out behind him into the main tunnel, lurched to his feet, and started doubling back through the maze.

He ran a half a minute down the corridors, huffing and stumbling over the rubble his pursuer had gored out of the earth, before the hunter caught up to him on the other side of the wall. Even separated by a layer of brick he could sense him. It came as no surprise when the stones toppled and the wolf leapt over them, but James McCrary's eyes went wide when his target greeted him with a crazed smile painted with blood and a gasp of flame.

The hunter cursed at his lack of protection against the heat but was thankful that the hasty burst did not burn as hot as the last dozen. He whirled behind Casey and hit the opposite side of the tunnel, pulling a gust of dust from the cracks and smothering the fire that lingered on his arms. He made sure to hit the Cultist with the same cloud, but it failed to slow him. Casey's hands were already glowing, pressing red-hot towards him, casting bright shadows along the walls.

His back already flush against the tunnel, James dug his fingers into the stone and broke the wall apart, hoping for a deluge. The flood that came, though, was of light rather than water—a blinding dawn that seared their eyes. The hunter dove aside as he winced, and twin blazes blew out into the daylight. He moved almost immediately to take hold of the adjacent rubble, ready to bury the pyromancer once and for all, but as the sunlight cooled over his vision, his eyes tightened upon the spot where Casey had stood and found nothing.

"Casey," he heard himself growl, the name scraping his parched throat. He crept into the fracture in the tunnel with predatory caution, peering out into the white city.

The hole opened into a canal between two rows of high buildings obscured by flurrying drifts of snow. A bridge stretched over it farther on. James spotted a cluster of cars parked along it, but no other traffic. The lead car had held a stalwart old man with a bird's neck and a warrior's heart. James could make out a wide impression in the snow below the bridge where an impatient elven royal had leapt from the span and broken his fall with fire, then a host of tracks where the pack had stampeded down the canal to the entrance almost a quarter mile down. One set of them was light and direct, the marks of a determined woman with an elegant mind and a spirit to match. Close behind hers, a man's lopsided trail stood where the commander had staggered with one arm in a sling and the other toting a gun. The last footprints stumbled around the ice, slipping some here, sliding completely there, the path of a certain initiate. He could even see a break in the stride where Robert had stopped to catch his breath.

The hunter's eyes scanned the entire trail in a single heartbeat before he detected the tracks running opposite the others. He followed them up the canal to the bridge, barring snowfall from his eyes and gazing farther up. Beyond the bridge, a car park eclipsed the moon.

When he climbed towards the building, he caught sight of Casey dashing inside. His adrenaline rush cut the chase down to an instant. He turned up and up and up each floor all the way to the top, never losing sight of his quarry, but he could feel the moon leering at them with sickening curiosity. Even beyond the clouds, its gaze burned into him hotter than any flame Casey had thrown. He glanced to the gargoyles' domain then back to the sky, grimacing. Casey, though, seemed to have a certain proclivity for chases, for rooftops, and for scènes à faire.

"Are we dogs or gods?" he huffed, stopping at the center of the vacant rooftop. "Cause this must be what it's like when gods meet." The cars had been sparse on the lower levels, but here their arena lay bare, untarnished, decorated only by the white petals the sky cast down in approval.

In one hand, he held the Eye of Vaos, in the other the old god's Talon. James' hands lurched out to stop him, but when the black blade tapped the surface of the Eye, both ancients doubled over in agony.

"Can you feel it, James?" he strained, carving away an edge of the gem. "This is the blood of the mages, but what's inside us? Ours is the blood of *gods*." He took a second slash at the stone.

"You need mageblood to kill me," James challenged him, pointing Yang.

"I need mageblood to *show* you," the Cultist said, taking a deep gash from the Eye and sending the hunter's free hand to his temple, "so that you can understand before you die." He himself almost stumbled from the sensation.

James straightened into a fighting stance, attempting to tap into elementality, but every whisper of the Eye shattered his concentration. "Whether I get it or not," he said, tilting, "you can't live. You know that."

"Maybe." Casey's brow wrinkled while he took another sliver of mageblood from the gem. By now a line of violet residue had amassed on the edge of the dagger. "This." He lifted it so that James could see. "This is what we're made of. We wouldn't be here without this. We wouldn't be in such deep shit without this." He ran his tongue along the length of the blade, taking in every bit of mageblood he could, then let the eye drop to the ground. Even then, his vision started to shift. The blue gave way to darkness as the pupil consumed the iris and then the white turned to grey. Casey felt the change even if he couldn't see it. His eyes felt as cold as ice. The chill only startled him at first. Soon, he shivered. "I hope one day," he told the hunter who could only watch, wide-eyed, "that people will understand what I've done."

The air that came to him plunged deeper and stronger than ever before, but it felt shallow in his chest. He did not feel the air come in to relieve his lungs. It seemed more like drowning. But the air did come in, and as he connected to his energy, he felt flames leap to his hands out of nothing. The light that flickered from the heat shined radiant blue, almost white, the color of lightning. Unfazed by this peculiarity, Casey threw his hands to the ground, tilted his head back, and a roar of ice-blue fire the size of Solomon the Great escaped from his jaws.

It burned hotter than anything either ancient had ever witnessed.

Even from meters away, James shielded his face, dazed as he was by the inferno.

The swath the pyromancer cut through the air steamed where the fire had erased the snow. Even on the ground the ice sublimated. The fire in Casey's hands danced with excitement as he reclaimed a smile. "If that doesn't convince you, I don't know what will." He took a single step, stiffened an arm, and a blue blaze rolled forwards with the sound of a meteor.

James put as much concrete between the two of them as he could gather in a breath, a barricade two meters high and four meters thick. The tidal wave of fire crashed against it, splashed around the top and sides, curled around far enough to bake the hunter alive, but it stood. The flames peeled back before they could devour him.

He baulked at the power behind the Cultist's casts, his endurance, his focus—his speed. Casey appeared to his left with a double helping of fire and unleashed it upon him. James doubled the amount of earth he'd just summoned and broke the roof's foundation by peeling it up from the ground. It stopped the fireburst, but he felt the edge of the roof crumble behind it and go toppling down. Casey, however, did not fall along with it. Instead, he materialized opposite his first wall and the hunter found himself cornered.

Another wall went up somewhere between the magnitude of the first two, absorbing Casey's feint before he wheeled around to the last side of the box and poured a scorching avalanche into the stone trap. James fell backwards, grabbing the ground through what snow was left, and threw up a sheet of rock. He watched the fire swell over the lip of the wall before receding, and he regained his footing just as Casey came over the edge in a flourish of white.

He had nothing left with which to defend himself. The walls around him had thinned the ground as much as it could stand. This high above the earth his element met its limitations. If he pulled out any more rock from under them, the whole section might collapse. So when Casey landed in the ring, James rushed to meet him.

He lashed out one arm to deflect his opponent's, felt the heat of his punch go screaming into the air, and pulled Yang close to the Cultist's face. Casey bounded backward, smacking against the perimeter and losing his footing, and the hunter bolted after him for another strike. His opponent ducked the slice with ease and twirled behind him, raising his hand to bring down fire. James beat back blindly, pushing him back even more. When Casey came with another set of blows, he'd freed a combat knife from his boot.

An unexpected jet of fire shrieked from Casey's mouth, missing James by a hair. Then the elementalist threw a fist earthward, sending out a molten shockwave. Springing over it, the hunter came with the unnamed knife raised, missed, and hurled it after him while Casey circled around the edge of the box. Off-balance, he brought his Talon up to meet Yang. The two grazed each other, and the deathly sound sent each man reeling to an opposite corner.

The flames fled from Casey's fingertips as the dust around James settled to the ground. He held the blade up while the two cowered, inspecting it for a moment, and his eyes shook as they stared.

"Mageblood?" asked Casey.

James rolled his wrist and tightened his fingers around Yang. A gift from Uwe to him. A steel weapon with a mageblood core, designed for an ancient to wield. When the twins came into contact, the steel was enough of a buffer to protect him, but when they met with another weapon crafted from black, or better yet another ancient…

He rushed at his opponent, aiming to plunge Yang into his chest. It missed him and his Talon, but when Casey struck back James parried, and the ringing brought them both back to their knees. Then they were up again, too addled to cast, but animal enough to snarl and snap at each other with steel and mageblood before the blades met again and put them down once more.

The Cultist came up quickly this time, ravenous with his dagger outstretched. The hunter leaned away and felt death skirt his throat. This wasn't a fight that he could win. The mageblood made Casey's casts stronger and faster, and even without them he could slash just as swiftly. James couldn't kill him without changing something. A mindset, maybe.

The rooftop rumbled in spite of his dizziness. As soon as his black boots were planted in the snow, he felt his mind race for the pillar just under them at the near corner. He cracked the column with a thought.

At first, Casey only lost his balance before the second pillar broke, the ground began to lean, and he realized what was happening.

James was prepared to destroy everything around him to fulfill the hunt. This time, when the building fell, he'd make sure Casey Aduro fell with it.

His opponent's focus shifted from the pillars to his prey. Once the fourth support started to give way, he charged. Once the last one bent, the hunter could pull the whole floor into the river. The Cultist refused to let that happen.

James dodged the Talon once, twice, threw Yang out in a feint, and dodged a third time as his reach went out to the farthest column. He could almost feel it grazing against his mind as easily as he could've felt it on his fingertips. Then Casey proved that an animal's will was as unpredictable as nature in moments of life or death. When Yang came back to drive him off, he threw his hand up to catch it, howling, then extended his other hand as far as it would go, far enough to puncture James in the gut again.

His mind broke. His energy collapsed around him, buried him. He lost sense of the stone under his feet. The pillar at the end of the roof may as well have been the moon. An unfamiliar pain rocked up from his stomach and through his blood all the way to his mind where it held him and shook him and pressed his thoughts into paste.

In front of him, he watched through a haze as Casey pulled Yang from his own trembling, seeping hand and pitched it over the edge of the roof. Even in the fog of death, James could feel the heat that swarmed up around Casey's hands washing over his face. Then the genocidal animal plodded after him with his eyes leaking black and his hands bleeding fire.

To the end of his life, he'd hate him. He'd hate him with every breath.

Here, on his knees, James let the bastard get close enough to strangle him. The heat was enough to cauterize his open wounds.

Casey eyed him for a moment, reining in his smoldering rage, considering just how close he'd come. The hunter's face was a sickly brown, his skin dried out from the scalding heat, his dark eyes murky and dim. They spoke of mortality, of eternity, and all that was between.

Then, just as his Talon shot out, the film passed from over his eyes. Lionesque and supreme, James saw Casey for what he was.

Prey.

Casey lost the feeling of the ground under his feet as the hunter tackled him, driving him back against a barrier. He pulled in the Talon like a scorpion's tail, piercing his back just before they hit the stone and it splintered like glass, forcing the air from his lungs.

James shook from the pain, but it was nothing compared to what lay ahead or below. In the next moment, he toed the edge of the rooftop, felt the time come, and sent the rest of his strength into quaking legs. When he leapt, he sent a tremor rolling down the building that the city could feel for miles around.

He heard Casey curse as he shoved him away. He heard the hiss of heat come from above as the other ancient struggled to stay aloft. Then he looked to the earth—as welcoming as it had ever been—and thought urgently to reject its invitation.

There was a way. Uwe had tried to teach him once how to cast earth in freefall without a stance or without a connection to the element. It was difficult, but possible. He'd never tried it before.

James stretched his hand out for the ground, sent his vital force into every inch he could reach. The pavement was bitter and stiff, hardened by the same snow that brushed around the edges of his face and made it hard to forget that he was falling. Fast.

But the earth would save him. How could it ignore him? He'd been so loyal.

Above him, Casey burned like a rocket, so far above him it hurt to imagine. He was slowing—he was surviving—while the hunter fell.

The realization broke his focus at the wrong moment. He no longer felt any connection to the earth racing up to meet him now with an asphalt smile and snowy lips. Somewhere, the moon watched it all. It was smiling. It was laughing. It was peeking through the clouds to see how he would finally die.

The force was nothing short of colossal. His body broke the fall that his mind could not manage to fathom. Where he had not been able to soften it, the concrete split and fractured to match his bones. He rolled with a soundless scream onto his back, stopping only when he hit the Talon still lodged in his spine. He turned back over, too far gone even to shake. He didn't register the footsteps edging towards him, but he could not ignore the blade being wrenched from between his shoulders.

Casey pushed the broken thing onto its back and stood over his quarry. It tried to turn its head to look him in the eye but could not move its neck anymore. Its gaze remained out over the river with the white-capped buildings bearing witness to its execution. It wondered if Uwe had felt this still and calm when he'd gone.

When the fire sprang to Casey's hands, arms, and shoulders, the pain was almost welcome; anything to distract James from the feelings inside and remind him that he was still alive, choking on agony and writhing with a broken spine.

"I promised you a quick death." The black tears stained the Cultist's pallid face as he watched an all too familiar struggle. He swallowed the lump in his throat. "You'll burn like the rest of us." He sweltered under the blue mantle as it expanded, wrapping him like a cloak. The moment he lifted his hand to the hunter, he felt something off about the heat. His arm jerked back reflexively against the spike of pain. He tried to reduce the flame's intensity but found that it only grew brighter. All the fire was there, but he could do nothing to quell it.

"No." His animal panic became instantly human.

When one limb recoiled from discomfort, the lapse of concentration brought down his protection over another section. His right arm held until his fingers and hands and wrists and arms and elbows and shoulders and chest and neck and chin and cheeks and ears and nose and eyes and brow and scalp swam in a twelve-hundred degree shroud of pure sunfall.

He spun back, flailing, trying to wrest back control, dispel the flame, cast it off, get rid of it.

The snow peeled away around him as if to retreat. His breaths stopped coming in. Somewhere in the distance, he heard something like a death knell echoing in his veins. There was something like a bell chiming, chiming, chiming in his blood.

Then the fire ignored his command outright. The conflagration bit into his skin with all the fierceness of a beast held against its will. The moment it came unchained, it was hot enough to melt iron.

He felt the bell on the horizon clamor, started to scream something before he fell on bended knee and yielded. From the corner of his eye, James saw in Casey a primal fear. It was the kind of horror that frightens away a man's faith in the seconds before his death. Most terrifying of all, though, he watched the Cultist try to tell him something.

But the fire consumed him utterly. Not a sound escaped. The only parts of him strong enough to weather were his bones and his blade. The Talon sank into his ashen grip as the flames rushed up and away into the heavens, his black husk curled back into an unnatural shape and hardened, and the Flamestorm subsided forevermore.

* * * *

The hunter lay near him for seconds that seemed hours and minutes that seemed years. He drifted in and out of dreams, filling the nightmares of his past with the horror of his present reality all while he waited to die. It hadn't even occurred to him that the others might find him there, signaled by the geyser of fire that had erupted forth from the now-dead ancient.

He heard their shouts arrive like murmurs, their shapes resembling shadows, and when Michelle tilted his head towards her, her warm hands felt cold like metal. She was saying something, the same thing over and over again—something comforting, no doubt. He spoke out before he could understand it.

"Robert." The voice was weaker than he'd expected it to leave him. The sound drained hope from him. Still, the noise came in clear once he'd spoken. "Faolan."

"We found them," she said with eyes wide and brown. Dirt framed her face and a few cuts lined her brow, but she seemed largely unharmed. He grinned, or at least thought that he did. "They're okay. The elves are with them." She refused to let a tear fall while his eyes were open, but he could see them welling up in her cheeks as her lips tightened. Then he spotted Bailey and some of Faolan's guard behind her, and they answered his next question.

As one of the elves approached with medical supplies, Michelle ran her hands over every injury on his body, not knowing where to start. The katana's grievous puncture was enough, but the knife wounds, the broken bones, the burns...she stuttered at the sight of it all. Bailey looked away out over the river when the hunter tried to make eye contact with him, and James' vision sank into the earth.

"Alvin," he mumbled, no longer fighting the energy draining from his shell of a body.

Michelle shook her head.

The sensation returned to his stomach just long enough for him to experience pain before the throb warped. He'd never had this feeling before. Something like epinephrine, but different. An adrenaline for his battle with death. Anesthesia for the final hunt.

He started to tell the reader something when she pressed a heap of cloth into his gut and recoiled. Over her shoulder, though, he noticed another figure standing in front of the others. A tall, burly man. He was a dwarf with fiery hair, dark eyes, and a ridiculous smile. He was applauding his very death.

"My favorite thing about theatre," Uwe's specter said, "is that you can always find redemption in the finale. You about ready?"

"I'll be quick," he answered him. The others jumped at the utterance.

The vision nodded. "Take your time." He laughed, adding, "I've only been waiting a few years."

"Who told you where to find me?" he said, ignoring the answers Michelle and the others put to him.

"I asked a sheep. He sent me right over." When the hunter laughed, the muscles didn't stop twitching, so he shivered for some time after the humor had left him. He heard an elf swear and pull a hand around to his back. When Michelle moved over his line of sight, Uwe had disappeared.

She was still there, though, kneeling over him, shaking from fear or grief or cold or some combination of the three, and the tears were spilling in spite of her. The others had started weeping long before she did.

The ground slipped from under him as they tried to lift his body, but the sudden curve in his spine made him cry out.

"No," he chided them, waiting for his back to find the gentle earth again before continuing. "Chelle," he managed. The light in his eyes was fading now. She leaned in to hear the words that threatened to do the same. "Don't give Robert a gun. Ever." She found herself smiling, laughed suddenly, and broke the dam for the rest of her tears. "Send me home," he requested after half a decade in exile. She nodded, wordless. "Give my money to Diana Pascal," he made her promise. She did.

Then James McCrary the Stoneslayer let his neck fall to the side so that he could see the sky. The clouds were clearing, taking the snow along with them. The moon couldn't see him here, though, not with the car park behind him. Even so, he strained to find it. If nothing else, he wanted an opponent for his last hunt.

He'd always imagined himself dying under a full moon, a spectacle in a stone arena for a malevolent god.

Chapter Thirty-Eight
The Father

"They sent *you*?" said the reader, incredulous and short of breath. She stood petrified behind her desk as a man in black entered Mythic's lobby.

"They did." He cocked his head to one side and examined her. His mouth smiled even though his eyes did not. "How are you?" he asked in an almost unplaceable accent.

"Fine," Michelle answered, still enraptured. Her hands flicked up to the bandages on her face. "I wasn't hurt. Seriously, at least."

"Good," the man said, still smiling with only the bottom half of his face. His trimmed, black beard curled up with his lips, but the thick eyebrows only sloped down and away. He kept the rest of his hair cropped and combed. It matched his business attire well. He turned from her and headed towards the lift without another word.

She watched him go with his hands folded behind his back in the dark sleeves of his jacket, gripping one another firmly.

"Will you join us?" he asked, letting his soft, intense voice bounce off the marble walls. "I've asked that everyone be present."

Michelle nodded, ignoring the fact that he did not look at her when he spoke, and fell in behind him as he punched the call button for the elevator. His eyes gazed straight ahead; she could see them in the golden reflection of the doors.

"You're not..." she hesitated. "They didn't send you—" His sudden glare stopped the words in her throat. "Walter, Xiang, and Casey

314

betrayed the organization, but they're all dead now." The man in black's eyes lingered on her for a moment, too dark to read. She'd tried before, she recalled, without ever having any inkling of success. His were where eyes went to die, to be lost in the depths of a soul beyond legibility. She almost fell prey to them again before the lift doors spread, revealing a tall man wrapped in gauze who was supporting himself on crutches. A timid initiate stood at his side.

"Michelle," Robert sang when he saw her as if he hadn't already seen her that morning already, as if he'd never seen her in his life. She returned the look, blushing. Meanwhile, Gerard almost toppled over.

"Jesus, Joseph, and Mary." He stood dumbfounded for a moment before the man in black stepped into the lift and pushed him stumbling against the wall. He didn't have the presence of mind to wince as he shifted back. He was too busy sweating.

"Gerard," the man said, bowing his head and choosing the executor's floor from the panel. "You're the initiate," he confirmed with Robert, who lifted his head to nod before pausing.

"You're the courier from Berlin?" he asked. Gerard and Michelle's eyes fell on him like daggers.

"This is Europe's *patriarch*," Gerard informed him through gritted teeth.

"Oh, fancy-schmance," Robert said, shaking his head in affirmation. "Hey, that's pretty outrageous. Aren't there just three patriarchs in the whole world?" The man in black shifted his focus back to the elevator doors. "They never tell me anything," he complained. "Would've at least had a shave." He began to voice another excuse before Michelle nudged him to be quiet.

The initiate sank into her touch, rediscovering his smile. He tried to catch her eyes in his while the lift went up, but her concentration remained forward as well. After a dozen floors of silence, he attempted to break the tension.

"I had fun last night," he said, beaming like a clown and finally drawing her attention. Her glance held more shock than he'd anticipated. The panic left her and inhabited him before he could blink. "What?" he stammered, looking around. Gerard's face glowed red, white, and purple all at once. Then Robert turned and saw the patriarch staring him down.

His lips curled in a voiceless *oh* as the man's eyes dug into his. "Is there a thing with office romances?"

The doors slid open before the initiate could finish digging his own grave, leading Michelle and Gerard to rush through to the door and into the hallway beyond.

"Aaron," Gerard started, "something you should know before we begin—"

Before any of them could register the glow of a diamond, the patriarch shouldered by and a blue spark sprang up from his fingertips, leaping to the opposite doorframe. He pushed his way inside, his eyes ticking around the many chairs lining the office where there'd once been a desk. He checked the plastic sheet taped over the fractured window, but the only soul he found inside was Thomas Bailey.

"The elves," Michelle began. "As we would've told your courier," she went on but stopped short as Aaron raised his hand.

"I know you weren't expecting me. That's why I came. Because *I* expect a swift and elegant resolution to this ugly fuck of a mess." He turned, still smiling. "I don't blame you for letting Faolan escape. We'll apprehend him in due time. For now, I'm trying to pull together some slight idea as to what happened here. How it happened. Who was the cause. What is the solution. The most immediate facet of that problem being one Gerard Jones." He turned to the accused Cultist. "Why are you with us here today?"

He didn't have an answer, but Michelle spoke up for him.

"We've done our best to resume operations with an already decimated staff. Gerard is acting as our interim courier during what has been a hellish transition."

"Well, I guess he proved himself more than capable running errands for the Cult of the Apocalypse." Gerard tried to break eye contact while the patriarch watched him but found himself unable. Before he was aware of it, his mind had slipped from under his guard. "There are circumstances, I grant you, under which we would review a suspected Cultist's intentions. But…" he glanced over to the reader as if to instruct a child, "understand that an innocent man, a dead man, and a dead Cultist each do us the same amount of harm, which is to say none at all. A live Cultist, on the other hand, does all kinds." He turned his attention back to

Gerard who was still paralyzed under his scrutiny. "So the most prudent decision we as protectors of the world can make is to kill first on suspicion and deal with the guilt later. That is our *charge*," he concluded, pointing a finger at the ex-courier.

As he approached, he detected Bailey on his right, lurching forwards in a chair, Michelle behind him, arms outstretched, and even the initiate ready to intervene. One jolt could stop Gerard's heart permanently. Recognizing this, the accused looked up to his patriarch with deference in lieu of defiance, nodded, and knelt.

Aaron lowered his hand. "Stand."

Gerard's eyes came up to meet his, his brow wrinkling in confusion.

"We are men, not beasts. The thing that separates us most from the Cult is that our form of 'mercy' isn't a knife in the side." The patriarch still looked troubled, but as Gerard rose he placed a hand on his shoulder. "Your mother is safe?"

He hesitated to respond. "Yes, sir. Took a bit of searching, but we got her back safe and sound."

"Good." Turning to Michelle, he asked, "Has she been under observation?"

"Of course," she confirmed. "Both she and Gerard have been under my supervision. No signs of sabotage thus far."

Aaron nodded, though he was not completely comforted by her diligence. "I'm the only man in this hemisphere who can absolve a Cultist. He and his mother should have been in cages or boxes for the last few days. Remember that, the next time you want an innocent man to live." He took a moment to settle after the moment's agitation then gestured for everyone to sit. "As of this moment, I trust every man and woman in this room." Gerard, Michelle, Robert, and Thomas exchanged looks of relief before he continued. "But you're the branch of Mythic that almost let half of London die. Explain."

Michelle did her best to untwist her lips. "As Faolan explained it to me, our priorities were to close off access to the tainted water. Keep as much of it out of public hands as possible. We've accomplished that, with marginal success. Warned people about contamination, blocked off mains, drained as much as we could into the ocean, but the fact remains: there's mageblood out there."

"Mythic: Defenders of London, but no friend to the whales."

"We've encountered a few cases of consumption so far, but nowhere near as many as expected."

The patriarch pressed his hands into his back and looked down, nodding—the closest he'd get to an apology. "So…this wasn't an uprising. At best, it was preparation for another campaign. Even if it was, we mitigated enough damage that we have no business calling it that."

"My understanding," Gerard volunteered, "is that this was all just a Cultist trick. A chance for them to capture a Ciric royal alive. For them, all the death and destruction was just icing on the cake."

The skin around Aaron's eyes wrinkled. "All right, then. Casey's dead, his courier's dead, his mandor's dead, the Sewick coven is extinct, and the executor that let it all happen for a mageblood addiction has been rightly dealt the same sentence. I'd say we've earned a reprieve."

"I agree," said Michelle. "I think the Cult's operations will subside for the time being."

"And the stolen artifacts?"

One of the chairs scraped back as Bailey stood and handed over a black satchel. "The Eye of Vaos and The Talon of Vaos." He looked Aaron in the eyes, bowing back to his seat after a moment. "Both mageblood. It—"

"I know what mageblood is." He pulled the Eye from the bag and turned it over a few times before dropping it back in. "You'd all do well to keep your knowledge of it to a minimum. The heads of Mythic, a few executors who have dealt with it directly." He shrugged. "That's everyone who needs to know about mageblood." His hands darted back behind him. "It's a weapon, as dangerous to the wielder as it is to anyone else. You've all seen proof of that." He looked to the space where Walter's desk had once been. "I'll move these somewhere safer and separate them for now. For your own safety, none of you will know the new locations." The others nodded in understanding. "Now," he muttered, "are you in a position to resume normal operations?"

Michelle blinked. "Our staff was half what it should've been beforehand. How are we to operate with even less than that?"

"We'll replenish your ranks in due time," Aaron reassured her. "I'm not in a rush to dirty a branch you've just cleaned up." The reader nodded, bowing her head. "In the meantime, I think you've got everything you need to keep this city safe." Her eyes came up to meet his. "I see in this room a set of people who have had their mettle duly tested. A loyal people." He turned to Gerard. "I see a courier, tried and tested. Not sure I can say we've ever had a Cultist defect on our payroll before." The cocky Englishman stifled a chuckle. "I see a hunter," he stated, looking to Thomas. His eyes turned over to Robert, grinning wide. "A driver," he said with less confidence. "And an executor." Michelle's lips parted in shock. "You can do a reader's job in your sleep," he told her. "Literally." Finally, his smile reached his eyes. "You were born for it. I only wish everyone involved in this latest triumph could see a proper reward." The temperature in the room seemed to drop alongside the mood.

"Alvin was a dear friend and a trusted servant of Mythic. He will be missed," Michelle agreed.

"And the hunter," the patriarch was quick to remind her. "James McCrary? The man suspected of murdering Čeněk Holub in defense of the Cult."

The freshly-appointed executor stood in spite of the patriarch's authority. "Whatever James' mistakes were in the past, he showed himself a true and loyal hunter in the end." She let the patriarch's eyes consume hers, let his mind survey hers from her most active thought to her deepest memory. "He sacrificed himself so that this city and this Earth would be safe."

"For now," Aaron answered, satisfied. "And yet, you transferred a sizeable sum of money to an account back in the States. In New York, to be precise."

"James had two final requests: that we send his body home and that we make sure to take care of the woman he loved. We did just that."

"Well," the patriarch conceded, "I hope that she loved him as much as he did her. At any rate, I doubt Walter will miss his retirement funds." He shrugged again and started to leave. "If you see Faolan, let him know that the sooner he sees me, the sooner I'll stop stepping on his toes."

"As far as I could tell, it seemed like he was going to try and go home to Cire," Michelle told him.

"In that case, I might not find him alive." Before he left, he turned to

Michelle once more. "Goodbye, my love. Hope to you see you again."

Then the patriarch vanished as quickly as he had appeared, almost as much a phantom as the ancients of old. Robert stepped after him as the lift doors closed, scowling. "Who was that?"

Gerard laughed after a long bout of tension. "That was the patriarch of Europe," he exclaimed, which still meant less than nothing to the initiate. "The *senior* patriarch. Aaron Reid."

"Hunh," he considered the information a moment before looking to Michelle. "He has the same name as you." The reader glowered at him three full seconds before he understood. "Oh, fuck me." She'd already buried her face in one hand. He felt the skin on his face go hot. "What I said could've meant anything!" he argued as Gerard erupted into laughter again.

Michelle peeked between her fingers as the no-longer-ex-courier continued to jeer at the initiate-driver. The commander caught her attention. "How'd we do?" he asked her, pale of face.

"All right, I suppose." She wiped her hand across her eyes and sat back down. "I don't think he'll look into Diana, but it's out of our hands."

"He's the greatest reader of the last century," Gerard chimed in.

"If the century's two greatest hunters can die, then its greatest reader can be deceived. We've done our part." The words seemed to assuage their fears at least somewhat. "Loyalty," she admonished them. "The world rewards you for it. We have to believe that. Or I do, at least." She swiveled to the window, to the panel patched with tarp where James had forced out Xiang. She smiled at the handiwork before checking the sun's position. "It's still early. Gerard, your first duty as courier: put on a record for us. And for the love of God, no bloody Dvořák." The others agreed in murmurs as he limped to his feet. "We've got a lot of work to do. I say we enjoy the moment."

"Why this one?" Robert asked her.

"Most of these are fucked," Gerard cut in from the shelf. "Dunno who could've done that," he added before anyone could point a finger at the culprit. "Ah," he said, spotting an intact disc. "Dvořák!" he called out.

"Forget it," Michelle surrendered. Gerard shrugged and spun the disc up anyway. "At this moment," the executor continued, "the sun is rising over the east coast three thousand miles away." She winced as the sudden sound of strings warmed the room, but her discomfort gave way to amusement. The orchestra swelled in their ears. The strings were songbirds curling above the hunt while the brass mimicked the bellows of the beasts. The woodwinds were their whispers between blows, the drums the pounding of feet and hooves. The symphony spoke of the New World: a primal, beautiful place governed by the whims of man and animal alike. It reminded them of a far-off world they'd never visited, a home to them even if they hadn't been born there.

"Yesterday, a certain driver picked up a young woman from New York and helped her gather her things. Now that woman is being taken to the house we bought for her. I like to think that the instant she sees it, she'll remember the name of the man who was willing to die to get it for her. The man who saved the world. We are some of the only people who will remember him. I hope not one of us ever forgets his name."

* * * *

"James McCrary." It felt unnatural as it left Diana's lips. She hadn't spoken it more than twice in the last five years.

The name came to her before the car even stopped, when the driver in the front glanced back at her and smiled. He was hideous but handsome, a mask of scars and burns on an unmistakably beautiful face and one unusually long ear. He looked as though he could have been a prince in another life.

"It's all right," he told her. "Everything is all right. It's all yours," he sang, trying to excite her.

She held a finger up to her lips and hushed him, only half-present, and opened the door while the wheels were still rolling.

Her bare feet touched down on cobblestone, moved straight through the yellow winter grass, fallen leaves, pine straw, and the circle of soil beyond that. She ignored the stone walkway that snaked through the yard far up to the house, immense in modesty, padding along only when it curved back across her path.

It was the house he'd promised her, the home they'd built in words whispered between them, nestled in the afterglow of passion. She marked each feature with growing anxiety. The grey house, the blue shutters, and porch that wrapped around to both sides. It wasn't the house that surprised her most, though. The sight that plucked the air from her breast and made her shake more than the Carolina winter was the man sitting at the top of the stairs, hidden in a long, black coat.

"James," she said again, within earshot now, and watched the man drag his head up from his chest.

He thought at first that he was waking into another dream or that he must've actually died. He found that he'd forgotten her name. He could recall everything he'd ever learned about her before, but the name didn't come to him until he hit her eyes.

"Diana." The green displaced everything around her. The dark trunks of the trees, the gold grass, the rainbow of foliage; they were colorless before her. He'd seen her eyes in dreams, nightmares, and waking visions and had never forgotten the fire they ignited within him. He felt the adrenaline kick out from his heart and rock him onto his feet.

"Wait," she objected as he stood, eyeing the crutch tucked under his arm. She couldn't have stopped him. Even under his jacket he appeared as a man broken and misshapen. Only his heart held its same structure. She couldn't stop him lumbering towards her as he lost his footing. She pressed a hand into his chest as he collapsed on top of her, but she couldn't stop his fall entirely. She was strong enough to hold him up, but her legs began to shake under his weight.

"I'm sorry," he stammered, struggling to lift himself from her shoulders. Gradually, she helped him to stand, supported by his metal braces, and watched him tremble. "I've been waiting," he told her. "Five years, I've been waiting."

"*You've* been waiting?" The inquiry left her in a puff of hot breath. She folded her arms both for warmth and for protection. "Where have you been?"

Her anger lashed him like silk. Even enraged, the tint of her accent and the timbre of her voice were welcome abuse. He smiled in spite of his pains. "Zurich, at first." This she already knew. "Then Berlin for a while. For a long while. Then England. Now here."

He watched for a reaction as her eyes burned up at him. They glowed brighter than any emerald a wind elementalist could wield.

322

"We were here," she maintained.

"Yeah," James admitted, lamenting their time apart. "We were."

She caught herself, refreshed her reason with a sigh, and turned back to him. "Why did you have to wait so long to come back?"

"I couldn't support us," he explained. "Not doing what I did. I—"

"I know what you do." His heart tapped once, loudly, against the inside of his chest. "I always knew. You hurt people. Killed, maybe. I knew that. I still loved you. What was worse than that was leaving. To know that you could hurt *me*."

"I had to find a way out. Then things went wrong and I couldn't risk them hurting you."

"I waited years for something. Anything. A call."

"Dangerous..." he muttered.

"A letter."

"You don't have to wait anymore."

"You couldn't have left at a worse time."

"Diana," he surrendered, "I'm not human." She scoffed in agreement. "I'm not. I..." He licked his lips, fumbling with his words. He understood, at once, the frustration of a man who couldn't make others understand his transgressions. Casey Aduro's plight. "I'm a Mythopian," he spat out at length. The word itself seemed to quiet her. "I'm stronger and faster than normal humans. I can do things normal people can't." A sudden string of tears warmed her face. "I can move rock with my mind."

"I know," she smiled despite herself, stunning him. "I knew it."

The hunter's instincts directed his hands to the blades that were not there, tucked away for safe keeping along with the rest of his weapons and the rest of his old life, the life he'd killed once and for all in London. His conscious mind suppressed the reflex and loosened his tensed hands. "How could you possibly know?"

"The ground shook when our son was born." She laughed at first, elated at the joy of confession. Then her smile retreated and left her reddening eyes alone against his.

James felt his heart broil, his stomach twist, sensation racing through his blood. "You what?"

"I was pregnant when you left. I had a boy," she said, restraining a smile. "I waited four years for his father to return."

All the weight of dragonfear couldn't compare to the feeling James experienced in that moment, though fear was not a factor in the slightest. The worry resided in Diana who could only stand while the hunter's mind danced behind a stone expression. His quivering arms held firm on the crutches.

"We've been waiting for you. We've never stopped waiting." She searched his features for understanding or repudiation, discerning nothing. "I know that what we had was brief—"

He moved as swiftly as only an ancient could. On fractured legs, he swooped her up and lifted her into a cool, sweet kiss. She tasted sweeter than any hunt ever had. Even in the empty, cold air her fragrance filled his lungs. Warm tears poured between them. He felt the heat of summer on his face when he kissed her and saw vernal beauty in her eyes when he pulled away.

They stood apart from each other for some time. The phoenix of their love shielded them from winter, let the hunter forget his injuries, let her forget her loneliness. Then his fingers drifted across the small of her back, and they laughed in unison.

Their hearts baked the air in their lungs and sent it out in clouds of steam. "I love you," he told her and left her breathless again. "I love you so much. My whole life I never felt like I belonged anywhere on this Earth. Like, because of what I am….I didn't deserve a home or a family. I spent my whole life trying to find a place to belong. But I belong here. I do. I belong with you. With both of you."

"I would've waited a thousand years for you."

Every word they spoke was as true as the last, but none hit James harder in his life than the next.

"Would you like to meet your son?"

Diana choked back her tears with a smile.

Chapter Thirty-Nine
The Son

Once he'd pawed the sleep from his eyes, he could see the car clearly again. He jolted awake as he noticed that the seat next to him was empty. His mom was nowhere to be found. He leaned up to question the ugly driver, cowering from his face. The funny-eared man smiled.

"Your mother's outside," he said. "Go and track her down."

Out the opposite window, he could see the enormous house. It was more like a castle than anything he'd seen in storybooks. It wasn't as big as the buildings in the city, but the yard surrounding it and the trees tucked around the sides only added to its grandness.

He pulled his boots on, tucked the untied strings in, and opened the door before shooting the chauffeur a final glare. "It's all right," the man said. "Everything is all right." Then he set out to rescue his mother. Maybe he'd even get to explore the castle.

The boy sighted his target quickly enough. Once he'd moved around a set of trees, he found her standing in front of a large, crooked man in a long, black coat. His heartbeat sped him behind a tree. He glanced around at the bare foliage that presented little in the way of cover. Still, the environment here was denser than it was up north. He remembered watching the trees spring up and the ground become red, yellow, and orange the further south they moved.

When he peered around the large tree's base, he could see them squaring off. Neither spoke much, but he couldn't make out what they did say. He watched his mother for a moment. At first, he could only see her smile, but soon he detected the tears as well. Then she spoke again and the man in black lunged at her like a wolf.

His speed defied perception. The boy pulled behind the tree again and blinked several times. He'd never seen anyone move that fast. Still, the drum of his heart reminded him that his mother was in danger. He whirled back around to help her, but the two had separated again. This time they were laughing.

While his heart settled, he started to circle closer so as to intercept their conversation, but the sound of the man's voice drove him into a crouch. It vibrated through the ground as if he were roaring, although the man was speaking as softly as he could. When his mother spoke again, she sounded like a mouse in comparison.

Then her eyes fell upon him, as if she'd been aware of him all along. The man in black followed her gaze, and soon James McCrary and his son locked eyes.

The hunter was too shocked to smile.

"Come here," his mother beckoned him.

The pup stood, abandoning his game, and shuffled towards them over the shoestrings that had already come loose from his boots. He planted his hands in the pockets of his hoodie and broke eye contact with the man.

"This is James McCrary," Diana told him as he pulled his small body against her leg.

"Hello, sir," he mumbled, still staring him down.

"Hey," James replied, still frozen. His greeting brought the boy's eyes back up again. He noted the older man's short hair and scratched his own shaggy fro as if to boast the longer mane. "What's your name?" James asked, noticing the boy's eyes. Rings of the father's brown emanated from their centers, wrapping around the mother's green. His skin, too, rested between the dark tone of his father's and his mother's golden-white.

"Heath." He tried to keep his eyes on the man's longer this time but soon broke off again.

"Heath," he echoed with joy bubbling up in his throat. He briefly glanced up at Diana, melting in delight at her expression. "Do you know who I am?"

"No, sir."

"I'm your father."

This time, when the boy's eyes went to his, they did not leave. He stared, wide-eyed, while James knelt down on one leg with considerable effort.

"I was gone for a long time. I had to find a way for us to be together. And safe." He extended his arm. "I'm gonna be here from now on."

Heath inched forwards, watching his father, before coming into the embrace. James held him for a few seconds, and the boy's arms stayed at his sides. Heath could feel his father grunt in pain and tried to pull back, but the hunter hushed his injuries and hugged him tighter. "I'm sorry that I was gone," James blurted. "I'm so sorry."

The boy struggled more, forcing his father's arms apart, then threw his arms around the hunter's neck. Entangled, father and son breathed in unison. Diana watched James' lips broaden into a smile. Over his shoulder, Heath's did the same.

* * * *

Heath was the first to storm the castle. He rushed in ahead of his parents and had swept through most of the building before they'd cleared the foyer. He claimed an empty room on the second story that would have been a guest room if not for his unexpected existence. From there, he could even see the clearing in the trees behind the house where a pond had been dug and dredged. Not very large, James admitted, but big enough for fishing or swimming. Heath had never been swimming before. His father promised to teach him once his body had healed.

Diana marveled at the house's every detail. She struggled to believe that it had been constructed before they'd ever dreamed of it all those years ago. James had plans to make it even closer to her vision once they'd settled in. Thanks to Mythic and Faolan, he had the money to do whatever they wanted with it. More exciting than the house, however, was the prospect of living in the house with her lover and with her child. She wanted more than anything to watch Heath grow as well as to have brothers and sisters he could grow alongside. The instant Heath disappeared again, she pulled James into an empty room with the ravenous look of a lioness and locked the door behind them.

Later on, the two of them emerged out into the cold of the living room to find their son hauling firewood in from the dark. Diana helped him place the next bundle into the fireplace. When the boy asked his father to light it, he told them both to stand back. He hadn't cast fire in almost a decade, but he was determined to raise the boy without fear of his heritage. He steadied himself with one crutch and blew a plume of deep red over the stack. It splashed over the wood for a few seconds and left a burning patch. Then the hunter blew on the logs to spread the blaze and the fireplace warmed to a glow, holding back the night for a while.

Diana and Heath watched in muted astonishment. Their eyes twinkled after the fire somewhere between disbelief and horror. When James turned to them, the fear gave way to admiration. Diana rushed to him and wrapped her arms around his waist. Heath stood with the stiffness of a gargoyle, worshipping the flames as if he'd never seen a fire in all his short life.

James gathered them around the warmth to explain what he was, what Heath was, and what he could become. He described his upbringing to them, his discovery, his initiation, his training, his indoctrination. Often Heath would fail to understand him, or else he'd understand more than Diana wanted him to. In time, though, they both understood James McCrary.

To them, he was a hero. A knight just like the ones that the boy had read about in children's stories or the more complex legends his mother told him. To be the son of such a man made his pretend fantasies a complete reality. The possibilities consumed him. Diana's love for James only deepened as she better understood him. He was a hunter, not a killer. He protected people from what threatened them, preserving as much life as he took, and more.

The more he told them, the tighter she clung to him with unearthly strength, the closer Heath drew to hear his words. Eventually, though, the night and the stories exhausted even the hunter's son. Heath slept at his mother's feet on his father's coat, dreaming of Mythopia.

As the fire faded, James pulled his love up to him and pressed his lips against hers. Atop a dragon's corpse he hadn't felt this victorious. He asked her to marry him. She responded, half-awake, that it was funny he thought it needed to be asked.

Then the hunter sank into a dreamless sleep.

Epilogue
The Moon

He woke into a nightmare.

The warmth of the fire had been replaced by cold, black, and stillness. He could hear the wind outside. Beyond it, he thought he heard a cry.

The hunter nudged Diana away, rolling up from his broken spine to find that his son had vanished.

Before she could even open her eyes, he'd already reached the back of the house. The moon invited him out into the bleak knot of trees, lighting a path out into the wood. He barreled down the trail without crutches, hobbling, pressing his broken body step after step after step, baring metal fangs for the world to see.

The call assailed him, that familiar howl. A feral blast from the darkness echoed in his blood.

Soon he could see it, as well. The forest opened into a glade not far from the house, a pond within the trees. He saw the crescent moon floating in the face of the water. He watched it for a moment before a shuddering heap at the edge of the pond reddened his eyes.

James staggered around the water, dashed to the figure, and turned over the boy who was wrapped in his coat. His son trembled as the cloak opened, revealing the hideous mark that had been left on him. On his bare skin burned a red scar—a large 'V' branded into his chest.

The hunter dropped his blades. Yin and Yang shrieked as they met the sand, roaring for the ancient blood seeping from the boy's wound.

"Heath."

The son could not stop his bleeding just as the father could not stop his tears.

He clutched Heath against his chest and threw his head about. His foggy eyes lanced out into the oblivion of the forest, challenging whomever would threaten his progeny, but the woods would not answer him. The soundless trees were there only to bear witness.

He heard footfall somewhere out in the arcane reaches of the forest, too quiet to identify, too distant to chase.

There was something out there watching them, there was something out there hunting them, and there was that familiar feeling in the hunter's heart reminding him that it would never, ever stop.

So there stood James and Heath with the burden of their blood, held by the reach of the world. There stood the hunter and his son for all time, caged in the endless hunt. There stood the father weeping, the son bleeding, and the white moon smiling over an infidelitous Earth.

About the Author

Brandon Smalls has loved telling stories since before he had the words to tell them. At four, he recited fairy tales. At five, he created picture books. At ten, he wrote his first novel and imagined the fantastic climes of Mythopia for the first time. By the time he finished high school at sixteen, he'd already completed another novel and expanded the world of Mythopia even further.

In the years since, Brandon has discovered countless mediums for his storytelling, ranging from acting on the stage and the screen to writing and directing films. He has found the most creative freedom, however, while writing his novels. *An Infidelitous Earth* marks the first look into a world that burgeoned into being faster than he could learn the words to describe it.

A native of LaGrange, Georgia and a graduate of Davidson College, Brandon currently lives in New York City where he acts, directs, and writes.

Contact Information

Primary website: http://www.mythopiaseries.com
Fan site: http://www.facebook.com/AnInfidelitousEarth
Instagram: https://www.instagram.com/brandonasmalls/
Twitter: @brandon_smalls4
Author Email: mythopiaseries@gmail.com

CPSIA information can be obtained
at www.ICGtesting.com
Printed in the USA
FSOW01n2105040417
32741FS